Anton Koffield stepped to the vault door and slowly, carefully, spun the dials one by one to set up the combination. Then, slowly, carefully, he checked through all the numbers, one after another. "That looks right." He stepped back and pulled the lock-open lever.

They could hear the dead bolts inside the door pull back and *thunk* into place.

Norla found that she was holding her breath. There could be anything, absolutely anything in there, from the DeSilvo-in-his-coffin tableau that Bolt had described, to some damned-fool practical joke. That would appeal to DeSilvo. It was the sort of thing he'd do.

Koffield pulled hard on the vault-door handle, and the door swung open. And inside—

Inside was an utterly empty room. There was nothing there but a set of stairs, leading down into the ground.

The three of them stood there, staring.

Norla turned to Koffield. "Don't tell me *this* is what you thought you'd find."

Novels by
ROGER MACBRIDE ALLEN

The Torch of Honor
Rogue Powers
Orphan of Creation
The Modular Man*
The War Machine (with David Drake)
Supernova (with Eric Kotani)
Farside Cannon
The Ring of Charon
The Shattered Sphere
Caliban
Inferno
Utopia
Ambush at Corellia*
Assault at Selonia*
Showdown at Centerpoint*
The Game of Worlds
The Depths of Time*
The Ocean of Years*

Published by Bantam Books

THE
OCEAN
OF
YEARS

Second book of
**THE CHRONICLES
OF SOLACE**

ROGER MacBRIDE ALLEN

BANTAM BOOKS

THE OCEAN OF YEARS
A Bantam Spectra Book / July 2002

ISBN 0-553-58364-6

Published simultaneously in the United States and Canada

Bantam Books are published by Bantam Books, a division of
Random House, Inc. Its trademark, consisting of the words
"Bantam Books" and the portrayal of a rooster, is Registered
in U.S. Patent and Trademark Office and in other countries.
Marca Registrada. Bantam Books, 1540 Broadway,
New York, New York 10036.

PRINTED IN THE UNITED STATES OF AMERICA

OPM   10 9 8 7 6 5 4 3 2 1

To Matthew's Aunts and Uncles—
Edie and Connie,
Carl, Jim, and Chris
for all the good times, past and future

ACKNOWLEDGMENTS

I would like to offer my thanks to all those who had a hand in making this book better than I could have made it on my own. Thanks first and foremost to my wife, Eleanore Fox, who made it possible to do the work, and to our son, Matthew, who did his exuberant best to make it most entertainingly impossible to get anything done at all. Thanks again on another score to Eleanore, for performing much-needed surgery on the manuscript. Thanks also to my father, Thomas B. Allen, for reading the book and making many valuable suggestions. Charles Sheffield made sure that a certain semi-mathematical puzzle didn't stretch the rules *too* far.

Thanks to Michael Shohl for his patience, courtesy, and poise in difficult times, as well as for his clear and direct editorial notes. And thanks to Juliet Ulman of Bantam Books, who took the ball and ran with it, just as the clock was running down toward the deadline.

—*Roger MacBride Allen*
Takoma Park, Maryland
December 2001

TABLE OF CONTENTS

He hath set eternity in their heart, yet so that man cannot find out the work that God hath done from the beginning even to the end.   —Ecclesiastes 3:12

That which is hath been long ago; and that which is to be hath long ago been: and God seeketh again that which is passed away.   —Ecclesiastes 3:15

Wherefore I saw that there is nothing better, than that a man should rejoice in his works; for that is his portion: for who shall bring him back to see what shall be after him?   —Ecclesiastes 3:22

DRAMATIS PERSONAE

Note: A Glossary of Terms and Gazetteer of Places and Ship Names, along with a Chronology of Key Events, appears after the main text of the book.

Wandella Ashdin—historian and expert on Oskar DeSilvo.

Ulan Baskaw—Scientist who lived approximately five centuries before the main action of the story. Little is known about her—it is not even certain whether or not Baskaw was a woman or in fact a man. Baskaw invented many terraforming techniques that were later appropriated by DeSilvo. Baskaw also discovered certain mathematical principles underlying the science of terraforming.

Jerand Bolt—Starship crew member stranded aboard Asgard Five, later recruited to serve aboard the disguised *Dom Pedro IV*, AKA "Merchanter's Dream."

Alber Caltrip—Alias used by Anton Koffield aboard the disguised *Dom Pedro IV*.

Lieutenant Commander Burl Chalmers—Head of section in Kalani Temblar's office at Chronologic Patrol Intelligence Command Headquarters.

Norla Chandray—Second Officer aboard the *Dom Pedro IV*.

Sindra Chon—Starship crew member stranded on Asgard Five by equipment malfunctions aboard her ship. Later, recruited along with Jerand Bolt to serve aboard the disguised *Dom Pedro IV*.

Oskar DeSilvo—Architect and terraformist of the previous centuries, and director of the project to colonize Solace. He managed the centuries-long project by using cryosleep and temporal confinement, arranging to have himself revived from time to time in order to oversee critical points in the process.

Neshobe Kalzant—Planetary Executive, Solace.

Anthon Kolfeldt—Variant spelling of Anton Koffield name used in Glistern rhymes and stories for children. The Glistern convention in writing is that Kolfeldt is the evil monster, while Koffield is the historical figure.

Admiral Anton Koffield (ret)—A retired officer in the Intelligence Command of the Chronologic Patrol, and former commander of the Chronologic Patrol Ship *Upholder*.

First Officer Hari Leptin—Alias used by Captain Felipe Henrique Marquez aboard the disguised *Dom Pedro IV*.

Captain Felipe Henrique Marquez—Captain of the *Dom Pedro IV*.

Dixon Phelby—Cargo officer aboard the *Dom Pedro IV*.

Commander Karlin Raenau—Station commander of SCO Station, orbiting Solace.

Hues Renblant—Disaffected officer aboard the *Dom Pedro IV* who seeks to resign from the ship's company.

Second Officer Leona Sendler—Alias used by Norla Chandray aboard the disguised *Dom Pedro IV*.

Captain Olar Sotales—Director of the Station Security Force aboard SCO Station.

Yuri Sparten—The former assistant to Karlin Raenau, commander of SCO Station. Now assigned to serve aboard the "Merchanter's Dream," the name under which *Dom Pedro IV* is traveling. Although he has no interstellar experience, he is posing as the "Dream's" captain. His parents, as children, were refugees from the fall of Glister.

Lieutenant Kalani Temblar—An investigator working for the Chronologic Patrol's Intelligence Command.

Clemson Wahl—Starship crew member stranded on Asgard Five by equipment malfunctions aboard his ship. Later, recruited along with Jerand Bolt to serve aboard the disguised *Dom Pedro IV*.

Lira Wu—Very junior crew member serving aboard the *Dom Pedro IV*.

THE TIMESHAFT WORMHOLE TRANSPORTATION SYSTEM

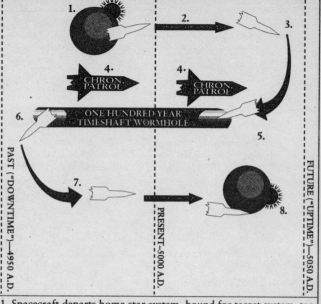

1. Spacecraft departs home star system, bound for target system, ten light-years away. Crew enters cryosleep hibernation and/or temporal confinement for duration of voyage.

2. Spacecraft travels for fifty years at one-tenth light-speed, thus traveling fifty years uptime and a distance of five light-years.

3. Spacecraft reaches timeshaft wormhole, midway between home and target systems. Captain is revived briefly to pilot ship through timeshaft.

4. Both uptime and downtime ends of wormhole are guarded by Chronologic Patrol ships.

5. Spacecraft drops through timeshaft and is propelled one hundred years downtime, into the past.

6. Spacecraft emerges from wormhole, fifty years before its departure from its home system and one hundred years before it enters the wormhole. Captain returns to temporal confinement.

7. Spacecraft onces again travels fifty years at one-tenth light-speed, again traveling fifty years uptime and five more light-years.

8. After traveling for one hundred years shipboard time, spacecraft arrives at target system a few days or weeks after departure in objective time. Crew is revived from one-hundred-year hibernation to find less than a month has passed.

THE
OCEAN
OF
YEARS

PRELUDE

DIAMOND REDUX

Office of the Planetary Executive,
Solace City, Solace.
5340 A.D., Terrestrial Common Era

Neshobe Kalzant, Planetary Executive of Solace, leaned back in her office chair. She read, once again, the letter found in the tomb of a man who had not died.

The man who had brought her the letter, the man to whom the letter had been written, stood before her desk, his posture rigid, his expression utterly unreadable. But for all of that, Neshobe knew what he wanted.

It was a long letter. She skimmed through it, letting phrases jump out at her.

> . . . *my tomb was not my tomb . . . It is no one's tomb. The ashes are as false as the reports of my recent death.*

"Recent" indeed. The letter had been discovered over a hundred years after it had been written. But there were strong reasons to believe the writer was still alive, in some form of suspended animation.

> . . . *I have failed. Failed utterly and ignobly, failed because I ignored facts I did not find convenient,*

failed because I believed I could make the world, the universe, fit the mold I decreed.

But I have . . . learned far more secrets than those that Ulan Baskaw taught me. There is much to be found in the most secret places of the Grand Library, and in other archives. You need only look to the events of the Circum Central incident to know that is true. The ships you called the Intruders did indeed exceed light-speed.

"This exceeding light-speed business," Neshobe said to the man standing in front of her desk. "They gave up even *trying* to do that thousands of years ago. But you believe him."

"I was at Circum Central," he said quietly. "I saw it."

Neshobe hummed tunelessly for a moment, staring at a patch of nothing just over her visitor's left shoulder, and then went on reading. She skimmed down, past the writer's boasts, and into his confession. She had to read the words again.

The collapse of Solace is coming. I believe that now. But I also believe that it will serve as a wake-up call, a warning to all the worlds . . .

She blinked, lost her place, and tried to settle herself. She had known for a long time, down in her bones, that the planet she governed was too far gone to recover. But the writer was the man who had quite literally made her world, who had directed the terraforming project. To have *him* admit it, from a hundred years in the past— that cut deep. If he had known, back then, it would fail—why hadn't he stopped it?

But failure is not mine alone. Humanity itself is failing. The enterprise of our interstellar civilization is subject to the same physical and mathematical laws as Solace. All our worlds are doomed. . . .

Well, yes, that was the news her visitor had tried to bring to Solace. It was the letter writer who had prevented him from delivering the warning. She skipped back and forth through the letter. The writer's defense of himself was a mishmash of tortured logic and special pleading. No need to go through it again. She skipped to the end. Where the Great Man offered up a deal.

> I have great good to offer, prizes of knowledge and technology that I alone can give . . . but much of what I can offer will not be accepted willingly. Drastic ideas will not be possible until the situation is desperate. . . .
> Seek me out. I live, but slumber. I am hidden, but hidden where you can find me. Find me, and together, we can do great things.
> . . . Hate me, forgive me. Feel what you will toward me, and I will accept it. There are larger matters at stake, and my own guilt and shame do not matter.
> Only one thing does matter.
> Seek me out.
> With heartfelt respect, I remain
> Your sincere admirer
> Dr. Oskar DeSilvo

Neshobe Kalzant set the pages of the letter down on her desk. She looked at the man who stood before her, at Admiral Anton Koffield. "Who knows about this letter?" she asked.

"You. Me. Wandella Ashdin, Norla Chandray, and Captain Marquez. No one else. The various support people know we found something, of course. They just don't know what."

Neshobe swiveled her chair about to stare out at the endless rain.

Oskar DeSilvo, the man who had written the letter, had designed the Diamond Office they were in, the mansion of which it was a part, and the city that formed the view seen from it. That is to say, the view she would be seeing right now, if not for the endless rain. In a sense, DeSilvo had made the rain as well. DeSilvo had directed the terraforming of Solace—and, according to the letter, had not had the courage to admit that fundamental flaws in the process had made it a predictable, mathematical certainty that the planet's climate and ecology would collapse. *Always rain where you don't need it, and never where you do.* That was the Solacian proverb meaning nothing ever went right. The weather problems were bad enough, and persistent enough, to shape the words people lived by.

Here it was rain. *Sure as rain in Solace City.* That was another proverb. Elsewhere it was killing droughts, or coastal inundation, or massive algae blooms. Everywhere, the climate was unraveling.

"You believe him," she said to her visitor. It was not a question. She spoke without turning around, and kept staring out the window.

"Yes," said Anton Koffield.

"And the climate projections?" She couldn't bring herself to say the rest of it—*the climate projections that say the planet will collapse.*

"Confirmed and reconfirmed, over and over again," Koffield replied.

At last she spun about in her chair. "So there is no hope," she said, "except for what a genocidal maniac offers us from a hundred years in the past. And he won't give us what he has—whatever that might be—unless you go and find him first."

"Yes. He implies that faster-than-light travel is the least of it. But Dr. DeSilvo has been prone to exaggerate in the past."

There was understatement for you. "And in spite what he's put you through, you want to go after him." *Or, more likely, because of it.* DeSilvo had done a lot to Koffield, and done most of it from a distance. He had in effect framed Koffield for the destruction of the Circum Central wormhole. When Koffield had discovered that the planet Solace, DeSilvo's masterpiece, was doomed to failure, he had taken passage aboard the *Dom Pedro IV* to fly to Solace and deliver a warning. But DeSilvo had stolen Koffield's evidence off the ship, sabotaged the *DP-IV*, kept it from flying through a timeshaft, and marooned the ship and crew 127 years in the future—all in the interests, so DeSilvo claimed, of preventing the panic Koffield's "false" warning would produce. Unfortunately, the warning was proving to be all too accurate. "Or *do* you want to go?" Neshobe asked.

"I don't feel as if I have a great deal of choice. We must find out what technology he has found. He has a faster-than-light drive. He implies there is more—but FTL travel, all by itself, could change everything. *Everything*. Yes, there is a chance that it's a fraud, a trick. But if it's real—then millions more might be saved who otherwise could not be evacuated."

Neshobe nodded. There were endless questions, any number of ways that FTL might prove useless, or prove to be a fraud. But the chance was well worth taking. "Agreed. You must find DeSilvo."

She turned her gaze back toward her desk, toward other objects pulled from DeSilvo's false tomb. Books and a datacube. The datacube was in fact the cube that Koffield had intended to bring to Solace. It was the very cube DeSilvo had stolen. DeSilvo had, apparently, placed it in the funerary urn as a sort of confession of his guilt. One of the printed books contained the same data as the cube. The other three books were by Ulan Baskaw—an author Neshobe had never heard of, before all this had started. She had died centuries before DeSilvo was born—but still he had managed to steal from her, as well, plagiarizing her books—the books that now sat before Neshobe. He had used them as a guide for terraforming Solace—but had ignored all the warnings they contained, the proofs that the technique had to fail. "These books," she said, putting her hand on the titles by Baskaw. "These *copies* of these books. Where are they from?"

"It's more a question of *when* are they from," said Koffield. "They have printing dates showing they were printed off 110 years ago, and chemical analyses of various sorts confirm that."

"So these aren't the originals."

"No. Presumably those are still in the Permanent Physical Collection." The PPC was a gigantic space habitat, a huge cylindrical space station, orbiting Neptune, back in the Solar System. In it were stored physical printed copies of every book the collectors could obtain. Nearby, also in the orbit of Neptune, was the PPC's digital equivalent, the Grand Library. DeSilvo had erased Baskaw's books from the GL's digital equivalent—but he had forgotten to destroy the PPC's physical copies.

"So the copies you read, you consulted, are still sitting on a shelf in a giant library orbiting Neptune."

"Presumably."

"Good," said Neshobe. "Very good. Because I—we—have other problems. I've discussed your information, your evidence, your warnings, with the leaders of all the major parties, and all the other power factions. All very quiet. No one wants it to leak prematurely. Half of them don't believe any of it. Mostly the spaceside people, who don't experience the weather problems, and would get buried in refugees one way or another if we evacuated the planet."

"How could they not believe evidence this strong—"

Neshobe held up a hand to silence him. "Because they don't," she said. "I agree your evidence is solid, and our scientists on Greenhouse have fallen in love with the models based on Baskaw's work. But life would be so much better for so many people, if only it were all wrong, and you were a fraud." She stared at him a moment. "Life would certainly be easier for me, I can tell you. So we need proof you didn't fake the whole thing. Proof that you were there on the PPC, when you said you were, and that the books were there too—and better still, that they are still there, on the shelf, right where you left them. Bring that proof back, and *maybe* we'll have enough proof to convince the unbelievers—or at least silence them."

"That's not going to be easy," Koffield said.

"No," she agreed. "But we need it done. Enough so that I'll have to make it a condition for assisting you."

He considered for a moment, then nodded. "Very well," he said. "Whatever evidence there is, we'll get."

"Good," she said. "How long until you'd be ready to go?"

Koffield frowned. Neshobe had the impression he had expected her to need more convincing—but running the planet had already convinced her of how bad things were. Any tiny chance for hope was worth reaching out for.

"Well," Koffield said, "there's a lot of research we have to do, a lot of planning. We'll need a ship—"

"We'll refit the *Dom Pedro IV* for you. *How long?*"

Koffield looked flat-out startled. Plainly, he was not used to being interrupted. "About two months. But that's assuming we can get—"

Neshobe Kalzant let him see the fear in her eyes, even as she read the cold, hard, anger in his. Koffield had his own reasons for wanting this trip. Oh, yes, indeed. She thought of the other passages in that letter, the one that spoke of the crimes DeSilvo had committed against Koffield, all for the common good.

"You'll get," she said, "whatever you need." She reached out to her desk and touched the letter again. "You command the mission, Marquez commands the ship. Just so long as it all stays very, very, quiet—and you bring back whatever it is he's got—and proof of your claims."

She remained there for a time, long after Koffield had left. There was a lot to consider. Koffield, for one. He had played things square up to now—but there would certainly come a time when his priorities no longer coincided with hers. And he would be out there, somewhere, far beyond the Solacian system, out from under the watch they had kept on him.

Or maybe there was a way to keep the watch going. They needed someone on the inside, on the ship. But Solacian politics more or less guaranteed that whoever they put aboard ship would be working for more than one master—and perhaps would feel no loyalty to her at all. Tricky however she did it. She thought for a further time, then spun about in her chair, putting the rain, the endless rain, at her back. There was one fairly obvious candidate. She spoke into the empty air. "Commander Raenau, on SCO Station," she said to the listening Artificial Intelligence. "Place the call."

Felipe Henrique Marquez, master of the Timeshaft Dropship *Dom Pedro IV*, was waiting for Koffield in the aircar that had brought him to the Executive Mansion. The rain blew in the door as Koffield stepped inside.

"Spaceport," Koffield said to the car's controls, and sat back in the seat facing Marquez.

"So what do we get?" Marquez asked.

"Everything," said Koffield. "Blank check, with a few conditions. And I assume we'll find some other strings attached, sooner or later. But we'll get all the help we need, and the *Dom Pedro IV* will get a full upgrade."

"Very good," said Marquez. "I just wish she'd have a full crew."

"How many do you think will want to stay behind?" Koffield asked.

"Two at least," said Marquez. "With the two who died on arrival, that leaves us short four crew before we even boost for the wormhole."

"We can't sign any new crew," said Koffield, his voice hard. "Not on Solace. We've been through that. Sign up four new crew, and we'd get spies on board for four different factions."

"Maybe five factions," said Marquez, with a tired smile. "I agree—reluctantly. No new crew. We'll have enough security problems without them."

"Agreed. Kalzant wants the operation kept quiet— nearly as much we do."

Marquez nodded. There were as many reasons for keeping the operation secret as there were ways it could all go wrong.

And there were *plenty* of ways for it to go wrong.

SIX MONTHS LATER

CHAPTER ONE

THE REALMS OF THOR

A shaft of silver that gleamed in darkness, a javelin thrown across the black of space, the great ship hurtled down toward a hole in the sky.

The *Dom Pedro IV*, flying under a false name and false pretenses, dropped toward Hanson's Timeshaft, more formally known as TR-40.2, in the Thor's Realm Timeshaft Wormhole Farm. She was the *DP-IV* no more, so far as the outside universe was concerned. She flew now under the name "Merchanter's Dream." And if that was the third most common name for a ship in all of Settled Space, that could not be helped—and perhaps it would be very helpful indeed.

Norla Chandray sat in the copilot's seat. She had the very distinct feeling that she was not much help to anyone at the moment.

Captain Marquez sat next to her, in the pilot's seat, seemingly imperturbable, but with a hint of tension, excitement, hovering there beneath the surface. "Give me a final check on all externals," he said.

Norla ran her boards, blipped through all the telltales and camera ports. "All retractable external devices retracted and stowed."

"Close forward view shields," Marquez ordered.

Norla activated the proper controls. Overhead, the

shutters swung to over the *Dom Pedro IV*'s—no, pardon, the "*Merchanter's Dream's*"—forward observation dome. The massive shutters clamshelled shut, ready to protect the bow of the ship against the nothingness that loomed just ahead. The *thud-clack thud-clack thud-clack* of the shield latches locking down boomed out, transmitted through the hull of the ship.

"Forward view shields up and locked," Norla reported, quite unnecessarily. If Marquez couldn't tell for himself that the shields were up, he had very little business flying a timeshaft ship.

But Marquez knew his business, even if he hadn't flown a timeshaft transition in the last 128 years—no, longer than that. Add another forty-plus years since we boarded ship, Norla told herself, and shook her head. Even if the thought was precisely accurate, it still didn't make sense. But it didn't matter. Not now. Right now all that mattered was that *she* was the one who had never flown a timeshaft transition before this trip. But that was about to change.

"Very well," said Marquez. He pressed the general intercom button. "All hands, this is the captain. Final strap-in warning. All hands to timeshaft transition stations. We're going in." He turned toward Norla, and grinned at her, an expression of manic enthusiasm, tinged perhaps with a hint of worry. And even above and beyond the mere question of deliberately dropping a multimegaton ship through a black hole and back several decades into the past, there was plenty to worry about.

Marquez glanced over to the comm officer's station, where Admiral Koffield was sitting. There was distinctly very little for a comm officer to do at this point. They had sent and received the standard arrival signal and mirror reply to the Chronologic Patrol ship on station, here on the uptime end of the timeshaft. Any further communication at this point would almost certainly mean out-and-out disaster, with a volley of railgun fire about to slam down into them. Koffield sat where he was because it was a convenient place from which to watch the proceedings.

If it became anything else, it could only mean the game was up, almost before it began.

"Ready for the timeshaft, Admiral?"

Admiral Anton Koffield smiled, as open and relaxed an expression as Norla had ever seen on the man. "Long past ready," he said. "We have to get through here before we can get where we're going. Let's do it."

There was an odd eagerness in his voice. Somehow, Norla found herself reminded of a restless child on a long trip, asking over and over again — "Are we there yet?"

Well, they wouldn't be there for a while yet. They had a lot of hoops to jump through first. But she had no doubt whatsoever that what Anton Koffield was eager for was to get back in the fight, back in the hunt.

He had been waiting for a long time. In a sense, he had been waiting two hundred years, and showed no sign at all of tiring. Norla was glad that Anton Koffield was not in pursuit of *her*. She had no doubt that everyone else on the ship felt the same way. Koffield was not the sort of man one wanted to have as an enemy.

"All right, Officer Chandray. You heard the man. Let's do it!"

"Yes, sir," she said, feeling far less enthusiasm than she heard in the voice of the two men. Were they really that excited by the prospect of what lay ahead—or were they just doing good jobs of acting?

Besides all that, there wasn't much for her to do at the moment. They were already dead on course toward the timeshaft, falling like a stone—indeed, faster than any stone could fall on any respectable world—toward their rendezvous with a tiny hole in space and time.

Norla checked her boards. "Four minutes to ship's rated redline," she announced. With every moment that passed, the *DP-IV* was falling faster, streaking closer to the timeshaft wormhole as its gravity field pulled them in toward itself. The thruster power that would be needed to break free of the wormhole was likewise growing, moment by moment. In less than four minutes, the variables of time, distance, velocity, and time available would all converge, producing an imaginary red line in the sky, drawn around the wormhole. Pass the redline, and it would be physically impossible to break free of the wormhole.

The ship's rated redline was the ragged edge, where if all systems worked perfectly, if nothing failed under maximum strain, if no strut snapped, if no power coupling blew out under emergency maximum, the ship could survive.

As the ship continued its headlong fall, the *DP-IV* would cross the theoretical redline, the point beyond which *no* ship, of *any* description, could possibly escape, where even infinite thrust applied in an infinitesimal amount of time would not be enough to let a ship break free.

Of course, merely getting as close as they were to the ship's rated redline meant any attempted approach abort would be close to suicidal. Only if the choice were between certain doom and a hundred-to-one chance for survival would the dangers of an abort be worth the risk. And though as yet the point was academic, it might not stay that way. There was the small matter of the Chronologic Patrol Ship on station, here on the uptime side of the timeshaft. If the CP ship decided, for whatever reason, that it didn't want the *DP-IV* boosting through the wormhole, it might order an abort, even now. In such a case, the CP ship might elect to eliminate the problem altogether, by simply blasting the *DP-IV* out of the sky . . .

"Three minutes to ship's rated redline," Norla announced. Three minutes for the uptime ship to notice there was something not quite right about the *DP-IV* and open fire, or send the *DP-IV* an autoabort order that she would ignore—or obey—at her peril.

The ship's external ports were all secured, but the *DP-IV* still had a few detectors active, microlenses that extended only a few molecules outside the hull, peeking through pinhole-sized ports in the hull and feeding visual, radio, and infrared-band data back into the ship through data cables thinner than a human hair. The microsensors had only limited sensitivity, but they were far better than nothing, enough to confirm the ship's course down toward the timeshaft-wormhole nexus—and also to keep an eye on the CP ship. If the CP ship moved against them, they might not be able to do anything, but at least they would know about it.

But the CP ship stood aloof, passive. No doubt the warship was watching them, probably using them for a gunnery tracking target, but it did not interfere with them.

"Two minutes to ship's rated redline," Norla announced.

Of course, the CP ship was only the first and least of the dangers they faced. There was the timeshaft wormhole itself to get through—and then a world, a universe, of danger on the other side of the wormhole, and eighty-three years in the past.

Nor were all the dangers outside the ship. Norla spared a glance away from her displays to look toward Yuri Sparten, seated there next to Koffield.

When Neshobe had authorized the refitting and upgrading of the *DP-IV*, Koffield had warned there would be strings attached. Sparten's presence was proof of that.

Planetary Executive Kalzant had asked to see the mission's deception plan—and had sent it back with one very large alteration. Yuri Sparten was to join the ship's company, and would pose as captain of the ship "Merchanter's Dream" in the presence of outsiders. This, Kalzant explained, would provide a certain amount of legal cover to the mission, in the event that the deception was uncovered. Sparten was a citizen of Solace, and was hurriedly commissioned into the planetary defense force. The commission provided at least a legal argument that the *DP-IV*/"Merchanter's Dream" had some sort of government authority for operating under a falsified name.

None of the ship's company were particularly impressed by the explanation, and no one was in the least grateful for Sparten's presence. Literally from the first moment Anton Koffield had set foot on SCO Station, the main orbital facility for Solace, Sparten had been watching him.

Whatever official duties he might supposedly have, it was plain enough to all involved that Sparten had been forced on the crew, for the sole purpose of continuing to watch Koffield. But for whom, and with what precise purpose, Norla could not say.

And then there was Hues Renblant, nominally the first officer of the *DP-IV*, seated at the nav station. Renblant was angry, but there was nothing new about that. Hues Renblant must have been born angry—and he refused to believe anyone but Koffield could be blamed for their predicament. He had spent the last months telling anyone who would listen—and was allowed to get close enough to listen—that it was all a fraud. Koffield had faked the whole show, had sabotaged the *Dom Pedro IV,* invented all his so-called evidence, tarnished DeSilvo's name—and had done it all just to rescue his own reputation after the Circum Central debacle.

Renblant had no desire to stay behind in the Solacian system, and had no desire to stay aboard the *Dom Pedro IV* so long as Koffield was there, and Marquez was very definitely unwilling to let him deadhead all the way to Earth—which left one unpalatable option. His contract allowed him to be put down at a way station—and Asgard Five was it.

He plainly resented Norla being where she was, there in the copilot's station, but Renblant had dug himself into that hole. *Let* him not like it. That was where Marquez had wanted her, and Marquez, after all, was the captain. Still and all, having Renblant staring daggers into her back until they reached Asgard Five was not exactly going to put Norla at ease. She was glad they were to be rid of him soon.

"One minute to redline."

But there was no point to calling out the rest of the countdown. They could all read a clock display, and besides, the CP wouldn't cut it that close. If the CP ship was going to do anything, they would have done it already. They were going in. Either through the timeshaft, or crash-landing onto the black hole that underlay the wormhole. And she was going to see it. That was the breathtaking part. Back in her world, in her time, no one but the captain ever got to see a timeshaft drop.

Norla had never flown a timeshaft drop, awake or frozen. She should have done one drop in a cryocan, on the way to Solace—except something had gone wrong, terribly wrong, with the ship's systems. Sabotage. And the *DP-IV* had done the full run in normal space, without dropping back through time. The ship, and all aboard her, had been marooned in the future. They had all stayed in cryo too long.

Ever since she had nearly died as she came out of cryo, some small part of Norla had been whispering to her larger self, telling her that she would never again have the courage to lay herself down in the coffinlike confines of a cryocan. And that would have meant that she could never again cross between the stars. She would have been a stay-behind, marooned not only in time, but in space.

But then had come the Solacian offer to refit the *DP-IV*, and the news that they were installing a temporal-confinement system big enough for the entire ship's company. Back in the previous century, when the *DP-IV* had first boosted for Solace, temporal confinement had been ruinously expensive. It took too much power, and the equipment was too big and heavy. The standard operating procedure for timeshaft ships had been that all crew members and officers had to fly in cryocans. Only the captain traveled in temporal confinement, so he or she could be revived quickly in case of emergency.

But the *DP-IV* had gotten herself stranded in time, thrown into the future. Surprisingly little had changed in the intervening decades, but sometime during the 128 years after the *DP-IV* had departed for Solace, the power costs for temporal confinement had dropped, and the equipment had gotten smaller.

It still wasn't cost-effective to use temporal confinement on all the colonists on a five-thousand-person transport ark. On a monster ship like that, the colonists still had to fly in cryocans. But then, there weren't that many colony ships going out anymore, anyway. On a smaller craft like the *DP-IV*, with ten or twenty aboard, these days, everyone flew in temporal confinement.

Beyond question, temporal confinement was vastly superior to getting stuffed into a cryocan. However, the temporal-confinement fields interfered with the timeshaft wormhole's portal nexus and the timeshaft wormhole itself. In fact, a TC field would "interfere" so energetically that the resulting energy release would tear the ship apart, down to the subatomic level.

Therefore, the ship's temporal-confinement system was powered down during the transit of a timeshaft wormhole. The entire ship's party could witness the run through a timeshaft wormhole, an event heretofore witnessed only by the captain.

"Redline," Norla announced. Their way was forward, and no choice.

The ship was battened down, all hardware retracted, all shields up, exposing as little as possible to the violent stresses of a drop into and through a black hole. They fell toward it, faster and faster.

Norla flipped her screens to exterior visual. The little peek-out cameras, their lenses still extending out of the hull, if only by micromillimeters, gave a reasonably clear view, but there was surprisingly little to see. The black hole itself was, of course, invisible. The portal nexus they were to pass through, in essence the door backward through time, was likewise too small—and orbiting the wormhole too fast—to be visible. There had even been two other ships that made the run just ahead of the *DP-IV*, an hour or so before, but even on extreme magnification, there had been precious little to see of their passages. Twice they had watched as small silver oblong shapes moved through space, and then vanished as they intersected portal nexi.

But now those ships were gone. The only other visible object, aside from the stars in the sky, was a far-off dot of light that was the uptime Chronologic Patrol ship, one of the uptime-downtime pair guarding this wormhole.

Norla found herself staring at the dot of light that was

no doubt watching them. For the hundredth time, Norla told herself that it was perfectly normal and to be expected that there should be a CP ship on station. Still, given the history of the *Dom Pedro IV*, and given the past activities of many of those aboard her, that dot of light was all it took to get everyone nervous, even after passing the redline.

Try as they might to hide it, Norla could read that emotion on every face. She looked again toward Koffield. Correction. Make that every face but one. What did he think, and feel, when he looked at an uptime patrol ship? He had once commanded such a craft. He had done his duty, and his job, and done them well— but it had not ended well, for him—or, really, for anyone.

But it wasn't really the uptime ship that was the problem, and never had been. The whole point of the Chronologic Patrol, of the CP's complex wormhole portal guard system, was to keep the past from learning about the future. Uptime patrol ships asked very few questions. It was the *downtime* ship, on the other side of the timeshaft wormhole, that could give them trouble during interrogation.

Norla flipped her screens away from the exterior pickups. The view outside might not be much, but the symbol-logic graphics told a far more dramatic story. It showed their rapid acceleration toward an invisible dot straight ahead. They were coming up on the singularity itself, dropping toward it fast, damned fast. The display also showed the CP ship's likely firing solutions if it didn't like what it saw, and showed the ship's redline, now far astern.

Like a bat out of hell looking to dive back in, they fell toward the wormhole, utterly committed. Nothing could stop them.

Norla checked her boards. Still on course, still showing an all-green board. She glanced over at Marquez, the veteran of endless timeshaft transitions. He might easily see something she had missed. More than likely, she could read a warning of doom from his face more easily than she could off the display screens. His expression was serious, even grim, but he was calm, almost at ease.

Now the tidal stresses on the ship were starting to make themselves felt. Creaks and groans echoed up from the lower decks as the hands of unseen giants grabbed at the *DP-IV* and sought to pull her apart. The ship was built to take it, but no ship ever made could hold together for long under such punishment—one reason that timeshaft ships made their runs at the highest velocities they could manage.

The whole ship was beginning to vibrate, thrumming with the stresses pulling at it. Something broke loose and crashed into a bulkhead, but Norla didn't look up from her displays. There was no time to deal with whatever it was anyway. In fact, it was too late to deal with anything. This close to the wormhole there were no course adjustments they dared make. The *Dom Pedro IV* was as unsteerable as a bullet shot from a high-powered rifle. She had been aimed and fired, and now there was no way to turn her, to guide her, to speed her up or slow her down. She would hit the target, or she wouldn't.

Norla flipped over to visual again and stared ahead. She could never hope to see the singularity itself, but the folklore was that, sometimes, in the last few seconds of a timeshaft drop—there! There it was!

It was the timeshaft portal nexus, the door through which they had to pass. It was a flattened pale grey oval, orbiting the singularity at fantastic speed, swinging around in its impossibly close orbit, closing in to meet the *DP-IV*, their paths set to intersect perfectly at exactly the right—

And they slammed into the portal. The exterior display went black, the main compartment lights cut out, there was another crash somewhere in the darkness, and someone screamed and cried out behind her. They hit so hard that Norla thought for a moment that they had missed, that they had crashed into the singularity itself.

No, she told herself. *If the black hole was going to kill us, we'd be dead by now.* Hit the singularity, and your ship would disintegrate in the moment between two heartbeats, between two thoughts. *There wouldn't be time to realize we were dying.*

The lights came back on. The ship bucked and quivered, shrieking and groaning, feeling as if it were going to shake itself to bits, as the tidal stresses of the wormhole reached out, trying to tear the ship apart. She glanced over to Marquez again, and was startled to see the manic, leering grin on his face. His mouth opened, and it looked as if he were shouting with excitement and pleasure, but it was too damned noisy in the command compartment for her to hear it. She watched him in astonishment. He was enjoying this.

Not knowing whether that should reassure her or terrify her, Norla turned back toward her displays. The exterior view was gone, but her pilot's symbol logic was still up and running. And it showed all normal. Apparently, it was supposed to be this rough a ride.

The shuddering, roaring transit went on and on. To Norla it felt more like a long, drawn-out crash into a wall than a passage through a gate. Norla knew, as a matter of logic, that they were inside the timeshaft wormhole now. There was no way to see out, and indeed nothing to see, but just outside the hull of the *Dom Pedro IV*, the years were running past, and running backward.

She tried to grasp that, tried to understand what that meant. They had set a course that led back through time. They were sailing against the current, in stormy seas, across a short stretch of the Ocean of Years.

The shaking rose to a crescendo, another alarm started hooting, and two or three indicator lights on Norla's display, lights that had been solid green, started to flicker over into amber. Norla caught a whiff of what smelled like burned plastic.

And outside the years were falling away, flowing backward, waves pulling themselves away from the shore, coursing home into the deeps, burying themselves in currents that were themselves melting into the past.

And then—

And then, time running backward intersected with

normal time. A ship from the future decanted itself into the past. The shaking stopped. The fabric of the ship creaked and groaned as the tidal stresses melted away, and the ship shot away from the downtime end of the timeshaft, rising up out of the wormhole. The exterior view displays came back to life, and showed them flying up, out, toward the friendly, familiar stars—and into a time past, a time they did not know. Most aboard the *Dom Pedro IV* had lived through this time before, but had done so frozen in cryo, or in temporal containment.

Indeed the *Dom Pedro IV* had lived through this time more than once. At this very moment, that past version of the ship was out there. Elsewhere in the cosmos, that previous *Dom Pedro IV* was sailing on through the darkness toward Solace, all aboard her frozen in ice or frozen in time, none of them aware that they were already decades overdue, already marooned in their own future.

But it didn't matter. That was the whole point of traveling through timeshaft wormholes. The timeshaft itself was totally isolated, light-years from any star. It would take long, weary years for the *Dom Pedro IV* to travel from this point to her destination, long enough that she would be back in the year she had started from by the time they arrived. Their previous selves, in that previous ship, were likewise light-years away, so utterly unreachable that they might as well not exist. The light-years themselves, the vast distances, were barrier enough to prevent the *DP-IV* of the present from having any contact with the *DP-IV* of the past.

Norla forced herself to stop worrying about esoterica, and focus on the matters at hand. The downtime Chronologic Patrol ship was just coming into view on her symbol-logic screens. They were in the past now, and this CP ship was entitled, empowered, and expected to ask all the awkward questions that the uptime ship could not. There were a lot of questions that no one on board the *DP-IV* would want to answer. They could get into massive amounts of trouble if the downtime ship got too inquisitive.

Or maybe not, she thought. They had left Solace as it was just beginning its slide into ecological collapse, and they were in search of the man responsible for that failure. The world they had left behind might well be nothing but a hellish wilderness of death by the time they returned, a world of starvation, refugees, and riot. Compared to what life back on Solace might become, spending the rest of their lives under Chronologic Patrol interrogation sounded downright cozy. And the chance of catching the man who had done it made the risks seem acceptable to Norla.

Flying under the false name "Merchanter's Dream," the *Dom Pedro IV* boosted away from the timeshaft wormhole.

CHAPTER TWO

BODYGUARDS

Anton Koffield watched the displays as the *Dom Pedro IV* emerged from the timeshaft, and unclenched his fists as he read the symbol indicators that told the tale of a ship that had made it through. They were well and truly on their way.

He flexed his fingers, and rubbed them together, working out the tensions. The passage itself had held no fear for him. It was what the passage symbolized that had gotten him so keyed up. The move through the wormhole meant that he was well and truly in pursuit; the hunter, and no longer the prey.

By any rational measure, one passage through one wormhole was the most trivial milestone he would face on the journey ahead. It was the least of all the challenges on his way forward into darkness, his journey up and out of the plots and the mysteries that had wrapped themselves around him. But if he were to have the slightest hope of tracking and capturing Oskar DeSilvo, then first he had to overcome all the other challenges that stood in his way—and that included the quite routine business of transiting several timeshaft wormholes. He would have no chance of facing the greatest of dangers that lay ahead if the first and least of the needful steps defeated him.

Koffield had harbored the quite irrational fear that he would be stopped somehow before he could make the passage. Perhaps it was because so many cruel surprises had jumped out at him since that first day of the *Upholder* incident, so many long years ago. He had been trapped and tricked and turned back so many times—and always, it seemed, it had been Oskar DeSilvo there, waiting in the background, watching for Koffield to spring the trap DeSilvo had set and baited. Koffield had almost come to expect ambushes around every corner, hidden trickery in the safest of places. The ground had opened up under his feet so many times that there was no longer anyplace to stand that he fully trusted.

But DeSilvo isn't within light-years of us, Koffield told himself. *And some time has passed. It's even possible that he's dead again—even permanently dead this time—by now.* That idea hadn't occurred to Koffield before. The notion of a dead DeSilvo had its attractions; there was no doubt of that. But a dead DeSilvo would also seriously interfere with Koffield's plans. There were questions—urgent questions—they needed to ask the man. In his last communication, from beyond his falsified grave, DeSilvo had claimed to hold the keys to many treasures. *Let the man live,* he thought. *At least until I find him.* That notion cheered him, and he focused his attention once again on more immediate concerns—such as maintaining good relations with the ship's commander. He would be asking a lot of Marquez in the days and months—perhaps years—to come. It would only be prudent to work on keeping the man happy.

He turned to face Captain Marquez. "Nicely done," he said. "A good, clean transit run."

Marquez, clearly pleased with himself, his ship, and the words of praise from Koffield, made a graceful little shrug, lifting his shoulders and turning his palms upright. "Considering the state of the timeshaft, I think we managed all right," he said.

"Better than all right, from what I remember from pilot reports," Koffield said. "Thor's Realm has always been a rough patch."

Marquez nodded solemnly. "Yes, and a little rougher now than it was. Too much traffic, and a timeshaft cannot age gracefully."

Koffield cocked his head noncommittally. "That, I cannot judge, my friend. I've transited other Thor's Realm timeshafts—but never this one." If the idea was to keep Marquez happy, then the last thing he wanted to do was get drawn into the oldest of debates over timeshaft travel.

Theory said all timeshafts should be so much the same as to be indistinguishable from each other. But nearly all timeshaft captains claimed otherwise. Some wormholes were smooth and easy, others tight, rough, choppy. Every pilot had a theory about what caused the variation. Some—apparently including Marquez—even believed that the timeshafts themselves were aging, slowly decaying, wearing out as the long decades and centuries passed—though theory said that was impossible, too.

Koffield elected not to worry further about it. Some mysteries persisted, and that was all there was to it. He was far more interested in the mysteries he had some hope of solving—and there were plenty of those.

An alert tone buzzed on the comm console behind him. He spun about in his chair. Their expedition was already facing its next challenge—and one that was far more likely to give them some trouble.

"The downtime Chronologic Patrol ship is sending its automated info-query," he announced, no doubt unnecessarily. Everyone on board knew the downtime ship would query them—and everyone knew just how heavily armed a CP ship was, in the event it didn't like the answers it got.

Of course, what really had everyone worried was that the query-and-response system was automated on both ends. It would be the patrol ship's ArtInt asking the questions, and the *DP-IV*'s ship's Artificial Intelligence that would be giving the answers—and ArtInts did not make the best liars.

Ships' ArtInts, ShipInts, were designed, built, and programmed to be even more obsessed with protecting causality than the Chronologic Patrol itself. A ShipInt's primary function, above and beyond merely maintaining and operating its ship, was to prevent the past from being contaminated with knowledge of the future.

Usually, this was a fairly straightforward matter. A ShipInt would, for example, keep its ship's main communication systems locked down until the ship had passed through to the downside end of a given target wormhole. But time travel was a complicated business, and sometimes the demands on a ShipInt grew complicated as well—and that could lead to problems.

In the course of her journey to Solace, the *DP-IV* had been sabotaged, time-stranded in the future, and had two crew members die while coming out of cryosleep. The *DP-IV*'s ShipInt was expected to protect its crew—and the deaths had certainly struck hard at whatever it used for a psyche. Then, just before her present journey, something had happened that was almost as traumatic, from the AI's point of view. The ship had undergone a major upgrade and overhaul. It meant yanking some subsystems and hardware that had been installed centuries before, and replacing those with wholly new technology, four or five generations more recent than what it replaced. It would be difficult for a ShipInt to integrate the new gear under the best of circumstances—and circumstances were far from the best.

Each of these crises would be enough to give any ShipInt pause. Taken all together, the combination of shocks would make even a wholly stable ship's Artificial Intelligence twitchy, and that much less predictable or cooperative. Adding to the problem, ShipInts were programmed and built to grow increasingly suspicious, to the point of paranoia, with each additional perturbation from the normal operation of the ship.

With all that it had been through, the *DP-IV*'s ShipInt might already be edging toward complete psychosis, toward a point where it would regard the entire universe

as merely an elaborate plot designed to trick it into
something it wasn't supposed to do.

But even under those circumstances, the present Ship-
Int was too much part of the ship to risk replacing it, too
much woven into the detection systems and operational
controls. Any attempt at replacing it would be closely
akin to trying to perform a brain transplant on the
ship—which the ShipInt might, understandably, interpret as someone trying to do something that violated the
ShipInt's programming: a circumstance in which a ship's
ShipInt was programmed to self-destruct, taking the ship
with it.

Therefore, despite all the drawbacks to so doing, they
had left the old ShipInt in place. It was the proper course
to take, but it left the crew of the *Dom Pedro IV* in the
awkward position of hoping that an increasingly paranoid Artificial Intelligence would lie convincingly
enough to keep the cops from getting curious.

They had one thing going for them: a strange little
loophole in ShipInt programming called the "smuggler's
out." In order to remove any incentives for criminals to
engage in the major crime of casuality violation as a
means of getting away with minor offenses, ShipInts
were permitted to lie—about anything and everything
except times, dates, and matters pertaining to time
travel. They could lie about who they were, and what
they were doing, and where they were going—but they'd
damn well better not lie about when they were from.

Before the *Dom Pedro IV* had left Solace, her ShipInt
had been programmed, briefed, and bargained with by
the best ArtInt psychs in the Solacian star system. They
were reasonably certain the ShipInt was still sane and that
they had convinced it to stick with the "Merchanter's
Dream" story, but there was still the danger that it could
fall victim to a fit of honesty.

Anton Koffield found himself holding his breath as he
watched the display indicators report on the data transfer between the *Dom Pedro IV*/"Merchanter's Dream"
and the Chronologic Patrol ship. He sensed motion be-

hind himself and glanced back. He was not at all surprised to see Marquez there, a worried expression on his face, as he watched the displays for himself.

The transaction was over almost before it began. The main screen flipped over to text mode, showing the queries from the Chronologic Patrol ship in blue, and the responses from the *DP-IV*/"Merchanter's Dream" in green, both colors scrolling far too fast to read. It seemed as if the whole ship's party was holding its collective breath as the blur of text flew by. But then it was past and done, and one word, writ large, appeared on the screen.

APPROVED.

All strictly routine, of course. Everything had gone as planned. Maybe that was the surprising part. Sooner or later, Koffield knew, something was bound to go wrong. It was hard not to expect it to be sooner. *It's been a long time since things went right,* Koffield told himself.

And if things were going to go right, they would have to be kept secret. Who they were, what their ship was, what they were after—all of it had to be quiet, for complex and interlocking reasons.

First, DeSilvo himself might be watching for them, through an ArtInt programmed to monitor ship arrivals in the Solar System, for example. Far more importantly, they were after DeSilvo in large part to obtain suppressed technology. They didn't want to attract the attention of whatever authorities did the suppressing—and they didn't want to be prevented from getting the hardware.

Further, they didn't want to cause a panic. They were, after all, dealing with apocalyptic news: Baskaw's work had proved, with mathematical certainty, that not just Solace, but every terraformed world, was doomed. If that got out, it would mean trouble. It could cause wars, revolutions, chaos through Settled Space. Any local authorities who got wind of what they knew would, quite sensibly, clap them in irons at the very least to prevent all of that. Some authorities might well reflect on the fact that dead men told no tales.

Koffield knew that he, personally, had to keep his identity secret. He was still remembered, in certain quarters, as a combination boogeyman and Flying Dutchman. Wildly lurid and inaccurate versions of how he had wrecked Circum Central, doomed the planet Glister, and then vanished, still circulated. They would attract a great deal of attention if he came back to life a century-plus after vanishing.

Long ago, Koffield had run across a quotation from a near-ancient statesman. "In wartime," the statesman had written, "truth is so precious that she must be protected by a bodyguard of lies."

That idea had always appealed to him. The aphorism said a great deal about the ultimate purposes of secrecy and deceit, and also served as a strong reminder that there was much in human pursuits that never changed. The near-ancients might not have understood the operation of a timeshaft starship, any more than Koffield could sail a nineteenth-century oceangoing vessel. But the words reminded him that there was no stratagem, no tactical bluff, no outright lie, that had not been used time and again over the long millennia of human history.

Whatever gambit they tried, it was all but certain that someone had tried it before. And that meant the odds were very good that their opposition, possessed of vast experience and long memory, had encountered it before and would be ready for it.

It was going to take long and careful planning, and very sharp work indeed, in order to get past them.

Norla Chandray leaned back in her pilot's seat and let out a sigh. They were through. It was done. She glanced over at Koffield and read the expression on his face. By this time she knew him well enough, barely, to know what was on his mind. She had heard him speak of the way ahead, the challenges before them. Anton Koffield saw the passage as merely one early move in a game that was barely begun.

Norla shrugged and smiled to herself. That might be

Koffield's take on the passage. It wasn't hers. She likewise felt relieved to be through the wormhole, but perhaps for somewhat more immediate reasons.

To Norla, the passage *was* the game—and she had
won. Now she knew, really knew, that she was a pilot,
and a starpilot, too. She had gotten her start as an interplanetary pilot—and everyone knew that interplanet
was where the washout candidates from interstellar service wound up. She had gotten her starside certificates
much later than most, and done so by virtue of taking
the exams repeatedly—despite the strong discourage-
ment of the test proctors. While, technically speaking,
the regulations permitted candidates to retake the exams, it simply was not the done thing. But Norla had
gone ahead and done it. The choice had not made her
popular—but, on the fourth try, it got her a starside cer-
tificate.

The *Dom Pedro IV* had been her first—and so far
last—starside berthing. And on the first run with Norla
aboard, the *DP-IV* had gone and gotten stranded 127
years in the future. Suddenly everything Norla knew
about ships was more than a century out-of-date.

But in spite of all that, here she was, on the pilot's
chair aboard a ship on the downtime side of a timeshaft.
She had taken a ship through a wormhole—and no one,
anywhere, could say that a woman who could do that
wasn't a pilot.

All very well and good, but this was no time to rest on
her laurels. There was work to be done. First off, she had
to find Asgard Five. It was out there, somewhere on the
downtime side of the hole.

Koffield came over and stood behind her as she
started the job. She instantly got a strong signal, and had
a position and course plotted in nearly as fast.

"Quick work," Koffield said to her. "A second Alaxi
Sayad."

"Thank you, sir," said Norla. It was an obscure enough
reference that she was sure no one else on board would
know what it meant. But Koffield had told her stories.
Sayad had performed miracles of detection and plotting

aboard Koffield's old ship, the *Upholder*. Koffield had always held Sayad in high esteem, and Norla was sincerely proud to be compared to her.

On the other hand, most things with Koffield had their dark side, even his compliments. Sayad had been killed in the line of duty, scant minutes after doing the work that had so impressed Koffield.

Marquez checked the status boards, and then nodded toward Norla.

"Let us pay a visit to Asgard," he said. Norla engaged the preset course, and the *DP-IV* commenced her boost away from the wormhole and toward Asgard Station Five.

The station was roughly eighty astronomical units from the wormhole—nearly twice as far as the distance between Pluto and the Sun at closest approach. Even at top acceleration, the *DP-IV* would take nearly a week to get there.

Basic physics dictates that wormholes could not be closer than about a quarter light-year from each other. The Thor's Realm Wormhole Farm encompassed a dozen wormholes, and the volume of space under Farm jurisdiction was roughly ten cubic light-years. But even in the midst of so much isolation, the Chronologic Patrol imposed harsh security on wormhole stations. No ship was allowed to approach a wormhole station except on a direct path through the wormhole from the uptime end to the downtime end, and then straight in to the station. If a ship approached from outside Wormhole Farm space, without having transited the timeshaft, the CP would blow it out of space without warning.

As with all other wormhole stations, Asgard Five carried no detection or communications gear, beyond a carefully shielded interior telephone system. Robotic e-ferrets scuttled endlessly over the station, searching constantly and tirelessly for comm systems. The whole system was there to prevent someone using radio to beam in information, and thus get future knowledge into the past. Doubtless there were other security procedures, there for the same purpose, that outsiders didn't know about.

Norla stared glumly at her displays as the *DP-IV* came about and headed toward the station. It was not pleasant to reflect on all that security. Even if it was not intended to protect against the sort of schemes that Koffield had in mind, the mere fact that so many were watching so intently made it just that much more likely they'd see something. And there was a lot those aboard the *DP-IV/* "Merchanter's Dream" did not want seen.

Captain Marquez stood resolutely behind Norla Chandray, his hands firmly folded behind his back. He was determined to avoid interfering with her as she performed the docking maneuver. He doubted that any ship's captain had ever been fully comfortable with handing over a closing maneuver to a subordinate.

But this time, at least, he need not have worried. The "Merchanter's Dream" eased into a docking berth at Asgard Five. The docking clamps boomed down into place, securing the big ship to the station's exterior cageworks. A smooth, steady bit of piloting. "Nice work, Officer Chandray," Marquez conceded.

"Thank you, sir." Chandray checked her boards. "Ship's ArtInt reports safe docking and a good pressure seal. The station's systems are jacking in. Stand by—there. We're clear to open our hatch to the station."

"Why then, let us go do so. Officer Chandray, if you'd be so good as to stay at your post and stand the first watch, I'd like to take our first station party over." He glanced at Hues Renblant before he went on. If ever a man wanted off a ship, it was Renblant—and Marquez wanted no reluctant members in his crew. "We have some business to attend to, and I'm sure that at least some of us are eager to get on with it."

They were trying to act normal, and one of the normal things a ship did was to drop off and pick up crew—and Hues Renblant was determined to hold Marquez to the letter of his employment contract. That document included the "prevention of stranding clause" that gave Renblant the right to be put down "at any intermediate way station or port of call where he might reasonably expect to obtain further employment, provided that appropriate notice is given of the intention of the officer to resign from the company of the ship, and so long as the officer continues in diligent exercise of his duties until arrival at such way station or port of call."

A contract was a contract, and no one could find an escape clause that applied to the situation. Despite the security risks, Marquez had to agree to let Renblant disembark at the station. Fortunately, the contract did not require him to let Renblant deadhead all the way to their final destination, though Renblant had tried to make that claim. Otherwise, they would have been forced to leave him off at Earth. That, of course, would have been a thousand times worse, from a security point of view. And a thousand times better, from Renblant's perspective—and Renblant knew it. That they would not grant him transport to Earth had quickly become another of his grievances.

It was bad enough that they had to take him as far as Asgard. Marquez hated to do it, but he knew—and Koffield agreed—that they had to allow Renblant off or risk the collapse of morale among those who remained aboard, who would quite rightly see themselves as prisoners.

Asgard Five had started out as headquarters for the construction team that had built the wormhole, and it had grown from there, built out of whatever bits and pieces of ships and cargo carriers that came to hand. Some of the station was purpose-built modules, hauled to Asgard for the express purpose of adding them to the station. But most of it was made from left-behind hardware, bits and pieces of ships and cargo carriers that had made it through the wormhole but had been abandoned in place—ships and parts of ships that had been damaged during transit through the wormhole, ships whose entire crews had died, and ships that had plain run out of fuel, or financing. Any spacecraft that suffered bad luck but survived the wormhole wound up becoming part of the station.

In effect, the "Merchanter's Dream" was docked to a starship graveyard, an agglomeration of derelict spacecraft, welded and bolted and docked and bonded to each other any which way. It was a depressing thought, even to those of the station's visitors not given to superstition. So far out from everything else, light-years from the nearest star or planet, it was hard to keep one's imagination from dwelling on the endless cold and dark. Huddled up close to a black hole, even a station assembled from nothing but brand-new, purpose-built modules would likely have felt haunted.

It was the same story at nearly every wormhole station. Worse, perhaps, were the wormholes that did not have the traffic to justify a station. There, instead of a station built of wrecks, there were just the wrecks themselves. You could see their blips on radar, and it was easy to imagine them as they were, cold and dark, tumbling through the void, endlessly orbiting the wormhole that had killed them.

Marquez had fretted himself with the thought of haunted wormhole stations so often that the idea was almost comforting, in an odd sort of way. He knew, in his heart, that a wrecked spaceship was dead metal, scrap that might as well be reused, and nothing more. He could enjoy the little *frisson* of dread, imagining the dead crews lurking in the corridors of their salvaged ships, and then turn the fear off and move on.

No, it was the new worries, the *realistic* worries, the ones concerned with possible, even probable, dangers, that had him jumpy. He glanced to his right, at Hues Renblant. The soon-to-be-former officer had the strap of his duffel bag over his right shoulder, and the weight of the big bag was nearly bending him double. Renblant would no doubt be far more comfortable if he set the bag down while waiting on the hatch and lifted it up once the hatch opened—but that would have delayed his departure from the *Dom Pedro IV*/"Merchanter's

Dream," perhaps by as long as several seconds. A blind man could have read Renblant's eagerness to be gone.

Marquez let out a sigh. No, ghosts need not trouble him. Not when the living were clearly more than willing to provide that service. Then he glanced to his right, and Yuri Sparten. "Ready for your first performance, Captain?" Marquez asked him in a near whisper.

"Quiet, sir, please," Sparten replied in even lower tones, without looking at Marquez or shifting his expression. "It's just possible they're already monitoring somehow. We really shouldn't give Them any reason to pay attention to us," he whispered to Marquez.

Marquez smiled. Why should They—whoever They were—monitor a perfectly nondescript ship like the "Merchanter's Dream"? Well, it was perhaps right and proper for an officer working undercover—double cover, if Marquez's suspicions were correct—to exhibit a certain paranoia. And no doubt the lad would have been nervous no matter who he was really working for. Impersonating a ship's captain was a serious bit of fraud to commit, no matter how good the cause.

The airlock's inner hatch swung open, and Renblant was the first one through it, moving with quite indecent haste and no respect for protocol. "Captain" Sparten should have been the first to go enter the lock, but Renblant got there first. That in and of itself would have been sign enough of things amiss, to anyone who knew Renblant. No doubt Hues Renblant felt the irregularities aboard the *Dom Pedro IV* were egregious enough to free him from any demands of ship's etiquette.

No one else tried to shoulder past the "captain." To Marquez's eye, Sparten looked particularly young and nervous as he stepped from ship's steel into the station. Marquez followed him into the lock, watching his back, literally and figuratively, and Koffield brought up the rear.

Marquez watched Renblant as he fidgeted in the lock chamber, waiting for the outer door. Renblant took the whole situation as a direct insult, aimed precisely at him. A man who felt like that might decide the rules did not apply, that he was entitled to break them, or even that he had a moral obligation to break them, for the sake of the greater good.

And a man who started thinking that way could put them all in danger.

Marquez was not in the least bit sorry to have him off the ship.

CHAPTER THREE

ALL THEIR SINS
REMEMBERED

The idea, Koffield reminded himself as he brought up the rear of the little group boarding the station, was to behave normally. But what was "normal" in a place like Asgard Five? Wormhole stations were not places where the social graces were much overpracticed.

Their party crowded into the airlock and Marquez made his way through a thicket of arms and elbows to the command panel. He worked the controls, sealing the inner door behind them. The inner door swung shut and sealed itself.

So much for behaving normally, Koffield thought. Long before, Marquez and Koffield had decided to keep the ship's airlock sealed at all times, rather than following the more common procedure of leaving the hatches between ship and station open to allow free access. But there were captains who elected to keep their locks sealed. After all, the technical skills and the personal ethics of wormhole-station personnel were often indifferent at best. It would be assumed that "Captain" Sparten was worried about keeping his ship's air supply from leaking out, and/or cargo pilferers from getting in. It couldn't be helped. They couldn't allow the "Merchanter's Dream" to be boarded or inspected—especially by the likes of wormhole stationers.

As the lock cycled, the tight quarters of the lock chamber, the crowded-in knot of nervous men, the faint whiff of fear-sweat irresistibly reminded Koffield of his first encounter with men who chose to live cut off from all others.

Long, long before, back on Earth, Koffield had been a very young Chronologic Patrol officer-in-training. As part of that training, Koffield had served with a Customs inspection team in the Indian Ocean. The idea was to learn something of the basic procedures—and of the tensions and dangers—of boarding and inspecting a vessel, without the expense of packing cadets off into interstellar space.

Their team was assigned the task of boarding merchant ships and spot-checking their manifests against the actual cargo. The inspectors searched diligently, and ran all the proper checks. They did not ever find anything beyond the most trivial of violations, nor had they expected to do so.

And yet all the crew aboard all the ships had always melted away whenever possible. The ship crews worked so hard to avoid the Customs teams that once or twice Koffield wondered if they had boarded automated ships, with no one aboard but the captain. It was plainly obvious the men—and they were nearly all men—had something to hide. As Koffield had gradually learned, that something was themselves. Practically the only people willing to endure the isolated, largely anonymous, and usually solitary life aboard an ocean freighter were those with a tax judgment, or a lawsuit, or an ex-spouse, or an ex–business partner, or a conscientious and thorough sheriff, or the like, waiting out there in the real world.

That was even more true for the denizens of a wormhole station. Places like Asgard Five were where you went to get away, to hide. People who had no place left to go, who had something they could not bear to face, or who simply could not work up the courage, or the cost of a ticket, or the luck—to get back aboard a passing ship.

The advantage, so far as Koffield was concerned, was that the folk aboard the station weren't overlikely to notice if anyone in their party happened to act a bit out of character. Koffield was particularly worried about Yuri Sparten. He was crowded up against the young man, and it would have been hard not to give him a thorough looking-over. Koffield did not expect to be impressed, and he was not. Yuri might be wearing the cap and the uniform, but he did not look remotely like someone in command. He was plainly young and inexperienced.

Very inexperienced. This was, in point of fact, the lad's first-ever trip out of the Solacian system. And yet, there he was, playing at being a starship captain!

Koffield was certain that Sparten had been assigned to watch him. No matter. Let him have a front-row seat, and watch as closely as he liked. So long as he didn't get the chance to talk about it with outsiders.

Pressure equalized, the outer door of the lock swung open, and the party from the "Merchanter's Dream" entered Asgard Five. Koffield was not surprised to find there was no reception committee waiting on the station side of the lock. Perhaps the stations was understaffed, and there weren't enough warm bodies around to provide the usual courtesy of a welcome. Or, more likely, the crew wasn't much given to socializing for its own sake.

They stepped from the hatch—Renblant again in the lead—into a long corridor that took a couple of sharp turns necessitated by the need to connect the main lock complex with a docking port on the far side of an over-size cargo bay.

As they walked along the access tunnel toward the main lock complex, Koffield managed to drift back enough to let everyone else get ahead. He was much less interested in protocol and respect to rank than he was in keeping an eye on everyone—a job best done from the rear. He was not much surprised to find the party pausing as it came out of the tunnel. Hues Renblant, though he might be eager to lead the way, had never been on

Asgard Five before, and he stood irresolute, in the center of the lock complex, not at all sure of which way to go. Quite automatically, Renblant looked to his captain for guidance—and then realized what he was doing, and blushed furiously.

For all his talk of getting free, free, free, of Marquez and the *DP-IV* as soon as humanly possible, his first reflex had been to turn to Marquez, Captain Marquez, for guidance. Even worse, Marquez was the only one of the group who had been there before, and knew the way. Marquez, allowing himself a smile, eased himself to the front of the group.

"Come, my friends," said Marquez. "This way."

The little group made its way deeper into the bowels of Asgard Five Station.

The lighted sign over the compartment hatch read MEETING ROOM FOUR—RESERVED FOR MERCHANTER'S DREAM DISEMBARKATION CONFERENCE. Relieved to have finally arrived at his goal, Renblant pushed open the hatch and stepped in, followed by the rest of the shore party. He watched as Sparten, Koffield, and Marquez filed in. Marquez shut and locked the door, and the three of them sat at one long side of the conference table, Marquez in the middle, Koffield to his left, farthest from the door, and Sparten to the right.

Renblant sat down on the other side of the table, in the middle, facing Marquez. "All right," he said. "Let's get this over with. What's your offer?"

Marquez settled back in his chair, smiled blandly, and folded his arms in front of his chest. "Offer? What offer?"

"Don't play games," Renblant snapped. "Your offer for my silence."

"Funny thing about silence," said Marquez. "It's an odd commodity. The less there is of it, the less it's worth."

Renblant frowned. "What are you talking about?" he demanded.

"You spent the last six months talking to anyone who

would listen about your accusations," said Marquez. "Like the old saying goes, the cat's out of the bag—but you want to charge us for putting it back in, and pretend it never got out."

"Your people had me watched!" Renblant said. "You kept me cooped up where I couldn't talk to anyone from the outside."

"That didn't stop you trying. I think you even succeeded, once or twice. There were a few news stories that had to be hushed up. And none of it made us think you *wanted* to keep quiet. Do you know the old saying about Caesar's wife?"

Renblant was confused. "Ah, no," he said.

"They said it wasn't enough that she was innocent. She had to be above suspicion. I sort of feel that way about a starship crewman looking to receive a large silence payment. How do you feel about that?"

This was not going the way Renblant had thought it would. He glanced toward Koffield. He had expected Koffield to be the one doing the talking. "The things I said. Why penalize me when they didn't actually hurt you? After all, you *did* hush them up."

"For the time being. Things do tend to leak, sooner or later. But certainly the fact that you spoke before—and that you said such unkind things about the admiral— make your promise of future silence far less reliable and valuable."

Renblant swallowed hard, and realized that he was sweating. None of this was according to plan. He opened his mouth, but no useful words came out.

"Why don't *you* make *us* an offer?" said Captain Marquez. "What do *you* think your silence—or rather, your promise to keep silent—is worth?"

Renblant blinked hard, and then managed to stammer out a figure—a figure toward the middle-low range of where he had intended the deal to be made.

Marquez smiled coldly and cocked his head to one side. "Oh," he said. "I see. Well, why don't you try again?"

• • • •

Koffield was largely content with the end result of the negotiation. The deal they finally cut was long, tedious, detailed—and far less lucrative than Renblant had expected.

Ships and crew bought and sold silence contracts all the time. However, one thing did make this deal special: After all, the secrets being protected concerned the fate of worlds, not who was sleeping with whom, or price-fixing on transport fees. Renblant did not know the whole story—far from it. But even the bits and pieces he did know could lead a moderately patient researcher toward the truth—that the collapse of human civilization outside the Solar System had already begun, unnoticed. And that perhaps, not so far in the future, humanity would be extinct outside the Solar System.

Koffield watched Renblant as the session ended and they gathered up their belongings and left. He hoped, for Renblant's own sake, that it had occurred to the fellow that others besides his old shipmates would wish him to keep silent. It would also be best for Renblant if it occurred to him that there were surer ways of ensuring his silence, besides paying for it. If Renblant did choose to talk, and wasn't careful about whom he chose for a listener—well, it would likely be the last talking he ever did.

Koffield saw the scowl on Renblant's face as he signed the agreement and shoved it back across the table for Marquez's signature. Koffield had not the slightest doubt that Renblant intended to violate their agreement the first chance, and every chance, he got. But, fortunately for all but Renblant, he was going to be doing that talking in a place where no one was likely to listen. He wondered if Renblant knew what he was letting himself in for. Anyone who wasn't solitary and twitchy when he or she came aboard Asgard Five was all but certain to get that way after a month or year on the station, floating there in the dark between the stars.

Koffield devoutly wished Renblant a long wait between ship arrivals. Koffield had done a lot of homework on the subject, learning all he could about the patterns of ship arrivals at the station. He had very carefully timed out their voyage so as to produce the highest possible odds of an extended stay for Renblant. The longer he was stuck there, the longer it would be until anyone heard his story.

The four men put their notes and agreements away. Marquez signed and thumbed the payment plaque, stood up, and handed it to Renblant. Now they came to the trickiest part of the whole affair. The agreement concerned silence and secrets on specific topics, and those secrets were itemized in the agreement—with the result that it could not be brought out in any sort of hearing or trial without defeating the purpose of the agreement. The time-honored solution was to make a further agreement, about the agreement.

Marquez started a witness recorder, and spoke for its benefit. "With the signing of a sealed agreement, and the transfer of the agreed amount, I, Felipe Henrique Marquez, do conclude this agreement with Hues Renblant, as of the date and time indicated on the witness recorder making this record. Hues Renblant, will you speak?"

"I will speak," he replied. "With the signing of a sealed agreement, and the transfer of the agreed amount, I, Hues Renblant, do conclude this agreement with Felipe Henrique Marquez as of the date and time indicated on the witness recorder making this record."

And it was over. Somehow, not just the closing statements, but the whole meeting—the verbal jousting, the dickering, the fussing over the precise language of the agreement—had had the feel of ritual to it, of sympathetic magic, of a thing played out in the hope that it might actually work. Say these words, make these promises, make this offering of just the right size, in just the right way—not too cruel, not too polite—before your opposite number. Perform the purification incantation in precisely the approved manner, and then the problem would vanish. All could go on about their business, all their sins washed away, forgiven and forgotten.

But no. That was not the way of it, and it was vital that he bear that in mind. Hues Renblant was an angry man and blamed Anton Koffield for his predicament. Renblant would remember all their sins for a long, long time.

CHAPTER FOUR

RECALLED TO LIFE

"Did you get the job done?" Norla asked, as Koffield and Marquez made their way into the *DP-IV*'s wardroom. With the ship powered down into station-dock mode, she had gone off duty and found herself something to eat. She had figured the returning party would stop there.

"Yes, we did," Marquez said as he poured himself some coffee and sat down across from her. "We've said all our farewells and kissed Renblant good-bye. And we had a pleasant little surprise. There is actually some Earthbound cargo we can carry waiting here for transshipment, and we've contracted to do the job. The station's cargo boss will start loading us at start of main shift tomorrow. Sparten's still in the cargo office, finishing up the arrangements."

"Is that good?" Norla asked. "I thought we were just going to let Renblant off and be on our way. Taking on cargo will slow us down."

"Not by very much," Koffield said mildly, bringing his own coffee to the table.

Norla smiled and shrugged. It went without saying that they were already years, even decades, behind their quarry. What difference could another day make?

"And it will make us a bit more believable as a cargo

ship if we actually have some meaningful cargo on board," Marquez added. "I never did think the stuff they put aboard at Solace was all that convincing."

Norla could see his point. There wasn't much from Solace that couldn't be gotten better or cheaper on Earth. "What about the warm-body issue?" For purposes of informing as few people as possible of the situation, no new crew members had been signed up on Solace. But with the departure of Renblant here, and the others before Solace departure, they were going to be distinctly shorthanded.

"I got the impression that there were some possibilities," Koffield said. "But it's highly likely that they'll want us more than we'll want them."

Norla hesitated, then decided she had to speak. "Sir, I think we might want whoever we can get from here, and want them more than you realize."

"What do you mean?" Koffield asked. "We'll have a much better choice of recruits in the Solar System."

"Yes, sir. That's just the trouble. I think there are a few consequences of that you haven't thought through all the way."

Marquez looked sharply at Norla. "If the admiral hasn't thought something through all the way, it'll be the first time ever."

"No it won't," Koffield said. "Far from it. If she's spotted something, I want to know about it." He turned back to Norla. "What is it you think I've missed?"

"That the potential crew members we'll recruit from back in the Solar System will have a lot more choice as well. No offense, Captain Marquez, but the *Dom Pedro IV* isn't exactly the latest model."

"Not by a couple of centuries," Marquez agreed.

"So she's not going to be a draw for top-flight crew looking for cutting edge. No one we sign here is going to have a chance to turn us down for a better offer. They won't even have a chance to look us over too hard, if we ship out in a day or so. But time works against us in the Solar System. We expect to spend a good chunk of time in the System, doing research on DeSilvo—and then, if

we're lucky, we'll head off to wherever the clues lead—
that is, if we even find any clues. We might have to head
back to Solace and start over. Whatever we do, we likely
won't be acting like a freighter by the time we leave.
We're going to seem suspicious as all hell. And whoever
we try and sign will have a lot of time to check us out,
think it over, and ask questions—in places we don't want
them asked."

Marquez frowned and looked to Koffield. "She makes
some good points," he said.

"There's another issue," Norla said. "I'm not doing
more than guessing at this next. I want that made clear.
No one has said anything, or hinted at anything. But.
What makes you so sure all of our present crew are definitely going to stay aboard, come what may? They're
merchanter crewmen, not explorers out to search the unknown or heroes looking to revenge ancient wrongs.
And whatever happened or happens to Solace isn't their
problem. They have been marooned in their own future—but they will have the chance to go home, at least
in a sense. Most of the crew is from the Solar System.
And we might be in the System for months—before we
launch off for the stars know where. A lot of motivation
to go ashore—and not much to stay on board. No one
has said they want off the ship—but human nature is human nature, and they'll be facing a lot of temptations. To
be blunt, we could wind up without enough crew to fly
the ship."

Marquez grunted sadly. "All true. But even so, surely
we should be able to sign some crew in the System."

"But who would those crew be?" Norla demanded.
"Who would they be working for? If I were the Chronologic Patrol, I'd get curious about a ship like ours. Admiral Koffield—you served in CP intelligence. Wouldn't
you have worked very hard to get a set of eyes and ears
aboard a ship that didn't seem to have any good reason
for what it was doing, and didn't have good answers to a
lot of simple questions?"

Koffield nodded. "Yes, I would. We'll do our best to

avoid getting noticed—but we'll have to assume that the CP will spot us the moment we arrive in the System. Any crew member we take on in the Solar System could easily be a CP agent."

Norla frowned. "I thought so. And there's more. To be more direct than I ought to be, just for a second, I know both of you—all three of us—believe Yuri Sparten is here to watch us, and the only question is—who for? And Wandella Ashdin—well, she's not crew, she's a passenger. The foremost Solacian expert on DeSilvo, and we'll need her expertise. She practically worshiped the man—until we came along and rubbed her nose in the proof of his crimes. She's friendly enough—but I don't know that she ever really forgave us for destroying her illusions—and people have a way of talking themselves out of things they can't bear to believe. How far can we trust her? Will she give us all the knowledge she finds— or will she hold back something that makes DeSilvo look bad, or maybe she'll decide we got it all wrong, and he doesn't deserve us chasing after him?"

Koffield frowned. "We've discussed this. We've planned all along to set someone to 'assist' her—to watch her, look over her shoulder."

"But that someone will have to be someone that you—that we—can trust. Which subtracts one more from the very small pool of trusted people we can send to do *other* work besides hold her hand. We're going to need more warm bodies than we have—and I think we'll lose bodies, not gain them, before we leave the Solar System."

"So we scrape the dregs of Settled Space off the decks of this station and sign them up instead?" Marquez demanded. "You don't exactly get high-quality people in a place like this."

"We don't have much choice," said Norla.

"That's true in more senses than one," Koffield said. "I think Officer Chandray is right, Captain Marquez. We have to recruit crew here. But the pickings are going to be slim."

"Not so bad as you might think," Norla said. She pulled a small datapad out of her breast pocket and handed it to Marquez.

"You've already been browsing the station's staffing data?" Koffield asked.

She shrugged. "I didn't see much point in bringing up the problem if there wasn't any way to solve it."

Marquez scrolled the personnel listed on the datapad, glancing through the service record summaries. "It says here twelve transients eligible for transfer are currently resident in the station. And how many of them do you think might be usable, if we lower our standards enough, perhaps?"

"Six of them I'd reject out of hand, just on service record," Norla said.

Koffield took the datapad from Marquez. He looked over the screen. "That many?" he asked. "I only see three I'd red-flag immediately."

"I agree." said Norla. "Three are scratches because it's completely obvious they are disasters that have already happened and are waiting to happen again. But then another three were born on Earth. I looked them over, and what they've done to try and get back. Sign any of them, take them back to the Solar System, and I'd say the odds are about 80 percent they'd make Renblant look like he was taking his time going ashore."

"That's pretty hard-edged," said Marquez. "And here I thought you were the sentimental one."

"We're on a tough mission," she said, her tone a trifle defensive. "I think we're going to be shorthanded. Maybe shorthanded enough to get us in trouble. But that's no reason to run a very expensive back-to-Earth taxi service for hard-luck cases. Especially when doing so might leave us even more shorthanded, and closer to trouble."

Marquez was still studying the pad. "There's one Earth-born transient you didn't downcheck," he objected.

"Jerand Bolt. His record doesn't exactly say 'homesick' to me," said Norla. "More like 'tourist.' He's al-most never signed up to crew on a ship that's going someplace he's already been. And he's had at least five chances to go over the side in the Solar System. Never taken any of them."

"But he's never been stuck in one place this long, ei-ther," Koffield observed. "And he's got a medical down-check."

"Cryosleep averse," Norla agreed. "But it doesn't have any bearing to service on our ship. We're upgraded to temporal confinement."

Marquez smiled "Thank you, Officer Chandray, for reminding me, but I was aware of that fact. You like this fellow," he said, tapping his finger on the datapad.

Norla turned her hands palm up in a studiously non-committal gesture. "I like specs I see, for him, and two or three others on that list. Bolt's sheet says he's a born wanderer who's been stuck here forever. I read that as in-centive to stay on the *DP-IV*, not cut and run. But what's on the pad doesn't mean Bolt or the others are still up to spec. Still, it couldn't do any harm if someone went and talked to them. Someone fresh to the problem, with a clear objective in mind."

Koffield cocked his head and looked at Norla quizzi-cally. "I think, Captain Marquez, that I just heard the sound of someone volunteering. And her suggestion re-minds me that your pilot is likewise a born tourist—who has never actually been aboard a wormhole station. Or am I reading too much into your word choice, Officer Chandray?"

Norla grinned back at both of them. "No, sir, I don't think you are."

"Well, I don't see how a pilot is much use to us at the moment, seeing how the ship is docked to the station," said Marquez. "But I'm just the captain of the *Dom Pedro IV*. No authority here. I think we'd better wait for Captain Sparten of the 'Merchanter's Dream' to come back aboard. If we're pretending he's captain, we'd bet-ter pretend to ask his permission."

• • •

Jerand sat down at the smaller of two tables in the Transients' Wardroom of Asgard Five. His friends were already there, and he greeted them with a cordial smile as he removed his plate, cup, and utensils from his tray and stacked his tray with the others in the center of the table. For whatever reason, on this station, it was simply not the done thing to eat from dishes that sat on a tray. To do so would mark one out as an unmannered buffoon— at least on Asgard Five. Jerand had served on many ships and stations that cared not at all about such matters, but it was always wise to follow local custom.

He took his first bite of food and happened to glance casually up at the wall chronometer as he did so. He made the calculation without thinking, without any conscious choice at all. Five years, two months, seven days, three hours, two minutes, fourteen seconds.

There were times Jerand Bolt deeply regretted ever learning the simple mnemonic tricks that allowed him to keep track of precisely how long he had been on the station. But it was too late, far too late. The techniques were burned into his memory, down at the level of reflex. He could no longer look at a clock without automatically updating the count.

It was scarcely an exaggeration to say that the figure also represented how long he had been scheming and fantasizing over a way to get off Asgard Five.

Jerand Bolt was the senior transient on station, but that status brought few privileges. It certainly did not entitle him to permanent resident status. He could die of old age on Asgard Five and still be listed as a transient. Mostly what being senior transient brought him was the repeated chance to see transients who had been there less time leave before he did.

He glanced around the table and considered his companions. Biylert Stanless: three years, two months. Sindra Chon: two years, four months. And Clemsen Wahl, on station a mere five months and two weeks, so short a time that there was still some rational point to counting the weeks.

There were eight other transients on station, but the four of them didn't socialize much with that group. They were seated at the larger table in the Transients' Wardroom, but they might as well have been behind a steel bulkhead for all the conversation that passed between the two groups.

Long ago, Jerand found himself thinking of the two groups as the Malfunctions and the Volunteers—though he had never used either term with any outsider. Sometimes he wondered which of the mental labels was the more ironic.

The four Malfunctions had wound up stuck on Asgard due to real equipment failures, and no fault of their own. Jerand's cryocan, for example, had nearly killed him, and the malfunction had triggered a well-known immune reaction to cryonic medications, and thus left him with a permanent medical downcheck for travel via cryocan. The others were likewise forced ashore by equipment failures or supply shortages that had left their ships with more crew than the ship could safely transport between the stars. When the choice was to beach one crew member or to risk the lives of the whole crew, the math was pretty easy. It could be something as simple as a slow leak in the oxygen top-off tanks, leaving the ship without adequate reserves for a decades-long interstellar passage. That was what had gotten Sindra stuck.

The Volunteers, on the other hand, had all elected to depart their ships—at least to hear them tell it. Jerand suspected all of them had been invited to leave their ships in the strongest terms possible. To hear the Vols tell it, none of them had ever shipped with a competent captain, or on a properly maintained ship, or used any piece of hardware that wasn't broken before they got to it.

Jerand and his companions had long ago heard all the Vols' stories. It was, as much as anything, the sincere desire to avoid hearing them again that caused the four Malfunctions to sit at a separate table, and to otherwise avoid off-duty socializing with the Vols as much as possible.

On duty, there wasn't much choice, one way or the other. All the transients drew the same duties—any and all unpleasant, low-skill, nonautomated jobs. The permanent staff neither knew nor cared which transient did which job. They didn't even rate human attention when it came to work assignments—the station's auxiliary ArtInt handled the transients' worksheets without human intervention. Malfs and Vols were thrown together during work hours.

"So what's the story on the arrival?" Sindra asked, shifting over a bit to give Jerand room.

"The *Merchanter's Something-or-Other*," Jerand said as he reached for his fork. "Don't know much more beyond that."

"Well, I do," said Clemsen, the eagerness in his voice plain to hear, even in the near whisper they all employed, more or less automatically, whenever any Volunteers were in earshot. "Inbound from Solace. Not many ships from there, these days. Outbound for the Solar System. Letting down an officer—and he didn't look half-sad to be leaving. I saw him coming down a corridor, looking real glad to be here instead of there."

"Malf?" Biylert asked eagerly. "Or Volunteer?"

Clemsen shrugged. "Vol, it looks like. I sort of drifted by station ops and chatted with him while he was getting prelim processing. He didn't say much—who would, with your ship still docked? But I got the idea there was something plenty strange on their ship, even if there wasn't anything wrong. He's in guest quarters tonight. My guess is he'll be at the other table"—he jerked his head toward the Vols—"by lunchtime tomorrow."

"Great," Biylert growled. "Another character we won't be on speaking terms with."

"Maybe, maybe not," Clemsen said. "But there's one other tidbit I did pick up. Jerand—her name is the *Merchanter's Dream*. And she's all temporal confinement. No one flying in cryo."

Jerand looked up sharply, and it was a struggle to keep from dropping his fork. His cryo downcheck had kept him stranded here all this time. Temporal confinement ships were few and far between—and none of the ones that had docked at Asgard in all that time had been looking for new crew. He opened his mouth and shut it again, unable to make the words come out. Suddenly, there was a ray of hope, a key in the lock—and he couldn't dare ask the question that might make it all go away. If they weren't taking crew on, then it wouldn't matter. But if they were . . .

"So they need bodies?" Sindra asked, plainly ready to risk the answer. "They recruiting?"

"Oh, yes," said a new voice, from behind Jerand's back.

Jerand nearly jumped out of his seat. No one had moved quietly enough to surprise him in a long time.

"Yes, indeed, we are doing just that."

Jerand turned around in his chair and looked up to see a stranger, a woman with short blond hair, wearing a uniform coverall of a design he had never seen before. He noted the words MERCHANTER'S DREAM on a rather drab and uninteresting shoulder patch. "You're doing what?" he asked. "And who are you?" But deep in his gut, instantly, he already knew the answers—and that was just as well, for his heart was racing so fast and so loud he wasn't sure he'd be able to hear her reply.

"I'm an officer on the *Merchanter's Dream*," she said. "And we're definitely looking to recruit." She nodded to Jerand. "You're Bolt," she went on. "I want to talk with you."

INTERLUDE

DESILVO

Eighty-seven Years Before
Temporal Confinement Chamber,
Undisclosed Location

Dr. Oskar DeSilvo moaned and muttered in his sleep, pursued by his dreams. He laughed, cried out, then shouted in alarm and sat bolt upright in his cot, suddenly drenched in sweat, his heart pounding.

He slapped on the light and tried to calm himself. The dreams were starting to get to him, even if he couldn't remember anything at all about them. Chasing. That was the best he could recall. But was he the pursuer—or the pursued? He had a vague sense that he shifted from one role to another as he dreamed.

He glanced at the clock to see what time it was, and laughed at the futility of the gesture. The question *what time is it?* had no meaning, and far too much meaning, inside temporal confinement. He had been in here about two days, subjective time, and he was running a confinement of approximately one to fifty-two hundred—a century going past outside for every week inside the confinement. According to his chrono displays, in the outside world, just over twenty-eight years had passed. The end not yet in sight.

He got up off the cot, stretched, and began his morning exercises. Twenty sit-ups. Oskar DeSilvo took his health very seriously. He knew himself to be in astonishing good health for a man his age—even if he himself was not entirely clear what age he was. According to the chronologic display, it was at present the year 5254—no, there, it had just rolled over! It was 5255, and Oskar DeSilvo had been born in the year 4893. That gave a crude figure of 362 years old, but of course, it was meaningless. By that logic, he had aged fourteen years since yesterday!

He finished the sit-ups and began a series of stretching exercises. Thanks to timeshaft wormholes, cryogenic canisters, and temporal confinement, Oskar DeSilvo had traveled back and forth through large swathes of the years between his birth and the present day, over and over again—but he had been frozen solid for much of that time, or else held in temporal confinement. A lesser but significant factor had been relativistic effects: repeatedly traveling for years at a time at 10 or 20 percent of the speed of light threw off age computation by a significant amount. And more than interstellar travel had confused any calculation of his life span. He had also done before what he was doing now: used temporal confinement and cryo without going anywhere, merely waiting out events, skipping over years and even decades, until this or that project had come to fruition.

But never had he waited out this much time. Twenty-eight years was longer than he had ever time-jumped before—and he wasn't anywhere near done yet.

In part, he was awaiting Anton Koffield, who was, in this year of 5255, in cryogenic storage aboard the *DP-IV*, en route to Solace. It would be another eighty-odd years before the *Dom Pedro IV* arrived. Sooner or later, Koffield would find the clues that he, DeSilvo, had left behind there. Those clues ought to lead Koffield straight back toward the Solar System, and from there . . .

DeSilvo smiled as he began jogging in place, imagining

all that was in store for Koffield. It might even kill him.
His main plan was dependent on Koffield surviving, but
even if the Koffield gambit failed, even if the system's
manual release failed, then the temporal-confinement
system would automatically release DeSilvo some years
late, and he would work from there.

Besides DeSilvo had more reasons than Koffield for
time-jumping such a distance. His projections and fore-
casts had proved so disastrously wrong in the past, and
this time he had to be sure.

DeSilvo bathed in the tiny folding refresher, and prepared his morning meal in the galley-cubby, then went
straight to his small folding desk—not a long trip, as the
entire confinement chamber was scarcely three meters in
any dimension. Data had been accumulating "overnight," and he was eager to get a look at it. It was difficult, though by no means impossible, to communicate
from one side to another of a temporal confinement, and
Oskar had made certain arrangements to receive data
covertly from a number of sources. He scanned the information eagerly, hoping to spot something definitive,
something that could make him certain he was right—
but he soon gave it up as a bad job. There was nothing.
Twenty-eight years was barely enough time to establish
trend lines, let alone reach conclusions, on the experiment he was running.

Experiment! An experiment with the entire human
race serving as the test population. But he dared not act
until he was certain. No rash mistakes. No hubris. Not
this time. Or was it hubris to let things alone, to let
things go on as they were for another hundred years?

If so, let it be. He dared not interfere. Not again.
What if he was wrong again—or what if someone else,
in the ninety or so years he still had to wait, found another answer? No. He would extract what he could from
the spotty data that managed to reach him—and then
emerge, as planned.

With luck, Koffield would be there. And he would
show Koffield what needed to be done. Koffield would

see, would understand, would accept the necessity of following the orders of Dr. Oskar DeSilvo. He would accept his proper role as DeSilvo's subordinate.

Oskar DeSilvo smiled. Somehow, the time remaining suddenly did not seem so long.

on her tongue, even if she did, it almost seemed rehearsed.

thoughts became more and more confused, and that
the vague hand-shaking, too, also was a part of

CHAPTER FIVE

EIGHTY YEARS AT A COCKTAIL PARTY

It was obvious there were some funny things happening
aboard the "Merchanter's Dream," but Jerand Bolt
didn't like to ask questions until he had learned as much
as possible on his own. Sindra Chon felt the same way,
but it was clear that Clemsen was bursting with curiosity, much good it would do him. No one aboard was
willing to tell them anything.

But some things didn't need telling. It was clear to see
that their "captain," Yuri Sparten, didn't know one end
of a starship from another. He leaned on his first officer
so hard it was a wonder that they both didn't fall over.
Jerand soon got the very distinct impression that the so-
called first officer was in fact the ship's master. The first
officer was calling himself Hari Leptin, but it was hard
not to notice that he often failed to respond to that name
on the first pass.

Clemsen claimed to have watched as "Leptin" mis-
spelled his own name on a shipping document before
hurriedly correcting himself.

The second officer, the blond woman who had recruited them—she was certainly in on it, whatever it
was. She had handed out the name Leona Sendler, but
somehow, she wasn't convincing. The name didn't roll

off her tongue when she said it. It almost sounded rehearsed.

Although he became more and more convinced that "Leptin" was the real captain, he was also starting to get the feeling that he wasn't the ship's ultimate commander. Jerand was inclined to name the passenger who called himself "Alber Caltrip" as the real leader. He was better about keeping up appearances than the others. You couldn't catch him out the way you could with "Leptin." He answered to "Caltrip" smoothly and perfectly, as if he had been born to the name, and not been assigned it at the start of their present journey. He played the part of a rich man with a touch of wanderlust most convincingly. But things that others did made Jerand wonder about Caltrip. The others all deferred to him, for a start. And Jerand had noticed that one or two of the other old members of the crew slipped now and then, and addressed him as "Admiral." That was hard to miss. At a guess, Caltrip had hired the ship to take him to Earth, for whatever reason, and had reasons for keeping it secret.

Still, Jerand wasn't much concerned at first. If the officers wanted to play at disguises and dress-up, and some of them got sloppy about it, that was their problem. If they wanted to call the ship by this name instead of that, what difference did it make? Ships did such things once in a while, usually in hopes of dodging taxes somewhere or other.

In the meantime, Jerand felt himself sliding easily back into the long, punctuated rhythms of life aboard a timeshaft ship as the journey of the ship that pretended to be the "Merchanter's Dream" rolled on.

Predeparture was resupply and systems checks, and, for new crew like the three Asgard Malfs, a chance to get familiarized with unfamiliar hardware. Then came the *boost phase*, accelerating away from the station. *Postdeparture* was a month of hard work, preparing the ship for the decades-long transit to come. Storing cargo in protective cocoons, cleaning and adjusting and powering down systems that were vital on arrival at the destination but would not be used for many long years. Searching endlessly for tiny flaws and malfunctions that might grow into huge ones, if left to themselves. Arguing over and over with the ship's Artificial Intelligence, which always wanted more repair, more replacement, more upgrade. In Jerand's experience, all ShipInts were twitchy and overdemanding—but the buzzbrain on this tub went right to the edge.

Then, at long last, came *dormant cruise*, as both ship and crew powered down for the long, long ride between the stars, with the ship in the care of the ShipInt and the crew in one form or another of suspended animation. A given ship might use the old and highly unpleasant version of cryogenic canisters, or the vastly better system— if power-hungry—form of temporal confinement, but either way meant bypassing the endless and tedious years of travel between the stars.

A smart captain—and, it would seem, either Sparten or "Leptin" was that much, at least—made sure the crew had a few days of tailing down and rest after the rush of postdeparture. Bolt had served on ships where the captain, under some misplaced sense of order and efficiency, had ordered the crew into their cryocans directly after their final work shift, as if it would slow down the ship if they had a few days of light duty before freeze-down. Of course, all that did was ensure that the crew would wake up with the same stiff muscles and sore backs and empty bellies they had entered the cans with decades before. But the "Merchanter's Dream" operated under more humane and sensible policies.

Every other phase of the journey was in large part familiar to Jerand, but temporal confinement was new to him, and he found himself looking forward to Confinement Day with eager anticipation. Jerand Bolt, if he was anything, was a sucker for new experiences.

The work schedule for the night before Confinement Day included only the lightest and slightest of last-minute details, all quickly completed. The rest of the evening was dedicated to all the things they would not have in confinement—good food, privacy, and enough room, for starters. On cryocan ships, the Last Night before Cryo-day generally included an all-hands meal, with the entire ship's company together one last time before they entered the cans. In the cold and the dark of a cryocan, a person was alone, and, in cryodreams, often desperately lonely. And there was, after all, something like a one in five hundred chance that you'd never wake up. Last Night might well be just that. It gave you a chance to say your just-in-case good-byes.

But an all-confinement ship required a different psychology. They were all going to be jammed in together for a good long while.

Besides which, the crew of the "Merchanter's Dream" was sliced up into three distinct groups that did not socialize with one another. There were the officers and passengers in one group, the original crew members—and the three Malfs, who had signed on at Asgard.

The three new arrivals had found their fellow crew members a remarkably tight-lipped group, quite unwilling to talk about anything besides shipboard work. Nothing about their personal lives, nothing about the ship's previous ports of call or its present journey.

So the Malfs found themselves holding a Last Night dinner by themselves, and falling instantly, Jerand discovered, into the old habits of life aboard Asgard Five, of a life and a universe that was Us against Them.

"Can someone please tell me what is going on aboard this ship?" Clemsen demanded as he reached again for the bottle of wine. It had been a good meal, the best that could be drawn from ship's stores, and now they were relaxing over the remains of dessert, stretching out their Last Night together just as if they were about to enter those five-hundred-to-one cryocans in the morning.

"No," the other two replied in unison, before they all broke up in laughter.

"What's your conspiracy theory on this one, Clem?" Sindra asked with a smile.

Clemsen shrugged. "Who needs a theory? Can you

give me a theory besides a secret plot that explains why they all have phony names? Or why practically the only cargo on board is stuff they picked up at Asgard? Who'd boost for Earth with empty cargo holds?"

"Ah, it's a tax dodge," Sindra said. "Or else some of 'em—maybe all of 'em—are trying to back-immigrate into the Solar System."

"Think so?" Jerand asked. "Hadn't thought of that, but it could be." The preferred method was to sneak back in, then pretend you had never left the System, but had just spent time in an orbiting hab or station, since there were no restrictions on intrasystem migration. You simply reappeared one day and started using your ID again as if you'd never left. "That would explain the phony names."

"Can't be," said Clemsen. "Can't back-immigrate to a place you've never been. You wouldn't have an existing identity to step into. And our fearless Captain Sparten ain't never been to Earth."

"How do you know that?" Sindra demanded.

"I ran into him when he got lost on G Deck. I helped him find the command center," Clemsen said, with such a determinedly straight face that Jerand had trouble believing the slander. "He was acting friendly, and we starting chatting. That right there is just like a captain, don't you think? Having a nice little visit with a newbie crew who has to help you find your own command deck? I was really convinced."

Sindra held a finger to her lips and pointed to the compartment's comm panel.

Clemsen waved her off. "So maybe they're bugging us. They'd have to know any crew they signed that had working brains would wonder what the real deal was. They're walking around carrying signs that say IT'S SURE MYSTERIOUS. They expect we won't talk? Anyway. I have my nice little chat with Cap'n Sparten, and I made some dumb joke about being careful we didn't take orbit around the fourth planet instead of the third—and he said—'But we are sending a team to Earth.'"

"We got us a captain who doesn't know Earth is the

third planet?" Sindra asked, and let out a low whistle. "I just changed my mind. I don't wanna go."

Clemsen grinned. "You should have thought of that about 8 billion kilometers ago," he said. "Sparten could be plenty smart, but he's not from Earth. So that lets back-immigration out, for him at least. And I don't think many of the rest of this gang are Earthers."

"The Admiral," Sindra said, flat-certain. "He's from Earth. Even he can't hide all of his accent all the time. And Second Officer Sendler, the woman who signed us. I'd put money on her. Maybe one or two of the other-ranked crew—but hell, they talk so little it's hard to judge."

"I wish to hell someone *would* talk," Clemsen said. "I want to know what's going on."

"Ask the second passenger," Jerand said. "Maybe she'd tell you. She was pretty talkative before Sendler showed up and shooed me away."

"*Second* passenger?" Clemsen demanded. "You mean, besides the Admiral?"

"Yep. Middle-aged woman. I don't think I was supposed to see her. I was doing some checks on the starboard-side plumbing up on C Deck, and walked past a cabin that had the door open but no one in it. The place was like a blizzard hit it. Papers and books and datapads everywhere, notes stuck to the bulkheads. She had the desk folded out, but you couldn't even see it for the stuff that was on it. Then this nice old professor type shows up and starts twittering on about sorry she had left the door open, she had just gone down the hall to wash her hands, and sorry the place was such a mess, and wasn't it all going to be a most exciting trip—and then Sendler pops up around the turn in the corridor, shoos the nice old lady back into her cabin, and tells me to get back to work. I don't think we were even supposed to know she was on board."

"We'll all be in the same compartment tomorrow," Sindra objected. "She'll be right in our laps."

"So they wanted her under wraps from us until to-morrow, when they'll all be there to sit on her if they have to," Jerand said. "And I can't blame 'em. Trust me, she'd have told the whole tale in about four minutes if Sendler hadn't shown. They must have had an ArtInt doing a watch on her cabin. Only way Sendler could have shown up so fast."

"That's pretty paranoid," said Sindra.

"Like I said," Clemsen replied. "Come up with a theory to explain all this that isn't a conspiracy. Something big is up."

"So maybe there is," Jerand answered. "What's it matter, anyway? We're off Asgard. We're on a ship, and we're going somewhere."

"Not just somewhere. We're going to Earth," Clemsen said.

"Never seen it, have you?" Jerand asked.

"No," said Clemsen. "And I can't wait."

"Yeah," said Sindra with an affectionate chuckle. "It's quite a place. Pass me the rest of that wine and I'll tell you all about it."

Admiral Anton Koffield, alias Alber Caltrip, could not suppress a smile as he reached over to shut off the mike in the compartment where the Malfs were holding their Last Night dinner. Their guesses were good, as far as they went. The trick would be in not giving them any chance to make their guesses better. And, no doubt, the best way to do that would be to keep them all very, very busy. Easy enough to do after Confinement Day, when all hands would be kept busy preparing for Solar System arrival. But during Confinement Day—well, Jerand Bolt had been right to say that Professor Wandella Ashdin would require the closest of supervision. For a half a minute, Koffield allowed himself the luxury of imagining Ashdin bound and gagged, clapped in irons to keep her from talking. But no, he regretfully concluded. They needed to keep her happy. They needed her expertise.

What they didn't need was what they would get tomorrow unless steps were taken—a liberal demonstration of the woman's very big mouth.

Koffield sighed. He'd have to talk to her. Maybe—

maybe—if he spoke to her directly and firmly, one more time—she'd actually come to understand the importance of keeping her mouth shut unless and until the ship was outward bound from the Solar System. Anton Koffield, who had fought the only space battle of note in the last two hundred years; who had pulled that battle's only surviving warship, the crippled C.P.S. *Upholder*, back from the brink of disaster and guided her home again; who had held her shell-shocked crew together by sheer force of personality; the selfsame Anton Koffield stood up and headed toward Wandella Ashdin's cabin, intent on conversing with her—and dreading the ordeal ahead.

Confinement Day began. As per orders, all hands bathed vigorously, changed into fresh clothes, ate their fill of tasty food, and brought along one small bag each, containing whatever they might wish as entertainment during a period of enforced tedium and proximity. Clemsen laughed it all off, mocking the way the authority figures were ordering them to relax and enjoy themselves. But Jerand could not help but notice that the crew members who had done a confinement run before were all taking their preparations very seriously indeed, and he decided to do the same, trying to be very thoughtful about what he packed.

Just before the appointed time of 1100 hours, he joined the rest of the ship's complement—crew, officers, and passengers alike—as they converged at the hatch to the ship's all-hands confinement chamber. As per standard operating procedure, the captain and first officer were in pressure suits so as to save time getting through the lock to the ship's main command center in case of emergency—and also because the confinement chamber was close-enough quarters that there would barely be room to suit up in any event. The crew of the ship's company wore standard duty coveralls.

A rating opened the hatch, and everyone filed inside, following the conventional order of officers, passengers, crew. There was little conversation.

They found themselves in a compartment barely large

enough to accommodate everyone. Even an advanced and superefficient temporal-confinement system was a massive power hog, and so the confinement chamber was built as small as possible. The chamber was spherical, with the passenger deck occupying a large cylindrical section of its interior. Life-support equipment occupied the space over the passenger deck, and the temporal-confinement field generators took up the belowdecks space.

Light-duty acceleration couches were set in a circle around the perimeter of the passenger deck, with their feet facing in toward the center. Three small folding tables, with even smaller and ricketier-looking chairs, occupied the center of the space. All the furniture was latched to the floor, holding it in position, but allowing it all to be rearranged or stowed if need be. There was a small chemical toilet on one side of the chamber, and a smaller stand-up galley directly opposite.

The compartment was equipped with its own airlock, sealing it off from the rest of the ship, just in case of a long slow leak that might empty the ship of air over the many years of the journey.

There was a low murmur of conversation as they all found their places and strapped themselves in. Two crew members sealed the outer airlock hatch, and everyone aboard watched as they pulled the inner hatch and sealed it shut—sealing all of them in for several decades of objective time. Inside the chamber, the time would pass more quickly—although, Jerand guessed, it might not seem like it was moving all that much faster after the first twelve hours or so of subjective time.

"Captain" Sparten and First Officer "Leptin" stood by the control panel by the airlock and did their final checks of ship's systems, working through repeater screens slaved into the ship's main command deck. From where Jerand was strapped in, it didn't seem as if Sparten was making much effort at all to pretend he knew the business better than Leptin. Well, if they were going to let the charade take a backseat to doing the job properly, that suited Jerand. At last, they came close to the end of the checklist. It was time for the main shipboard gravity generators to shut down, leaving the chamber, and the entire ship, in zero gee. Cutting the gee field saved power, and also prevented the gravity system from interfering with the temporal confinement.

"All right, everyone strapped in?" said Leptin, looking around the room. "Stand by—powering down gravity generators in five seconds. Five, four, three, two, one—powering down."

It took a few moments for the gee field to fade away. Jerand felt some odd sensations in his stomach and his inner ears, but the discomfort soon passed, to his relief. Like most spacefarers in an era of commonplace gravity generators, Jerand had but little experience of zero gee, and he had been worried as to whether he would have lost his adaptation.

"Gravity system powered down," Leptin announced. "Stand by for temporal-confinement field activation. Everyone all set?"

There was a general murmur of agreement, though Jerand could not even imagine what one might do to get set for such a thing as time slowing down by a factor of ten or twenty thousand.

Even so, the response seemed to satisfy Leptin. He turned and nodded to Sparten.

"TCF generator to preactive mode," said Sparten, flipping another in the rank of switches on the TCF control panel.

"Let's pop on the comparator chronos, shall we?" said Leptin. "Just so we know the damned thing is working." He threw a switch, and a large display panel set into the wall by the galley came to life.

It displayed the time and date in three columns, under three headings: GREENWICH MEAN, SHIP'S RELATIVISTIC OBJECTIVE, and SHIP'S TEMPORAL-CONF SUBJECTIVE. For the moment, the second and third columns were in lockstep, counting off the seconds, with the Greenwich Mean Time display already nearly an hour ahead. They had spent the last month boosting up to about 15 percent of light-speed before shutting down the ship's main engines, and .15 of C was more than enough for relativistic effects to start building up.

And, of course, there were a lot more than three clocks that could have been displayed. Asgard Five, light-years from any appreciable mass, besides the merely planet-size mass of the wormhole, billions of kilometers away, was in a volume of space as nearly "flat" as it could be inside a galaxy. As a consequence, time there ran just a trifle faster than on Earth's surface. And, of course, the timeshaft wormhole was a connection between two points in time. Which time was "correct"—the downtime end, the uptime end, or the moment frozen in the ineffable span that linked them? Passing through the mass of a wormhole slowed all the clocks on board, adding yet another variable.

It was scarcely an original thought, but Jerand could not help but wonder, with so many possibilities to choose from, how anyone ever knew for sure what time it was. Which clock was "right"? He knew that the correct answer was "all of them," but even knowing, down in his gut, the way only an interstellar traveler did, that time slowed at high velocities and in large gravitational fields, that answer did not satisfy. It stood to reason that there was some place, or time, or dimension, where the measured time was the correct time.

The near-ancient philosopher, Einstein, had decreed that there were no privileged frames of reference, and no one had yet proved him wrong—but that wasn't enough to convince Jerand. Not even his own life experience could do that. After a lifetime of dealing with every kind of time dilation and chronological distortion imaginable, he still couldn't shake the gut feeling that, somewhere, someone knew the correct time.

Well, whoever that someone was, he or she definitely was not aboard this ship.

Besides, there was a fourth column on the display, with the heading CONFINEMENT RATE. It showed the value 1:1. When that ratio changed, timekeeping would turn twice as complicated.

"Confirming intrachamber volume at vacuum. Withdrawing umbilicals from outer chamber hull." There was a pair of dull thuds as the cables providing data and power connections between the chamber and the ship withdrew. "Chamber now on internal power. Stand by for magnetic levitation activation."

"Stand by for pusher rod withdrawal," said Leptin. "Ladies and gentlemen, the maglev field ought to be able to hold the chamber in place without any problem—but let's not give it any problems. Please remain seated and strapped in. No bouncing off the bulkheads, if you please." The scuttlebutt was the maglev system was a trifle underpowered, and might not be able to hold the inner chamber rigidly in place if stressed by rapid or violent movement inside the chamber. "Pusher rods withdrawing."

There was a rapid-fire series of bangs, split seconds apart, as the rods snapped back into their recesses inside the inner chamber. Now the temporal confinement chamber was simply floating in zero gee, surrounded by a centimeter of vacuum and the outer chamber hull beyond that. Potentially, any slight movement inside the chamber could be enough to set the whole mass moving, bouncing it off the outer hull, and perhaps causing serious damage. But the system had been designed to prevent that problem.

"Maglev engaging," Leptin announced.

There was a odd, low-frequency shudder that moved up the scale to a deep, bell-like tone, and then a much higher, sweeter ring that seemed to come from everywhere and nowhere. Jerand realized it wasn't like a bell—it was a bell, the hull of the chamber vibrating in reaction to being struck by the force of the maglev field.

"Stand by for temporal confinement in ten seconds," said Leptin.

And what logic in a ten-second countdown when it was the very length of the second that you were changing? But there was no time to think about the nature of time—

"Confinement in five! Four! Three! Two! One! Activate!" Leptin stabbed his finger down on the button.

The lights dimmed for a moment, then steadied, and Jerand felt a kick in the base of his stomach that might have been a real phenomenon, and might have been his psychological need to feel something. No one had ever quite settled the question of whether or not it was possible to feel a temporal-confinement field. Some people claimed they could.

But there was at least a clear visual indicator of what was happening. The comparator chronometer was going crazy, the Ship's Relativistic Objective accelerating to the point where even the hours were a mere blur, moving too fast for the numbers to register. The Greenwich clock was ramping up nearly as fast. And the confinement ratio was ticking up right along with them. Already it had gone from 1:1 to somewhere upward of 500:1, and was still moving higher. Even as he watched, the ratio shifted over to four digits, and just kept climbing.

Jerand frowned. The numbers all looked very impressive—but where could they be coming from? The inner confinement chamber had cut its last physical connection to the rest of the ship, and thus, the outside world.

He turned to the man seated next to him, the cargo officer, Dixon Phelby. "Excuse me, sir," he said. "How are they getting those time data points? Are all those just some sort of estimate or projection?"

Phelby laughed. "They'd better not be, or else we're going to have some navigation trouble. You need some real fine-tuning to control temporal confinement properly. The confinement rate isn't perfectly stable. It can 'hunt' a bit—and little mistakes end up getting big fast when you're dealing with ratios like that." He gestured toward the display.

Jerand was unnerved to see that the ratio was now shown as well over 2000:1, and still moving upward at blurring speed. The Shipboard and Greenwich clocks were now moving fast enough that the days displays were moving too fast to read. "I can believe it," he muttered. "So how do they get the data?"

"Simple enough. There's an emitter on the inside of the outer chamber hull sending signals at a specific frequency in the X-ray range. There's a very well-shielded window in the inner chamber with sensors that can pick up everything from X ray down through ultraviolet to visible light to infrared to radio frequencies. We know what wavelength is being sent, so we can read the confinement ratio just by dividing—or is it multiplying?—the frequency that we're receiving on this side. The signal itself can carry whatever data you like just by pulsing on and off. We do the same trick in reverse to talk back with the ship. And if the comm link fails for whatever reason, the confinement automatically powers down, so we don't overshoot because we don't know what time it is." Dixon's smile faded a bit. "Believe me," he said. "You don't want to overshoot."

It was an intriguingly cryptic remark, but there were other wonders—extremely disconcerting ones—that were seizing Jerand's attention. Now the confinement ratio was up over 9000:1, and still climbing. Even as he watched, the ratio added another digit. *Time is moving more than ten thousand times as slowly in here as it is out there. In the two minutes I have been sitting here watching the numbers move, two days have passed on Earth. They've worked a full shift on Asgard Station since Phelby finished talking.*

"How high a confinement ratio are we going to get?" Jerand whispered. Somehow the sheer magnitude of the forces at work made him want to keep his voice down.

"Ideally, 17,532 to one."

"How did they pull that number out of the hat?"

"Simple. It's just 365.25 days times twenty-four hours times two. That comes to two years an hour. They could crank it higher—but it gets too expensive. On the old ships, when just the captain was in confinement and everyone else was in cryo, they used to spool it up to maybe 500,000 to one, maybe more. It used to be that the largest shipboard confinement was just about big enough for one person, and the power demand for it was just about as high for a million to one confinement ratio as it was for a piddly little ten thousand to one rate. With that situation, you might as well crank it up all the way. And they couldn't ramp up the power or tune the rate. They'd just cut it on and off through external controls. The captain would only experience a few minutes of subjective time, even on a hundred-year-plus transit."

"So what changed?"

"They figured out how to do bigger confinements, and figured out how to reduce the power consumption drastically for lower-rate confinements. This setup draws less power than an old-style half-million-to-one confinement big enough for just one person. But if you cranked this confinement to anything much over 30,000 to one, the power demands would go past terrifying to obscene. So they try to strike a balance. Most captains figure two years an hour is fast enough. When we left Asgard, we were eighty-three years downtime in the past from when we're going. So forty-one hours and change in confinement gets us there—or gets us then, I should say. Not too bad."

The confinement ratio was still climbing, but the rate of increase was leveling off. It went from 12,000:1 to 14,000:1 at an almost leisurely rate, and then floated gradually upward, more and more slowly, until it came to rest at 17,532:1, and then started drifting up and down a point or two from that rate.

A new display popped up—CONFINEMENT DURATION. This one had two subwindows, GREENWICH and CONFINEMENT-SUBJECTIVE. Jerand shook his head. Clocks and more clocks, he thought. The more ways they measured time, the more Jerand wondered if there was any real thing to measure.

But there were realities back of it all. Scarcely ten minutes had passed inside the temporal confinement as the confinement ratio ramped up and then stabilized, but two months and eight days—no, nine days, ten days— had streaked past on Earth. Another twenty minutes in here, and women on Earth who had been virgins when the ship's crew had stepped inside the confinement chamber would be giving birth to full-term babies. In the forty-odd hours Jerand would spend in confinement eighty years would pass. Those women would pass into old age and die. Their children would grow, mature, raise families, become grandparents, and die in their turn. Whole nations would rise and fall, political movements would sweep across whole planets, grip all the people in feverish excitement, then fade away into oblivion.

But even that was not the worst, the strangest of it. The whole point of the timeshaft-wormhole network was to provide the illusion of rapid interstellar travel. The ship's present journey might take eighty-three years, but thanks to their drop back into the past, the ship would arrive mere weeks or months after her departure. In the normal course of things, the ship would deliver her cargo and passengers, take on new shipments for the next port, and then launch again to spend decades in transit, traveling through years where she had been once before. Then the ship would drop down another timeshaft, back into the same past where she was right now—whatever "now" meant.

These were indeed years Jerand had lived through before, many times. He had ridden aboard a dozen timeshaft ships, shuttling between the stars, dropping back through the wormholes, falling through the years, passing himself coming and going—but never within light-years of his other selves.

Even the limited sort of time travel made possible by the timeshafts could induce multiple duplicates. Jerand had spent a goodly part of his time aboard Asgard working out his own personal chronology. According to his calculations, he had reached his own personal multiplicity record between June 4 and September 23, 5298, Earth calendar, a period during which he had served aboard the old *Dawnstreaker Seven*. During that period of time, there were no fewer than five *Dawnstreaker Sevens* moving through space, and no fewer than seven Jerand Bolts—two of them serving as junior crew aboard other ships.

But, as best Jerand could figure, he had been frozen solid in cryo aboard all of those ships during just about all of those voyages. There might have been a two- or three-day period in August of that year when there were two of him, light-years apart, but both awake and active, but between timeshafts and relativistic effects, it was damnably hard to work the thing out with any precision.

But this. This was different. Now he was awake indeed as he ghosted through the fast-moving years. He would live through 5298—and 5297, and 5299, and 5300, and on and on. Out there somewhere, right now, multiple copies of his past self were slumbering in the cold and dark, coursing between the worlds. But each beat of his heart took nearly an hour of their time. He would live through 5198 again—but the year would take all of thirty minutes to pass. He might take a nap and miss a decade's history.

Jerand forced himself to push the thoughts away. It was all too disconcerting, too disturbing, too frightening to pursue such ideas any further.

Jerand had always been better at direct action, dealing with the matter immediately in front of him. He had never been much for confronting the big abstractions. He preferred problems he could see and feel and touch, situations on a human scale—situations between people.

And there was plainly a lot going on between the people on this ship. He needed to understand the game being played. He needed a better understanding of the players, and the game pieces. For that matter, it could help if he could tell which were the players and which the pawns.

He hardly knew where to begin. But it almost did not matter. Any bit of gossip could be the key in the lock, the missing piece of the puzzle.

He caught Phelby's eye again, and nodded toward the ship's second passenger, the nameless middle-aged woman of vaguely academic appearance. "So who's the mystery woman?" he asked.

Phelby's open and friendly expression closed up tight as the pressure doors on an airlock. "Don't know much about her," he said. "Just a passenger, as far as I know."

"Oh," said Jerand, and let it go. Phelby's answer had told him something: Phelby was a terrible liar—but the man was at least willing to make the effort to dissemble. Bolt stored the information away. Any bit of knowledge might be useful.

Not deterred, Jerand considered a more direct approach. He could go up and talk to the female passenger—the professor, as he was coming to think of her. But he could read the tension in Phelby's posture, the way the Admiral was, even now, watching Jerand watching her. They were on guard. If he tried, they'd shoo him away, probably even issue direct orders to stay away from her if he forced the issue.

Jerand Bolt had always prided himself on following orders—even if there had been times when it had taken some creativity and literalistic interpretations to manage it. It was often easier all around if the order were never issued. Better not to push, so the powers-that-be wouldn't push back and issue inconvenient orders in the first place.

Besides, in these close quarters, it was hard not to learn something about her merely from observation— and it would be damned hard for them to lock them all in the same compartment and then order him not to look at her. And so he did—discreetly, from a distance, with a casual glance now and then. He had no doubt at all that he had been correct in his first impression. She was obviously some kind of academic.

She looked to be the slightly scatterbrained sort, judging by the muddle of datapads and research notes she was struggling to control in zero gee. It was also plain to see that she had little or no experience of weightlessness. He could read that in the greenish and sickly cast to her complexion, in the difficulty she was having in managing her notes and materials, and even in the awkward way she had adjusted her lap belt.

Sindra drifted past the professor, intent on nothing more nefarious than browsing in the galley for a snack. The professor instantly scrabbled together all her notes, trying much too obviously to hide them from someone who wasn't looking. Subtlety and discretion were other things the professor wasn't good at.

Jerand glanced at Sendler out of the corner of his eye,

and was not in the least surprised to see that she was poised as if to intercept Sindra. Plainly, the professor had gotten a talking-to, but even so Sendler was still tasked with watching her with all the intensity of a divehawk. Plainly, they feared she still might blurt out something she shouldn't, even after being lectured.

But look who was doing the watching. Sendler—a senior officer. The only plausible reason not to assign a low-ranking crew member to such a baby-sitting duty was that the crew weren't fully in the picture either. Whatever the secret was, not many knew the full story.

He was going to have to wait a while and look sharp for his chance to learn more. Waiting was all any of them could do for the time being. He let out a weary sigh and glanced at the chronometry display. One hour and forty minutes had passed since they had entered the chamber. Outside the temporal confinement, something like a year had passed. But there was a long way yet to go. And there was nothing to do but watch the hours crawl past, and the years rocket by.

Eighteen confinement hours, and thirty-odd Greenwhich years later, Jerand had reached a few more conclusions—though not about the professor or the real nature of the voyage of the "Merchanter's Dream."

He had, however, concluded that, taken in and of itself, temporal confinement was not much as an experience. While it was a vast improvement over the dangerous and physically draining business of travel by cryocan, tempo confinement was excruciatingly dull. Jerand had read somewhere that someone had compared it to spending decades at a cocktail party held in a room too small for the event. At the time, he had dismissed that as a rather weak witticism, but now he was prepared to view it as nothing more nor less than the grim truth.

The lights had been dimmed for a time, and the air temperature lowered, to simulate "night," and then the lights had brightened and the chamber had warmed again to signal the start of "day," but, somehow, there in confinement, neither mind nor body was fooled by the light and temperature cues.

It wasn't just Jerand, either. None of the confinement chamber's occupants seemed able to settle into any sort of routine. They dozed fitfully during the "day" part of the cycle, and fidgeted all through the "night." Some read, or watched and listened to various sorts of entertainments on their datapads—but Jerand had always gotten too restless to be able to read or view anything on a cramped public conveyance.

The galley was too small to serve everyone at once, and, anyway, the center tables were too crowded for the whole ship's company at once. Meals had to be served in shifts, and, in between preparation, the actual eating of the meals, and then cleanup, the various meal calls all blended together.

Between the crowding, the ceaseless small activity of meal preparation, and the randomizing effect of zero gee, with small personal objects and bits of litter floating off in all directions, it was all but impossible to keep the chamber tidy. Nor was it practical for anyone to bathe, or even to change clothes. By the end of the second "day" cycle, the compartment was getting distinctly ripe.

Tempers were likewise deteriorating. One minor disagreement over a card game nearly came to blows, and was only resolved when "Captain" Sparten ordered the two crew members involved to move to opposite sides of the compartment.

Jerand Bolt was surprised not at all that Clemsen was one of the two disputants, but he could have almost wished that Clem had picked a fight with Sindra or himself, rather than with one of the ship's original crew. The ship's company had been more or less self-organized into three groups—the officers and passengers, the veteran crew, and the Malfs—before confinement. That pattern had hardened with every passing hour. It was easy to imagine that, if confinement lasted long enough, there would be three armed camps, at each other's throats. But no. The Admiral—he was plainly the real man in charge, whoever he was—the Admiral would never let it come to that. That was a man who knew how to deal with people. He'd handle things, if it got to the point where things needed handling.

For about the thousandth time, Jerand checked the chrono display. *Only forty-three years to go,* he thought, as his eyes fell upon what seemed to him to be the most meaningful of the measures on offer. It said something that all the irony, all the gallows humor, had fallen away from thinking that way. It might well be literally true that the years were passing as fast as hours, but it was likewise true that the hours felt like years.

Somehow, it seemed appropriate that Jerand slept through the end of it all—if one could really call what he did sleeping. He dozed fitfully in his chair, opening his eyes now and again whenever someone bumped against his chair, or some machinery or other switched on and off. The passing time twisted and tangled together into a formless, half-waking dream that fled from every effort at recollection.

But then, he was awake, fully and truly awake, to see "Captain" Sparten, suited up, preparing to do arrival safety checks out in the ship. Even as Jerand blinked and rubbed his eyes, the inner hatch came open, and gusts of bitingly cold air from the long-powered-down corridors of the ship rushed in. The frigid blast of air was a shock, a tonic, and he was instantly alert.

They had arrived. The Solar System, and Earth, awaited them.

At a rough guess, Jerand Bolt had slept, however fitfully, through the last ten years of the trip.

CHAPTER SIX

ALWAYS HALFWAY THERE

Protocol required that Captain Yuri Sparten be the first out of the confinement chamber. A proper respect for safety dictated that he go out with his pressure suit sealed, cycling through the airlock by himself to do basic safety checks. Outside the confinement, the ship's systems had had eighty-plus years to deteriorate. The telemetry piped through to the confinement chamber hadn't reported any significant problems—but there were bound to be any number of small systems failures. Add enough of those together, and leave them alone long enough, and they could equal a ship-killing disaster.

They would do a full maintenance sweep of the entire ship as they decelerated through the outer reaches of the Solar System. In fact, what a timeshaft ship's crew did, mostly, was prep a ship for her decades-long sleep at the start of the interstellar transit, powering system down, repairing worn parts, cocooning everything against the cold and dark. Then, as the journey drew to a close, the crew would repair everything that had gone wrong anyway.

First things first, however. It fell to the captain, as the person who best knew the ship, to do a fast, preliminary check of the environmental systems, and then to power up the heaters, the ventilators, the artificial-gravity system, and all the other machinery needed to keep humans alive and well billions of kilometers out into the darkness.

The inner airlock door closed behind him, and Yuri Sparten had to study the outer door controls for a moment before he was sure how to work them. *The person who best knew the ship. What further point in* that *charade?* he wondered. They were going through motions so as to fool the Asgard recruits—and it was as plain as day on Solace they were not in the least bit fooled.

But Koffield insisted that the game go on—and so it did. So be it. He would play "captain" for at least a while longer. Marquez had briefed him carefully and walked him through all the procedures before the start of confinement, but none of that was the same as doing it.

So now I get to do it. He smiled without pleasure and opened the outer hatch.

In spite of all his mental preparation, it was still a shock to see the interior of the ship so changed. While Yuri had been sweating out two days in a pressure suit, eighty years had passed out here, eight decades without light or heat, without movement or life.

Utter blackness blanketed everything. The only light source was his helmet lamp, casting great looming shadows off every handhold and hatchway. There was a thin dusting of frost on nearly every surface, and the ventilator grilles were caked with the stuff, a centimeter thick. Yuri scratched at the frost with a gauntleted finger, and was surprised to see that it was too hard to scrape off. Every drop of moisture in the air had long since frozen out.

Yuri checked his suit's exterior temperature gauge. It showed -103 degrees centigrade, far above the ambient temperatures in interstellar space. Even in standby mode, the ship's systems generated enough waste heat to warm things up substantially.

He pulled himself forward along the corridor, using the handholds, moving toward the new auxiliary control room, installed at the same time as the confinement chamber. It was one deck up. He came to the companionway leading up and pulled himself along the pitch-black stairway. He came to the next deck, and kicked off the bulkhead to sail along the corridor toward aux control.

He pushed open the hatch and pulled himself into the control room. He powered up the compartment lights, killed his suit lights, and activated the operations boards. He ran the prelim checks, and was pleased to see a very clean board, only a few ambers and one or two reds in a wall of green indicators. Given eighty years, it was inevitable that a few things would wear out or break down, but the *Dom Pedro IV*—no, strike that—the "Merchanter's Dream"—was in good shape.

"Confinement, this is Sparten at aux control. It looks like our ship came through just fine. Starting power-up of environmental systems. Stand by for artificial gravity in thirty seconds, mark."

"Glad to hear it, *Captain*," said Marquez's voice through his earphone. "We'll be glad to get our feet under us."

"Sparten out," he said, not wishing to spend needless words with Marquez. He brought up the gravity system, and then light and heat and air circulation.

Once he was done, Yuri lingered for a moment in aux control. For a brief time, at least until he reopened the hatch to the confinement chamber, he was well and truly in command of the ship. That was worth savoring.

And there was something else. Auxiliary control had something not found in many compartments of the ship. A viewport. Yuri worked the ship's attitude controls to bring the ship about so the viewport would face straight into their direction of travel, then swung open the viewport's protective shield. He stood there, watching, as the heavens outside wheeled silently about, and a single star, brighter than all the others, slid out into view, and then came to rest, a gleaming, perfect dot of yellow, centered exactly in the port.

The Sun. Earth's Sun. The star that warmed humanity's home world, that had lit all the days of human history before the leap across the stars. The home star. Yuri,

born on Glister and raised on Solace, had never seen it
before. There it was, its light falling on him. He reached
out his gauntleted hand and touched the viewport,
strange emotions coursing through him. There were
things he meant to do in the realms of Sol. Things that
Marquez and Koffield would not like at all.

Anton Koffield waited and watched as intently as everyone else, and let out the same weary cheer, and the same
sigh of relief as the inner hatch reopened. Sparten already had his helmet off as he came inside, and he was
smiling and gesturing that all was well. A wall of frigid
air rushed into the confinement chamber, flushing out
the warm, damp miasma of too many people together
for too long.

It's finally over, he thought. Even Anton Koffield had
found himself starting to feel anxious, restless, as confinement wound down to its end. It had been just one
more step on a journey that had already been prolonged
to impossible lengths.

Koffield had been delayed for over a century en route
to Solace, then for months in the Solace system, then for
weeks transiting to Asgard. And then this leg, a subjective two days to cross eighty years. He felt as if he had
been trapped inside a monstrous version of Xeno's para-
dox, where each stage of his journey was half as long as
the one before it, but an infinite number of ever-shorter
distances lay before him, leaving him always halfway
there.

Now we've arrived, he thought. *At long last, I've
reached the first stage of the search itself.*

There would be further delays—some he could fore-
see, and no doubt others that would come as unpleasant
surprises. Transits inside the Solar System, negotiations
for permission to enter this archive or that research center, struggles to get past bureaucratic barriers. All of
them would soak up time.

But not yet. Today was for rest, for clean clothes, for
sleeping in a proper bunk rather than in a stuffy com-

partment of restless people. And tomorrow would come the next stage in the journey.

And after being locked up with the entire ship's complement, Koffield realized that one part of the equation needed more attention than he had given it. *People.* They had nearly had one fistfight in confinement. It was mere luck that things had not boiled over even more.

Koffield could see very plainly that it was going to be up to him to try and put things right. And he could also see where he would have to work hardest, and soonest. He watched the three Asgard recruits—the Malfs, they called themselves—filing out of the confinement chambers. *Let them get some rest first,* he thought. *But best not to wait too long.*

He made the interval as short as he decently could, sending voice messages that "invited" the four Asgarders to visit his cabin six hours after departure from confinement. Officially, they were off duty, resting and washing up. But none of them refused the invitation, and all of them arrived within seconds of the appointed time. No one spoke, aside from a muttered word or two of greeting.

Anton Koffield looked from one face to the other, trying to read what he could from the expressions of the three people crowded into his tiny stateroom, and once again, he considered his words carefully. He needed to tell them as much more as they needed to know, enough to keep them happy—but little enough to keep them out of trouble.

Besides all that, he would have to look beyond just those who would hear him now, and bear in mind that the odds were good that at least one member of his audience was likely to report what he said to others. It might not be for months, perhaps even years, but it would almost certainly happen.

The room was quiet, and all eyes were on Koffield, standing at one end of the small compartment. They were waiting for him to begin. "I want to start by apologizing," he said. "I should have spoken with all of you before we left Asgard. It was an error in judgment to leave things totally unexplained for so long. And I want to start by saying I know none of you are fools," he said. "Fools would have missed the odd things going on aboard this ship—but I have no doubt you have noticed them all." His certainty was based on the fact that he had been listening in on their private conversations, but never mind.

"You have no doubt made some shrewd guesses as to what is going on. I strongly suspect your guesses are wrong, simply because you have nowhere near enough information.

"I do not propose to tell you anything more. That is for your safety as well as ours."

"Sir, excuse me, sir," one of them interrupted. It was the youngest one, Clemsen Wahl. "How is keeping us in the dark for *our* safety?"

Koffield nodded. "Fair question. Modern interrogation techniques allow the interrogator to map the associative paths, and trace the *connections* of knowledge. In other words, they can map out the position of a certain piece of knowledge in the brain, though they cannot read off that piece of knowledge directly. But they *can* know for certain if a subject has told all he or she knows about a given subject, simply by seeing how much of the portions of your physical brain mapped to a given topic have become activated as you discuss the subject. If we tell you nothing, they will see from your brain mapping that you know nothing. They will know for sure you are not deceiving them.

"Those who know more will be subject to—unpleasant—handling if they are caught, and interrogated, and they resist. Those of us who do know all, or nearly all, have carried our knowledge here of our own free will, knowing it could endanger us. You did not make that choice."

Wahl frowned. "So we're just supposed to play along, totally ignorant, forever?"

Koffield rubbed his hands together anxiously. "Once we have reached a point where the danger of exposure is past, or at least greatly reduced, I promise that we—I— will tell those who wish to know all—or nearly all, that we know. I'm not going to hand out security combinations and defense setting. But for the time being, we believe that our silence is your safety.

"I can tell you now we are looking for something. We are looking for information. All our studies so far indicate that what we seek, or at least leads to it, will be found in the Solar System, scattered about in several archives and research centers and similar institutions.

"I can also say that we mean no harm to Earth, or to Solace, or to any innocent persons. Our primary reason for secrecy is to avoid the dangers of false rumor and panic. Our studies might—might—reduce or eliminate certain dangers. But to discuss them in public would cause panic and disruption, and simply make matters worse."

"That sounds like what you'd tell us if you were up to something that *was* intended to hurt a lot of people and were trying to keep it quiet," said Bolt.

"You're quite right," said Koffield. "All I can suggest is that you have now met us all, and have had a chance to consider what sort of people we are. If we seem like thieves and murderers, then denounce us. If we seem like people trying hard to do something quietly for the sake of public calm—then I would ask that you join us, and help us, and be patient with us."

It seemed to mollify them, and it was all true as far as it went. Koffield did not choose to tell them how many laws their ship was breaking, or how likely it was that their "research" would pit them against the Chronologic Patrol. No need to mention that, if successful, it would render the entire fleet of timeshaft wormhole ships, the ships to which they had dedicated their working lives, utterly obsolete.

"I doubt there's much point in asking who you are," said Bolt. Plainly he was the leader of the group. Koffield knew he would do well to treat him with careful respect. "I won't bother. But can you at least tell us, clearly and directly, who is actually in charge?"

A sensible sailor's question. One of the most dangerous things in space is an unclear or uncertain chain of command. "I can tell you that some of us are using assumed names. Others are not, because their real names aren't known to anyone we're likely to encounter, and there seemed no reason to create additional confusion.

"As regards the chain of command: I wish to remind you that there is such a thing as guilty knowledge, and that possessing it without reporting it makes you an accessory before the fact. Fraudulently posing as the officers of a ship to the authorities is a crime everywhere. While you're considering that, I can tell you that First Officer Leptin is a fine officer who has served in a senior position, that Captain Sparten has in the past served in a more junior capacity, and Officer Sendler will obey orders from both of them. I can also say that I am not in the chain of command. However, as the man who chartered this vessel, I would hope that the captain would listen carefully to my requests. Is that good enough for you?"

Bolt shifted uncomfortably in his seat and nodded. "Ah, yes, sir. I think it tells us everything."

"Good," said Koffield. "Now then. We're about a week out from Neptune, our first port of call. We need to visit the orbital stations there. We plan to leave the ship in orbit there, and send research parties to other sites in the Solar System. I—we—have not yet determined who will go in which party. It is likely, though not certain, that I'll use all of you. Under the terms of your contracts, you may decline extended service off the ship without penalty. We will honor that clause. You can refuse to serve on a given assignment—but you will not be able to choose your assignment. Is that clear?"

There was a mumbled chorus of assent. "Very well," Koffield said. He stepped toward the compartment's door and opened it to signal the meeting was over. "I believe that is everything. If you have any questions, please don't hesitate to ask me." He smiled. "But if I were you, I wouldn't count on getting answers to all your questions just yet."

"Ah, thank you, sir," said Bolt. "I think." The group got up, muttered their thanks and farewells, and headed out the hatch to the corridor beyond.

As he watched them depart, Anton Koffield could not help but think of all the questions he had that had no answers yet. Starting with—who was he going to send where?

Three hours later, Anton Koffield crumbled up about his hundredth sheet of notepaper and heaved it toward the recycler bin. At the rate he was going, he would deplete the ship's supply of paper before he got the job done. Probably it would have been better if he had started out with a datapad, something with a screen he could erase and reuse. Or even a storage sheet, that could retain the images of the text and doodles drawn upon it and then call them back up as needed.

But somehow he needed old-fashioned paper for this job. Part of it was his instinct for security. Paper, once run through the recycler, couldn't be "un-erased" the way nearly all digital storage could be.

He stood up to stretch his back and allow himself a chance to pace back and forth. *Who went where, and with whom?*

He had asked himself that question so often that the meaning threatened to drop away from the words, leaving only a pattern of pleasant sounds, a mellifluous mantra, behind. And it seemed such a simple question, even a trivial one. But, plainly, if he chose wrong, it could lead to serious problems. Even, perhaps, to the project being detected—and *that* could have consequences so grave as to be beyond imagining.

After the disaster at Circum Central, after he had guided the stricken *Upholder* back to the Solar System, Koffield had found himself very much at loose ends. The powers-that-be had pinned a medal on him and promoted him for heroic service—and then devoutly wished he would disappear and stop embarrassing them. He had received no formal assignment, but protocol declared that an active-duty officer of his rank receive invitations to certain social events. For the most part, such invitations had been accompanied by some sort of signal that the hostess hoped he would have the decency not to show up.

But sometimes there were no such hints, and Koffield would go—only to find his place card set at the very worst table at which it was socially possible to seat an admiral, and that his table mates were invariably likewise embarrassments of one sort or another. He had always marveled at the social calculations and political judgments required to work out such massively complex seating arrangements. He'd sit there, working out in his head the number of possible seating combinations possible for a group of, say, 209 people at twenty-two tables set for ten each. How to factor politics against fashion? Rank against fame? Personality against ego?

Now he was beginning to appreciate even more the sort of problems that his unwilling hostesses had faced. Arranging the seating at a big dinner party was even more complex than his current problems—and at a sufficiently high-ranking dinner, the stakes might be nearly as high.

Start over, he told himself. *Three initial sites to search.* He started with a blank sheet of paper and set the name down again. The DeSilvo Archive in the Grand Library orbiting Neptune, the Permanent Collection, also orbiting Neptune, and three sites on Earth—the Planck Institute in Berlin, the Port-au-Prince Library of Terraforming, and the DeSilvo Monument Museum Archive in Rio de Janeiro. The Earth sites he could treat as one destination. The *DP-IV,* still flying as the "Merchanter's Dream," would dock at the Grand Library. The other two groups would each need an auxiliary ship, and each ship would need at least one pilot. *All right then,* he thought. *Assume—pray—we get some leads. That could mean we'll need to do follow-on searches elsewhere in the Solar System.* That meant all the aux ships would need sufficient power and stores for, say, two full round-trips Earth to Neptune. He noted that down. What else? *We have to leave at least three crew aboard to maintain the ship and to look legal if the local authorities check up. We've got a total of sixteen people on board, so all told, a maximum of thirteen that can be assigned to the research teams.* But some of that number would bear watching—and some would have to be assigned to do the watching. Could he pair up the trustworthy and the suspect while getting the studies done—or would he run out of spies before he ran out of unreliables?

He went back to the stack of stiff-backed crew cards he had ordered the printer to kick out on heavy storage-sheet stock. Each card was slightly larger than a playing card. On one side was the crew member's name, a holographic photo of him or her, and basic biographic information. The other side listed current crew assignment and work history, efficiency ratings, and so on.

But Koffield didn't need to examine any of that information. He knew it all by heart. All he really needed was the names and the faces printed on a stack of cards he could sort and shuffle and arrange as needed.

Of those aboard, he felt certain that he could trust two—Captain Marquez and Norla Chandray. Both were good, reliable allies—but neither was trained for this sort of silent, invisible, backstairs war.

Wandella Ashdin was, from the point of view of secrecy, a walking security violation, an indiscretion waiting to happen. And yet they needed her skill and knowledge if they were to track down Oskar DeSilvo. She, of course, would work the DeSilvo Archive in the Great Library.

That completed the list of those aboard who had the full knowledge of the discoveries on Greenhouse. No one else knew it all, but some at least knew a good-sized portion of the story.

Yuri Sparten certainly knew enough to make shrewd guesses about the things they had kept from him. He had played well the part of puppet captain, and had done nothing to betray Koffield's trust—yet. But it was the job of a double agent to appear utterly reliable. Koffield still did not know where the man's ultimate loyalties were. They would have to go on as they had, making good use of Sparten, and telling him what he needed to know, but still holding back whatever scraps of knowledge they could. It was a balancing act on a knife's edge, but there were no real alternatives.

Cargo Officer Dixon Phelby was bright and willing enough, and was privy to nearly as much as Sparten. Phelby had no axes to grind, no hidden agendas—at least none that Koffield was aware of. Koffield had seen the type before—the born tourist, who saw the whole universe as a vastly entertaining puzzle to be solved. Could Phelby really be that calm, that detached and matter-of-fact? Or were there hidden depths of passion, of anger, of wrong deeply felt that cried out for revenge? There was no way to tell.

That brought him to Jerand Bolt and his friends. Koffield knew from his eavesdropping that they had already started asking some awkward questions—but he had expected nothing less. He would not have wanted them as part of the ship's crew if they were capable of missing all the plainly unusual and suspicious circumstances aboard the "Merchanter's Dream." But that didn't make their curiosity—and even nascent paranoia—any less awkward.

As for the remainder of the crew—he shuffled through the rest of the cards and glanced at the surnames once again. *Aziz, Barimo, Lipser, Sherdan, Tugler, and Wu.* He knew the data on their cards, but that was all. He knew next to nothing of their natures. It shamed him to admit it, but as people, they were all but unknown to Koffield.

As a ship's officer, Koffield had always prided himself on knowing the members of the crew. But he had traveled as a passenger on the *DP-IV*'s journey to Solace, and, as per usual procedure with passengers, he had gone into cryosleep before any of the crew. Then, after Solace system arrival, the *DP-IV* had remained in the outer system while he departed for the planet itself, accompanied only by Norla Chandray. He had scarcely spent any time with the crew prior to the ship's departure on its present journey—and he had discovered just how thoroughly crews keep their distance from passengers—especially passengers with as alarming a history and reputation as Admiral Anton Koffield, victor of the battle of Circum Central, the supposed scourge of the Glister system.

Looked at one way, they had all been traveling together for centuries. But in all that time, Koffield had scarcely spent an hour in conversation with any of them. Regrettable, though understandable under the circumstances. In any event, it left him with no way to judge their suitability for this duty or that. All he had to go on was their service records—and Anton Koffield knew just how chancy that could be. He would have to assume ·hat any of them could become a problem at any time.

The odds were good that some or all of the original crew, or any or all of the Asgard Malfs, might elect to stay behind in the Solar System. It would be difficult to stop them, short of force—and crew locked down in the brig for the duration of their stay would do no one any good. Nor would crew members that deeply discontented be of much use on the next leg of their quest. That was something to bear in mind: He would need to offer both carrots and sticks to keep enough crew on the ship.

He shuffled the deck of crew cards, arranged them, rearranged them, considered the results, and adjusted them once again. Somehow, somewhere, there had to be a winning hand that he could deal—if only he could recognize it when he saw it.

INTERLUDE

REPORT IN TRANSIT

The first report traveled on a journey of such length and duration that it could only be described as a saga, but no one bothered to pay it any mind. Every trip between the stars was a journey of heroic proportions, but even the star-journeys of humans were not paid much attention. The journey of a message, a mere collection of encrypted ones and zeros, was not worthy of even that much regard.

The covert receiver bolted to the exterior of the Grand Library picked up the coded transmission and stored it until it received a query ping from a certain Chronologic Patrol Operations ArtInt. The receiver then shifted to transmitter mode for a few thousandths of a second and squirted the report to the CPO ArtInt's storage array. As per agreement, one copy was stored away for CP use, if it proved to hold anything of interest, and another copy was squirted to Message Vault Dispatch, controlled by yet another ArtInt that read the report's unencrypted dispatch heading, then picked the fastest route for the message. As it happened, an outbound ship, the *Neu Hoch Leipzig XXI* had departed for the intended destination only a few weeks before and was still within easy radio messaging range. Message Vault Dispatch combined the report in a queue with other messages for the destination, and, just before the *Neu Hoch Leipzig XXI* moved out of effective range, MVD lasered the whole queue to the ship in one shot. The *Neu Hoch Leipzig XXI*'s receivers picked up the queue that held the report and duly stored it in her highly secure Message Vault. The whole process was utterly automated and never came anywhere near the notice of the busy crew of the ship.

Shortly thereafter, the crew of the *Neu Hoch Leipzig XXI* set to work powering down the ship for the long lonely run through the decades to Thor's Realm, and a drop down through the years via the timeshaft wormhole there, followed by decades more spent in transit to the Solacian system.

Thanks to the drop through the timeshaft, the ship arrived within message range of Solace a mere week or two of objective time after her departure from the Solar System. The *Neu Hoch Leipzig XXI*, while still well out from Solace, commenced beaming the contents of her message queue toward Solace.

Solace MVD received the queue, and, reading the dispatch header on the report, relayed it with the rest of the traffic for Solace Central Orbital Station. SCO Station duly received the subqueue containing the report and dispatched the various items to their respective final destinations.

Thus, after a journey spanning light-years and decades, the report wound up in the arriving-info queue—the inbox—of Captain Olar Sotales, commander, Station Security Force, SCO Station.

The report chanced to come in during the night cycle, and so Sotales did not see it until he eased his way into work midmorning the next day. When his duties kept him up half the night—as they often did—Sotales used his privileged position as the boss to come in late if there was nothing pressing. He saw no merit in arriving at the crack of dawn with his head in a muddle.

Sotales was a short man, burly, olive-skinned, black-haired, with a beaklike nose and a slightly pop-eyed appearance. His bushy black eyebrows accentuated hard grey eyes. His face set naturally into an expression somewhere between suspicion and violent anger. He might have been an equally effective interrogator if he had been two meters tall with a dazzling smile, but it seemed unlikely.

Sotales grumbled past his aide and the guard outside his door. He plopped down at his office chair with the distinct air of a man who did not wish to be where he was. The sweep the night before had gone reasonably well—but, in Sotales' present opinion, not well enough to justify keeping him up until three in the morning.

His aide appeared with a tray holding his breakfast and morning coffee—no mere automated service for the head of security—and wisely beat a hasty retreat without attempting to engage his superior in conversation. Sotales paid the man no mind at all, but sipped at his coffee as he started scrolling through the overnight updates.

He came to the newly arrived report in due course, and chuckled quietly to himself. *Save me from well-intentioned amateurs.* All the classic signs were there: The unimportant reported in endless detail, the key details hurried over as if barely of interest, the overly elaborate efforts to phrase things so as to conceal how little was said, the very official-sounding bureaucratic language that tried to make things sound important (thus justifying all the effort and expense of the operation), the somewhat contrite closing section, apologizing for the shortage of hard intelligence in this report, and promising more solid information next time. All the report really said was "we got here safely and I'll write later when there's some actual news."

Sotales shook his head and set to work on his omelet. Well, it did no harm, really. The sender had been careful to omit any references that the Chronologic Patrol would likely have on any keyword watchlist. He instead referred to Subject 1, Subject 2, Vehicle A, Destinations I and II, and so on. The CP's people would no doubt be able to put it all together in the space of a few heartbeats—if, at some point, they decided it was worth their trouble. But the Chronologic Patrol as yet had no reason to do so, and the sender had given them none.

It was a complicated game that Solace, and all the other minor worlds, played with Chronologic Patrol Intelligence Command. The CP provided comm facilities and other resources in places, such as the Solar System, where Solace couldn't manage the financial expense or the expenditure of political capital needed to set up their own operations. The CP kept copies of whatever it passed along—but didn't read 99 percent of what it collected. There was simply too much of it, it was too deeply encrypted, and too much of it was idle chitchat.

But—they would keep the report stored away, and they would expect SCO Station Security to alert them to anything of interest to the Chronologic Patrol. If, years or decades later, the CP discovered that Solace had been holding back on intell, and then went back in their files, took the effort to decrypt something, and found out things they should have been told—well, the CP had ways of making things very unpleasant indeed.

He snorted, hit the "store file" key, chased the last bit of egg about his plate, rang for his tray to be removed, and turned to other matters. Sotales had not the least expectation that he would ever need to see the report again. Let it gather the digital equivalent of dust.

Mere hours after it had completed its epic journey, the report was shunted from Sotales' inbox down to the electronic archives. But, though Sotales was unaware of it, the report's travels were far from over. It, and many of its fellows, had other journeys to make.

CHAPTER SEVEN

PLAYING IT CLOSE

From the Journal of Admiral Anton Koffield (ret.)

August 1, 5341 (Earth Standard Calendar). Aboard
the Auxiliary Lighter *Cruzeiro do Sul*, off the *Dom
Pedro IV*, in transit from Grand Library to Earthport
High Station.

*Just as I expected, nothing is going according to
plan.*

Anton Koffield hesitated a moment, and stared at the
bulkhead, but then continued to write.

*That is, perhaps, a rather flippant way to start a
new journal, but somehow it suits the mood of this
moment. The ancient jibe—situation desperate, but
not serious—seems to suit somehow. All my careful
fussing over mission assignments and logistics has
flown out the window—along with two crew
members—and yet it doesn't seem to matter. The two
deserters, crew members Lipser and Barimo, went
out the proverbial hatch at the first possible moment
after the DP-IV's aux ship #3, the* São Paulo *(no*

sense in not calling things by their right name in this journal), docked with the Grand Library. Half an hour later, they were aboard the first ship headed toward the Inner System. At a guess, they'll be shopping for new identities on Ceres within another week.

Marquez (who is still not used to being called Leptin—or First Mate, for that matter) was even less surprised than I, and admitted to having assigned the two departed to the first aux-ship transit for the express purpose of giving them a chance to get it over with. At least, as he put it, "now we know where we stand."

Back in the Chronologic Patrol, of course, what Lipser and Barimo did would be a court-martial offense. But the DP-IV is a civilian ship—and after what this ship has been through, I can scarcely blame them for wanting to get out, get home—or at least get to where home used to be—while they had the chance. Lipser and Barimo were simply lonely, desperate, and scared. I have felt that way often enough in recent times and I find myself feeling a surprisingly strong sense of sympathy with them.

The two of them left behind a pathetically apologetic note, explaining what they had done, and promising to keep silent about the ship's adventures in the Solacian system. Obviously, neither of them would stand a chance up against serious interrogation—but they were trying to vanish, and I think they will manage it. The odds are at least fair that the Chronologic Patrol will never know there were such people. And, if the CP does find them, it is likely to take them a while. With luck, we'll be on our way—somewhere—by then. We can at least hope to leave the CP a long, cold trail to follow.

As a result of Lipser and Barimo's departure, I was forced to reshuffle my carefully worked-out mission assignments at the last possible moment, and I have strong doubts as to how good my revised dispositions will turn out to be. But under the circumstances, I doubt any possible disposition of the available personnel could be relied upon.

Now comes the hardest part of command—awaiting results. I have set my forces in motion and given them their instructions. Now all that remains to be seen is what else will fail to go according to plan.

Our own party is well on its way toward Earth, and I have spent half the journey thus far fretting over my own inadequacy for the task at hand. I have wished over and over again that I could have sent Wandella Ashdin to do the Earthside research, but that was plainly impossible. Her expertise will be put to far better use at the Grand Library's DeSilvo Archive—and, to be blunt about it, the woman shouldn't be left unwatched while in possession of secret information. It would be the height of folly to set her loose on Earth.

Earth. Even for me, the mere mention of the name is tinged with excitement, with wonder and mystery. And I spent my youth there, traveled there, know all about it—or at least fancy that I do. Neither of my two companions—Dixon Phelby and Clemsen Wahl—has ever been to the Solar System. Neither of them can repress his excitement.

My companions are more than a little distracted by playing tourist on the home world. I can't blame them. The very idea of a world where any of a dozen cities has a population larger than one's entire planet, where there are more forms of life than there are living individual humans on many worlds. Imagine, one species on Earth for every human on Solace! A place where humans fit, where they belong, without the struggle of terraforming, without the endless struggle to keep the ship's or the habitat's or the station's life-support system running. Where the air is sweet and clean and breathable, and life blossoms everywhere on its own, without having to be wheedled and begged and cosseted . . .

Their excitement is as understandable as the desertion of Barimo and Lipser—and closely related to it. The Solar System in general, and Earth in particular, are magnets, drawing in the curious, the romantic, the dispossessed yearning for home. Earth is Home, in a very real way, for all of us.

I believe that the fact that it is my actual and literal home, that I did live there, makes it a more distant place for me than for the others. You can't go home again.

When I came back to the Solar System with the Upholder, I never visited Earth, but remained in the Outer System, spending my time in the various habitats and bases orbiting Neptune. Which means that it has been over two hundred years since I last walked the home world.

Two hundred years. Time for civilizations to rise and fall, time enough for languages to evolve into entirely new forms, time enough for change to remake the world, and then have the world remade yet again by yet more change. Time enough for me to be, not merely an uncle to my sister's children, but a great-uncle, a great-great-uncle, a great-great-great-great-uncle to her distant descendants, collateral descendants so genetically remote from me that any resemblance to me would have to be put down to coincidence.

But of course, I have no idea if any of her children did leave descendants. It seems likely that there are still strong social pressures to discourage the procreation of children. Earth does not want a growing population. It could well be that my entire family line has died out, and there are no more Koffields in Germany—or the place where Germany was, two centuries ago. After all, that is long enough for a nation to vanish as well. Depressing thoughts, those. Such reflections and speculations have made me feel more cut off, more rootless, than I have felt in a long time—and it has been a long time since I have felt a strong sense of connection to anyone or anything.

Perhaps that is the reason I have started this journal—unless I have done it merely to pass the time on a long journey. But I think it more likely that I have done so in order to feel connected, ordered, linked to the things I set down in words. I never much cared for the task of maintaining a ship's log, back in the days when I commanded the Upholder. *Now I find I miss it. Though, of course, I have set down more personal observations and emotional reactions in these few pages than I ever did in all the shipboard logs I ever kept.*

But, reading back a paragraph or two, I find that I have misstated the case. I do feel connected. I have the strongest connection and commitment to our quest, our mission—and to the people caught up with me in the midst of it. Norla Chandray, Captain Marquez—even Dr. Ashdin and the cheerfully sardonic Dixon Phelby. Even our putative "captain," Yuri Sparten. Maybe it is nothing more than the fact that we have all been wounded by the same thing— by the same man—but yet it is enough to create a fraternity, a secret society, open only to those who have been hurt by Oskar DeSilvo.

Sparten, I suspect, would not count himself among that number, but he is, even if he does not know it. It was, after all, DeSilvo who actually ordered the destruction of Circum Central. Whatever injury that did to the planet of Glister must rightly be laid at DeSilvo's feet, and not at mine. The descendants of Glister survivors have blamed me for their disasters—even I blamed myself. But it was DeSilvo who did the deed.

That DeSilvo was the guilty party, and not I—that is one of many things that Sparten does not know, one of many secrets pulled out of what purported to be DeSilvo's funerary urn. Only four of us—myself, Norla, Ashdin, and Marquez—know the full story,

*for the full story is too dangerous to be shared. The
rest of humanity, Sparten included, must be left to
guess.*

    *That I was blamed for everything that went wrong
on Glister after Circum Central—that is the gravest
of all the injuries DeSilvo inflicted upon me.*

Anton Koffield stared at the words he had written on the
datapad, and struggled with the temptation to erase
them all. Why in the name of stars and sky had he written all that? He could not recall when he had ever written so much about himself.

But then he saw it. He looked around himself, at the
main deck of the auxiliary lighter, at Clemsen Wahl and
Dixon Phelby playing a game of chess. Not so very long
ago in his own experience, he had been traveling aboard
this very craft. That time he had journeyed with Norla
Chandray as his sole companion. She had watched the
way he had acted then and realized that he was preparing for battle. And now, here he was again, once again
aboard the *Cruzeiro do Sul*. And once again, he was
preparing to fight. Except this would be a spy's war, a
covert war, winnable only if the enemy never knew the
war had so much as happened. And Spymaster Anton
Koffield's only weapons were people, to be briefed,
aimed, and fired off into the cloud of secrets to find and
seize their targets. By sizing up the personalities, the
moods, the abilities of his people—and of himself—he
was taking inventory of his weapons.

Koffield shrugged and slipped the encrypted datapad
inside his tunic's inner pocket. Perhaps that was why he
had done it. Or perhaps that theory was itself merely another defensive layer of emotionalism, explaining away
what embarrassed him.

It didn't really matter.

What did matter was that, at long last, he was finally
on the trail of his tormentor, Oskar DeSilvo.

• • •

The Permanent Physical Collection
PPC Habitat
Orbiting Neptune

"Okay," Sendler said, her voice muffled by the breathing mask. "There's the Class A Reading Room we've been watching for, up ahead. We'll make camp there."

Her two companions were too tired to make any reply. They simply nodded and followed behind until they reached the room. The notice painted on the airlock in prim, careful letters read

READING ROOM J-23-S12/c1A
FICTION AND LITERATURE BY AUTHOR
THURBER TO THYLSIT

"Sendler"—Jerand Bolt no longer had the slightest doubt it wasn't her real name—"Sendler" leaned wearily against the Reading Room's airlock as she activated the controls and waited for the lock to cycle. She was hunched over to compensate for the weight of her over-size backpack, and Jerand knew his posture was not likely any better. He and Sparten simply came to a halt when Sendler reached the lock. They stood there, like exhausted pack animals that dared not lie down for fear they'd lack the energy to get back to their feet.

The hike so far hadn't been easy on any of them. But they were making progress. Another half a day and they'd be clear of the main fiction section.

The airlock hatch slid open, moving as slowly as the three travelers, and they all stumbled into the chamber. The outer hatch sealed, and a shimmering grey field materialized in the overhead bulkhead. It moved down from the top of the chamber, rippling over their bodies, setting the hairs on Jerand's arms on end. The pressure-curtain field moved down toward the deck, crackling and fizzing as it went. The field pushed the exterior pure nitrogen "air" out through the floor valves, and drew in the Reading Room's breathable oxygen/nitrogen mix behind itself.

The curtain field finished its work and vanished into the floor. The three tired travelers clumped into the Reading Room, yanked off their air masks, and unceremoniously shed their gear. They dropped their backpacks onto the deck, sat in the reading chairs, and peeled off their hiking shoes. None of them stripped off their jackets or hats, and they all pulled their gloves back on as soon as they'd stripped off their backpacks and masks. The stacks, and unoccupied Reading Rooms, were held at five degrees centigrade. The Reading Room's heating system came on automatically when it was occupied, but it would take a while to warm the room to any sort of comfortable temperature.

Jerand looked at his two companions and forced down a smile. Nothing to be gained in laughing at his superiors, and no doubt he looked as bad as they did. None of them were used to hiking as a form of transportation, or the awkwardness of moving in gravity one-third as strong as Earth's, or the fiddly adjustments required by the breathing masks, or, most especially, the physical demands of walking with large and heavy backpacks. Each of those new things required a surprisingly large amount of effort. Stacked one on top of another, they left the PPC Team flat-out exhausted.

Ever since their arrival at Alexandria Dock, the PPC's main entrance complex, Jerand had been warned repeatedly that the PPC was run for the comfort, convenience, and safety of the books, and not that of humans. He had seen a lot of evidence to support that warning, from the pure nitrogen atmosphere and frigid five-degree temperature maintained in the stacks, to the low-gee field used to reduce strain on bindings. Large areas of Alexandria Dock maintained breathable air and civilized temperatures for the human staff, but not the stacks. It had taken some real effort to get this far—and they hadn't even reached their destination yet. It took some time to get around the Permanent Physical Collection of the Grand Library.

The facility that became the Permanent Physical Collection had originally been intended merely as a storage site for the text that had not yet been scanned into the Grand Library's digital collection, but it swiftly evolved into something more, into a defense against the human urge to improve on what already worked, the impulse to develop new, better, faster—and incompatible—ways of storing information.

One information technician had estimated that all the information in the twenty-kilometer-long PPC habitat, all the words and pictures stored in the tens of thousands of kilometers of shelving, could be stored inside a single maxidense datacube ten centimeters on a side. But the trick would be in getting the information back *out*.

If the compression or encryption or indexing or display systems failed, if the data was damaged by a stray cosmic ray—or if someone simply dropped the cube from a great height onto a hard surface, or exposed it to extremes of temperature, or if it were lost or stolen—then the cube would no longer hold the wisdom of the ages and the history of the race. It would be a paperweight, a doorstop.

The Permanent Physical Collection was the near neighbor—and poor relation—of the Grand Library, which, in effect, consisted of multiple copies of just such a datacube. The stored information took up about .0001 percent of the Grand Library's volume. The rest of the GL was given over to all the hardware and facilities and staff living quarters and repair centers and so on required to ensure access to the data in the cubes.

If, somewhere down the line, someone decided to redesign the "standard" dataport, or to use a different voltage, or to rewrite the retrieval protocols, and elected to abandon all effort at backward compatibility so as to make new and improved features available, then the GL datacubes, though they were working perfectly, would still be rendered useless.

And even if the cubes survived undamaged, with all data and indexing intact, and the hardware and software required to access the data still worked—then still the cubes would fail to preserve all the data in the original works because some forms of information would likely not have been perceived as data in the first place. On a near-ancient paper book, for example, the composition of the paper might tell something of the book's history. The binding technique used, the style of type chosen, the composition of the ink—all might speak of how the book was made, or even who made it—or if the book was real or a forgery. Notes scribbled and then erased in the margin, the pages the book fell open to—those too might be of significance. Even the dirt on the pages could have meaning, because different ages had different kinds of dirt, and the sort that was found provided evidence as to when the book was read. It was not unknown for scholars to detect latent fingerprints, and thus to identify the actual scholar who had consulted the work a thousand years before.

Beyond question, there was great value in storing words and images and sounds and smells and all other records as digital files, and indeed the PPC's human staff and ArtInts worked endlessly to scan and digitize vast amounts of data from the collection for the Grand Library. It was far easier to do a computer search of a datacube than it was to do a hand search through physical books—and it was far easier to make a backup copy of a cube. Both the Grand Library and the Permanent Physical Collection had great value.

The most current versions of the PPC's datastore and the Grand Library's digital collection were shipped out to every human-settled star system at least once a year, thus providing massive redundancy and a precious resource for scholars throughout Settled Space. A copy of the latest version of the Grand Library Cube was already aboard the *Dom Pedro IV*/"Merchanter's Dream" for transport back to Solace.

There was also a physical "backup copy" of the PPC—a duplicate facility buried under the Lunar Farside. The theory was that any catastrophe that could wipe out both a habitat orbiting Neptune *and* a deep bunker inside the Moon would not likely leave many human survivors behind to worry about what had been lost. But even aside from the various one-of-a-kind artifacts stored in each facility, the two collections were never perfect copies of each other. Too much material came pouring endlessly in to both locations for that to be possible.

The best estimate was that only 63 percent of the PPC had actually been digitally stored. That left more than one-third of the collection completely invisible to anyone who did not actually visit the PPC. Worse, the PPC's indexing system was far from perfect. Earth's population had been in decline for thousands of years, and as an inevitable result of that, universities and other scholarly centers would merge, or shut down altogether. And that often meant the sudden donation of a million-volume library to the PPC. Any slight flaws—or yawning gaps—in the cataloging of the donated libraries were, in such cases, inherited by the PPC, and the staff, human and robotic, would be swamped by the sudden, urgent need to sort and shelve the books, and clear the receiving bays at Alexandria Dock, before the next shipment came in.

One full squadron of mobile ArtInts, three hundred units in all, had no other task than to scan the shelves for miscataloged books and pull them for recataloging and reshelving. They had been slowly falling behind the need for their services for the last century or so.

As a result of these and other problems, a significant but unknown number of books were miscataloged, or even completely uncataloged. Fortunately, the vast majority of these "lost" books were actually shelved in the right subject area. They were there to be found—if one made the journey to the PPC, then hiked through the stacks, and finally browsed the shelves.

It was the hiking part that was getting to Jerand. A life spent largely aboard starships and space stations had afforded him little chance for walking long distances. It was possible to lease small ArtInt-controlled travel carts at Alexandria Dock, but the rates were breathtakingly high. Besides which, there were only two-seater carts available at the moment, and the Dock staff hadn't seemed eager to rent two carts to one party. Sendler hadn't pushed too hard. Jerand thought she had started backing off the minute she realized the carts were controlled by built-in ArtInts that could not be shut off. What was she up to that she didn't want a robotic member of the library staff to see? And would she want to keep Jerand—and Yuri Sparten—from seeing the same thing?

" 'Welcome to Reading Room J dash twenty-three S dash twelve, slash c- 1-a' " Sendler read out loud, off a sign by the door. "Real nice homey welcome, isn't it?"

"Very sentimental," muttered Sparten, still slumped over in a chair and leaning his arm on the conference table. "I'm all choked up."

" 'This Class A Reading Room provides a general meeting room and eight private bunk rooms, each with two beds and two study system-link research carrels. Mattresses are provided, but not bedding. Other facilities include a small kitchenette for heating and preparing travel rations, a full bath, and complete power service.' Well, it looks like we've really moved up!"

"Did you say full bath?" Jerand asked. The night before had found them at a mere Class C Reading Room—one open room with a table and four chairs, a microsized refresher and bathroom, and no facilities for heating food. Their midday rest stop had been a Class D, about which the less said the better. Jerand had missed his last chance at a shower before departing the "Merchanter's Dream"—whatever her real name was. That was getting to be several days ago.

"I *did* say full bath," Sendler replied with a grin. "And as soon as the heaters get this place up to a decent temperature, I'm going to pull rank and get first crack at it."

Jerand glanced over at a weary "Captain" Yuri Sparten and saw no visible reaction. *Very interesting. How the devil did you pull rank on a commanding officer—unless he* isn't *the commanding officer?*

Jerand Bolt stored that bit of information away with

all the others. He stood up, grabbed his backpack, and started rummaging through the travel rations, looking for something that might benefit from the use of actual cooking facilities.

After a roaring hot shower each, and an adequate meal together, the three of them turned in for the night, each in a private room—and Jerand Bolt instantly discovered he was not used to having a room to himself. He had been looking forward to the chance to curl up in bed with something good to read, but somehow, once there, he couldn't work up any enthusiasm for reading.

Maybe it had been so long since he could read in bed that he lost the knack. Jerand had bunked with Clemsen Wahl aboard the "Merchanter's Dream," and back on Asgard Five, too, and it had always been close to impossible to concentrate on the written word while Clemsen was rattling off so many spoken ones.

Here no Clemsen prattled on. Here Bolt had a bed larger than he had slept in for years, and even a spare bed on the other side of the room. A study carrel stood at the foot of each bed, and a large worktable stood in the center of the room, providing the most basic of all research tools—a convenient surface upon which to spread out materials. The room was large enough for two researchers to share comfortably for weeks on end—and Jerand had it all to himself.

But instead of luxuriating in the peace and the quiet and the privacy of his accommodations, Jerand was restless, wide-awake. He shut the datapad full of stories he had been trying to read. Might as well give it up. There wasn't anything in it that could catch his interest. *Biggest library in the universe, and I can't find a thing to read.* He smiled at that, set the datapad on the nightstand, and turned out the light.

But sleep would not come. The darkness too dark. There was no glimmer of light from anywhere. It wasn't just the actual darkness that was bothering him, either. The bedroom was a windowless box, inside the larger windowless box of the Reading Room, and *that* box

was inside a sealed cylinder twenty kilometers long, and
the cylinder was orbiting Neptune, out in the far darkness, the Sun merely a largish dot of light set in the
blackness.

People weren't meant to live in such darkness. No
wonder they were all nuts back at Asgard Five. That far
from any real light, watching for the lights of ships to
come through the ultimate darkness of a black hole—of
course they were twitchy out there. No, the *real* wonder
was that anyone living the space voyager's life held on to
any bit of sanity at all—

Jerand swore to himself, rolled onto his side, and gave
his pillow a good hard punch. He'd drive *himself* crazy if
he didn't stop going on like that. Fine thing when a dark,
quiet room was all it took to send him that far off the
deep end. What could be better for sleeping than dark
and quiet—

He sat bolt upright in bed. Suddenly he realized it
wasn't quiet. He could hear someone walking, very quietly, just outside his door. He heard the low rumble of
the bedroom door opening and shutting, the click of the
latch dropping shut—and then he could hear that there
was someone in the room.

He started to reach for the light, but a voice in the
dark stopped him cold.

"Don't," said Yuri Sparten. "Leave it off."

Jerand heard a quiet *click-click. The door lock,* he
told himself. More steps in the absolute blackness, then
the reading light over the worktable came to life. There
was Sparten, his back to Jerand. Sparten turned around
and faced Jerand. He was wearing infrared goggles, but
he pulled them off, folded them up, and tucked them in
an inside pocket of his tunic. He reached into another
pocket, and for a split second that lasted forever, Jerand
braced himself for the sight of a weapon. Sparten was
going to execute him, silence him, eliminate him, before
he could reveal their secrets. They could dump his body
in some obscure corner of the stacks, and it could easily
be years before anyone found the corpse—

Sparten's hand came out, holding what appeared to

be a pack of playing cards. He held them up so Jerand could see them. "Out of bed, Bolt," said Sparten, and something in his voice made Jerand move as quickly and obediently as he would have if Sparten had been holding a gun on him. "Go over there. Grab a chair, and sit down at the table. No—other side. I want your back to the door."

Jerand did as he was told. Sparten moved around the table and sat on the other side, so he could watch the door. He adjusted the lamp so the light speared straight down at the table, putting his face half in the darkness. The light reflected off the tabletop just enough to cast huge, dim, looming shadows everywhere. He started dealing the cards.

"You couldn't sleep," said Sparten. "Neither could I. Too keyed up, and this place is just too quiet. I heard you moving around, and came next door. We decided to play cards. We closed and locked the door to keep the noise down as much as possible. Pick up your cards. We're playing Wormhole." Jerand obediently picked up his cards, and some corner of his mind found the time to notice that he'd never seen cards like these before. They were circular, and didn't have the usual suits marked on them. Instead they each showed a glyph in the center of the card, and repeated around the periphery. There seemed to be four different glyphs—a blue galaxy, a red five-pointed star, a green crescent moon, and a yellow comet. *How am I supposed to play with cards like these?* An absurd worry, of course—but just the sort of thing his subconscious would throw up to try and keep him from facing larger worries.

"What's going on?" he asked, not daring to take his eyes off the cards.

"I needed to talk to you. Talk to you away from Chandray. This is the first chance I've had, and I wanted to take it, in case there isn't another."

"Who's Chandray?" he asked, though of course he already knew the answer. But the question seemed to be expected.

"Norla Chandray. Our fearless leader. The one who's been calling herself Sendler."

Jerand had thought he was afraid before. He'd been wrong. In that moment, he finally understood what real fear was. He felt the first twitching of the trapdoor swinging open beneath him. This was the start of conspiracy, of secrecy and plots and spying. And there was nothing he could do to stop himself from falling into it. He might flee the room, yell bloody murder, call for Sendler—for Chandray—but what good would it do? He would be picking sides—but he did not know one side from the other, or what it was all about. Maybe Chandray was under orders to kill both of them if there was a disturbance. There was no way to know. But he did know Sparten didn't plan to hurt him—yet. It was all he had to go on. It would have to be enough. "Go on," he said. And just like that, he was cooperating, listening, enlisting, albeit passively, in whatever plot Sparten was part of.

"Leptin's real name is Felipe Henrique Marquez. He's the captain. The ship's real name is *Dom Pedro IV*. Those names mean anything to you?"

"No." But it helped. *Chandray. Marquez. Dom Pedro IV*. It was good to know the true names of things. He stared at his cards and figured out how the glyphs and marks corresponded to the suits and ranks he was used to.

"Didn't think so—though it used to be the *DP-IV* was a sort of famous ghost ship, for a while back on Solace. Never mind. One more name. Alber Caltrip. The one you call 'the Admiral.' Someone must have slipped, and you overheard it. Well, he's an admiral, all right. Admiral Anton Koffield of the Chronologic Patrol. Ever heard of *him*?"

Jerand shifted his gaze from his meaningless cards to look Sparten in the face for the first time. Koffield? *The* Koffield? Maybe sometimes it wasn't so good to learn all the true names.

There wasn't a spacer anywhere in Settled Space

who hadn't heard the name *Anton Koffield*. The Circum Central Incident. The only man to blow a timeshaft wormhole. The story was he had doomed the planet Glister, cut off their best supply route, starved the planet. Sometimes they said he had done it because he had gone crazy. Or else because he was stopping an invasion by some weird alien species called the Intruders. But no one, before or since, had ever seen any sign of any alien species more advanced than a slime mold, let alone one that could fly spaceships and attack a time-shaft wormhole, the way the Intruders supposedly did. One story was Koffield had imagined the Intruders *because* he was crazy—but supposedly there were all sorts of instruments that recorded the Intruders—and they were real enough to have destroyed another Chronologic Patrol ship and some transports, and beat the hell out of Koffield's ship too. *None* of the versions of the stories held together all the way. Probably the confusion, the mystery, around the story was part of what kept it alive.

"Wait a second," Jerand protested. "That was a hundred-plus years ago. Koffield's gotta be dead, or at least way old by now."

"Stranded in time," Sparten said coolly, staring at his cards. "The ship that took him to Solace—the *Dom Pedro IV*, in fact—malfunctioned. Missed its timeshaft drop and just kept going. Sabotaged, probably. The ship got to Solace—but it showed up 127 years late."

"But she would go totally off course! There's no way a ship that missed its timeshaft could—"

"Could ever reach port at all. Of course not. The chances of it happening would be billions to one, proba-bly longer. That's why it had to be sabotage. Very deli-cate, precise sabotage, designed to get the ship where she was going—just way too late to do any good."

"What—what sort of good?"

"I don't know it all," Sparten said. "I know some, from what I saw, and a little more from what I was told."

"So what does it have to do with Koffield?"

"That's kind of involved," Sparten said. He arranged the cards in his hand, and played one of them, setting it faceup on the table. The seven of stars. "Play a card," he said. "It doesn't matter what."

But somehow, suddenly, it did matter. Jerand suddenly realized he was playing two games at once—maybe more games than that—and he wanted to play them all well. A light suit of the same rank would negate a dark suit. He played the seven of crescents. "Involved how?" he asked. He pulled his cards in close to his chest to keep them hidden. It occurred to him that everyone was playing that way, in all the various games that were under way. In close to keep anyone from seeing. Maybe in so close it was hard to see your own cards.

"Koffield claimed he had come to Solace to warn people that something terrible was going to happen to the planet's climate—but he got there over a century late—and somehow, nearly all his evidence vanished en route. The thing is, a lot of terrible climate problems *did* crop up in that century-plus, and there was at least some surviving evidence—not solid *proof*, but some fairly good clues—suggesting that Koffield *had* predicted the disaster, long before it happened. But it *could* also be that he was pulling some sort of trick—writing down bad stuff that had already happened, and then faking it all up to *look* like it came from 127 years in the past." Sparten set down a card.

Jerand frowned. He couldn't tell if it was a deliberate play, and Sparten had made a mistake, or if he had just thrown down whatever card came to hand. *Why does it matter how well I play this game?* he asked himself. But it did matter. "A con job," he suggested as he scooped the card Sparten had discarded.

"Exactly. No one could figure out a motive for his doing such a thing, but the things he was warning about were supposed to be so big, and so horrible, that no one could believe them. And don't ask me what the bad stuff was, because no one told *me*. I'm not quite sure how

much the people who briefed me knew themselves."
Sparten picked up Jerand's discard and threw down another himself. "It all got dumped in the lap of Solace's government. They had to decide what to do. There were two basic possibilities. Koffield was lying, or he was telling the truth. *Both* possibilities seemed implausible. But if the Solace government guessed wrong, there'd be big trouble. If he was lying, and they fell for it, they'd waste resources that could have gone toward the real problems—and just fixing the real problems could bankrupt the planet. If he was telling the truth and they ignored him—well, as I said, I don't know the whole story, but a bankrupt planet is better than a planet with everyone dead."

"*That* bad?" He had another chance to negate Sparten's play—unless Sparten was trying to trap him. But the trap was very long odds—he played the negater.

"Might be," Sparten said, glancing down at the cards on the table. He laid down the lady of comets.

Jerand grimaced. Almost, but not quite, the card he needed. "So the thing to do was check Koffield out. And they put you on it?"

"Right."

"Who's 'They'?"

"Never you mind that."

"Why? You a spy or something?"

"No," said Sparten, a note of irritation in his voice. "At least, I wasn't then. Now, I suppose . . . anyway, they put me on it because I happened to be involved already, and happened to hear a few things. They wanted to have as few people knowing the story as possible. If they used me, they wouldn't have to brief someone else and add to the number of people who might blab." Sparten played another card—one that *had* to be a mistake.

"So you check him out." Jerand pounced on Sparten's discard, maybe a bit too eagerly.

Sparten didn't notice. "So I try to. I watch him—but Koffield is nobody's fool. He keeps me at arm's length, and meantime they start checking out the information Koffield still has. Part of it has to do with Oskar DeSilvo. Heard of him?"

"Yeah. Famous terraforming scientist."

"Right. Wandella Ashdin is a big expert on him and—"

"Let me guess. She's the other passenger on the 'Merchanter's Dream'—the *Dom Pedro IV*."

"Very good. But the point is, what Koffield has to say about DeSilvo checks out with what Wandella knows about him. *Everything* checks out—or at least it seems to. There's no way to know for sure. So the problem gets kicked all the way upstairs to the Planetary Executive. *She* decides Koffield should head out to Greenhouse— it's a large moon of a gas giant planet in the Solace system. It's got a lot of sealed habitats on it. It's where a lot of bioresearch goes on. The whole place is basically one big research center. They figure that, out there, they can best evaluate the little evidence they have. And nearly everyone in the know—including Ashdin and me—go along for the ride."

"So they ship you out to this moon." *And so you're all together where you can be watched at the same time, and you're all very, very, far away from the on-planet press.* "So what happens there?"

"I don't know all of it, but I can tell you some."

Why are you telling me any of it? Jerand thought, but he did not ask. He could guess. "Go on."

"We get to Greenhouse, and there's a big meeting. Everyone gets all excited about some math that Koffield does for them. They're all convinced it explains all sorts of things about how terraformed planets and habitats behave. They all think it's very important. Probably it is. When we left for Earth, they were still going at it, and they all kept saying the new approach could keep them busy for years."

Jerand looked at Sparten, and saw his expression had gone almost totally blank. There was something more, something deeper, that Sparten was leaving out. But later would be time enough to dig for it. Let Sparten say what he had to say. "That's nice," said Jerand. "A bunch of scientists get excited. So what? What's the big deal?"

"I'm coming to it," Sparten said, the irritation plain in his voice. "While we're there, it turns out that they have to blow a habitat dome because its ecosystem has gone bad. Mold and bacteria have taken over, or something. And it turns out that DeSilvo's tomb is in this dome. And for some reason that I don't know, *that* gets Koffield all excited. He spots some clue, I guess. He decides that he has to go get a look at the tomb immediately, even though they're already halfway set to blow the place. It's very hairy, very dangerous. They don't want to let him go, but he pushes hard, Chandray pushes hard, and they agree to let him go."

"You try to go along, but they cut you out."

"Right. *But* they take Ashdin along, because she's such a big DeSilvo expert." Sparten was talking fast, the words spilling out, as if they had been bottled up too long and were eager to escape. "They go into the dome, it blows, and they come out afterward. I know *that* much for sure. I talked to witnesses later. But as to what happened while they were in there—no one, not even Ashdin, has talked. I've checked every way I could. I had to piece it together, a little bit at a time, and some of it I still had to guess at. But it's pretty clear they get to the tomb. And while they're there, they put in an emergency call to Captain Marquez, aboard the *Dom Pedro*. *Why* it was an emergency, what they said to each other, I have no idea.

"The three of them come out of the dome after it blows. They get tossed into quarantine for a month—but that's no big mystery. Standard procedure after being in a contaminated zone. But they take some objects *into* quarantine with them."

"Things they found in the tomb?"

"Yeah. And I know what, too. At least some of it. After the dome was blown, a repair team went in and patched up the permanent structures—including the tomb. They took pictures of the damage. I've seen them.

Nothing really got hurt—*except the urn holding DeSilvo's ashes had disappeared.*"

Sparten looked Jerand straight in the eye. "Now think about that. DeSilvo's a hero all through the Solace system. The tomb was a major monument to him. They despoiled his grave. But no one arrests them, or charges them, or even mentions the vandalism publicly. They hush it up. The records I was able to check show that the urn was returned, or maybe a duplicate put in its place, very quietly, a few days after our friends got out of quarantine.

"Koffield heads straight back to Solace—and sees to it I don't go along. No one but Marquez goes with him. The people who should know think he might have had a private meeting with the Planetary Executive, just the two of them. If he did, he convinced her there was a problem that needed money thrown at it. Because a few days after *that*, the Solace government starts paying to refurbish and refit and upgrade the *Dom Pedro IV* and get her launched for Earth."

"So there was something in the urn. Something that got Koffield's group heading for the Solar System, searching for something. So what was it?" Jerand asked.

"I don't know. That's what I want *you* to find out," Sparten said.

Jerand stared at him in shock. "*Me? How?*" *And why?* he asked himself. *Why the devil should I get mixed up in the middle of all this?* "And wait a second—if you're working for security, and it's the Solace government sending the, ah, *Dom Pedro* out—why do you need spies? It's the same government, isn't it?"

Sparten frowned. "There's government, and government," he said. "There are a lot of factions, a lot of power bases. I could explain the ins and outs of the situation on Solace, but we'd be here all night and halfway into morning."

"You're asking me—you're *ordering* me—to choose your side when I don't even know what the sides are! Or what the fight's about."

"The fight is about saving Solace," Sparten said.

Plainly the words were meant to be grand and impressive, but somehow they just wound up sounding pompous. "Solace is in big trouble. I am part of a group that believes the present government is chasing after big, grand plans that will waste our resources and not really solve the problem."

"So you want to stop whatever it is that Koffield is trying to do?"

"No, not necessarily," Sparten replied. "We have no idea *what* it is he's trying to do—but we *need* to find out."

That much, at least, was a motivation Jerand could understand. *He* needed to find out, too—if only out of sheer curiosity. But no need to give up his bargaining situation just yet. "That at least gets us started on why *you* need me," he said. "But why do *I* need to do it—and how do you suppose I can do it? You're the spy. They must have given you *some* training. What can I do that you can't?"

"How you do it is simple—not be Yuri Sparten. Chandray suspects me. She'll be watching me—not you. When's she looking over her left shoulder to see where I am, you peek over her right. She'll send you to do things she wouldn't trust me to do. She'll make a mistake. Watch for it. Keep your eyes open—you do that pretty well already, without being told."

"I get the idea. It might get us—get you—somewhere. But why should I do it?"

Sparten set down another card and took up Jerand's discard. "Because I saw your file when you signed on—and because you swore an oath. 'Merchanter's Dream' is the legally registered name of the starship that brought us here, and I am the legal and registered master of that vessel. I'm the captain, and I'm giving you an order—and the file says you make it a point of pride always to follow orders."

The silence after that speech was long. Jerand Bolt could have answered it any of a half dozen ways—but he did not. Silence was plainly wiser. Silence? No, better still—misdirection. And maybe a chance to tweak

Sparten's nose a bit while he was at it. He took up the jack of galaxies Sparten had just played, sorted it into his hand, and then laid the run of cards down on the table.

"Wormhole," he said. "I win."

CHAPTER EIGHT

SCHOOLS OF THOUGHT

DeSilvo Archive
Grand Library Habitat
Orbiting Neptune

Wandella Ashdin's pocket comm bleeped. "Yes," she said to the empty air, trusting to the comm to accept the call and send her voice.

"It's me," said Marquez.

Who else would it be? Ashdin asked herself. Plainly, Koffield had told Marquez to keep an eye on her, and the man was taking his duties seriously. It seemed as if he was checking up on her every five minutes. "Of course it's you," she said. "Just making sure I'm still here?"

"No, I knew that already," he said cheerfully. "The comm units do position reporting. I just wanted to bring in the latest from the Earth group."

"Are they there already?"

"No, still thirty-six hours out. They're just checking in. Encrypted message. But, our, ah, friend had a query for you. Shall I bring the message up?"

Wandella didn't even bother suggesting that he read it over the comm system. It was beyond imagining that he'd tolerate any such breach of security. Not when he couldn't even bring himself to pronounce Koffield's name near a microphone. "Do I really have a choice?" she asked.

"No," said Marquez. "Not really. I'm on my way." The comm bleeped again, to indicate the connection had been cut. Marquez would be there inside of five minutes.

Wandella Ashdin leaned back in her chair and sighed wearily. She looked around, as if to regain inspiration from her surroundings.

The chamber had been DeSilvo's private study. She was sitting in the very study that the Great Man himself had used, sitting at his desk and in his chair. Soft music played. The lighting came from just behind her right shoulder, light of the perfect color and intensity for a scholar at work. The light automatically adjusted itself, shifting its position of origin whenever she changed position, even adjusting for the sort of screen or page she was reading.

Fresh hot tea sat in her cup. The room temperature was precisely right. And best of all, she was surrounded by original source materials.

She was in paradise—at least in what she had always imagined her own personal paradise to be. Oskar DeSilvo's own personal *sanctum sanctorum*, and she had it all to herself. Well, nearly all. Marquez and the others from the ship intruded, but they didn't really count. She was the only scholar in the place.

But she wasn't enjoying it.

Dr. Wandella Ashdin had spent her professional life studying the life and career of Oskar DeSilvo, and she had done it from light-years away from the main sources of information. It was all very well to be a scholar with unlimited search access to the library update datacubes the Grand Library shipped out every year or so. Each new cube contained incomprehensibly vast amounts of information—but in a sense, that was part of the trouble. Something new about DeSilvo was there in nearly every update cube—but finding it could be nearly impossible. The indexing was never what it could be, and no search system was ever as good as it was supposed to be. One could easily spend a month teasing out three or four worthwhile bits of data from the mountains of fluff.

And fluff there was. DeSilvo was still an important enough historical figure to be written up fairly often. Every new datacube usually contained at least one popular book or datapad file about him. It was rare indeed that any of them contained anything that was both new and accurate, and rarer still anything new and accurate that was also of the least significance. But still, the chance was always there.

And there were plenty of areas in the record with room for improvement. There were long stretches of DeSilvo's life, mostly those times he was involved in an intense, rigidly scheduled construction project, wherein she had a literally minute-by-minute account of his movements and actions. But there were other parts of his life where weeks, months, and even years were largely unaccounted for.

Here she had been able to fill a half dozen of the gaps in just a few days of work. Perhaps even more satisfying, she had been able to fill several gaps—and correct several outright errors—in the DeSilvo Archive's own official biography. That was what scholarship was *for*—to find the truth, to set the record straight, to further understanding.

It wasn't meant to be something done in support of hole-in-corner games, secrets and spying and plots. And yet here she was.

But even that was not the worst of it. She was here to study the Great Man himself. But the reason he merited such intense study, the reason it was worth the effort needed to get her here, was the abrupt change in his status—to that of Genocidal Monster. She had been there, in the room, when that damned Anton Koffield had opened that funerary urn and pulled out the evidence against DeSilvo. Worse still, the same urn contained DeSilvo's own *confession* of his terrible crimes. There was no escaping *that*, no explaining it away as a misunderstanding or a misinterpretation of the facts.

She frowned and glanced at herself in the elaborately framed mirror that hung at seated eye level to the right of DeSilvo's desk. *Explain it away?* she asked herself, appalled by her own mental turn of phrase. *Is that what you'd do if you could?* She shifted uncomfortably in DeSilvo's extremely comfortable chair and looked herself in the eye. Wandella Ashdin worked hard to be an honest scholar—honest enough at least to try to face her own preconceptions, the blinders formed by her enthusiasm, her hero worship. Well, the question was moot. DeSilvo's confession had seen to that.

And yet—and yet—there was still a part of her that longed to defend him, to fight back against his detractors. Her instinct was always to go to the sources, to check and cross-check the facts. She'd start to work and then, the thrill of the chase would take over, as she swam through the endless seas of data and record, zeroing in on *the* fact, *the* datapoint—and then she would blink, and look again at her work, and realize she had just spent another day strengthening the case against her hero, Oskar DeSilvo. It was all most confusing and dispiriting at times. The pursuit of Truth with a capital "T" wasn't supposed to be so—*ambiguous*.

But, feelings to one side, she was learning more and more of the Truth, and in ways that were likely to advance their current mission. Indeed, Wandella Ashdin was beginning to suspect they had all underestimated the stakes in the game they were playing. The fate of a world might be the least of it. DeSilvo had been doing his own hush-hush research, there at the end—though about what, she could find no clue.

The door slid open without warning, and in came Marquez. Wandella glared at him, but otherwise did not protest—this time. He hadn't used the annunciator on any of his previous visits, and Wandella had grown tired of arguing with him about it. Plainly, coming unannounced was part of his strategy for keeping an eye on her, and Marquez wasn't going to back down on anything concerned with *that* duty.

"So what's this message?" she asked.

"Read for yourself," he said. He pulled a sheet of message paper out of his breast pocket and handed it to her, still folded up.

Wandella knew the drill, and played along. She carefully shifted her body to put her back between the wall and the paper, and then unfolded it, careful to hold it close to her chest to prevent the printed side from being visible from any angle she hadn't blocked. She saw at once the paper was from the *DP-IV* and the message headers showed it had been printed into clear direct from the encrypted signal. Never would Marquez have dreamed of printing it off a Grand Library terminal, or even dreamed of letting it pass through the Library's data system. Encryption was all very well, but Marquez saw no reason to test the opposition's decryption skills.

That, of course, assumed that there *was* such a thing as an opposition—something of which Wandella was far from convinced. There had not been the slightest sign that the Chronologic Patrol, or any other security organization, had taken an interest in them. But Marquez, she knew, could not be dissuaded on any question of security.

Not that it would have done any hypothetical opposition much good if they *had* read the message. Koffield had written it in such a cryptic manner that Wandella herself had trouble parsing the sense of it.

APPROACHING DESTINATION. LOCAL SITES REQUESTING PRELIM SCHEDULE INFO. NEED RANKING OF SITES. ADVICE ON ADDS/DELETES, ALSO ON ADDITIONAL LEADS.

As best she could make out, he was in contact and negotiating with the various libraries and institutes to arrange visits. They wanted to know when he wanted to show up. Before he got back to them, he wanted her advice on where to go, and in what order, and on what new places he should try, and what currently planned ones not to bother with. Her researches had suggested a few changes to Koffield's search plan might make sense.

Marquez cleared his throat and put out his hand for the paper. "I must ask that—"

"You needn't say it," Wandella cut in as she folded the note back up and returned it to Marquez. "I won't work on it until I am back aboard ship, and I will use only the ship's communications systems to draft and send the reply."

"Very good," Marquez said. "Then I needn't disturb you further. I will see you back at the ship this evening."

Wandella Ashdin allowed herself a small, ladylike "hmmph," and a frown. Marquez bowed very slightly and left the room, closing the door behind himself.

"Back at the ship" indeed! She found it galling in the extreme that she was required to sleep in her spartan cabin aboard the *Dom Pedro IV* when she had an absolutely splendid suite of rooms available to her in the Grand Library.

Well, no point trying to do anything further at the moment. She had lost her train of thought. A visit from Marquez always left her agitated. Besides, it was nearly time to leave. Wandella powered down the last of her equipment, and walked slowly down the carpeted corridor toward the main entrance vestibule of the DeSilvo Archive.

She pressed the transit call button, and opened the door onto Scholar's Way, one of the main long-axis transit corridors of the habitat. Her irritation grew as she stood there, waiting, for a transit cart to arrive. After an interminable wait of nearly thirty seconds, one of the ubiquitous vehicles eased up to the door. Wandella stepped into it and sat down. "Marlowe Refectory," she said, making no effort to keep the annoyance out of her voice. No point being polite to a machine! Especially one that kept her waiting so long. The very idea.

As it happened, at that very moment, aboard the Permanent Physical Collection Habitat, Norla Chandray's party was just staggering into the spartan confines of Reading Room J-23-S12/c1A, after a ten-kilometer hike with full packs and breathing masks in near-freezing temperatures. No doubt they would have had only somewhat limited sympathy for Dr. Ashdin's suffering. On the other hand, entire schools of academic thought, pro and con, had been built around the statement that "all experience is relative to its context." And any marginally competent experiential relativist would have argued that, by the standards of the Grand Library, Dr. Ashdin was entitled to find the delay scandalous.

To put it bluntly, it had not taken long after her arrival at the Grand Library for Dr. Wandella Ashdin to become spoiled, and that was by no means surprising. The Grand Library had been designed for the specific *purpose* of coddling people like her.

The Grand Library was the digital-data companion to the Permanent Physical Collection. It was, in effect, that hypothetical maxidense ten-centimeter datacube, containing all the knowledge of the ages—or at least as much of it as could be stored as binary bits. The digital files themselves were stored in several duplicate datacubes, each actually about half a meter on a side. For convenience and redundancy, dozens of copies of the Grand Collection, as it was known, were scattered about the station.

Ironically, given that what the Grand Library was built to contain took up much less room than the PPC, the Grand Library was about 20 percent *larger* than the PPC.

A good part of the remaining 99.9999 percent of the Library habitat's volume was taken up with opulent setting that served no real purpose beyond display. The swank ballrooms, gleaming conference rooms, glittering dining halls, breathtaking observation decks, and so on occupied roughly a quarter of the habitat's volume. Supposedly, they were there as a tribute to knowledge, as venues to celebrate the scholarship that went on in the library. Put more bluntly, big fancy public spaces served to impress people, and holding splendid occasions in the Grand Library's very grand rooms usually made fundraising much easier.

The Grand Library was a long way from being fully

digital, and it maintained large collections of physical objects. The DeSilvo archive included physical papers of all sorts—personal letters, maps, drawings, as well as various physical artifacts, geologic samples, and even preserved biological samples of species important to this or that terraforming project. The DeSilvo Archive was a museum, and there were many others like it, each devoted to a particular scientist or scholar or area of study.

But all those functions took up only a bit more than half of the habitat's volume. The rest, as one anonymous wag once put it, was merely there to provide the scholars with nearly enough room to spread out their papers. And it was not only their papers, but all their data that needed spreading-out as well. Various disciplines relied on massive displays, or huge holographic tanks, in order to achieve the desired resolution for their data and simulations. Nearly all of the scholars desired privacy—and privacy gobbled up a lot of space.

In other words, when viewed as a complete system of research material plus researchers plus the infrastructure needed to connect them, the digital system took up just as much space as the physical collection.

Many scholars—though not so many experiential relativists—had made much of the contrast between luxurious conditions aboard the digital Grand Library and the relentlessly utilitarian facilities provided to those working in the Permanent Physical Collection.

The comparison was somewhat unfair. The PPC provided conditions of extreme luxury—for the books. But there was no getting around the fact that the scholars who delved into the digital had a far more comfortable time of it than those who grubbed around in the dusty stacks of actual, physical books. All the great libraries and research institutes experienced a similar division of their research materials. It was far from astonishing that the divide had left its mark on scholarship. But if all experience is relative, then the physical researchers could remain happy—so long as they never dared cross the line and experienced how the other half lived.

Wandella's transit cart pulled up in front of the Refectory. She got out, walked in, and breathed a sigh of relief. She was still in time for the first pouring of Early Tea.

The Permanent Physical Collection

Norla paused as the group came to an intersection, and checked the aisle, level, and corridor numbers stenciled on the wall, then quadruple-checked the grid address of their destination. Two intersections away. They were nearly there. And she had yet to tell her companions what, exactly, they were supposed to do there. She had to tell them now.

Norla had discovered something about paranoia: It was contagious. Out of all question, she had caught it from Koffield. And she had learned one other thing about paranoia: It led to moments like this one. She *had* to explain their mission before they reached the Geology and Terraforming Reading Room—and her paranoia-induced hesitation meant that she had to do it here, now, while they all wore heavy backpacks and breathing masks, while they were all cold and tired, and eager to get inside the Reading Room and rest. And now, right now, Norla would have to explain why they couldn't do that.

"Let's take a break," she said.

"But we're nearly there!" Bolt protested, his voice muffled by the breathing mask. "We're two minutes away."

"I know," said Norla. "I'm sorry about that. And I should have told you what I'm about to tell you sooner. But—well, I've been working too hard at keeping secrets."

The two men exchanged a quick, furtive glance with each other. With the breathing masks on, it was impossible to read their expressions, but plainly she had touched a nerve there.

"So what's the story?" Sparten asked. "What *are* we going to be doing?"

"Two main things," Norla said. "The most important is, getting more information." She looked toward Bolt. "There's a major terraforming crisis on Solace, and the Solacians need all the current data they can find."

She pulled a datapad out of her tunic. "This has got a list of every title on the subject of terraforming and climate engineering stored on the most recent Grand Library datacube shipped to Solace, about three years ago. We're going to get digital text on every terraforming book that *isn't* listed here. In other words, the texts that haven't gotten into Solace's copy of the Grand Library cube. We'll go down the shelf and see what we find that the terraforming people back on Solace and Greenhouse don't already have."

"So why do you have to tell us about that before we go in?"

"I didn't. It's the *other* job where that matters. There was some, ah, controversy about some information that—" what the devil was Koffield's cover name. It had completely slipped—no! That was it! "—that Alber Caltrip provided to the researchers on Greenhouse. It's in everyone's best interest to confirm his story as fully as possible. There are some who believe Caltrip's whole story is a fraud, and they are using that belief to block urgent work." *Like starting the evacuation of the planet.* But Bolt didn't need to hear about that part. "Caltrip reported himself as spending several days here, in the Reading Room we're about to come to. Proof that he was here would go a long way toward proving his story. So I need to check that room as thoroughly as possible for any remaining trace of his presence. We'd also like to confirm that the books he claimed to consult are where he said they were, and are still in the collection."

All that was true as far as it went. Norla saw no reason to tell Bolt the whole story, just at the moment. When he had first arrived on Solace, Koffield was carrying a sealed case, which he had thought contained a copy of a book he had found in the Terraforming Collection of the Grand Library's Permanent Physical Collection. The math and science in the book demonstrated that the techniques used to terraform Solace were fatally flawed, and the planet's ecosystem would fail within a few years or decades.

But when Koffield opened the case, the book and all the other evidence he had packed it in, were gone— stolen by DeSilvo, as it turned out. Koffield had managed to reconstruct many of the key math concepts, but that was not proof enough to decide the fate of a world. There were powerful people on Solace who wanted to deny the truth, who were determined to believe that the endless climate crises were merely a stretch of bad weather, a sign that a few details of the terraforming job needed adjustment. The deniers were a small minority— but there were enough of them to slow, or even stop, any effort to plan for the planet's evacuation.

"In short," Norla went on, "we need to find those books, and find proof that Alber Caltrip was in fact here."

"Come on. How many years has it been since he was here?" Sparten asked.

Norla very definitely didn't want to answer that question with Bolt standing there. *Oh, just over 128, I think. Best to leave it as vague as possible.* "I know," she said. "It's been a long time. But the Reading Rooms are a highly unusual environment. They are sealed between uses and all the oxygen-nitrogen is pumped out to keep the oxy from leaking out and contaminating the nitrogen atmosphere in the stacks. Only the Class A rooms even keep an oxygen environment between visits. The Class B Reading Rooms, like the one Caltrip used, are kept in low temperatures and a pure nitrogen atmosphere between visits—and the cleaning units check a visit counter, not a calendar, to decide when to do a full cleaning. Once every twenty visits, I think. The experts I talked to said there were about one in four odds that we could still find identity material from Caltrip inside."

"What's identity material?" Bolt asked.

Sparten answered, his voice short and impatient. "Flecks of skin or loose hairs you could get DNA from. Fingerprints. Papers in the trash can with his handwriting on them. Or maybe he scrawled his name on the wall in letters twenty centimeters high. *Caltrip Was Here.*"

Norla resisted the urge to snap at Sparten. She had to keep reminding herself that not everyone admired and respected Koffield as much as she did, Sparten least of all. He was a Glistern, raised in the belief that Anton Koffield had personally destroyed his world by wrecking Circum Central and thus preventing five rescue ships from getting to Glister. Fortunately, Sparten seemed to have come to see how simplistic that idea was. Five shiploads, or five hundred shiploads, of emergency supplies would not have saved Glister. Still, he was far from sympathetic to Koffield.

That left her with a Yuri Sparten who had all sorts of reasons to rebel. Push him too hard, and it was not beyond the realm of possibility that he could denounce them all to the authorities.

"Be careful what you say," Norla told him, her voice a study in control. "We are, all of us, in very deep waters here. We have to think everything through very thoroughly before we do it. All right?"

Sparten stared at her for the length of ten heartbeats. "All right," he said, in tones as icy as her own. He paused again, and then went on. "Is there really some chance there will be something left to find?"

"That's what the experts from Solace told me," Norla said.

"So you want us to stay outside the Reading Room while you search?" asked Bolt.

Norla looked at Bolt, startled. "What? Oh, no! Far from it. Then some damned paranoid could accuse me of planting evidence. I need you both wearing witness cameras and watching my every move."

Norla glared at Sparten. *Of course, you'd be doing that anyway,* she thought. "Come on," she said. "Let's go."

INTERLUDE

KALANI TEMBLAR

Chronologic Patrol Intelligence
Command Headquarters
(ChronPat IntCom HQ)
Lunar Farside

Kalani Temblar sighed wearily as she sat down at her workstation. She hesitated a moment, dreading the tedium that was about to begin. But there was no help for it. Girding herself for a long morning's work, she tapped at the glowing red spot on her console—the one marked NEXT PENDING QUERY.

The image of a timeshaft dropship appeared on the screen, along with several panels of text and several graphic displays. It would have taken her a good ten minutes merely to read through all the material, but she didn't have ten minutes, or even one minute. She glanced up at the upper left-hand edge of her display, at the box labeled NUMBER OF QUERIES PENDING. It showed 67. Even as she watched, it flicked up by one, to 68. She hated it when the count went up like that, before she could even get started grinding the numbers down. The input system tried to portion out the incomings fairly among the ops, and not dump more than an hour's work in any one person's queue. Today, it would seem, the

ArtInts had decided Kalani could consider sixty-eight ships in the next—she glanced up at the time display—hell, she was already behind. She had fifty-eight minutes to evaluate sixty-eight ships before moving on to the next part of her daily duties. She got down to it, staring grimly at her display, studying the data, trying to see if the ship on the screen was actually in some way suspicious.

Kalani didn't think much of her job, for the most part. Once upon a time, she had set to work on a new assignment by telling herself *Now I can do some good.* These days, when she arrived at the bull pen each morning and sat down at her workpod, her first thought was *How did I end up here?*

There was some merit to the question. Kalani had not sought out or received assignment into the Chronologic Patrol's Intelligence Service for the purpose of sitting in a windowless office and slogging through endless ship-movement reports.

The machines should have handled more of the work—or better still, all of it. At least in theory, Chron-Pat IntCom's Artificial Intelligences watched all the ships coming into or going out of the Solar System anyway. They were supposed to evaluate the available information on those ships and flag any and all that they considered "suspicious."

Understandably, if unfortunately for Kalani, IntCom's ArtInts literally had their paranoia setting adjusted to "high," with the result that, as best Kalani could tell, nearly *every* ship seemed suspicious. The ArtInts' rules for flagging ships had been tuned and retuned and tweaked endlessly over the centuries—but it was the nature of the universe to change, and the ArtInts viewed all change as potentially dangerous. Anything from a deviation in transit time to a statistically insignificant alteration in cargo ratios from a given ship's last run could set the ArtInts off. It required constant and ongoing adjustment to the profiling system to keep it working. Office folklore had it that one time the powers-that-be had shut down the profile-tuning department in one ill-considered

economy move. Within five weeks, IntCom's ArtInts
were slapping queries on literally *every* incoming ship.

Getting and keeping the ArtInts more or less under
control was often a case of two steps forward and one
step back. The best the profiling department could really
hope for was to get the ArtInts to march in place, to stop
adding reasons for flagging ships.

Kalani thought that over as she paged through the
queries, seeing nothing but the most trivial and innocent
deviations from an ArtInt's rigidly held idea of "normal." Many of the queries she could dismiss almost at
once. Most she could evaluate in under thirty seconds.

The fear of change was at the root of it. Impulsively,
she took up a stylus and scribbled on the storage sheet
she used as a notepad. She distilled the thought down
just a trifle as she wrote. *The nature of the universe is to
change, and the ArtInts view all change as dangerous.*
Yes. That was the way of it. True enough, and safe
enough. None of her superiors would argue with either
statement. But Kalani had come to another, and far more
dangerous, conclusion. You could substitute one term
for another, and come up with *the Chronologic Patrol
views all change as dangerous.* And *that* statement was
one she dared not commit to a storage sheet.

Kalani was something of a student of history in general, and of the Chronologic Patrol's history in particular. Going on for over two thousand years, it had been
the task of the Chronologic Patrol to protect causality, to
defend the past from the future, to prevent time paradoxes. The CP was further charged with the task of
maintaining the network of timeshaft wormholes that
made interstellar travel even remotely practical, and at
the same time made it at least theoretically possible to
damage or destroy causality. Those tasks the CP had always performed, and performed well.

But, somehow, somewhere—and not that long ago, it
seemed, only a few hundred years ago, as she read her
history—the CP had started down the road that led to
where they were: a Patrol that defended no longer just

against attacks on causality, but against *change itself*. There was an irony in there somewhere, but Kalani was not a person much given to contemplating ironies.

Kalani wondered exactly how and why *that* change had come. Maybe it was just the need to find a more relevant mission. Never, in all those centuries, had there been a documented case of successful causal derangement—an absence that led to endless, and inconclusive, debates. Some argued that the record demonstrated the dedication of the CP. Others argued—quietly—that the record proved that the CP, and all the endless and elaborate precautions taken against temporal interference, were utterly superfluous, that causality protected itself far better than mere humans ever could. But that was such rank heresy, and challenged so many deeply held beliefs at such a profound level, that it was not much discussed.

Kalani's own private opinion—one she likewise would never dare offer at the office, or most other places, either—was that the operative words were "documented cases." No law enforcement was perfect, no security system totally impenetrable. It stood to reason that, once a set of tools for time travel was in place, someone would find and employ a way to misuse the system.

Maybe the perpetrators had committed their crimes in ways that defied detection. Perhaps the cosmos itself took care of that detail for the time criminals. Perhaps what humans perceived as the universe was merely one of infinite universes, existing side by side inside an über-universe, a cosmos that contained all the sub-universes. If so, then perhaps the cosmos itself prevented causal loops by spontaneously generating whole, perfect copies of the universe that contained and confined the paradoxes, splitting off the jumbled causes from their awkward effects.

Some theories held that certain types of temporal paradoxes would cause the universe that contained them, in effect, to short-circuit, to self-destruct, to vanish altogether. If that were so, then *only* the universes in which no serious temporal paradoxes took place would survive.

All that was as may be. Kalani was cynical enough to believe in a far less drastic explanation for the lack of *reported* paradoxes: the CP was very, very, very good at hushing up its failures.

But, beyond all cavil, the CP was also very, very good at accomplishing its primary missions. And, in a way, that was what worried Kalani. Never in all of human history had there been a law enforcement or military service that had survived, even thrived, for so long. And in all the two-thousand-plus years of its existence, the Chronologic Patrol had held true to its charter: *to defend time.*

Until—until not so very long ago. Kalani had studied the archives of the CP as closely as she could, in her off hours and spare time. She could not name a specific date. It had taken her years of research before she could even put her finger on exactly what the change was. Now, she knew: Somewhere, in the last few centuries, that charter had been altered. These days, it was obvious, at least from where Kalani sat, that the CP had another mission: *to defend the status quo.*

Once she understood that, the pattern was plain to see. In politics, in scholarship, in policy, in technology, in ways large and small, obvious and subtle, the CP used its considerable influence to prevent change. Maybe it was just the inevitable ossification of a very old and rigid organization, conservative impulses accumulating over the centuries. It almost didn't matter. Because there was another thought that had popped into Kalani's head, not so long ago. Another thought she dared not commit to writing.

An army that changes its mind loses its way.

Merely thinking the words was enough to make her shudder, just a bit.

Best not to dwell on it. She focused in on her comfortably mind-numbing work, paging through query after query, one completely harmless ship at a time.

But then she came to ship number 57 in her query queue. Her hand hovered over the button for the *cancel inquiry* command that she had already used fifty-six times that morning—but then she pulled her hand away. There was something odd—no, several somethings odd—about that ship. For once, IntCom's ArtInts had found something.

She flagged the ship for further query. Once she got caught up with her routine work, Kalani Temblar promised herself, she was going to take a very good, long hard look at the Solacian Registered TimeShaft Dropship *Merchanter's Dream.*

CHAPTER NINE

THE DRUNK UNDER THE STREETLIGHT

The Reading Room didn't *feel* right. Jerand Bolt knew it the second they came through the inner door of the airlock and he pulled off his breathing mask. They had been through five or six of the Reading Rooms before, using them as midday rest spots and places to sleep. There was a sameness to all of them that transcended the differences in size, level of sanitary facilities available, and so forth. This one had that sameness too. But below the surface, somehow, it felt different. No, worse, it felt *wrong*.

"Here at last," said Sparten, pulling off his mask.

"We can't get comfortable yet," Chandray warned him. *No harm in thinking of her by her right name,* Jerand thought. *But if I slip and call her Chandray, she'll know that Sparten talked.* Never mind. That was a worry for later.

"Do both of you have your witness cameras recording?" Chandray asked. The witness cams were held on the side of the head with a strap, and were supposed to see and hear everything that the wearer did. They used the same sort of write-once tamperproof memory as in longwatch cameras.

"Started mine in the airlock," Sparten said, the fatigue in his voice plain to hear.

"Me too," said Jerand.

"Good," said Chandray, "then let's get started."

Neither of the others seemed to have noticed whatever it was that niggled at him. But they were a long way from help, and it was no time to take things lightly. "Hold it," Jerand said. "Something's not right in here."

"What do you mean?" Sparten demanded.

Jerand shook his head. "Can't put my finger on it yet. But something isn't . . ." A memory popped into his head, a bit of spaceside folklore he had heard from some old boozehound spacer or other. *Humans aren't too smart about smell,* the nameless, faceless voice of a memory had told him. *Brains aren't wired up for it, the way a dog or a cat is. We focus on sight and sound, too much sometimes, and push away the smells and the tastes and the textures. Don't forget your nose. Let the data get to you every way it can.*

That was it. The smell. The smell of the place was wrong, in some strange and subtle way that barely registered. "The air," Jerand said.

"Masks back on—" Chandray started to say.

"No," said Jerand, cutting her off. "I'm remembering more. It's okay to breathe. But I know this smell from somewhere. It won't hurt us, but—wait a second. The air in here, the oxy/n mix." That was the shorthand term for oxygen-nitrogen gas mixture. "It just got pumped in, right? This was all nitrogen until we activated the airlock, right?"

"That's right," said Chandray. "The Reading Room wasn't even sealed out from the stacks until we activated the lock for the first time. It just had the same pure nitrogen atmosphere as the stacks. Once the lock is activated, they use the same sort of pressure-curtain field as in the airlock and push the pure nitrogen out and pump in the oxy/n. The heaters come on, the scrubbers start running to pull out the carbon dioxide, and so on. Once we leave, the system scavenges the oxy back out and powers down until the next customer."

"So probably the nitrogen part of the oxy/n they pull from the atmosphere outside the Reading Room, from the book stacks," Jerand said. He was talking half to himself, struggling to figure it out. Then he saw. "But the oxygen. Where would the oxygen come from?"

Chandray shrugged. "From some sort of pressurized supply, I suppose."

That was it. *That* set off the memory he needed. "Now I remember," Jerand said. "I was on a ship, a timeshafter that hadn't gotten decent maintenance since the rocks cooled. The captain wanted to save some money and he bought a bunch of supercompressed oxy canisters that were decades past their safe-use date. The oxy from those cans smelled like this. A little metallic tang to it, like it had reacted just a little to the inside of the pressure vessel over the years."

"So what does that mean?" Sparten demanded.

"It means we're breathing oxy that's been sitting in high-pressure cans for, like, a hundred years."

"So what?" Chandray asked.

"I don't know," Bolt said. "But doesn't that set off a little alarm alert in the back of your head? It sure does in mine." He looked around the room more carefully. There was something else different. Something maybe even a bit more subtle. The whole room seemed gloomier, greyer, than the others had been. As if the light was—

He looked up. Two out of the ten light panels in the ceiling were dead, and three of the remaining ones gave off nothing more than a pallid yellow glow, rather than a full-blown bloom of light. "How long are those light panels supposed to last?" he demanded. "Half of them are dead or about to fail."

Not only the light, but the reflections from the light were different. The surfaces seemed flat and grey. He stepped toward the larger of two reading tables in the room and knelt to put his face near the table without actually touching it. "Dust," he said. "Not very much, but some." Then he looked down toward his feet and saw the floor was covered in the same stuff. Their footsteps had compressed it a bit, but not actually dislodged it. He cautiously ran a gloved finger over the floor. "It's adhering, just a bit," he said. *And just how long would it have to sit there for it to start bonding like that?* "It'd take a bit of scrubbing to get it all up."

"So what are you saying?" Sparten asked.

"I'm not saying anything," Bolt replied, letting his irritation show. "But the people who trained me used to say that one good way to stay alive in space is always to notice the local environment. And I've just noticed three pretty strange things about this one."

"What it all *suggests* is that this Reading Room has been used so little for the last century that they've never had to replenish the oxy tanks, or accumulated enough visits to trigger a maintenance visit," Chandray said. "Can either of you think of another explanation?"

Neither of the men replied. It struck Bolt that this discovery put Chandray in an interesting spot of difficulty. She obviously hadn't wanted him to find out just how long ago Koffield's visit had been. Now, right from the start, they were confronted with strong evidence that *no one* had been here for a long time. How was she going to handle it? He glanced toward Sparten. How much more complicated could the game of *he knows that I know that she doesn't know that I know* get? No doubt they would find out soon enough.

"Well," said Chandray, "this probably makes our job simpler. If hardly anyone has been here, it ought to be that much easier to find traces of Alber Caltrip."

"But *why* hasn't anyone been here?" Jerand asked. "None of the other Reading Rooms looked like this."

Chandray shook her head. "I don't know. But it's not on the list of things we were sent here to find out, and that list is going to keep us busy as it is. So let's get started."

She knelt, inspected the spot of floor in front of her to make sure it held no clues, shrugged off her backpack, set it down, and started to unpack.

Norla tried to ignore the two men watching her. It was true they were following her orders, and also true that the process required witnesses, but still it was unnerving.

All she could do was endure the stares of Sparten and Bolt and get on with the job. Adding to the small irritations, she had her witness cam strapped to the left side of her head. The strap was starting to itch, but adjusting it or scratching at the itch would send the recording image bouncing around, making it impossible to see what was happening—just the sort of thing that looked suspicious on a witness-cam record. She had so many other things to put up with that one more wouldn't matter.

She had chosen the Reading Room's compact galley as the place to start searching, hoping to find a fingerprint or a fleck of skin or a loose hair, but a careful examination of every surface a visitor might plausibly touch had come up empty. There was less dust here, though more than enough to blot out any fingerprints that might have existed beforehand. It would probably hide a fleck of skin, though she was fairly sure she would still be able to see any hair left behind.

The frustrating thing was they had no way to deal with dust that wouldn't ruin the evidence they had come here to get. They had only the hardware they had carried in. Norla had her forensic kit, but it didn't have anything that could deal with an even layer of dust spread over a large area.

A microvacuum might do the trick, or even a fine-hair brush, swept carefully over the area in question. The best she could do was blow on the dust—which would of course contaminate the area with a fine collection of biological evidence of her own presence.

They might have been able to rig something from a breathing mask—given time, tools, and a willingness to risk ruining the mask, with the result that one of their party would be stranded until an emergency crew showed up. No doubt there were all sorts of dust-blowers and vacuums and brushes somewhere in the PPC's book restoration office—but that would mean a round-trip hike of twenty kilometers, the loss of at least a day, and, worst of all, would require explaining to the PPC staff why she wanted to search for forensic evidence in their Reading Room. No. They had to keep this quiet, and that was that.

On the bright side, even her so-far fruitless search had produced one very interesting piece of evidence—or more accurately, the interesting absence of a certain piece of evidence. She did not wish to bring it to Bolt's attention, in the vain hope that he hadn't noticed it. There was not only a fine layer of dust that must have taken generations to lay down—there was a completely *undisturbed* layer of dust. Their party had left footprints and hand prints aplenty, and the marks were sharp and well defined. Obviously, no one else had been here since the dust had settled—and just how long *would* it take for this much dust to sift out of the air? No doubt any of the PPC's environmental engineers could tell her that—but she couldn't ask *them* questions, either. She shook her head. "Nothing here that I can find. A full squad of crime-scene ArtInts might, but I can't. Let's try the bunk room."

But there was nothing there. And nothing in the main study room. There was one slight piece of negative evidence, concerning the trash receptacles. When Koffield had visited the Reading Room, he had been working to keep his visit secret, and Koffield was a very thorough man. He had told Norla that he had packed out all his trash, everything that could link him to the Reading Room. Sure enough, the cans were empty.

Norla had saved the washroom and toilet facilities for last. Those were the places where a person was most likely to leave a loose hair, a fleck of dandruff, a spot of blood from a cut.

The washroom appeared spotlessly clean at first, and, thanks to some quirk in the air-circulation system, virtually no dust had settled there.

Even using enhanced-vision goggles that could magnify and refine what she saw any number of ways, Norla couldn't find a thing. She was about to give up the search altogether when Yuri Sparten, using nothing but the unaided eye, made the only discovery of the day. "What's that?" he asked, pointing to a small smudge on the mirror, just to the right of the washroom door at about shoulder level.

Norla, scarcely daring to breathe, leaned in for a closer look, tweaking the contrast on her goggles to make the spot easier to see. A fingerprint—no, *two* prints, one barely there at all, and probably not readable. The tips of the fingers were pointed up and to the right. It looked like someone standing in the doorway had casually rested his or her hand on the mirror, just for a moment, perhaps while looking out into the main room—to see if something he or she needed was on the main table, perhaps.

The two marks were as next to nothing as anything could be, just a pair of faint impressions on a glass surface. Yet they looked fresh and sharp enough that Norla checked to make sure everyone in her party still had their gloves on. But no, some other visitor had left those marks, long enough ago that there were no corresponding footprints in the dust outside the washroom.

All that suggested that they might be Koffield's prints. If—*if*—the fingerprints belonged to Koffield, then even the most determined disbeliever back on Solace would have to accept that Anton Koffield had been here on the PPC. And if he *had* been here, in the Geology and Terraforming Reading Room, then that went 99.9 percent of the way toward proving the rest of his story, in spite of all the evidence that had been destroyed and manipulated. And if his story were proved, they would have to accept that their world was falling apart. And they would have to act. Those two fingerprints might serve to save the lives of millions—*if* they were Koffield's—and if Norla could photograph them, or lift them without destroying them. It was a lot to have riding on her first attempt at fingerprint preservation.

"Nice find, Yuri," she said, almost in a whisper. It was the first time in a long time she had called him by his first name. "Let's see who those belong to."

• • •

The image scanner worked perfectly. Norla copied the print images to her datapad, and made backup copies to Yuri's and Bolt's datapads as well. That accomplished, she felt ready to risk lifting the physical print itself. It was a highly delicate maneuver. At Bolt's suggestion, she did two practice runs first, planting her prints on another patch of mirror, and then lifting those. The practice paid off: The prints Yuri had found lifted up onto the capture film perfectly. She stored the lifts away, each in its own sealed and labeled container, with all three witness cams watching the whole process.

With the physical print itself safe, it was time to see if she could get an identity match off the stored scan. She brought up the field print-matching system on the datapad. It was supposed to report matches within ten seconds, and took twelve.

It was the answer she wanted: the prints belonged to Anton Koffield—right hand, index and middle fingers.

Norla smiled and handed the datapad to Sparten. "Once again, nice work, Yuri. Thank you."

Sparten was clearly bemused. "You're welcome. I have to admit I feel funny about the whole thing. Seems strange for me to be the one who confirms his story."

"Someday soon, maybe you'll hear the *whole* story," Norla said. "I think you'll feel better about things if and when you do."

"I hope you're right," Sparten replied, with just a hint of the old edge in his tone.

Norla didn't care. She had her proof. It had gone so smoothly and easily, it almost felt like an anticlimax. But in truth, it was victory. All by itself, finding and preserving that little scrap of proof would be enough to change the entire political game board back on Solace. It would open a trapdoor under the deniers, and remove the only justification, however flimsy, for blocking the evacuation project.

But for Norla, that sense of victory was far from the whole story. Another, deeper emotion welled up from down below. *Relief*. She had always believed Anton

Koffield—believed *in* Anton Koffield—even when the evidence seemed against him. Still, the niggling doubts had always whispered from the dark corners of her mind, of her faith. It was an indescribable pleasure to have those doubts completely destroyed.

"Maybe we've found what we're looking for, but we still need to eat," said Bolt. "Mind if I run some ration packs for dinner?"

"Please do," said Norla. "Let's be extravagant and use fast-packs tonight." The self-heating dinners only took a few seconds to prep, and wouldn't require dealing with the Reading Room's water supply. Norla had tried a sample of the water, which had been in the storage tank for a hundred years. Not surprisingly, it had picked up a sharp metallic flavor. It didn't matter. Right now, just about anything would taste good.

There was an old saying that for a good meal, it didn't matter what you ate—it was who you ate it with. To that, Jerand Bolt was ready to add a caveat. It was what mood your companions were in. The discovery of those two fingerprints had somehow shattered the tensions that had hung over their group from the start. Jerand was only starting to get a feel for the politics of the group, and the way those politics shaded over into personal relationships. Plainly the mutual dislike between his two companions stemmed from the fact that Chandray was pro-Koffield, and Sparten was anti-Koffield—though, suddenly, less so than he had been. And with that easing of his views had come a distinct mellowing of his outlook—Chandray was plainly a lot happier as well. Suddenly the two of them were laughing, joking, smiling.

Jerand wasn't fooled into thinking all their problems were over. There were still some very deep games being played. But, maybe the two of them would start to see each other as members of opposing teams, and not simply as the Enemy. Or maybe they would be at each other's throats again tomorrow morning. Which meant he had best take advantage of what might be a very temporary truce and see if he could push them along into getting some plans made. He waited until they had cleared away the last of the rubbish from their fast-packs, and all three of them were enjoying the sweet tea Bolt had managed to brew using water from his backpack.

"So," he said. "You've got your first item checked off. You found your proof that Caltrip was here."

"Yes," Chandray replied. "And that proof is very important."

"Right. And we also know that hardly anyone—maybe no one at all—has been here since he was here, and he was here a good long time ago. Is that important?"

Chandray frowned. "It might be. I don't quite know what it means. It's certainly strange. We didn't expect it."

"And tomorrow, we go looking for books, right?"

Chandray nodded. "We go looking for the books Caltrip said he examined while he was here, and also for any books on terraforming that aren't on the list of titles that they already have on Solace."

"How exactly is that going to work?" Jerand asked.

"Simple enough," Chandray said. She reached for her backpack and pulled out three wands. Each was a flattened cylinder about twenty centimeters long, about three centimeters by one and a half wide in cross section. They were bluish-grey in color, and had a small status screen set into one end of a flattened side of the cylinder. "These are bookcatchers," she said. "They hold who knows how much data. I don't think you could fill one, if you worked all day and all night for a month. But when a unit is nearly full, this red light will come on, and it's time to copy what you've done to a datapad."

"Wait a second," Jerand said. He could see where Chandray was going. "I thought the whole idea of this place was to have real books with pages. What good is a data-grabber going to do?"

"You haven't quite got the whole idea," Chandray said with a smile. "The whole idea of the PPC is to have copies of books that are *permanently readable*, without needing any outside technology or storage or whatever.

And you're right. That boils down to words printed on pages. But words on paper are hard to manipulate—hard to copy, hard to search, and so on. And the pages can wear out—or be torn, or defaced, or removed altogether. So when they started this place, the Grand Library's PPC committee set up a very standardized but flexible data-storage format, and required that all books that were accessioned to the collection had to contain a permanent dataplaque, usually inserted inside the book's spine. The plaque is supposed to contain the complete text of the book. That means someone can use a gizmo like this"—she held up the bookcatcher—"and just wave it near the book, and retrieve a full copy of the text. Then you can take the bookcatcher home and plug it into a printer that can generate an exact physical copy of the book—or you can just read the digital copy stored by the bookcatcher."

"And that's what we're going to do," said Jerand.

"Right. For every title that wasn't in the last Grand Library datacube sent to Solace."

"I noticed you said every book is 'supposed' to have a plaque," said Sparten. "Some don't?"

"Some don't," Chandray agreed. "I've got a little gadget with me that can scan and store images of the pages. It can scan a good-sized book in about ten minutes."

"How many books—with and without plaques—are we talking about?" Jerand asked.

Chandray shook her head. "No way to know. Everything is supposed to be cataloged and indexed, and the PPC is *supposed* to be fully copied to the digital Grand Library—but it doesn't always happen. I read one stat that said one-half of 1 percent of the books in the PPC aren't cataloged. We've got about three hundred terraforming titles on our collection list. So the odds are there are four or five additional books past that. But it's not just quantity. Maybe none of the books will have any really useful data. And maybe missing book number five has the information we urgently need."

"But you're counting on the books being shelved

properly," Sparten objected. "Suppose the missing terraforming book we need got misshelved in thirty-
second-century misrepresentational semibiography five
kilometers from here?"

"Then we'd never find it between now and the Sun
dying," Chandray said dryly. "We've got enough worries. Let's not invent more."

They got started the next morning, suiting up in their
cold-weather gear, strapping on their breathing masks,
and trooping out into the stacks. All of them were eager
to get moving. It was, after all, the start of their third day
in the library, and they were finally going to where the
books were.

The stacks were a gloomy place. The lights were
rigged to heat sensors, and came on at half power as they
approached. If they stayed in place for a minute or two,
the lights would come on full—but they weren't standing
still, and that didn't happen much. Instead they kept hiking, and the lights behind them powered down again almost before they had passed. They walked in a dim
bubble of life that moved with them, hemming them in
with darkness all around.

The sensor light system did not work flawlessly—
more evidence that this part of the PPC was low on the
priority list for maintenance. At such times as when the
lights came on late, or went out early, or never came on
at all, they relied on their handlights to illuminate their
way forward. The shadows loomed up strange and dark
and tall beyond their bright and shifting beams.

Some of the shelves were full, top to bottom, end to
end, aisle after aisle, with neatly ordered volumes, all in
matched bindings. Other sections were empty, or nearly
so, with only a few stray books here and there on the
shelves, or even shelves completely barren, waiting for
the inevitable next expansion of the PPC's collection.

Now and then, they spotted a Library ArtInt prowling along the shelves, using its long telescoping arms to
pull books down for readers with enough influence to
rate ArtInt stack service, or else reshelving books that

were no longer needed. The ArtInts worked mostly by infrared, which meant they could and did work in the dark, by the infrared light cast by their own emitters. The weird, angular, many-armed shapes would loom up suddenly out of the shadows, and then vanish into the darkness, paying the travelers no attention at all.

In spite of its name, the Geology and Terraforming Reading Room was a long way from the Terraforming stacks. From what Jerand could read from the maps of the PPC, the actual books on terraforming were as far from a Reading Room as it was possible to get. They were in fact two decks down from the Reading Room itself. All in all, it was about a twenty-minute walk.

Jerand's leg muscles were still sore after their unaccustomed exercise, but the morning's exertion was just enough to work the kinks out without tiring him anew. He felt good, felt happy they were at last about to get where they were going. All their effort thus far led toward this moment, to three people hiking through kilometer after kilometer of darkened bookshelves, toward whatever secrets might await them up ahead.

He followed Norla Chandray around the corner into the terraforming section—and nearly walked right into her, because she had stopped dead in her tracks. He stopped hard too, and Sparten did walk into him—but Jerand Bolt scarcely noticed. He was too busy staring at the chaotic jumble up ahead.

The terraforming stacks were like nothing else they had seen in the PPC. Books were everywhere—shoved helter-skelter into the shelves, stacked on the floor, sitting in half-opened packing cases jumbled on top of other packing cases that appeared to have been dumped and left there in a great hurry a long time ago.

A fine film of dust lay over everything, thickest on the lowest stacks of crates, thinner on the upper ones. It was easy to see where later deliveries had disturbed the older dust. There were furrows of dust where new crates had been shoved on top of older ones. The repeated visits of library ArtInts were marked in tire tracks that crisscrossed the floor.

It was plain to read the story in the dust and the tracks and heaps of books: ArtInts merely dumping the books in the section, wherever they could, whenever a shipment of books came in. On Earth, somewhere, a research library would close, and months or years later, an ArtInt would drop a crate of books in the Terraforming stacks.

"I don't get it," Jerand said at last, breaking the long silence. "Why aren't the books on the shelves? What's going on?"

"They're not on the shelves because ArtInts do what you tell them to do," Chandray said bitterly. "Precisely, exactly, what you tell them to do. And someone told the maintenance ArtInts to do exactly nothing. Someone set maintenance to priority zero—and zero is what they got." She thought for a second. "Caltrip was here. He didn't describe anything like this."

"So this all happened since his visit," Sparten said.

"But if this area was priority zero, how did all these crates of books get here?" Bolt demanded.

"Different team of ArtInts," Chandray said. "Or maybe the same ones working under a different command system whenever there's a book delivery."

"But *why*?"

"To hide the books," Sparten said. "The books come in, they get dumped, but they don't get scanned or sorted or cataloged. The Permanent Physical Collection is supposed to be the central repository—but none of these books"—he kicked at one of the crates—"would show up in the catalog."

"I told you last night that we assumed there would be a few omissions or errors in our list," Chandray said. She shook her head. "But this—no one was expecting this. We figured the listing we got would be *basically* accurate."

"Instead, it left off stars know how many titles," Sparten said. "Thousands, maybe."

Chandray nodded. "And if the book *wasn't* in the listing, and you *didn't* come here, you'd never even know the book *existed*. *We're* only here because we're trying to be extremely thorough." She thought for a moment. "Between this and the Reading Room, it looks like no one has been doing terraforming research here since Caltrip was here."

Jerand felt as if he had no energy, no emotion, left. Especially as it was plain as day that the job ahead of them had just expanded by a hundredfold, a thousandfold. They would have to sort through all these books, work up some sort of handmade catalog of what had been dumped, before they could even begin to get copies of the books missing from their list.

He walked forward a step or two, brushed some dust off the top of one of the crates, and sat on its corner. "Oldest joke in Settled Space," he said. "A peace officer is walking his beat one night. He comes up to a streetlight, and finds a drunken man prowling around on his hands and knees, staring down at the sidewalk. 'What the hell are you doing?' the officer asks. The drunk says, 'I dropped my access pass half a block from here, and I'm looking for it.' 'Why look here if you dropped it over there?' the cop asks. 'Because the light's so much better here.' " He looked at his two companions. "I think every terraforming researcher in Settled Space must have gotten drunk on digital source material. They trust in what the catalog says, and none of them come here."

"Why should they?" Sparten asked. "Someone did something to the ArtInt programming, and made it too dark to see the books this far from the streetlight."

"From here," said Chandray, "we can see them. Maybe—maybe—one of them has the data we need. We've got to cross-check them. Every single damned one."

Jerand stood up and swept more of the dust of the crate he had been sitting on. "All right," he said. "We might as well get started."

CHAPTER TEN

LOST AT HOME

Berlin, Germany: Earth

Admiral Anton Koffield, currently known as Dr. Alber Caltrip, blinked, rubbed his eyes, and tried once again to focus on the datascreen in front of him. He shook his head to clear it, stared straight at the screen—and realized he could not even remember what he was reading.

He gave up. Plainly it was time, and past time, to stop work for the day—or the night, more accurately. His search patterns and info-hunter ArtInt programs had grown so complicated that he could barely keep track of them while fully awake, let alone when he was utterly exhausted.

He powered down the datapad and realized that he was yawning uncontrollably. *Rest,* he thought. *I need rest.* He stood from the desk and headed for the washroom. He prepared himself for bed as methodically as he did everything else—washing his face, cleaning his teeth, laying out his clothes for the next morning, adjusting the thermostat to a more comfortable sleeping temperature, setting the window opacifiers to block the early-morning sun, setting the comm system to capture and record all messages without disturbing him.

Then he lay down in bed—and instantly was wide-awake, eyes open, staring up at the featureless ceiling.

Snatches of thought flashed through his mind, ideas and plans and theories and search techniques and names chasing each other around and around. *Port-au-Prince after this, query the institute's director on further works with Baskaw as junior author, query Wandella on why she's following the Mars lead so hard, search on closed-loop theories and DeSilvo, Baskaw, DeSilvo, Ashdin, after Port-au-Prince we go to Rio, check on junior author Baskaw, DeSilvo—*

He cursed, rolled over on his side, and punched the pillow into a more comfortable shape. The hell of it was, their cover story was working better than their real work. In terms of data on terraforming, they already had whatever there was to be found.

The Max Planck Institute of Planetary Climatology had a fine library on terraforming, and a finer database of operational procedures—but obtaining them was almost too easy. A single polite request had resulted in the receipt of the entire set of digital files the next day. Since then, Koffield and his two untrained assistants, Phelby and Wahl, had spent five days skimming through a few of the top layers, hoping for luck to lead them forward—and luck didn't seem to be such a good guide as they waded through the endless torrents of information.

It was tempting to give it up as a bad job, but data on terraforming was vitally important back on Solace. The planet's climate and ecosystem were locked in an irreversible pattern of collapse. *If there's a way to stop it, it's in the data somewhere.* It startled him, threw his thinking off stride. The thought had flitted in and out of his conscious mind, seemingly of its own accord, as if it came from outside of him.

But no. The idea was his alone. Born in his unconscious, or his subconscious, or the place where dreams were made. But it belonged to him.

Do I really still think we'll find the cure? he asked himself. He wanted to tell himself that he had not ever truly believed in, or hoped for, such a thing. But Anton Koffield had always demanded honesty of himself. *Had* he hoped, without daring to admit it to himself? Did he, on some level, still hope?

He frowned up at the darkened ceiling. He had learned long before that sometimes a man *needed* to fool himself. A man in desperate straits needed to believe something—anything, just as a way to stay alive. A few self-delusions could be formed into a sort of psychic armor around the soul—fragile, temporary, and unreliable protection, perhaps, but far better than cold and deadly facts.

Koffield had not permitted himself any such luxury— or had he merely *told* himself that, and gone on believing in miracles just the same? A fog of unexamined desires and dreams, beliefs that no one dared examine, could swirl about deep down in the soul of a man.

And then, there in the darkness of a visiting professor's flat in Berlin, his delusions, his hopes fell away. He sat bolt upright in bed, swung his feet over the side of the bed, and stood up. He went to the window and flipped the setting back to full transparent. He stared down at the gleaming forest of lights that was Berlin.

Without admitting it to himself, he *had* been searching for the magic answer, the secret formula that would make it all go away. Nothing could stop the death of Solace now. While they might well find some nugget of data that could delay the inevitable, there would be and could be no secret formula, no magic potion, no long-hidden solution that would cure the dying world.

But even after all he had been through, all the unpleasant truths he had forced others to see, he had let lies and hopes reach him. They would find nothing new in the Berlin data. There was nothing there they didn't already have back on Solace, or at least 99.99 percent of it was back there, courtesy of the datacube copies of the Grand Library that arrived in-system every year or so. And, no doubt, it was all duplicated again in the data being collected by Chandray's team in the Permanent Physical Collection, and by Wandella's studies in the Grand Library itself. Even if there were some magic answer in that missing hundredth of a percent of information, it would take years of searching to root it out. They had allowed for that in all their plans. They would take all the data they could get, bring it back to Solace and the labs on Greenhouse, and let the scientists and their ArtInts comb through it all. That was their job.

But it's not your job, Koffield told himself. *Slowly but surely, you've been forgetting that.* The whole search for terraforming information was merely so much window dressing. It was a cover story, meant for anyone watching, and for Dixon Phelby and Clemsen Wahl, so they would have a story they and their interrogators might believe, if it came to that. But the real purpose was to search for clues that might lead to the present location of Oskar DeSilvo. And Koffield was forced to admit he had run out of useful ways to look through the Berlin data for DeSilvo three days before.

He turned away from the window and sat back down at the desk. He keyed on the comm system and called to Phelby and Wahl's room. After a moment the screen lit up and showed him a bleary-eyed Dixon Phelby.

"Yes—yes, sir?" Phelby asked, fighting against a yawn.

"We're leaving for Port-au-Prince via the first practical routing," he said. "I'll work that up and get back to you regarding scheduling first thing in the morning. As soon as you get up, get your bags packed, finish up whatever researches you're doing, and stand by to depart."

The yawn escaped, and Phelby blinked sleepily and nodded. "Yes, sir. Stand by for departure via first practical routing. Very good."

He cut the connection and stared at the blank comm screen. *Find DeSilvo.* That was all that truly mattered— for DeSilvo had offered promises of remarkable technology, and provided proofs of his claims as well. Maybe, just maybe, some of that technology could save some lives, even as whole worlds were lost. It was time to move, to search further.

• • •

But the next morning found Anton Koffield, not hurtling through the stratosphere toward the Caribbean, but instead boarding a bubbletop air-tour car at Port Templehof in downtown Berlin. The "next practical routing," as it turned out, wouldn't be available for another full day.

Koffield was not touring alone. Herr Fest, a cheerful middle-aged associate from the Institute, had made the arrangements and offered to come along in the capacity of tour guide.

"You are most quiet, Herr Dr. Caltrip," said his guide as the car lifted off. "Is there a difficulty?"

"Hmmm? No, no. I'm fine, Herr Fest. I was just wishing that I hadn't put my people to needless bother."

"Well, these things happen. They will enjoy the day's rest, I am sure."

"I suppose," he said. As with virtually every other junior military officer or enlistee in history, the younger Anton Koffield had suffered the frustration of "hurry-up-and-wait." Early in his career, he had sworn never to be the cause of any such muddle, and for the most part he had kept that promise to himself. But this time, he had gone and done the thing—and done it properly. Going off half-cocked, acting before thinking, rousting men out of their beds for no reason. A classic case. Why couldn't he have left a message for the two men to receive in the morning? Even that wouldn't have done much good at speeding things along, since there weren't any available seats on any practical route to Haiti for another twenty-four hours.

Way back when, a younger Anton Koffield had also promised himself to admit his own mistakes and not get caught up in the mystique of command and the need to preserve the image of the commander as infallible. And on that score at least he was able to keep his promise this time. He'd already apologized to Phelby and Wahl, and given them both the day off. He hadn't the faintest idea what they'd do with the time. But that had ceased to be his problem.

For his own part, the enforced delay allowed him a chance to indulge his own curiosity—and his own sentimentality. He had been born in this city, after all. He wanted to see it again.

Koffield had need of a guide. His birth had been more than two centuries in the past, and the streets he walked were not the ones he had once known. Roads, neighborhoods, whole districts of the city had been completely remade, or else erased altogether, to make way for new things built in their places—or, in some cases, for nothing at all.

It was oddly disturbing to realize that this tour around a city he no longer recognized was as close to a homecoming as he would ever have. It brought him face-to-face with more hard facts: He had no home, no family, no link to a past or relations.

"Here we are, Herr Dr. Caltrip," Fest announced. The aircar descended slowly, found itself over an open field, and came in for a landing. The door of the craft opened, and the two men stepped out. Berlin had always been a city that prided itself on large open spaces, but this was near to wilderness, a patchwork of small meadows, with forest encroaching all around.

"This is it?" Koffield asked.

"The locator-system is quite precise," Fest said calmly. "You are standing"—he consulted his datapad—"almost precisely in the center of Alde Hundertwasser Strasse, five meters north of the entrance to number 47. That is to say, that street and that building existed here 230 years ago. The area was declared an empty district, fully cleared during a six-month period in the year 5252, and then replanted with indigenous plants, as you can see." He looked up from the datapad. "I'm sorry there is so little left to see."

"Yes," Koffield said. "Very interesting." He knelt, and pulled a bit of broken old brick up out of the soil. Perhaps this little fragment was all that was left of the house where he had been born. Not quite knowing why, he slipped the piece into his pocket. There was nothing else to show that anyone had ever lived here.

"This, ah, Koffield, was your remote ancestor?" Fest asked.

"That's right," he replied, finding it strangely hard to keep his voice steady. "My great-great-great-great-uncle or thereabouts."

Koffield did not feel as if there was much risk in using the name. If Koffield had arrived under his own name, 130 years after his presumed death—that would no doubt have garnered attention. The mere former existence of someone *named* Anton Koffield was not what they were trying to keep from being noticed. They needed to hide certain facts that had highly tangential *connections* to that name. The cover story also had the advantage of being simple, straightforward, and, in essence, true. Koffield had lived in this place. If someone bothered to check that far, they would be able to confirm it—and likely that would be enough to satisfy anyone about the rest of the story.

Since Koffield had not the slightest idea if he had any living relatives at all, the rest could be tricky. But it could take months or years to establish that there was no record of such a person as an off-planet scholar named Caltrip. Nor was there any particular reason to assume Fest would pass such trivial tidbits to the authorities. From what he had seen of it so far, present-day Earth was a remarkably unparanoid place.

"Naturally, I was interested when I came across Uncle Koffield's name in connection with my research into Herr Professor DeSilvo's terraforming work. When I discovered there was a local connection—"

"Of course." Fest nodded. "But, as you can see, nothing remains."

"No," Koffield agreed. "Nothing does."

They returned to the car without further conversation and lifted off. "This is my first trip to Earth," Koffield said. *At least it's the first trip for Alber Caltrip.* "I am not at all familiar with the way you deal with—what do you call it—surplus housing?"

"There is no universally used general term. That one will do."

"Surplus housing, then. Not just the houses, but the

streets, the utility supply tunnels, the sewer lines—of the infrastructure. Is it always removed so completely?"

"Oh, by no means," said Fest. He thought for a moment, then turned and spoke quietly into the command panel for the aircar. "Your great-uncle's neighborhood is in fact somewhat unusual. Infrastructure is maintained for the most part. You will see." The aircar lifted, came about to a new heading, and moved to the east, traveling over woods, fields, and forests. After a few minutes' flight, it slowed again, and then stopped.

The car hung motionless, about a hundred meters up. Fest gestured down at the land below. "This is more typical," he said. He turned and again spoke quietly into the command panel. The car turned itself north and began moving forward at the pace of a man walking at a rapid clip. Koffield could see they were precisely over a broad avenue. Side streets intersected the main road at regular intervals. All the roadways appeared to be in excellent condition—but they led past nothing at all.

In between the roads, where the buildings once were, forests and meadows now grew. It was jarring to see wild nature neatly corralled and arranged inside a rectilinear grid. The surface roads were kept clear and were in use, though traffic was light. Koffield saw some sort of robot transport trundling along the avenue below. There was a small herd of deer in a block of meadow just below. They didn't so much as look up as the vehicle rolled past. Three blocks on, he saw a fox calmly trotting along down the middle of a side street.

"I don't understand," Koffield said. "Why go halfway? Why leave the roads and remove the places the roads led to?"

"There is a great deal more than the roads left behind. All the city utility lines remain intact. Even if they are not active here, they still serve other areas. The water lines, for example, need to be kept up even if no one in this area uses them at present. And our roads are *very* well made. It would be very difficult to rip them all up— and suppose that someday we need a road again? Or suppose someone decides to rebuild in this area ten years from now? Why not let the maintenance ArtInts maintain the roads and the power grids? If nothing else, it serves to keep underutilized repair machines busy and functioning, so we know they are functional and experienced when we actually need them."

Koffield shook his head and gestured at the landscape below. "All that seems like a tremendous amount of effort to go through, compared to the sorts of benefits you're describing."

Fest shrugged. "It's all automated labor. We have more land than we need, and surpluses of nearly everything else. Materials are mostly scavenged or recycled—again with automated labor. We can afford it. We have done it this way for generations, and it works. Why change? Why question it?"

"I suppose," Koffield said, all his doubts remaining. Two centuries past, they had not done things this way. If population decline caused an area to empty out, the area was cleared of anything of historic interest, and then torn down as completely as Koffield's birthplace had been. "Why are you so certain that the area *will* be reused?" he asked. "I was under the impression that your population was still declining. Has that turned around?"

Fest shook his head. "No," he said, and there was a slight note of irritation in his voice. "The decline continues. Many believe that because Earth is a mature culture, it is not much interested in children, or childish things. Of course, what children we have are loved and cared for. But as for why I am sure this area will be rebuilt—fashion, mere fashion. This district is all the rage, then that one, then another, then another. Someone will build here for the sheer novelty of it—and then others will follow. They will move, until today's fashionable district is vacant, and we will level it in turn."

Fest turned and stared out the window. Koffield got the distinct impression that the man did not wish to answer any further questions. Were children a touchy subject, or was the man merely annoyed at an ill-mannered offworlder questioning Earth's way of life? Whatever the reason, Koffield didn't really mind keeping quiet. Every reply Fest had supplied so far seemed to produce more mystery than information—and Koffield already had enough mystery to be getting on with.

Port-au-Prince, Haiti

"Pass the, ah, whatever it is, will you?" asked Wahl, barely slowing down his fork as it shuttled rapidly between his plate and his mouth.

"It's called *Riz Cole avec Pois*," said Anton Koffield with a smile, and handed over the serving dish. "You're enjoying the food, I take it."

"Yes, sir," Wahl replied, his voice a trifle muffled. "It's like I've never *had* food before."

Dixon Phelby chuckled. "Then what have you been eating all your life?" he asked.

"Fuel," said Wahl. "Nutrition paste. Food-substitute. This stuff"—he gestured with a forkful of his dinner—"is *real*. Fresh. It hasn't been in storage since before I was born. I can taste the ingredients one by one. Not at all like shipboard food."

"Yeah, it's good, I suppose," Phelby said.

"The meal was superb," Koffield said to Phelby. "Is that all the enthusiasm you can work up?"

"It's not the food, sir. It's, well"—he dropped his fork and pushed back his chair—"why can't we ever eat *inside* on this island?" The Haitian scholar's hostel service had assigned them a flat with a rooftop dining area, and it would appear that the server robots had been programmed to serve all meals out there unless it was raining.

"Ah, the view's great!" Wahl protested. Phelby would have felt a bit more convinced if the kid had lifted his nose up out of his plate long enough to look at it.

"Yeah, it's great all right," said Dixon. "I'm just getting a little tired of being out *in* the view all the time.

Scenery is supposed to be on the other side of a viewport."

"You've been in space too long," said Koffield, pushing back from the table himself. "Now, if you'll excuse
me, I'm going to move downwind just a bit and indulge
an ancient and barbaric vice."

Wind. A gentle breeze eddied past the table, and gave
Dixon the creeps. To a spacer, strong unexpected air currents equaled a leak, equaled death. His attitude toward
most of the things of Earth—or at least of Port-au-
Prince—were equally negative.

Dixon Phelby was a spacer, used to having solid, honest
bulkheads all around him, used to looking forward, eager
to see something new. He did not care for large open
spaces, or wind, or for what he privately thought of
"palaces of oldness"—monuments, museums, memorials.

It therefore pleased him not at all to be in Port-au-
Prince. It seemed as if none of the buildings were properly sealed in or roofed over. The place was all
verandahs, terraces, balconies, and plazas, with the
building tacked on behind, just for form's sake. The
whole place was built to make you look, and look, and
look again at the surrounding vistas.

He could understand that impulse, even if he did not
appreciate it. Once, Phelby knew, the place had been a
full-blown disaster area. Everything that could go wrong
with the local ecology had gone wrong—or, more accurately, everything wrong had been done to it. Overpopu-
lation, deforestation, erosion, toxic runoffs. But not
now. The land had been made new again, and kept that
way. The lush forests, full of insect life, birds, mammals,
had returned. The streams and waters ran crystal clean
down to the ocean. The areas given over to recreational
farming were productive, the soil well cared for.

He glanced over at Clemsen. The kid was so focused
on his food that Phelby was effectively alone—and he
felt the need for some companionship. He stood up from
the table and walked to the far end of the wide rooftop
garden, to where Koffield was engaging in his "barbaric
vice." The wind shifted, just for a moment, and a tendril

of the sweet, pungent smoke drifted back toward him. No one would ever be able to convince Dixon Phelby to stick a wad of dried leaves in his mouth and set fire to one end, but he actually rather enjoyed the smell of Koffield's cigars. Apparently, the old man had laid in a goodly supply of them from a nearby island as soon they reached the Caribbean.

"When was the last time you saw a proper sunset, Phelby?" Koffield asked, staring out to the glorious western sky. The colors ranged from cobalt-blue overhead to blazing orange-red at the horizon, and a line of clouds piled up toward the horizon only made the descent of the Sun more spectacular and dramatic.

"Not in a long time, sir."

"Nor have I. Not in a very long time." He puffed thoughtfully on his cigar as he stared out into the darkness. "I think it's nearly time to move on," he said. "Rio next."

"No luck here, sir?"

"No. I've been running data comparators. I doubt you'll be surprised to learn that the Library of Terraforming here on Haiti has very little that wasn't in Berlin."

"No, sir. I'm not even sure why this place is here, considering that they just duplicate the same data collections."

"It's here because this is Haiti," Koffield said. " 'The greatest terraforming success in history.' That's what they tell themselves around here. But, of course, what they did here wasn't terraforming."

Phelby nodded. He had heard it before, but he was starting to understand it, and believe it. Haiti was, according to Koffield, the success that had launched a thousand failures. Ecological renewal was not terraforming—but back then no one had really understood that, or been willing to believe it. The victory here, the creation of all this loveliness out of ruin and squalor, had led directly to the disastrous decision to remake Mars. "There's nothing new in their archives?" he asked.

Koffield shook his head. "No. Oh, there are a few

things no one else has. Some books, some data, a few bits of art, a few interesting artifacts—but well, nothing much on, ah, *our* topic of interest."

Amazing. Even out here, on the rooftop, in the gathering dark, and the wind blowing, after ten days soaking up the unsuspicious, unquestioning, unworried attitudes of Earth, Koffield was being careful. Just in case They—whoever They were—still kept watch. If They had ever been watching at all. But it didn't matter. Phelby understood that "our topic" meant DeSilvo.

"You haven't found *anything* worthwhile so far, sir?" Phelby didn't even bother to phrase it as "we." He and Wahl were window dressing. Koffield had given them a few make-work jobs, and stuck them with most of the dreariest drudge work of plowing through datafiles—but Anton Koffield had been doing all the real work, and there was no sense in pretending otherwise.

"I'm not quite sure I'd put it that way," he said. "I certainly haven't found what I was looking for—but beyond question I've found a number of things that I wasn't expecting. Quite possibly some very useful information. There's a—a *pattern* to how Earth has changed, and *not* changed, since I was last here. And that pattern would tell us something, I'm sure—if only I had wit enough to see it."

Phelby watched the blazing ball of the Sun drop beneath the far horizon. He looked up toward the zenith, where the first stars were already peeking out of the blue-black sky. " '*Who benefits?*' " he asked. "Back in Coldharbor Dome, my dad ran the company store. When a trader came in and made an offer that didn't make sense, a deal too good to be true, that was the question Dad always started with. 'Figure that out,' he'd say, 'and the rest will fall into place.' "

Koffield thought for a minute. "I believe," he said at last, puffing on his cigar, "your father had ahold of something there. I'll think on it. In the meantime—we get ready to head to Rio. The museum there is about him, after all. They ought to have *something* there that no one else does."

Rio de Janeiro, Brazil

Earth was a dream. The server floated up to Clemsen Wahl and proffered another of the delectable drinks whose name he could not quite pronounce. Caper-something or other. He smiled, took it from the server's upper deck, and leaned back again in his hammock. The apartment, provided for the use of visiting scholars, was beyond doubt the cushiest berth Clemsen had ever drawn.

The view from the balcony was breathtaking. The light was bright, clear, perfect. He looked down on the sun-kissed Atlantic, far below, at the glistening beaches of Ipanema, at the seabirds coursing overhead, at the perfect blue sky, at the pretty girls sunning themselves on the beach, and wearing very little while they did it.

But it was, perhaps, not the sights that he loved best, but the caress of the breeze against his skin, and the scent of salt in the balmy clean ocean air. Fresh air! Not from a tank or a hydroponics loop or pulse recycler, but air washed and made new by nature herself.

Rio de Janeiro was magnificent. Berlin had been marvelous, albeit in a serious, solemn sort of way. Port-au-Prince, jewel of the climate-repair project, had been achingly lovely. But Rio topped them all.

Yes. Earth was a dream, and Clemsen Wahl was seriously questioning whether he wanted to wake up.

"Wahl!"

Unfortunately, his superiors had other opinions on the subject. "Yes, sir, Officer Phelby! Coming!" He gulped down what he could of the drink, disentangled himself from the hammock, and hurried back into the main room of the flat they had been assigned. "Yes, sir," he said again. "Ready when you are!"

"So you were ready half an hour ago?" Phelby asked. "I've been waiting for you downstairs."

Clemsen gulped. "Sir? Sorry. I, ah, must not have heard the intercom on the balcony."

"Or in your sleep," Phelby growled, in a voice that was far less severe than his words. "Never mind. Come on. If we hurry, we won't be *too* late—and with any luck Caltrip will still be buried in the stacks. You might live to see tomorrow—if you don't keep *him* waiting."

Clemsen followed Officer Phelby out of the flat and into the lift. The door slid shut, and they dropped smoothly and silently down to ground level. The lift let them out in a small glassed-in vestibule. The doors to the plaza slid open as they approached, and they walked outside.

The building above stood on pillars, leaving the space below as a shaded open-air plaza, the sea breeze forever blowing through. It was immediately obvious why Phelby had not been too angered by the need to wait. The view from the plaza was every bit as spectacular as that from the balcony, although the sky and the distant blue horizon featured less prominently, and the nearly nude—or completely nude—sunbathers featured somewhat more. Clemsen lingered just a moment before entering their groundcar, and Phelby did not rush him.

The car started itself up as soon as they were inside. "Where is he now?" Clemsen asked.

"Still at the *universidade*," Phelby replied, pronouncing the foreign word with slightly exaggerated care. "My guess is that he's got another few megagigs of data for us to transfer. Probably no one has actually looked at any of it for a hundred years. Probably most of it isn't *worth* looking at." Clemsen had heard it all before, and he noticed that Phelby didn't bother with the pep-talk part of it, about the one unit of data hidden in among the endless dull statistics, or the correlations that might be drawn, answering as-yet-unanswered riddles, about how somewhere in what they were collecting was going to be the missing piece of a puzzle they were working on back on Greenhouse. Maybe the dullness, the sameness, of the work had beaten the true believer out of Phelby, or maybe his mind was simply still on the young ladies at the beach.

Clemsen's thoughts were certainly still on them, and on the heartbreaking loveliness of the utterly blue sky, on the astonishing quantity and variety of birds in the skies and the trees, on the food better than anything he had ever tasted. The groundcar wheeled them around the improbable splendor of the Lagoon, and toward the three-thousand-year-old *Nueva Tunel* through the seaside mountains.

And they want me to get back in a grey steel can and leave all this? he asked himself. Even to ask the question was to answer it—or at least, to ask it was to hear what his heart would answer.

The odd thing was that it would be so easy to run away from the team and stay behind on Earth. They had been welcomed everywhere with open arms, almost no questions asked. Earth people didn't seem to have any sort of identity cards, or security checks. That had seemed utterly unlikely at first. Surely there was some sort of hidden identity sensor—a transceiver worn under the skin, perhaps.

He had dug into the question during research time that should have been spent on the Admiral's work, and established the astonishing truth that there were no such identity systems. The best explanation he could find was, in essence, that only societies with wide gaps in income needed identity systems, because they were primarily used for allocating resources. Earth was so rich, and all the people of the planet so well provided for, that a universal identity system was more trouble than it was worth.

No ID scans. No one checking up. All he would have to do would be to pick a horizon and run over it—no. He pushed the thought away.

But, of course, the thought would not stay away.

The car rolled on, moving slowly, and the pretty girls sashayed along the sidewalks at languorous speed.

CHAPTER ELEVEN

ADVENTURES IN SERENDIP

Permanent Physical Collection
Orbiting Neptune

Jerand dropped the case of books down on the wobbly portable table and straightened up wearily. He pulled a grimy cloth out of an inside pocket and wiped off the faceplate of his breathing mask. Mostly the effort had the effect of smearing the dust around, rather than cleaning it off, but still it was marginally easier to see. A droplet of sweat formed on the tip of his nose, and he couldn't reach through the mask to wipe it off. He resisted the temptation to shake his head to dislodge it. If he did, the drop would splash on the inside of the mask and further obscure his vision. He considered peeling off the mask and holding his breath in the pure nitrogen atmosphere long enough to wipe his nose, but that might well knock the sweat onto the faceplate, and his hands were so grimy by now he'd likely leave behind more sweat and crud than he'd clear away. Best to just hold still and let it drip off—there it went. Good.

Jerand Bolt had learned long ago that there were times when it was absolutely necessary to take pleasure in the tiniest of victories.

The good news was that there were a slightly larger

number of victories to cherish. The first was that Norla had found Baskaw's books, right on the shelf where they belonged, right where Koffield had said they were. Unfortunately, they weren't so lucky as to find Koffield's fingerprints on the books, or any other identity material. But only someone utterly determined not to believe would demand to have that last link in the chain as well—and probably such a person would find reasons not to believe Koffield's story, even then.

The box on the table represented the second, and smaller, victory: It contained the last set of books they had to sort through. Everything else had been examined, at least in a preliminary way, and shelved in something like a logical manner.

The miserable job was nearing its end, but Jerand Bolt dared not even think the thought, let alone speak it out loud. There had been enough bad luck already, without going out of his way to jinx things. Say the words, and probably a battalion of ArtInts would come around the corner with fifty freshly delivered cases of books.

He looked up to see a very weary-looking Norla Chandray walking toward him. "Last one, Officer Sendler," he said.

"Good," she said.

"What sort of shape is the shelving work in?" he asked.

"Yuri's nearly caught up," Chandray replied. She patted the side of the box. "The sooner we get this lot sorted, the faster we can get all three of us on that job and get it done."

"Sounds good to me," Jerand said. "Then all we have to do is check every damned book we've just sorted and cataloged against that list of yours."

Chandray groaned. "Don't remind me. But we'll leave that until after we get a good night's sleep. We're all too punchy for that kind of work now anyway."

"I was hoping you'd say that," he said. "Let's get at it."

He opened the box and looked inside. As with too many of the other boxes, there was no inventory sheet, no listing that gave any clue of what was to be found inside. They'd have to sort them as best they could by hand. He starting pulled books out of the case.

"Not another one of these," Jerand muttered.

"Another of what?" she asked.

Bolt made no answer, but instead handed her a slim volume with a faded blue fabric cover. On the front cover, and on the spine, were two words. TERRA-FORMING in large letters, and in smaller type, NEMO. There was a small symbol, a star in a circle, on the spine.

"How many of these have you come across?" she asked.

"At least five so far, including that one," he said. "Got ˙ts of copies of other books, of course. Every time a library closed, it would send its books here. Lots of dupes. But none of the copies of *this* one have had call numbers, or listing codes, or filing cues. I still haven't figured out where to shelve them or catalog them."

Chandray frowned, her expression hard to read through her grimy breathing mask. "So where did you put the others?"

"In the problem stack, end of the last shelf of the section."

"I'll take it," she said. "Maybe I can figure out where they go."

The Grand Library
Orbiting Neptune

It was late in the night cycle. The lights had dimmed, the air temperature had dropped a bit, and the general background hum of the station had faded away to almost nothing.

Wandella Ashdin did not notice. She had not noticed much of anything external for a long time. She took another sip of her tea, quite unaware that the service ArtInt had refilled the cup three times in the past hour.

She was but dimly aware that she had wandered off into the great forest of knowledge. She had very nearly forgotten why she was in the Grand Library, but that was understandable. The whole huge edifice of the Grand Library was built for the express purpose of letting her—urging her—to forget everything that went on outside. All she was truly aware of was the chase itself, the tracking down of answers to questions. Whether the questions themselves had any relevance, she no longer knew or cared. She was a carefree and careless child, racing about in a perfect garden, chasing whatever butterfly came closest and looked to be the biggest and most gaudy.

In short, she was off on a tangent.

But it would be the tangent itself that ultimately reminded her of her purpose—and, as chance would have it, the tangent in question would prove utterly central to the matter at hand.

The Grand Library had been called a womb, a tomb, a fortress, an ivory tower, a walled garden, a cave where the inhabitants could and did refuse to see the shadows on the wall cast by those outside. Those metaphors, and a dozen more, for good and ill, were commonplaces of comparison, and they shared more than a little truth. She had every imaginable facility and virtually no distractions. It would have been all but impossible to resist the temptation to wallow in it all, and Wandella Ashdin made not the slightest effort to resist.

It was easy for Wandella to imagine that it was all her just reward, her due and nothing more, after endless years mucking about in the toilsome academic backwater of Solace. Here, everything that had been hard was suddenly made easy. She had access to datasets and texts almost before she was finished asking for them. All the equipment and supplies, from the pads of notepaper to the Library's ArtInt datanet infrastructure, were new, gleaming, modern, functional, and elegant in design.

Everything was made easy. Everything, including roaring off on a tangent. Instead of struggling for weeks or months to dig up a reference—or worse, being forced to wait for someone else, on Greenhouse or Earth to do it—here, the references, the texts, the evidence just poured out of the datascreens at her. In the Grand Library, a question that might take a week to research back on Solace, and whose answer might be incomplete or ambiguous, was answered in the space of a heartbeat or two, and answered with clear, definitive authority and clarity.

Even the residual mysteries were dealt with in a most satisfactory manner. While it might well be logically impossible to prove a negative absolutely, to be utterly certain that no one had the answer, the Library ArtInts could come very close. Their data searches and statistical analyses provided confidence levels so high they couldn't even have been reported on the display system she used back on Solace. When the Grand Library research ArtInts reported that nobody knew the answer to her question, Wandella Ashdin could come very close to assuming the ArtInts were right.

But usually, there was something to be found, and usually the ArtInts could find it. A lead that would have trailed off into murk, fuzz, and nothingness back home would grow into a huge network of connections, leads, references, and documents. That was what made the tangents so tempting—as in the current case.

Because it was starting to look an awful lot as if Oskar DeSilvo had spent a goodly amount of time on Mars.

Mars. Red Planet. Ghost Planet. The Great Failure. Across all of Settled Space, on every terraformed planet, in every domed settlement, aboard every space habitat, they knew the saga of Mars, of the first disastrous attempt to remake a world in Earth's image, way back in the fourth millennium. But it went deeper than merely the story of an engineering failure. It was what came after the disaster, what the planet had become, that made the place, the planet, merely the *name* Mars a source of horrified fascination.

No one ever went there. Even two thousand years after the Failure, the Interdict was still in place. Only the occasional parties of researchers into morbid ecologies ever went through the long and tortured application process needed before one even made the trip—if one dared to make it. In the present era, two thousand years after the terraforming project failed, no one involved with terraforming would have any reason to go there. And it went deeper than that. No one involved in terraforming would want to get *near* the place. It was bad luck, bad history, a planet-sized monument to what could go wrong.

But DeSilvo *had* gone there, repeatedly, in the thirteen-year period between Koffield's departure for Solace and DeSilvo's own purported death, something more than a hundred years ago. It wasn't easy to prove. That was a lot of time for the trail to go cold—and he had worked hard to cover his tracks. But she had proved it.

She had never met the man. Up until a few months ago, she had been convinced that he had died decades before she was born. But for all of that, she knew him too well to be fooled by tricks she had seen him play before. It would take more than a few misleading—all right, admit it—falsified—diary entries to throw Wandella Ashdin off the trail. She had an encyclopedic knowledge of the man, of his movements, of how he liked to travel—and how he guarded his secrets.

Wandella Ashdin saw the patterns so clearly that the smoke and mirrors that DeSilvo had thrown up in the last century might as well not have been there. He had spent much of those thirteen years on Earth. Three times he had filed flight plans, reporting plans to travel aboard his private spacecraft, the *Cidade de Ouro*, to Ceres, the largest body in the Asteroid Belt, for this or that conference or professional meeting. Three times there were clear records of his departing Earth, and returning—but no extant record of his activities on Ceres.

Even way back then, Ceres had been called "the little world that keeps big secrets." Sited as it was more or less in the borderlands between the Inner and Outer Solar System, it had always been a favorite location for professional meetings that involved parties from both the Inner and Outer System. And, for much the same reason, it had always been a place that earned a nice living by not asking too many questions and not worrying too much about the plausibility of the answers it did get.

The same proud tradition saw to it that record keeping was more or less on the honor system—which, in theory at least, meant that DeSilvo could have stayed there all three times and yet never left a data trail. But DeSilvo was a public personage. He would have popped up in some sort of news report, or intelligence report, or group photo, or personal recollection written by another attendee. Wandella found no mention whatsoever of him on any of the three occasions.

And on all three occasions, the three bodies in question—Earth, Mars, and Ceres—were in orbital positions that put Mars directly between the other two. Once might be chance. Twice might be, or might not. The odds of its happening three times when DeSilvo happened to be going that way, and when, just by chance, there was no record at all of him appearing at the other end—well, calling the odds "astronomical" seemed appropriate.

And, before each trip, she had found purchases of equipment—decontamination suits, sterilizers, med kits—that would have been of little use on Ceres, but might well be in daily use on Mars, to the point of being used up, which would explain the repeated purchases. If he had merely been stocking his ship's emergency lockers, he wouldn't have had to buy new ones each time. And she had found ship's manifests and inventories from routine maintenance records, from just before the third trip, and one about six months afterward. They showed three disposable decon suits aboard *before* departure, and none aboard half a year later. Wandella could think of no plausible alternative to the obvious conclusion: He had used up all three suits in the intervening months—and you needed some sort of decon suit on Mars.

It wasn't much, even as a circumstantial case—but it was enough of a start to get her searching other places, for other bits of evidence that might fall into place. And so she had completely forgotten that she was supposed to be trying to find out where DeSilvo was now. She was utterly intent on finding out why he had been in a certain place well back in the previous century.

"I've got it!" a cheerful male voice called from the doorway. She looked up to see Marquez coming in. Marquez had got bitten by the Mars bug as hard as she had. The mere mention of DeSilvo's possible connection with Mars had been enough to turn him around completely, transform him from a surly baby-sitter to an enthused partner in the research. There was something about such a huge and distant catastrophe that drew people in—especially frustrated romantics, such as time-shaft dropship captains.

"Where?" Wandella asked.

"In the transport history section. When a ship is finally decommissioned, they're supposed to get the automated logs—and any ship's ArtInt debriefs. The logs stayed sealed for a hundred years—and so these were in the open file."

"From *his* ship?"

"Yup. The *Cidade de Ouro*. I got two sets of hard copies. One for you, one for me. Here."

He spread the pages out on the desk—DeSilvo's old desk. He pulled one sheet onto the top of the stack. It was filled with cryptic navigational notations she could not even begin to decipher.

But, plainly, Marquez could make sense of them. He stabbed his stubby finger down at one particular string of symbols. "There. That's it. Injection into Martian orbit. Right off the *Cidade de Ouro*'s auto-log." He riffled through the other sheets, found the one he wanted, and pulled it to the top of the stack. He stabbed his finger down again. "There. From the ShipInt debrief. It confirms the auto-log. These are both for the first trip. I'm going to go after the other two later."

"Excellent work, Captain Marquez."

"Hey, I'm not done," he said. He picked up one stack of papers and left the others for her. "I got a query running right now on the *Cidade de Ouro*'s ShipInt debrief."

Wandella nodded. The debriefings of the ShipInts

were done by other, larger and more powerful, ArtInts, skilled at sucking every drop of knowledge out of the ShipInts. If there was anything to find, and if Marquez had structured his query properly, the debrief file would have it. "Good," she said. "Now we *know*, for sure, that he went to Mars repeatedly. But the question is, why? Do you have anything on where he landed—or if he landed at all?"

"No, and yes," Marquez said, "and for the same reason. The manifests you found didn't list towed cargo, just ship's fittings and interior cargo—but the *Cidade de Ouro* was designed to tow cargo pods. A lot of ship's captains like to do a dodge with the pods. They claim the pod as a separate vessel put under tow, and report it as 'both received and delivered in a fully sealed condition.' They claim they never look in the pods, and they can't be liable for the contents of a separate ship. That gets them off the hook for lots of paperwork—and makes it that much easier to hide what they don't want found. So I haven't found anything on the exterior pods—and I'm guessing I won't. Because this"—he pulled out another sheet—"is a receipt from a ship broker in High New York Habitat, showing sale for cash of *five* heavy-duty one-shot landers, to an account controlled by DeSilvo's Solace terraforming operation. Big cargo landers, with one-crew personal ascent stages, specced for Titan."

"What does all that mean?" she demanded. She didn't much care for it when Marquez used technical jargon— or any other situation that required her to confess ignorance.

"A one-shot lander is just that—one use only. They use 'em to drop cargo onto an unprepared planetary surface, where there aren't landing pads or refueling depots. They go in, they land, and they stay where they land— until someone scavenges them for parts. But these landers had small upper stages, only big enough to return a pilot to orbit. And the Titan-spec is very interesting."

"How so? I thought Titan was much smaller than Mars."

"It is—about 20 percent the mass, and a third of the

surface gravity. *But* Titan has a nice, thick, noxious atmosphere, so a Titan-rated lander has to be able to tolerate that—and of course a Mars lander has to deal with atmosphere. *And* the designation *heavy-duty* basically means they double the strength of the structure. Figure in that they rate in about a 50 percent safety margin, and a heavy-duty Titan lander would be just about like a light-duty *Mars* lander. And these were *big* landers. Even if you only loaded them with half their rated cargo mass, that'd still be a lot of cargo capacity."

"I see it," she said. "But what about the other two landers?"

Marquez shrugged. "Spares? Maybe two trips we haven't spotted yet? Maybe he sent them in on autopilot? It's a hundred years ago. We might not get *all* the answers." Marquez checked his watch. "Gotta get back. We'll talk later."

"All right, Captain," Wandella said. "Thank you."

She barely looked up to watch as he left. Instead, Wandella Ashdin gloated over the material he had left behind. This was new. This was big. This was completely unreported information on DeSilvo. None of the biographies, none of the references, had this. No one had it. DeSilvo's reasons for going to Mars almost didn't matter. No doubt, they would turn out to be interesting. Whenever DeSilvo hid something away, it was for a damned good reason. But merely that she had uncovered such a major fact in his life—that alone would be big news. No other DeSilvo scholar had found it. But in just a few weeks' work, *she* had found it. Granted, Marquez had been extremely helpful, but *she* had been the one leading the charge.

She flipped through the other papers Marquez had brought her. Most of it was log entries or data summaries from the ship's auto-log and ShipInt debriefing. She couldn't make heads or tails of it, but that really didn't matter. Marquez could decode it for her, or she could find some helpful research ArtInt who could do it for her.

Then she came across a series of images Marquez had printed out. A spacecraft—it must be—yes, there was a label below—the *Cidade de Ouro*. A schematic of the model of the one-shot lander in question. And a photo of—of Solace?

Wandella frowned. Why in the blazes would Marquez give her an image of Solace in with this collection of material? Besides, on second thought, it didn't look quite like Solace. Far less open water, and the overall color was slightly and unpleasantly wrong.

And then she saw the label. It wasn't Solace. It was Mars.

Her mistake stunned her. She had confused her planet, her *home* planet, where she had been born, and her children and her grandchildren lived, with post-terraforming-collapse Mars. Did her own planet look that much like the corpse of a world?

It all came back to her, hard and fast as a punch to the jaw. Finding DeSilvo wasn't a game, wasn't an exercise in the techniques of academic detective work. It wasn't something she could put to one side while she indulged her curiosity. It was a race against the clock, with precious little time remaining. DeSilvo, if he could be trusted, had promised to release a treasure trove of technologies, including true faster-than-light travel. If whatever tricks he had could not save Solace, then perhaps at least they might save some of her people.

It didn't matter a damn whether or why DeSilvo had spent his vacations on Mars a hundred years ago. What mattered—and what she had not moved forward on by so much as a millimeter—was finding out where the man was *now*. She considered briefly the possibility that DeSilvo's trips to Mars had been to prepare a refuge, a hiding place. Perhaps he was down there now, in his cryocan, dreaming away the decades. She rejected the thought almost at once. Mars of the present day was a place of savage hostility to human life, and to machinery as well. Nothing that breathed, nothing that relied on moving parts, or electronics, could long survive on

Mars. DeSilvo would have been safer with his cryogenic canister in a tank full of sulfuric acid, than to have it sitting on Mars. Whatever he had been doing on Mars, it had nothing to do with where he was hiding.

She resisted the urge to sweep all the pages off the desk and onto the floor. Instead she stacked them neatly and placed them on a corner of the desk—with the image of Mars on the top of the stack. Let it stay there, to remind her.

Start over, she thought. *Tomorrow morning. Book one, page one, line one. From the top. Get some rest, clear out all this Mars nonsense, and get focused back on what we're supposed to be doing.* Marquez would be disappointed. He had been having fun playing detective. But he'd understand, and he'd agree. It was time to focus on serious business. For the first time in days, she thought of Chandray's team. She hadn't heard much from them, other than text messages that reported their progress slogging through the mountains of unsorted books. Guilt caught at her, hard. How easy she had had it, how much she had indulged herself, while they moved forward with that miserable job. But for now, she needed to get some food, get some rest, and be prepared to start fresh.

She powered down the lights and her datapads, and walked across the room toward the door—and paused by the bookshelf there. A polished gold-colored metal plate read BOOKS by OSKAR DeSILVO. It dawned on her that something had been bothering her about that shelf. Something wasn't right. *So what? So you don't like the bookshelf. No more tangents. Let it go, get some rest, and start fresh in the morning.*

But she paused there a moment longer. *Start fresh.* Getting her mind clear would be a big part of that. Now that she knew, consciously, that something was wrong with that shelf, it would worry at her until she solved it—and she sat facing that shelf, all day long.

And then it came to her. *That thin blue book.* A silly thing, a pointless thing—but there it was. She knew her man—and DeSilvo had never written anything short in his life. She looked at the spine. There were two words there. TERRAFORMING NEMO. Under *NEMO* was a very simple decoration—a diamond set inside a square. But if the author was Nemo, then what was it doing on this shelf? Perhaps it was a set of essays edited by this Nemo, and DeSilvo had contributed to it.

But then what was it doing on this shelf? She glanced across the room, to the far larger and fuller shelf of BOOKS WITH CONTRIBUTIONS BY OSKAR DeSILVO. There were hundreds of them. DeSilvo had been famous for doing essays and introductions and afterwords—and then reusing them all over and over again, all for the sake of getting his name on yet another book. This Nemo book belonged over there.

But everything in this room—*everything*—was supposed to be arranged as per the instructions in DeSilvo's will and testament. She had looked over that document, early on, on the theory that it was a good place to start looking for clues to where he was. She had not studied every line of every codicil, but it was plain that DeSilvo had been very specific about how things should be. She'd have to take another look at it.

In the meantime—she reached for the slim blue volume and pulled it off the shelf.

Something to read at bedtime.

INTERLUDE

KALANI TEMBLAR

Chronologic Patrol Intelligence
Command Headquarters
(ChronPat IntCom HQ)
Lunar Farside

"So, Kal, whaddaya got?" Burl Chalmers set his over-flowing sandwich down on a stack of datapads on the left side of his desk and gestured for her to sit down in the chair facing him. Chalmers was a big and untidy man, with an office to match. He ran Kalani's section, and, by all official measures, ran it well. How was something of a mystery, given the state of his desk and his files.

Kalani scooped most of the papers out of the chair, and then stood there for a moment, unsure where to put them.

"Dump 'em on the floor over there," Chalmers said. "Sit. Tell me what brings you in."

"A live one, maybe," said Kalani.

"Get out. You talking the real deal? Field work?"

"Maybe. Lot of background checks to do first," she said. "But I think it might be big. Ready to hear it?"

"Go," said Chalmers, and then picked up his sandwich again and started back in on his lunch. A blob of mustard dribbled out onto his shirtfront. He dabbed at it with a greasy napkin and settled in to listen while he ate.

Kalani checked the notes on her datapad. "Oddball ship, the *Merchanter's Dream*. Small freighter, size class three. Inbound from Solace. Not much traffic from there, these days. Not much cargo aboard, and most of it tranship stuff that was gathering dust at one of the Asgard stations at Thor's Realm. The Solacian cargo wasn't worth bothering with. Not for a startup ship with no capital reserves."

Chalmers raised his eyebrows. "Startup? That's oddball right there. I can't remember the last time I heard of a new ship out of Solace."

"You're right," she said. "You can't. It happened before you were born."

"So someone out there got ambitious. That it?"

"That's nothing," she replied, and went back to her notes. "This *Merchanter's Dream* isn't a new-built ship. Way old design, with a lot of recent—expensive—upgrades jammed in. Very pricey stuff—like a brand-new temporal confinement chamber large enough for the whole ship's company. That's real money. Plus she doesn't act like a cargo ship. She dumped her inbound cargo at Neptune Orbital Transfer Station, didn't even try to take on new cargo, and then moved over to the Grand Library."

"The Grand Library?" Chalmers asked. "What, the captain wants to catch up on his reading?"

"Maybe. We've got one unconfirmed report that the captain and two others flew from there to the Permanent Physical Collection. Another aux ship took off for Earth. Haven't tried tracing their movements yet."

"You'll have fun when you do try," said Chalmers. "No one down there keeps records, and no one can ever be bothered to tell what they do know."

"Wonderful," said Kalani. She had already been dreading the prospect of getting someone Earthside to assist her queries. Chalmers didn't make it sound any better than she thought it would be. She went on with her report. "So. A cargo ship that's not moving isn't making money—but this one's been docked to the Grand Library for weeks now. One passenger—"

"*Passenger*? On a little size class three cargo ship like that?"

"Told you it was oddball," said Kalani. "One passenger off the ship waved some credentials around and has been granted full researcher's privileges at the GL."

"Lots of weird," Chalmers agreed. "What's your read?"

"It's not about cargo, that's for sure. Someone who doesn't worry so much about money—which must mean some kind of government—sent the ship here to do some kind of research. One team to the GL, and another to the PPC, plus whatever the Earthside group is doing. And they did their best to give the ship some kind of pretext for being here."

"What's wrong with research?" Chalmers asked. "That's what the GL is there for."

"Research is fine. It's the cover story, and trying to do it on the quiet, that bothers me. Someone's trying real hard not to get noticed, but they're stuck with a ship and a cargo manifest and a set of behaviors that make it hard to manage."

Chalmers shoved the last bite of sandwich into his capacious mouth and reached across the desk, gesturing with his fingers for Kalani to hand over the datapad. She leaned forward in her chair and gave it to him, then watched him read it over as he chewed and swallowed.

"Well, you got hold of some funny goings-on, that's for sure," said Chalmers. "Not enough for me to send you out—and not *quite* enough to pull you off the Ship Query Queue. But take some of your copious spare time and work this from your desk for a while—quietly. It's still probably nothing—but you're right. There's more than enough funny business to make you wonder." He handed back the datapad, which now had a large greasy fingerprint on the display. "Get back to me with whatever you can develop."

"Any deadline?"

"Nah. Talk to me as soon as you have something to say, not before."

"Suppose they bug out before I'm finished looking them over?" she asked.

"Then we'll have a datafile next time they come through. We can nail them then, if it turns out they need nailing. Besides," he said, "it's just one little tramp cargo ship. If it gets away, it won't be the end of the world."

"Thanks," she said, taking the hint and standing up. "I'll keep you posted."

She headed back toward her workpod. Kalani *had* been hoping that Chalmers would pull her off the Ship Query Queue, but never mind. The main point was she had gotten approval to do an actual investigation—once she got her paperwork caught up. Her desk was starting to look as bad as Chalmers'. She set down the datapad that held the *Merchanter's Dream* data, and reached for the top item in her inbox.

And it wasn't until then that she thought to wonder how, exactly, he could know for *sure* that the *Merchanter's Dream* had nothing to do with the end of the world.

CHAPTER TWELVE
LOST AND FOUND

Rio de Janeiro: Earth

An apologetic Dixon Phelby stood at attention before Anton Koffield. "I'm sorry sir, but that's all I know. Clemsen Wahl skipped out during the night. I've checked everywhere I could, this early, and he's gone. I really don't know more about it than what's in the note."

A fine way to start off my last day in Rio, Koffield thought, sitting at the breakfast table on the balcony of his scholar's suite. He frowned at the note. It was a long, rambling apology that said nothing at all. His security training overcame a temptation to crumple the note up and throw it away. *Damaging or disposing of the note would be bad security and bad protection of evidence,* nagged a voice at the back of his head. True enough, but what did it matter? He set the note down carefully on the corner of his desk, more to keep the little voice from nagging at him than for any good it would do to preserve the note.

"Any idea where he might have gone?" he asked.

"Not really, sir," said Phelby. "He could be just about anywhere by now. The one bright spot is that his note promises he won't talk about us, or why we're here."

"He certainly won't talk to the authorities if he's on the run, in any event," Koffield agreed. "Not voluntarily. But I agree. I don't think he'd turn us in."

"No, sir. He was tempted by—well, all this," Phelby said. "But I don't think he'd betray us—even under pressure."

"All right, Mr. Phelby. It can't be helped. Just see to it that you stick around yourself."

"Don't worry, sir," Phelby said, with a rueful smile. "This is all very pleasant and lovely—but this much wide-open space gets me nervous."

"I'm glad to hear it. Go soak up some more nervousness. Wait for me downstairs on the plaza. Dismissed."

Koffield watched as Phelby turned and left the room, plainly relieved that he had not received a royal chewing-out.

Koffield signed wearily. So Wahl was gone. He was not much surprised. On reflection, he was mostly surprised that the lad had stayed so long. He had half seen it coming. In another sense, he was wondering why he himself had stayed so long. Rio had been just as much of a dry hole as Berlin and Port-au-Prince.

Or *had* they been dry holes? He couldn't shake the feeling that there was a pattern to the things he had seen, and that the pattern could tell him a great deal, that what he had already found was perhaps far more valuable than what he was looking for. Well, maybe. Either this was the land of Serendip, and he was too blind to see the precious jewels scattered about the landscape, or else he wasn't quite through torturing himself with hopeful delusions. But there was something more, something else gnawing at him. The inescapable sense that there was something he should be looking for, an angle he hadn't considered. Anton Koffield could not remember ever feeling so uncertain, so full of self-doubt.

He looked down and discovered that he had finished his delicious breakfast without being aware of it. Never mind. It was time to get moving anyway. He didn't want to waste time. *Last day in Rio*, he reminded himself. *Tomorrow, on to the Canberra Institute*. He put his hands on the table, set his feet, made ready to push himself back—and then stopped. He dropped his hands, let his feet relax, and leaned back in his chair.

No. Not Canberra, he thought. *Not anywhere. Wherever I go on this planet, I'll just find the same relentlessly helpful support, the same faceless ArtInt servants doing everything I wish, more good food, more pleasure and comfort, all of it over and over again. And the same huge reams of data, more massively redundant copies of what I have already. I'm being buried in duplicate copies of what I don't need.*

There was no point in moving forward. There was nothing more for him to find, searching the way he was.

But what other way to search *was* there? And what, exactly, was he looking for? He stood up from the table, stepped to the railing, and stared unseeing at the crystalline sea. His ultimate goal was unchanged: *find DeSilvo*. Find the man who had left Solace to die, who had hidden the truth, the terrible, inescapable, mathematical proof that all the terraformed worlds were doomed. Pry loose the magical answers the man had promised, learn all the secrets that the damned megalomaniac had stolen and squirreled away, and then—

—And then, never mind. Once he had squeezed DeSilvo dry, then would come a time for a more personal reckoning. But Koffield chose not to think quite that far ahead, for fear of seeing more in his revenge fantasies than he wished to know about himself.

Earth and the Solar System had been the unquestioned and obvious first places to look, perhaps for DeSilvo himself, or at the very least for information about him. The man had spent the vast bulk of his career here. There would be more to learn here about the man here than anywhere else.

Beyond all that, the Grand Library and the vast facilities on Earth herself made the Solar System the first port of call for research on any subject. That was why they had been so welcome, so accepted, so unquestioned everywhere they went. All the off-worlds sent their scholars here. What else would they do? What was one more clutch of researchers amongst the thousands here already?

And had that first, unquestioned, even unconscious decision been wrong? Koffield had half assumed that DeSilvo was actually somewhere on Earth. The man had always enjoyed his comforts, and valued his own safety. Where else but Earth could a gentleman find the most comfortable living arrangements—and be safest from the impending collapse of the terraformed worlds?

The only real question in Koffield's mind had been whether the man would be up and about, or still tucked away in some form of cryogenic storage or temporal confinement. It was fairly obvious that the man must have put himself in storage if he was expecting to be alive when Koffield found his letter, over a century after it had been written. But would he have revived himself by now? Or not?

DeSilvo had, after all, invited Koffield's searches, and at the very least would have a rough idea of when Koffield would start looking. Would he have arranged things to be awake and alert, ready for Koffield's arrival? Perhaps DeSilvo had even arranged some sort of signaling device—the stars knew how—to report when the funerary urn on Greenhouse that supposedly contained his remains was opened, and thus that Koffield was on the trail.

Koffield had been working on the assumption that DeSilvo was up and about and on the lookout for him. Koffield would not have felt comfortable about the idea of waiting about, frozen stiff, for a dogged and implacable enemy who was determined to hunt him down. But DeSilvo had in essence *invited* Koffield to track him down. How did *that* play into it?

And what if something had gone wrong with DeSilvo's plans? The Great Man was perfectly capable of making mistakes, of miscalculating—they all knew that perfectly well. And the last word they had from DeSilvo was from about 114 years ago. Plenty of time for unforeseen circumstances. What if some vital event had failed to take place, or some machine had broken—or what if the man had simply died of natural causes?

Koffield swore under his breath and turned to go inside. To the devil with it. Back to work. First step—alert the authorities concerning Clemsen Wahl. There would likely be very little they could do about it, and next to no chance they could find him, but it was important to go through the motions, if for no other reason than to keep the local cops happy. If he didn't report it, they might start thinking that Koffield had helped Wahl get away.

Next, cancel the arrangements for the Canberra trip. There was no sense at all in going halfway around the world to find yet another set of copies of what he already had. And then—then it would be time to think again, to start over, to ask himself once again what DeSilvo had done—and what DeSilvo would do.

The local cops made sympathetic notices, and promised to do all the sorts of things that never did much good. The run to Australia was easy enough to cancel, but it did leave Anton Koffield with something of an open calendar. He decided to head back to the grandly named, if modest-sized, Oskar DeSilvo Monument Museum Archive, if for no other reason than to say his good-byes and to tidy up a few loose ends.

The brief ride to Rio's Centro district gave him but little time to think, and Phelby's fretfulness did not make it any easier. Koffield was on the rear-facing seat, with Phelby at the rear of the car, facing forward. He kept staring at Koffield, then remembering himself and looking out the window instead, until his worried gaze slipped back to Koffield. Obviously, Phelby felt responsible for Wahl's departure. Koffield toyed with the idea of giving Phelby the bawling-out he was plainly expecting, just so the man would stop dreading it, waiting for the other shoe to drop. Instead, he decided to try talking sensibly. "Listen here, son. Stop tearing yourself up. You weren't under orders to watch Wahl. Even if you were, there's only one of you. There was no way for you to watch him every second. Short of locking him up, there was nothing you could have done to stop Wahl, once he had decided to vanish."

"The signs were there," Phelby said. "I should have been able to read them."

"Then I should have been able to as well," Koffield said. "I even did read them, a little. But I decided not to look too hard."

"Sir?"

"Again, short of locking him up—which I very much doubt the locals would approve of, and which would probably result in *our* getting locked up and *his* going free, and our receiving far more attention than we want to risk—I don't think we could have stopped him from running, even if you and I took heel-to-toe watches. And we couldn't have done that—not and gotten anything useful done. And if we *had* managed to keep him from running, what would we have on our hands? A surly prisoner, storing up resentments against us, who'd want to run anyway, and just might want to get even with us later. Do you think we need another Hues Renblant, telling anyone who'll listen that we're liars, cheats, and crooks?"

"No, sir."

"I didn't think so either. So half-consciously, I decided to let him go if he wanted—or stay if he wanted." That wasn't exactly accurate. Koffield hadn't even come that close to making a conscious decision about the matter. But it did serve the purpose of taking the blame, and the guilt, off Dixon Phelby. "Now he's out there, feeling bad about leaving us, trying to find a way to show some sort of residual loyalty—and the best way he can do that is to keep quiet."

"I guess—I guess I see, sir." Phelby was quiet for a time, quiet until the car brought itself to a halt by the entrance to the DeSilvo Monument Museum Archive. "What about me, sir? What if I decided to run?"

Phrased that way, the question could be taken as concerning the past or the future. Koffield chose to answer for the present, as clearly as he could. He pushed a lever, and the air-car's hatch swung open. "There's the open door, Mr. Phelby. The only things holding you back are your sense of duty, your oath of obedience to your ship's captain—and your knowledge of just how important our mission is. Take off at a flat run, and I doubt I could catch you. But how easy would it be to look in the first mirror you came to—or the second, or third, or hundredth?"

He looked the younger man straight in the eye. The two of them sat there, frozen. The moment stretched out, just long enough for Koffield to wonder if he'd bet wrong. Then the younger man slid away from the door, and gestured for Koffield to get out first. "After you, sir," he said. "They're waiting for us upstairs."

Senhor Vargas was indeed waiting inside, and quite eager to be of help in any way he could. "Good morning, Dr. Caltrip! Good morning, Senhor Phelby!" he started in as soon as he saw them. Would they care for coffee? The summaries they requested yesterday evening were available. Would they care to see them at once? Is there another query they would wish to make, before other duties called him away? Were their accommodations satisfactory? A pity young Senhor Wahl could not attend this morning. Senhor Vargas is sorry to learn that their youthful friend was indisposed. Was there anything that could be done to assist with . . .

Thanks be to the stars, Phelby read Koffield's mood and knew to lead Vargas off and give Koffield time alone to think. Koffield sat down at the main reading table in the Archive's small library and tried to soak up the stillness, the quiet.

He thought about all they had seen. There were hidden messages in it everywhere for him, of that he had no doubt. All that was required was that his wits sharpen enough to understand what was all about him. Even Wahl's departure should tell him things.

But even if such things might be important later, they were peripheral to the task at hand. Wahl's departure could tell him nothing about finding DeSilvo.

It was starting to seem that nothing of any description could lead him to the man. He thought again of the words of DeSilvo's letter, the words burned into his memory.

"Seek me out. I live, but slumber. I am hidden, but hidden where you can find me."

DeSilvo had a weakness for puzzles, for trick meanings. Was there some play on words, some double meaning that might give an answer? Koffield had worked through every syllable of that letter, looking for such things, and never found anything. But there was one thing—direct, clear, to the point. *Hidden where you can find me.* Not *where I can be found,* but *where you can find me.* The letter had been directed to him, to Anton Koffield, personally. *You* didn't mean any random person who read the letter. It had to mean no one other than himself. Was that mere overblown praise for his detective ability? Was it, as with so much of that letter, just meant as salve for Anton Koffield's ego? Or did the man mean something by it? Was it grounded in something?

Books.

The thought, the answer, came flitting up from his subconscious—but Koffield was not able to grasp its meaning. Yet, with that single word had come such a sense of surety, of confidence—he knew, he *knew,* the solution was there, in that word, if only he could find it. He froze, held his breath, as if the answer he sought might fly away if he moved suddenly and spooked it.

Books.

All right, books. What about them? He had searched through thousands of them, scanning the text through every sort of data sieve he could devise. Analyzing the text, the datafiles, every way he could.

Not text. *Books. It was the books that caught him the first time.*

And then he had it. That was it. Koffield felt his heart racing, wanted to pound his fist into the table, wanted to jump up and pace across the floor. But still he held stock-still, determined to think it through in cold, hard logic, get all the facts straight.

Get your thoughts in order. Think about the first time. DeSilvo had signed him up to work in the archives of the Solace project, and Koffield had thought of writing a book about the Solace terraforming project. In the course of his studies, Koffield had discovered that a great number of things had been left out of the archive index. Anything negative, anything that might put a bit of tarnish on DeSilvo's halo, simply wasn't listed. Koffield had decided to put together his own index—and in the course of doing that, he had found Ulan Baskaw's work. Three books, all erased from the Grand Library's records.

It wasn't supposed to be possible to purge a book from the GL's memory systems, and yet DeSilvo had done it. But DeSilvo had made a mistake. He had forgotten about the Permanent Physical Collection. Koffield remembered telling Chandray about it, a long time after the events. "... *a person who can manipulate a computer system that well tends to* think *in terms of computer systems and ArtInt operators. So much of what they know about the world comes to them through computer displays that they start to think that the world* is *what the computer and the ArtInt-ops tell them it is. If the computer records show that the book has been deleted, then it has been.*" DeSilvo had failed to consider the actual, physical book, the copies that still existed, there in the PPC.

The actual, physical book. He, Koffield, had fallen into exactly the same trap as DeSilvo had. Overwhelmed by the amount of data, faced with the absolute necessity of getting through as much of it as possible in the shortest possible amount of time, he had focused almost entirely on the digitized texts themselves—burrowing endlessly through the data, the words recorded in the computer memories to be sliced, diced, sorted, ranked, scanned, searched, and then spewed out onto datapad screens. Koffield had found the truth in a physical book the last time—and DeSilvo had as much as told him that was where to look now. It had been staring him in the face the whole time.

Staring him in the face. Koffield realized he had been looking blankly out into the middle distance. He shifted his gaze downward just a trifle—and found himself looking at a shelf of handsomely bound volumes. A gleaming engraved brass plate set into the shelf itself read BOOKS BY OSKAR DESILVO.

It couldn't be that easy. Koffield frowned for a moment. Easy? How many light-years, how much of his life, how much thought and sweat and determination had it taken to get him as far as sitting in this chair, staring at that shelf of books? Much harder, and the journey this far would have killed him. But even so, could it be that it would be as simple as looking in a book?

Moving slowly, carefully, as if still afraid that the train of logic might collapse if he tried to rush it too hard, Anton Koffield stood and crossed the room to examine the books. But what book would it be, and what *in* that book would it be? He stood before the shelf, staring at the thirty or so volumes there, thinking, not yet touching them. Perhaps, something that could not be recorded in a digital version—or at least, that normally would not be.

It might be something as simple—and as devilishly hard to find—as an old-fashioned microdot, disguised as a period at the end of a sentence. The near-ancients had perfected that one, shrinking a whole page of text down into something a tenth of a millimeter across. The information he needed could have been woven into a pattern in the paper, or stored as DNA code in a sealed micropacket sewn inside the binding, or actually be in the text itself, coded in some way dependent on the book's pagination—as simple as page one, word one, page two, word two, with the text or the pagination deliberately altered in the digitized version so the code would not work. If the possibilities were not infinite, they were vast enough that they might as well be. *I could spend my whole life searching this one shelf of books for a hidden message, and not find it,* Koffield thought.

Except—except that wasn't the way DeSilvo's mind worked—and DeSilvo had said "hidden where you can find me."

Let's just assume he means that. That he's hidden where you, Anton Koffield, can find him. No one else.

How would that work? To ask the question was to

know the answer. How had it worked before? Koffield thought back to DeSilvo's false tomb. DeSilvo had left what appeared to be a string of random characters chiseled into a wall, worked into a pattern of excessively clever symbolic representations. Except the string of characters had been the combination to the lock on the personal pack compartment built into Koffield's cryosleep canister. To Koffield's eyes, but to no others, that character string said THIS PROVES I STOLE FROM YOU.

And think about the timing. The universe believed that DeSilvo had died more than a century ago—because that was when DeSilvo made it appear as if he had died. DeSilvo would have worked at preparing his false tomb, written the letter found in it, and prepared whatever further message he had left for Koffield, all at the same time. To Koffield, the two might be separated by light-years and long stretches of time. But DeSilvo had made them all at once. All of a piece. And DeSilvo had a tendency to return to the same theme, the same ideas—the same tricks—again and again and again.

Yes. Yes. That would be the way of it. DeSilvo would do what he had done: leave a message, in plain sight, that would speak only to Admiral Anton Koffield.

He considered the shelf of books once again. Plainly, these books were meant more as decoration than as reading material. They were bound in the most elaborate and luxurious materials, tooled and embossed and worked about with gold leaf, synthetic jewels, holograms—in short, every bit of frippery available to the bookbinder's art. The titles of several were done in type and design so elaborate that it was difficult to read the words.

Koffield recognized several of the titles. Some were serious works of scholarship, some were credible accounts meant to educate the general public about terraforming—and some were the most egregious self-promoting fluff, part of DeSilvo's substantial contribution to his own hagiography.

These Koffield dismissed, at least for the moment.

Perhaps the clue he sought would turn out to be something hidden in the text, perhaps some subtle alteration in an edition published since Koffield's own disappearance, but that seemed unlikely. What he was after was something that would jump out at someone with a particular bit of inside knowledge but be completely passed over, not only by the casual observer but even by a scholar knowledgeable in the field. It seemed unlikely that DeSilvo would have counted on Koffield spotting a misplaced comma on page 234 of *Aspects of Theoretical Large-Scale Hydraulic Engineering for General Terraforming*. No. It would be something bigger, something more obvious—like a book that wasn't there, that should have been, or—*or a book that shouldn't have been there, but was.*

His eyes fell on it. The last book on the shelf, all the way over to the right. A slender volume, with a blue binding, much plainer and less elaborate than the others. TERRAFORMING, the spine lettering read. NEMO. And a small symbol, a circle inside a square, below the lettering.

He knew. He had no idea how, or to what, but he knew that book was the key. He pulled it down from the shelf. He started to read.

Two minutes later he slammed the book shut. He was breathing heavily. Sweat stood out on his forehead. Anton Koffield did not believe in ghosts. But he suddenly had the sense that he knew what it must be like to see one.

Ten minutes after that he was composing urgent queries to Ashdin and Chandray.

CHAPTER THIRTEEN

PHOEBE, LUNCHTIME, AND SWIFT

Aboard the São Paulo, *(Dom Pedro IV Aux Ship #3)*
Approaching Mars

Alone in the dark, in ship's night, the rest of the crew and passengers asleep, Captain Felipe Henrique Marquez glared out the forward porthole of the *São Paulo*, watching a green-red dot grow larger, and wishing, not for the first time, that he had never laid eyes on Anton Koffield. Marquez was used to giving orders. He did not enjoy taking them—and sometimes it seemed that Koffield had done nothing but issue orders since the day the two had met. It softened the blow somewhat that the orders were altogether sensible and necessary, and that Marquez knew, down in his bones, that the stakes could not be higher. And he had to admit that Koffield could not have treated Marquez with greater respect than he had shown.

But for all of that, it was galling for a man who valued his freedom as much as Marquez to find himself under the *de facto* command of another man, implicitly accepting Koffield's right to the leadership.

But, here he was, hurtling through space, once again obeying, without question, another of Koffield's detailed "requests." If the lives of millions—and revenge against

the man who had so harmed them all—were not at
stake, Marquez would have had half a mind to refuse.
That was why he had taken the graveyard watch for
himself on this trip. He had not been much interested in
company.

As per Koffield's "request," the *Dom Pedro IV*'s two
smaller auxiliary ships, the *São Paulo* and the *Rio de
Janeiro*, were joined together to form one larger and
quite ungainly craft, hard-docked together side to side
through their cargo locks so as to form a corridor between the two craft. Also as per "request," aboard the
joined ships were Marquez, Wandella Ashdin, crew
member Lira Wu, and the three members of the expedition to the Permanent Physical Collection—Second Officer Pilot Norla Chandray, Acting First Officer Yuri
Sparten, and Petty Officer Jerand Bolt.

They were flying toward the Inner Solar System, and a
rendezvous with the *DP-IV*'s third and larger aux ship,
the lighter *Cruzeiro do Sul*. Admiral Koffield and Cargo
Officer Dixon Phelby—but not that damned deserting
Clemsen Wahl—were aboard the *Cruzeiro*.

They had left the *DP-IV* herself behind, in orbit of
Neptune. Marquez could only guess what Koffield had
in mind, but whatever it was would likely be something
best done quietly. A few small auxiliary craft moving
here and there around the Solar System wouldn't be
enough to attract notice—but dropships the size of the
DP-IV rarely ventured in close to Earth, and she would
attract attention the moment she did so. So, in the interests of maintaining a low profile, she stayed where she
was, alongside the Grand Library.

And, of course, all this left the main ship—*his* ship—
in the hands of inexperienced and low-ranking crew—
Senior Acting Chief Petty Officer Sindra Chon, Petty
Officer Tamric Aziz, and three crew members: Zhen,
Sherdan, and Tugler. Chon had more years in, and had
served in larger vessels, than his other crew, and by the
merchanter's rules of rank and seniority, he had been
forced to recognize Sindra Chon's technical seniority and

place her over Aziz in nominal command of the ship—
something that might not sit well with the others, who
had served aboard her far longer. Marquez hoped and
believed that Chon, while acting as commander, would
have the sense not to give any actual orders.

Marquez had left eight separate maneuver sequences
stored in the *DP-IV*'s ShipInt. He fervently hoped they
would cover all the likely contingencies—though he had
very little data to go on.

One datum he did have was that red-green dot in the
porthole. Mars. The Ruined World. They were close
enough that he could almost imagine seeing a hint of
blue water, as well. And they would still be getting closer
for some time now, before they reached the rendezvous
point.

Why would Koffield pick a meeting point so close to
the planet, unless he intended for them to go there?
Maybe, just maybe, there was something in the orbit of
the planet he needed to see. On Deimos or Phobos, perhaps.

But Marquez had two other datapoints in stock.
Taken together, they shot down any such hopeful specu-
laton. The first was this: Two thousand years after the
Great Failure, it was still standard decontamination procedure to abandon in orbit any vehicle that had landed
on the Martian surface, and, if possible, to send it on a
destructive reentry path, to prevent any attempt by salvage crews who might be unwise enough to try and scavenge a lander left in orbit.

But the second datum was worse: The *Dom Pedro IV*
carried three auxiliary vehicles capable of landing on a
planet. Anton Koffield was flying here in one of them,
and had "requested" Marquez bring on the other two,
leaving the *DP-IV* without an escape vehicle in case of
emergency.

Marquez couldn't think of a single reason for bringing all three aux ships, and taking chances with the
DP-IV, unless they were going down to that damned
place, for whatever reason. One to do the landing, and
then be abandoned. One to serve as a rescue craft, just in

case. And one to remain in orbit, and get them all home, if they had to run a rescue and then dump the contaminated rescue ship.

Marquez had been very much intrigued by the story of the Ruined World, when they were safely back aboard the Grand Library. But, as they neared the planet, Captain Felipe Henrique Marquez lost all his enthusiasm for Mars.

A single light popped on, and a text message flashed on the heads-up display. *Long-range visual detection periodic intermittent target acquired,* it reported: a very long-winded way of saying the scanners had spotted a flashing light: the *Cruzeiro do Sul*'s acquisition beacon. Marquez didn't bother doing a naked-eye search: the scanners had much more sensitive vision than he did. The blinking light was more of Koffield's cautious and detailed planning. A visual beacon that was only bright enough to be detectable at this short a range ought to be much harder to spot or track than a radio transmission. This far from civilization, it didn't seem likely that anybody would be watching—but why take chances?

Marquez ordered up range-and-rate figures. Just under three hundred kilometers away, closing very slowly. Good piloting—extremely good piloting—from both ships.

No doubt Koffield would want them to take it slow and gentle during rendezvous and docking. The less energy they put out, the harder they would be to spot. But that could only delay the evil moment when the *São Paulo/Rio* complex would dock with *Cruzeiro*.

Marquez glared once again at the red-green dot up ahead. After all, once they were docked, it would be time to prep for their next destination.

Aboard the Cruzeiro do Sul

Norla Chandray staggered a bit as she helped drag the heavy packing case to one side of the *Cruzeiro*'s main compartment. Finally, they got the heavy case of

whatever-it-was moving and set it down by the starboard bulkhead. She paused there a moment and looked
around herself.

The *Cruzeiro* was a fat cylinder, fifteen meters high
and twenty in diameter. Topside was the docking system,
and a flat upper deck, open to space so that the *Cruzeiro
do Sul* could carry bulky cargo that would not fit inside
the ship strapped down to her upper deck.

It was also possible to deploy a habitable dome-
shaped temporary upper compartment, in essence an inflatable igloo, that sat on the open upper deck. When in
place, it was accessible from the main deck, via a ladder
through the topside hatch. Marquez had brought the
igloo along aboard the *Rio*, though he not yet deployed
it atop the *Cruzeiro*. Things weren't that crowded—yet.

The main deck, the ops deck, of the *Cruzeiro do Sul*
was little more than one big open compartment that
could be rigged as any combination of cargo space or
passenger facilities. This trip out, when it seemed likely
they'd need all the room they could get, the main deck
had been cleared of everything portable but a chemical
toilet and refresher, with the crew sleeping in sleeping
bags on the deck. The lighter had four portholes, set into
the hull at equally spaced intervals.

The pilot's station was built up against the hull between the only other two permanent structures on the
deck—the gangway leading down to the systems deck to
the pilot's left, and the main airlock and docking collar
to the right. The *Cruzeiro* was docked to the *Rio de
Janeiro* through this airlock, and the *São Paulo* was
docked to the *Rio*'s secondary docking port.

Below were the systems deck and engineering space,
and below that, at the aft end, the main ship engines.

What seemed a long time ago, and was a long way
away, Norla and Koffield had flown the *Cruzeiro* across
the Solacian planetary system. Back then, with just two
of them aboard, and no cargo to speak of, the *Cruzeiro*
had seemed like a huge echoing old barn. Now it seemed
crowded, noisy, and small. She looked around and
shook her head. Strange to be back here again—and

strange that this place should look so different, and yet the same. At least it didn't smell of book dust. It would take a few more showers before she would truly feel that the same could be said of herself. And at least she didn't have to wear a breathing mask.

Everyone, from the *São Paulo* and the *Rio de Janeiro* and the *Cruzeiro do Sul*, were crowding in through the hatches. And no wonder. Koffield had called a meeting—and it sounded as if some real answers might be forth-coming. Norla did a quick nose count. There were eight of them there, altogether. Somehow that seemed like not very many people to make the lighter seem so crowded—or to try and save so many lives.

There was one bright point—the word had come down that there was no longer any point at all in con-cealing the true names of ships or people, or in trying to hide that they were looking for Oskar DeSilvo. So many holes had been punched in all the secrets that further at-tempts to conceal would be pointless, and could serve to draw more attention to the real state of affairs.

But Norla could guess at another possible reason for letting the various cats out of the bag, a reason she didn't want to point out for fear of damaging morale: Koffield, for whatever reason, had concluded that they weren't likely to be returning to Earth, or to the Grand Library, or anywhere else in the Solar System. It was safe to tell all, if no one was going to get a chance to talk to anyone outside the ship.

Koffield stood in front of a packing case that had been shoved up against the port-side bulkhead. He had set up a portable display panel on the case and had a few other books and papers sitting on the case as well. He checked the adjustments on the display, then turned to face the others. Somehow, that was enough to get across the mes-sage that it was time to begin, and the murmur of con-versation faded away without further prompting. "Good evening," he said. "I just have a few things to say. I'll try to keep it short, but please, all of you—take a seat on a chair or a packing case or the deck if you like."

He paused while people settled themselves. "Before I

talk about why we're all here, and what brought us here, I want to talk about everything else that we have learned. Things that don't quite make sense. Every one of our three research teams found oddities—anomalies, if you want to use a grander term.

"Why do they build streets with no houses on Earth?

"Why is Earth making no move to correct her declining population? Why is security so lax, and why are the officials so welcoming and uncurious, everywhere we go?

"Why and when were the Permanent Physical Collection ArtInts programmed to do no maintenance work in the terraforming section? It was maintained perfectly well when I was there. It looks as if no one used the PPC's Geology and Terraforming Reading Room in the last hundred years. How could that be? Taking a broader view, why, everywhere in the Solar System, does it seem that the study of terraforming is turning moribund? We all found old research data—but virtually nothing current or recent. Terraforming will soon become a lost art if things go on as they are.

"There are other, more subtly strange goings-on, nuanced enough that I suspect it would be easy to charge off in the wrong direction if we dealt with them prematurely. Rather than point them out now, I want to think them through a bit more before I discuss them.

"For the most part, it seems to me the people in the Solar System aren't aware of how odd these things are, either because they take them for granted, after living all their lives with what they've always known, or because the anomalies are hidden away out of the public view. I'm not much for intuition—but I can't shake the feeling that those anomalies add up to something. I don't know what, just yet. I'll be thinking about those mysteries—and, when time permits, I want all of you thinking about them as well.

"All that to one side, there was another mystery, much closer to our main area of research: What the hell was Oskar DeSilvo doing, making repeated secret and solitary visits to Mars?"

He paused for a moment, and Norla glanced toward the porthole. Mars was out there, very close. Why *had* he gone? DeSilvo had made the trips during the time he was still trying to convince himself that Solace wasn't going to collapse, and maybe sliding over into the time when he finally admitted Solace was doomed. So why would he go and play tourist on the world that had suffered the most complete and most famous ecology collapse in history? It would be like a man wracked with guilt for murdering half the town making a pleasure tour of the local morgue.

Koffield went on. "Those are the questions we found. Let me turn to what brought me here, and caused me to bring the rest of you as well—an answer. An answer in a little blue book—or, rather, multiple copies of a little blue book like this one. It's a precise fascimile of the copy on display in Rio de Janeiro—and not *quite* an exact facsimile of most of the other copies that we turned up in the Grand Library and in the Permanent Physical Collection. And, I might add, once I knew what to look for, and made discreet queries, I was able to find copies in about a half dozen big physical-text libraries."

He held the book up high, then opened it up to show them the title page. He powered up the display screen, and it lit up with an enlargement of the title pager. "*The Science and Art of Terraforming*," he read aloud. "By Anon Nemo."

"A bit obvious, that," said Dr. Ashdin.

"Maybe to you," muttered Jerand Bolt. "It went past me. What's a bit obvious about what?"

"The author's name isn't a name," she replied. "It's words in Latin. A very ancient, very dead language, but you can trace back lots of languages of modern speech to it. Educated early near-ancients would know it, and even after it stopped being commonly spoken, a lot of words and terms were used in academic circles. *Anon* is short for *Anônumos*—our cognate is *anonymous*, obviously, and of course it means 'nameless.' And *Nemo* means 'no one' or 'nobody.' So a nameless nobody wrote the book."

"I don't think it was expected that everyone would catch the Latin reference," Koffield said mildly. "I think the purpose of using that particular made-up name was to keep the book from being cataloged under a name where it might be more easily found. And, consciously or otherwise, it's also a joke—or maybe a confession. But I'll explain those points in a minute."

Norla spoke up. "Ah, forgive the obvious question, but, well—*did* DeSilvo write this book? I mean, aside from the afterword? Is that why it's important?"

"I know Oskar DeSilvo's writing style better than I know my own," Ashdin said. "The opening passages sound like him, but the main text of the book isn't a bit like his work. On the other hand, the afterword is not only his style—he lifted some of it, verbatim, from other essays he's done. The afterword is DeSilvo—self-plagiarized DeSilvo—through and through."

Koffield set down the book and nodded. "I'm just as sure as Dr. Ashdin is that Oskar DeSilvo did not write the main text of this book. But let me go back a bit. I spent a great deal of my time on Earth slogging through endless data records, searching for some sort of clue that might lead me—lead us—to DeSilvo. A marginal note, a letter written to a colleague, a mention in a historical text—any sort of documentary clue. That's more or less what I sent the *rest* of you off to search for as well. And, so far as I am aware, none of us found any such thing."

Another murmur of agreement. "That's my fault," Koffield said simply, without any attempt at theatrics. "I sent you looking for the wrong things. Something I didn't realize until I spent a long time looking for them myself."

"And that book there is the right thing?" Sparten asked suspiciously. "What makes it right?"

"I should have been trying to think like the man I was tracking. I didn't," Koffield said. "I sent you looking for data, information. But Oskar DeSilvo has been playing games right along—with us, with the planet Solace, with millions of lives. I should have sent you looking for *puzzles.*"

"Wait a second," said Jerand Bolt. "When we got the queries from you, we went all over that book with everything we had. We did high-resolution scans of all five copies we had, and tried a maximum-res scan, before we left the library. Max-res is supposed to be like using a hundred-power microscope. I put the ArtInts to work examining the scan. If there was anything larger than an amoeba, a memory dot or a data-whisker physically hidden on or in the book, we'd have found it. Nothing. We spent most of the trip here going through the text for codes or ciphers. Even if it couldn't crack a given code, the text analysis system we used should have at least spotted that there *was* a code, a hidden pattern. We looked. We looked damned hard. There's nothing there."

"You're right," said Koffield with an odd, sad little smile. "Or nearly so. There's almost nothing there at all."

Norla spoke. "We did spot five little oddities—well no, as you say, *anomalies* would be the better word. They weren't just odd or unusual. They were things that were—well, willfully wrong."

Koffield looked at her thoughtfully. "Name them."

"Well, for starters, there's barely anything in it about terraforming. A few generalities at the beginning, but then it launches into a long screed on mixed-species population statistics in sealed domes—how the number of earthworms sets an upper limit on the number of rabbits per hectare, that sort of thing. I don't know if that counts. Maybe the publisher just stuck on a title with the word 'terraforming' because he thought it would sell better."

Norla looked to Koffield, but he didn't say anything. She went on. "The more obvious anomaly was the afterword by DeSilvo. It was there at the back of the book, but it wasn't cited on the title page, or in the copyright and catalog notice on the publication page. These last few weeks, I've learned more than I wanted to know about how libraries operate. Library ArtInts just look at the catalog data. They don't check the rest of the book. Without the catalog citation, DeSilvo wouldn't be listed as a contributor."

"You're right. He wouldn't be—and he wasn't. I made a very thorough check on that. Go on."

"Well, it's not anomalous, just sloppy, but the catalog description notice was so vague and uninformative that the book could have been listed almost anywhere. Go to five different libraries, and you'd find it five different places, if you could find it at all. It doesn't help that the title is almost entirely misleading."

"Right again," said Koffield. "I checked that, too."

For Koffield, his reactions were the equivalent of wildly enthused praise. Norla was starting to feel a bit like the teacher's pet. Not necessarily a good thing, if the others resented it. She saw Sparten glaring at her, and Bolt watching Sparten's expression with obvious amusement. Well, there was no help for it at the moment. "Then, ah, there were the dedications," she said. "Or epigrams, really."

"Dedications, plural?" Ashdin asked, clearly puzzled. "My copy only had *one* dedication. Not that I could make much out of it." She consulted her datapad. " 'To the noontime memory of looking straight up at what Swift predicted.' "

"We saw that one," Norla said to Ashdin. "One dedication per book, but in the five copies of the book we saw, there were three different dedications. Two of that noontime memory one, two of another, and one singleton. There's a different little symbol on the spine that goes with each particular dedication, probably just so you could distinguish them from each other without checking the inside pages." She turned back to Koffield. "*That's* the dedication anomaly. Different copies, otherwise identical, with different dedications. Officer Sparten suggested that might be some sort of ego game, or funding stunt—do up multiple versions and suck up to multiple friends and financial supporters." There, she had given him some of the credit. Maybe *that* would smooth his feathers a bit.

"That doesn't make any sense," objected Captain Marquez, blithely ruining Norla's attempt at peacemaking. He then charged in deeper, making things worse in the bargain. "If you're writing as—what was it?— 'Nameless Nobody,' then what good is the dedication going to do? *And* I take it those books ended up side by side on the shelf at the PPC. Whoever did it took a damn big risk. They'd be in six kinds of hell if Dr. Blank was all proud of the honor of getting a book dedication, and then found out later you'd dedicated copies to Madame Dash and Mr. Dot."

"Besides," Bolt put in, "that's not the sort of dedication you'd put in to honor someone or thank them. You'd write 'To Dr. Joseph Blank, with heartfelt thanks for all his support.' That stuff about the noonday sun is a private reference."

"But what does it mean?" Ashdin demanded.

Bolt shrugged. "It could be anything. Maybe Swift warned Anon Nemo not to go off to the park at lunch with Madame Dash because they'd look up and see her husband had followed them. And Swift got it right."

"Officer Sparten? Any comments?" Koffield asked.

Sparten shook his head. "It was just a thought. But I would say that if the book was intended for private circulation, instead of mass publication, that would reduce the risks of getting caught. After all, it took something like a hundred years for those copies to wind up side by side. And if you were publishing anonymously, you might still want to honor a friend or a patron. So Nemo did it this way because he couldn't reveal Dr. Blank's identity without revealing his own."

"Good points. But Officer Chandray said she had *five* anomalies. What was the fifth?"

"The publication date," she said. "Usually it's just a year. Sometimes a month and year. But all the versions of the book I saw show a full date." She checked the notes on her datapads. "Um—August 3, 5225. I checked a lot of other printed books. No one bothers setting the exact date down," she said.

"Notice anything else odd there on the publication page?" Koffield asked.

Norla shrugged. "Not really—except that the rest of the cataloging data was so sloppy and vague—why be precise about the one thing that doesn't matter?"

"Taken altogether, what it all says is that whoever did this book is an amateur," Bolt said. "Maybe what it means is that he or she doesn't know the etiquette, I guess you'd call it, of publishing. So what? I haven't heard or seen one thing that tells me why *this* book is important." He looked toward Koffield. "You pulled us from Neptune to Mars because of this book. No offense, sir, but—why?"

"Because of something I saw that no one else here could have. Something that wasn't in this book."

Norla had never seen Koffield this way. He was almost talking in riddles himself. The man was almost giddy. Maybe he had spent a little too *much* time trying to think like DeSilvo. Or maybe the man was just enjoying the moment, savoring an hour of victory after so many years of disaster. Taken in that light, she didn't mind at all that he wanted to have a bit of fun. Stars in the sky, the man had earned it. And it was plain to see that, right now, what Anton Koffield wanted was for someone to serve up the straight line. "What would that something be, sir?" Norla asked.

Koffield smiled. "The same words, in another book. Once you get past the opening passages—which I suspect *were* written by DeSilvo, and probably lifted from one of his books—the entire work is plagiarized, the whole thing, from top to bottom—from Ulan Baskaw's first, and least important, book—*Statistical Analysis of Species Populations in Artificial Environments*. The same words, just dumbed down a little. All the charts and tables and numbers and math taken out, leaving just a simplified version of the text."

Norla was shocked, and she wasn't alone. Enough of those present knew enough of the story to put the room in a stunned silence. Ulan Baskaw had lived and died five hundred years before, and almost nothing was known about her. It was not even absolutely certain that Baskaw was a woman. It was Baskaw's later work that DeSilvo had plagiarized years before, and used to build the world of Solace. And it was her final work—suppressed by DeSilvo—that proved, beyond doubt, that the ecosystem of Solace, and of every other terraformed world, would collapse. "But—but who else but you has *read* that book—I mean, in the last hundred years?" Norla asked. "Who else would be in a position to *spot* that?"

"No one, that I'm aware of," Koffield said. "Which means, I suppose, that the whole effort of getting the book printed, of shipping it out to libraries; of leaving the detailed instruction in his will that it be displayed with the other 'Books by Oskar DeSilvo' in Rio and in the Grand Library—another detail I checked on; all of it, from start to finish, was just DeSilvo's way of sending a message to *me*, here and now, in the present day, 113 years after he pretended to die."

No one spoke for a moment—everyone, no doubt, struggling as hard as Norla was to get their thoughts in order.

"I know it sounds lunatic," Koffield said. "Just as lunatic as the first message from DeSilvo we found, in his supposed tomb. It's fairly obvious he wrote them both at about the same time."

Norla saw Sparten's head snap up, and he stared at Koffield in shock. She saw Bolt watching Sparten. Both men were suddenly very alert. In that moment, Norla no longer had the slightest doubt that Sparten had in fact been sent to spy on them—and that he had tried to recruit Bolt. Koffield saw it all too—he must have. But he did not react. "I don't suppose there's any further reason to keep the details of what we found secret from this group. You all know too much already by now anyway. But I'll leave the details for another time."

That must have been a message that Sparten was going to have a hard time dealing with. *I'll give you what you've been chasing after for months a bit later. It's not really important anymore.*

Koffield was still talking. "I felt then, and I feel now, that the notion of expending so much time, so much effort, to send a message across such a distance of time

and space—and to do it so—so playfully, so whimsi-
cally—is madness. It seemed so deranged, that it would
almost be easier to accept and believe that I was a madman, that I was imagining this vast conspiracy that
stalks me across the years and light-years."

He sighed, and leaned back against the packing case
behind him. "Probably that's why I'm telling it all this
way, instead of just presenting the facts—no, the *riddle
answers*—I finally tracked down, after I stopped looking
for facts and figures. If all of you follow my logic, if *you*
see the same answers, then, unless we're *all* out of our
minds, it must be that the man who created the puzzle
was the madman—not the people who solved it."

"So what's the puzzle? And what's your logic?"
Sparten asked.

"And why did you bring us out *here*?" Marquez demanded, stabbing a finger out the porthole at Mars.

Koffield smiled. "Bear with me a bit longer while I explain my logic. My first point of departure was this: It's
been my impression DeSilvo never did anything without
a reason. He made plenty of grand-scale mistakes in his
time, but he always fussed over the tiny details, and
made sure everything was just right." He turned to
Wandella Ashdin. "Would you call that a more or less
fair assessment?"

Ashdin nodded. "I'd say so. He published books
about theories and ideas that were just plain wrong—but
his math was always right, and his indexes were always
superb."

Norla had to smile at that. Only an academic would
think of indexing as a personal attribute. "Very well,"
said Koffield. "With that in mind—" He tapped a control on his datapad. The blowup of the book's title page
vanished from the display panel behind him, to be replaced by three enlarged sections of three separate dedication pages. "There might be others, but in the samples
we had—the one I found in Rio, Dr. Ashdin's Grand Library copy, and the five found in the PPC—we find these
three different dedications. Though I think you're right,

Officer Chandray. 'Epigrams' might be closer than 'dedications.'

> "To Phoebe Long & Dee Latt,
> who cry midday havoc."

> "Low in the South, High in the West:
> to the red warrior under two companions at lunchtime."

> "To the noontime memory of
> looking straight up at what Swift predicted."

Norla had never been much for puzzles and word games. She tended to get impatient with the puzzle if she couldn't solve it at once and annoyed with herself if she got it wrong—or worse, if anyone else solved it first. And worst of all was struggling to solve a puzzle while someone who already knew the answer was watching. Under certain circumstances, puzzles could bring out the very worst in her—and these circumstances were pretty close to meeting that spec.

"For what it's worth," Koffield said, "the one I saw was the first one, about Dee and Phoebe."

"I'd read that as talking about two little girls who were fussy and cried a lot instead of taking an afternoon nap," said Lira Wu, speaking for the first time.

"Let me get this straight," said Bolt, staring at the display. "You're saying that all three of these riddles have the same answer?"

"That's right."

"Time of day," said Ashdin. "They all refer to a time of day. 'Midday havoc,' 'lunchtime,' and 'noontime.' "

"Those are all the *same* time of day," Norla said. "Noon. Something happens at noon. But noon where?" Norla had a spacer's appreciation for the fact that it was never the same time everywhere. Between differing day lengths for planets, time zone shifts on each planet, and the vagaries of relativistic time dilation, it could be damned near impossible to be sure what time it was someplace else. Suddenly, something popped into her head. Koffield had given a hint, and a big one. He had asked if she had noticed something else odd about the publication data page. "Can you bring up the pub data page on that display?"

Koffield tapped at his datapad, and the page popped up. She scanned down the various bits of officialese until she spotted the two lines she was looking for.

> *Published August 3, 5225,*
> *in the city of Greenwich, England.*

"Noon in Greenwich," she said triumphantly. "I saw a lot of pub pages. Hardly anyone reports the city of publication—and I don't think Greenwich is exactly a hotbed of publishing."

"And they don't set publication dates on Sunday either," Bolt said eagerly, looking up from a calendar display on his datapad.

"Good!" Koffield replied. "I didn't think to check that."

"Sunday, August 3, 5225," Norla said. "So that date is special, somehow."

"Odd, really," Ashdin muttered, half to herself.

"What is?" Norla asked.

"That August 3 wasn't August 14."

Norla looked at her in puzzled amusement. "I think you'll find that most days of the year aren't August 14. It's not that unusual."

"No, no, you don't understand. August 14 was DeSilvo's birthday—and he always liked making things happen on a date that had some significance to him. The day work first started on Solace, the ignition of the SunSpot over Greenhouse—that sort of thing. He delayed lots of things to August 14 over the years. I'm surprised he didn't set that date as the publication date."

"Maybe he couldn't," said Bolt. "Maybe that's the point. It really *was* an important date. Something did happen then, something he needed to point out."

"You've got all that DeSilvo info there," said Lira Wu, pointing to Ashdin's datapad. "Is August 3 a big date for some other reason?"

"You know, it does stick in my mind, somehow," Ashdin said, as she ran the search. "There was something—" She stopped in midsentence, and her face went white. "Oh, my. That's the day he died, exactly one year later."

Koffield looked surprised. "That detail I missed." He thought for a moment, then smiled at Ashdin. "And I think it was a message meant for us."

"But how could his death be—"

"What death?" asked Bolt. "I thought the whole deal was that he *faked* his death."

Ashdin looked stunned all over again. "My word. I'd forgotten that for the moment."

"So you're saying he chose the anniversary of this particular day as the one to fake his own death—just to send a signal to us, here and now?" Sparten asked.

"We're not saying anything," Norla said. "But there the two dates are—and Dr. Ashdin just got done saying how much the man liked—likes—marking anniversaries."

"So, somehow," said Lira Wu, "noon, August 3, 5225, Earth standard calendar, was a big important moment. Or at least an important moment in *Greenwich*."

"But what's important that happens in Greenwich?" asked Bolt, sitting next to her. "It's near Paris, isn't it?"

"London," Koffield said gently.

"What's the difference?" asked Bolt. "I'm just saying, wouldn't big important things happen in the big city?"

Sparten was checking his datapad. "Nothing much in the history files for that date," he said.

"Greenwich," said Norla. "What's important about—"

And for once, Norla was the one who solved the puzzle before anyone else, with one intuitive leap setting off the next, in something that was closer to free association than rational thought. *Greenwich is where they keep the time—universal time, official time, from there. Because that's where the zero meridian of longitude is—longitude! Phoebe Long and Dee Latt. Longitude and latitude. What about the other two? Does it fit?*

She popped on her datapad and read the second riddle again. "Low in the South, High in the West: to the red warrior under two companions at lunchtime." *Low in the South, High in the West. Right. That fits latitude and longitude, Red warrior? Look out the window. Mars used to be red, remember? God of War. Okay—what about the two companions? Are Dee and Phoebe—wait—the war god's companions!*

And the last piece fell into place. "Deimos and Phobos!" she shouted out. "Phoebe Long and Dee Latt! Phobos Longitude, Deimos Latitude!"

"What?" Sparten asked.

"Their ground tracks!" Norla shouted. "Don't you get it?" She pointed to the enlargement of the publication page. "At noon, Greenwich Time, on Sunday, August 3, 5225, Phobos was over such-and-such a Martian longitude, and Deimos was over such-and-such a latitude. Put them together—"

"And that's where *something* is on Mars," said Koffield. "Stars alone knows what. Well done. Full marks."

Sparten was working it out, thinking through the puzzles. At last he nodded, and smiled. "I get it. I get it," he said.

"But who or what is Swift?" Lira Wu asked.

"Of course!" Ashdin said. "Why the devil didn't I see it? An early near-ancient writer. Very much forgotten, of course, but he is remembered for what was really a very odd circumstance—a most unlikely circumstance. In one of his fictional works he described Mars as having two satellites, one orbiting—what was it—every ten hours, and the other in twenty-one and a half."

"So what?" asked Bolt.

"So he described them 150 years before they were found," said Ashdin. "I think he got pretty close on the orbital periods, too."

"He did," said Marquez. "The periods are about 7.68 hours for Phobos, and about 30.24 for Deimos."

Norla wondered how Marquez had known that—and then remembered he was a ship's captain who had just had a lot of free time in hand—while heading toward Mars. Of course the man had done his homework.

The main thing was, it all held together. It was lunatic, from start to finish—but there it was. She could understand why Koffield had wanted the rest of them to walk through it all. Doubting his own sanity was in and of itself a sign of sanity, when the answer was this crazy. If this much time and effort was poured into reaching *her*, personally, across such time and distance, it would be hard not to wonder if she were deluding herself, if her ego was running away with itself, and dragging her along with it.

"So, you must have done the math by now," Sparten was saying to Koffield. "Where on Mars?"

"Believe me, I want everyone checking my figures on this," said Koffield. "And it took me longer to set up the problem than it did to run the numbers. But, the results I got were"—he read them off his datapad, slowly and carefully—"eighty-nine degrees, fifty-three minutes, eighteen seconds west, and one degree, thirty minutes, twenty-five seconds south."

"Where's that?" Bolt asked. "What's it near?"

"Just north of Calydon Channel," Koffield said. "About five kilometers east of the Mariner City ruins."

"That tell you anything?" Bolt asked.

It seemed to Norla that Koffield stiffened, just slightly. "I beg your pardon?" he replied.

"Ah, do you know anything, sir? I mean, about what's at that location?"

"I do," Koffield replied. "But I'm not ready to discuss it."

"You just got done telling us there wasn't any more point to keeping secrets," said Sparten.

Koffield looked at Sparten, his expression utterly flat and calm. But Norla would not have wanted to be on the receiving end of that gaze. "You're right," he said at last.

"No more need for keeping secrets *that belong to us*. It happens that there might be—might be—another party's secret that came into my possession by chance. If it becomes necessary to divulge what I know—I will speak. Otherwise, I will not."

There was silence in the compartment for a heartbeat, and then another, as Koffield looked at Sparten, and Sparten stared back. At last the younger man nodded, and then busied himself by looking at whatever happened to be on his datapad's screen.

Norla remembered rumors—not rumors, not even rumors of rumors, but something closer to spacer's folklore, stuff she had heard when she had last been in the Solar System. Sparten wouldn't have been likely to hear it. The story was that the Chronological Patrol had once had some sort of installation on Mars, one they wanted kept very private indeed. There were endless variations on that theme, but that was the basic tale. It would be enough to explain Koffield's reaction. He wouldn't very much like the idea of betraying his old outfit.

"So you're figuring for us to go down there, uh, sir?" asked Lira Wu, plainly not liking the idea.

"Yes," said Koffield, nodding. "Not all of us. It will be a small team. We'll need to leave many, if not most, of the group in orbit. I'm going to ask for volunteers to contact me privately in the next day or so."

"Ah, sir—what about the one-use-only rule?" asked Bolt. A lander that had been to Mars wasn't supposed to go further than planetary orbit to bring the crew up for decontamination and return to their orbital craft. The lander was supposed to be sent on a destructive reentry trajectory. "Or are we breaking enough other rules that one more doesn't matter?"

"It matters," said Marquez. "There's breaking rules for good reasons, when you're ready to take the consequences, and then there's unleashing an interplanetary killer plague. That rule we don't break." He turned to Koffield. "But I can't afford to give one of my landers away for nothing. What about it, Admiral?"

Koffield looked at Marquez. "It might be both small

landers. If there is a planet-side emergency, it might well be that the second lander would have to go in for a rescue."

"Suppose the *second* lander runs into trouble too?" Bolt asked.

Koffield looked to Bolt and turned his palms up, empty. "Obviously, the *Cruzeiro do Sul* couldn't go down after her, or else we could all be marooned on Mars for good. If the second lander fails, that's that. So if we go down, we'll definitely lose one lander, and possibly two."

Koffield looked back at Marquez. "I can't in good conscience offer to buy or replace your landers, because I would have no way to pay for them. You know better than I do, Captain Marquez—I own barely more than the clothes I'm standing up in. I lost nearly everything the first time I was marooned in time, and lost most of the remainder the second. The Planetary Executive of Solace did provide me with a certain amount of discretionary funding—but nearly all of it has gone to paying for our transport on Earth—and to buying, as quietly and discreetly as I could, the specialized equipment we'll need for Mars. But the government of Solace *did* send us on this trip, and thus, in effect, hired your ship. I believe they would compensate you—though there is no way for me to guarantee that. And we might not make it back to Solace, for whatever reason. You might not *want* to go back there—and I couldn't blame you. But I believe they would compensate you. That's the best I can offer."

Norla raised her eyebrows. Koffield had just admitted his poverty, and his own lack of authority outside the group, in front of his whole command. Plainly, he had felt he had no choice but to play it absolutely straight with Marquez. In that, he was probably right. Marquez knew the score as well as Koffield did. *No sense in any of us trying to kid each other anymore,* she thought. Marquez nodded. "You're asking me to take lots of chances," he said. "A lot of chances." He considered for a moment.

Norla watched Koffield's face. There was a whisper of

desperation behind his hard and determined expression. If Marquez said no—

"We'll use the *São Paulo* first," Marquez said at last. "I never did like the way she handled on docking anyway."

CHAPTER FOURTEEN

FALLING DOWN

"I thought I'd get to go," Marquez said once again, standing in the hatchway between the *Rio de Janeiro* and the *São Paulo*. Jerand Bolt had to shoulder past them as he carried more gear into the *SP*. Bolt would have had to try hard not to listen in to their conversation—and he wasn't interested in trying hard at all.

"Small team," Koffield said again. "Besides, you're the only dropship captain we've got."

"Besides you."

"I think it's obvious I have to go," Koffield said. "DeSilvo's been sending messages to me. There might be something else down there that only I could spot, and—"

"I know," Marquez said, looking profoundly unhappy. "I know. It makes sense. I have to stay. I also know we couldn't stop you going no matter what."

You could probably still stop me, Jerand thought. He volunteered—everyone had volunteered—but he was having second thoughts, right on schedule. The idea of visiting Mars had been appealing in the abstract, but the closer they got to making the run, the less abstract it got. He carried the last of the gear into the lower deck of the *São Paulo* and started securing it.

Norla Chandray stuck her head out of the upper

deck, the pilot's cabin. "Getting close to ready?" she asked.

Bolt hooked a thumb toward Koffield at the airlock. "Still saying their good-byes."

"Oh, for the love of—" Norla muttered something under her breath, then spoke up again, in very carrying tones. "Admiral!" she called out. "Insertion burn in twenty minutes, and we've got a lot to do. We've got to button up now!"

"All right," Koffield said. He stuck out his hand to Marquez. "See you on the other side," he said.

Bolt didn't care for that turn of phrase under the current circumstance. It was an old dropship crewman's farewell, and meant nothing more than the other side of the timeshaft wormhole. Under the current circumstances, however, the other side could mean certain other things.

The two men shook hands. Koffield moved back from the hatch and swung it shut, then stepped back through the inner lock hatch and sealed it as well. He checked the lock's status display. "Airlock sealed and secure. *Rio de Janeiro* lock shows sealed and secure."

"Right!" Norla called out, her head still sticking down through the hatch. "Stand by for cross-check." Her head disappeared, then they heard her voice through the ship's intercom system. "*Rio de Janeiro* confirms airlocks sealed and secured on both ships. Clear for hard-dock unlatch." A loud series of clunks and bangs signaled that the hard-dock latches were withdrawn.

"Disengaging soft latches," Norla reported. "Using outgassing for separation." The second set of latches released with somewhat less noise and drama, and then, with an absurdly loud "pop," the two ships pushed away from each other, driven apart by the released air pressure between the two hatches. The *São Paulo* was clear, at the start of what would be her last flight. That would be all right—so long as it wasn't the last flight for her crew.

"Let's go watch," Koffield said, and headed up the ladder to the pilot deck. Bolt followed along.

The *São Paulo*'s pilot deck was formed by the upper third of the ship's cylindrical body, and the rounded overhead cap on the cylinder. It was close to being a fully glassed-in cockpit, with large portholes—windows, really—set into the rounded overhead bulkhead, and into the wraparound wall of the cylinder. Norla was front and center in the pilot's station. The hatch to the lower deck was in the center of the deck, and two other operator stations were arranged, 120 degrees to either side of the pilot's chair. Norla Chandray, intent on maneuvering the *São Paulo* away from the *Rio de Janeiro* and *Cruzeiro do Sul*, paid them no mind as she made some fine adjustment. Then she glanced back over her shoulder. "Secure yourselves for maneuvering," she said.

"You to the port seat, I think, Mr. Bolt," said Koffield.

"Yes, sir," he said. As was the convention on cylindrical ships, port and starboard were based on the position of the pilot's station. He busied himself with seat belts and straps for a moment, and then took the time to look out, and up, at the universe.

The view was spectacular.

Toward starboard and the rear, the combined bulk of the *Cruzeiro do Sul* and the *Rio de Janeiro*, still docked together, took up half the sky. The two ships were gleaming white cylinders framed against the jet-black sky, their portholes glowing with warm yellow light from their interiors, their red and green close-in nav lights blinking slowly on and off.

The two ships began to recede as the *SP* pulled herself away. Jerand Bolt was surprised to find himself choked up inside. Somehow, those warm, white, safe ships, framed in the velvet darkness, looked like home, like the best and last home he would ever see.

He turned his gaze forward, looking over Norla's shoulder. There, slowly growing larger even as the *Cruzeiro* and *Rio* fell behind, was Mars, now about the size of a full moon as seen from Earth.

Once, he knew, the planet had been red, and, after that, blue and green and white, the colors of a living world with oceans and plants and ice caps. There had been, for all too brief a time, fields and forests, clear-running streams, skies of bluish-purple and puffy white clouds instead of the salmon-pink produced by fine-grained airborne dust.

Now a sickly grey-green prevailed on the land, some of the old red was returning, and the oceans were cold and grey-green, flecked with ice, laden with leached-out minerals, home to nothing more attractive than huge mats of poisonous algae. The forests were stumps and rotted wood, the rivers flowed with green-brown water choked with more algae, and there was nothing on the planet clean enough to show as white. Even the ice caps were a dirty grey.

The Great Failure, indeed.

"What about surveillance?" Norla asked. "Can we talk about that now?"

Bolt had been thinking the same thing. There was still a strict Interdict on visiting Mars, and damn good reasons for it, too. It stood to reason there would be some sort of watch kept.

Koffield had been unwilling to discuss the matter until they were clear of the other ships. He was, after all, ex-Intelligence. Plainly he was very big on the concept of "need to know."

"Follow the flight plan, and we should be all right," Koffield said.

"Unless we're blown out of the sky," Norla said. "It's Deimos and Phobos, isn't it? By strange chance, the flight plan you gave me keeps Mars between us and both satellites the whole way down."

There was a minute of silence. "All right," he said. "It's time I briefed you. It's Deimos and Phobos. Or at least it was, two hundred years ago, last time *I* got the briefing. What they told me was that, back when the Interdict started, they were still dealing with the tail end of a squatters' rebellion. People who didn't want to get kicked off, or were determined to land on the planet and settle, in spite of the plagues. The problems were temporary, and they were damned if anyone was going to chase them off just because of a little mold problem."

Norla laughed. "That sounds familiar," she said.

"Doesn't it? In any event, the squatter rebels kept shooting down any free-flying Interdict vehicles, so they built hardened bases on both satellites. Dug in deep. Even a fair-sized nuclear weapon wouldn't do more than melt the sensors on the surface, and those could be replaced in a few hours. So Deimos and Phobos watch the planet, and a zone of space twenty degrees around it, and sends an alert if they spot anything. Both Phobos Station and Deimos Station are automated. Neither one can do a shoot-down on its own, but they can get authorization from Interdict Command back on the Moon, and then fire at will. The stations won't fire at anything that's landing, just in case it's misreading the situation—and besides, the odds are pretty good that Mars will save Interdict Command the trouble of killing whoever lands."

"What about free-flyers?" Norla asked. "Deimos and Phobos can't cover the whole planet."

"No, you're right. You can't see Phobos at all from the ground if you get a good distance from the equator, or Deimos either if you go well to the north or south." Koffield shrugged. "But there aren't any practical *trajectories* departing from the polar regions that the satellites can't track—and the poles aren't exactly the most pleasant places on the planet. The North Pole is ice floating on water, and there's some pretty nasty weather down south. Still, if they were doing things right, there would be a free-flying observation platform in high-altitude polar orbits. But *are* they doing things right?"

Koffield shook his head and answered his own question. "I don't know. It's been two thousand years since the Failure, and two hundred since I got a partial briefing as part of my Intelligence Service indoctrination. But it's damned hard to keep an operation that requires human oversight going for that long. You could set a team of ArtInts on the job, and they'd never quit—but you'd need human authorization for a shoot-down. My guess? Human nature has taken its toll. After a while the people on the ground stopped shooting down the spy satellites, because the people on the ground have all died of the slight mold problem, or something worse. There was still the problem with damn-fool tourists—but most of them died on the surface, or back on their own ships, if they made it to orbit. The problem of illegal landings tended to solve itself, in a very grim way—and so the people in charge relaxed a bit. More than likely, the Interdict system got scaled back during a budget review, and then revived after some sort of scare, but never got fully rebuilt, so now it's running on full automation, and they're low on spare parts.

"Someone looking for an excuse to save money would figure the satellite stations don't actually have to spot the landing or the takeoff, so long as they tracked a ship on a trajectory with a track that stopped or started on the surface. The satellites could spot a launch coming over the horizon, even if they didn't spot it on takeoff. That would be good enough, and a lot cheaper."

"So, they won't shoot at us until we're leaving," said Bolt. "That's comforting."

"We'll just have to time our launch so that we stay out of view from Deimos and Phobos all the way up, that's all," Koffield said calmly. "Once we're past Deimos's orbit, we'll be all right."

"Boy, that's even more comforting," Bolt muttered.

"If *that* makes you feel good, you'll love this," said Norla. "Right now, we've got the propellant tanks at 84 percent full."

Normally, the *São Paulo* and her sister ships used a reactionless drive, using a system that produced energy by reacting stored propellant. It was highly efficient, and the reactionless engines could run for days or weeks at a time if need be—but the reactionless drive could not produce anything like enough thrust per second to carry the ship to a planetary landing, let alone take off again. At such times, the ship burned the same propellant through good old-fashioned rocket engines, generating much higher thrust per second—at much lower efficiency per liter of propellant. In short, the rocket system was a fuel hog. Norla didn't want to use it a millisecond longer than she had to. It was a long way to the closest fuel depot.

"We'll have to burn about half the tank on the return trip, boosting back to a trajectory well outside Deimos's orbit, where the *Cruzeiro* can reach us without getting shot at, maybe," Norla went on. "But if we've to fly around looking for whatever the hell it is down there, we'll have to do it at high-hover, which translates into burning propellant just to stand still. Do that too long, and we don't get back. If I get down to tanks at 53 percent before we're on the ground, I'm doing a midair abort straight back to orbit."

"No! We land even if we can't get back."

Norla was surprised. It was not Koffield talking, but Bolt.

"We could still radio back information to the *Cruzeiro do Sul*," Bolt added.

"What stake have *you* got in it?" Norla demanded.

"The same one you do," he said. "You think there's a guy down there who could save lots of people, or maybe just a lead that could point us on the next stage toward finding him. If we bail out today, our odds on managing a second landing attempt go *way* down. Deimos will *have* to spot part of our departure track, and there will be that much less propellant to go around. Besides, once we hit atmosphere, the ship is contaminated—right, Admiral?"

Koffield nodded. "That's right," he said.

"Do you think Captain Marquez would allow even enough contact to do refueling between his ship and this one if we had mold spores on the hull?"

Norla frowned. "No."

"So that would leave them with the *Rio* to make the same try, except Deimos would be alerted, and the *Rio* wouldn't have any rescue backup."

"I see your point," Norla conceded.

"One other thing," said Bolt. "If what I heard was

right, this DeSilvo guy made at least three round-trips on one-shot cargo landers, and came back to orbit on personnel stages."

"So?"

"So those landers should still be down there, along with whatever gear they carried down, and whatever else was abandoned at the site—and those landers carry propellant hoses, same as we do. Those landers were designed to do landing and nothing else. These boats are mostly for space-to-space, with a landing capability compromised into the design. The landers probably had a better propellant reserve. Their tanks won't be empty. We *might* be able to rig something to refuel us on the surface."

"Would the propellant still be good after all this time?"

Bolt shrugged. "Why not? It's in the same kind of tanks as on this ship, and it's the same propellant. According to the logs I checked, these ships rode with full tanks all the way to Solace and back—more than two hundred years, ship's time."

"You've done some thinking on all this," said Norla.

"Yes, ma'am," Bolt agreed, but said no more.

"Admiral?"

"You're the pilot," he said. "It'll be a split-second decision, and we won't have time to debate. The ship will do whatever you decide. But there is one point I would like to add. We're coming in from the west, with the descent timed so that Deimos won't be able to see us in flight. Deimos will rise in the east about six hours after we land, and will have line of sight on us for about sixty hours after that, until it sets in the west."

"Right. We can't launch until then," Norla said.

"Won't there be instruments on Deimos able to spot the ship on the ground?" Bolt asked.

Koffield shrugged. "If they knew exactly where to look, and used extremely powerful instruments, maybe."

"But they could just run a comparator," Bolt objected. "Tell it to tag any differences since the last image run—and they'd spot recently landed ships."

"Wouldn't work. Mars has lots of weather. Clouds, winds, rain. Weather not only hides things while it's happening—it leaves the surface changed. Things get wetter, hills erode, mold growths shift and change. But getting back to my point. Deimos will be just below the eastern horizon when we put down. If we do scratch the landing and immediately head back to orbit, we'll have to fly east—flying more or less right at Deimos as she rises, and we'll be boosting at full power. That, I think, they could detect."

Norla's face went white. "I hadn't thought of that."

"Well, now you have," Koffield said calmly.

"And I think you've both made your point," she said. "When we go in, we go in all the way." Norla checked her displays. "And we're going to do it soon. Initial insertion burn in five minutes, mark."

The engines shut down, and the *São Paulo* slid smoothly into her transfer orbit. "Secure from maneuvering," Norla announced.

"Mr. Bolt, go below and get started with your pressure suit," said Koffield. "I'll come down and help you into the burn-off suit in a few minutes."

"Yes, sir," Bolt replied, with very clear enthusiasm. He had no intention of entering the Martian atmosphere until he had a full pressure suit on, sealed, and powered up. If something went sour with the ship's cabin pressure, he did not want to try breathing Martian air. And he was just as happy for a chance to do something besides watch that damn planet get bigger in the viewport.

He reopened the floor hatch and headed down the ladder to the lower deck, careful to reseal the hatch behind him. This was very much a time to make sure everything got done right.

With that in mind, he set carefully to work checking over his suit. It was important to make sure it was right in every detail. If all went well, he'd be in it for about the next sixty to seventy-two hours.

If things went a little bit wrong—well, he might be in it a lot longer than that.

• • •

Norla Chandray had half expected Koffield to start some conversation, once Bolt went down below, but he didn't. Whatever the loquacious, enthusiastic part of him had been, that part was gone now, sliding beneath the waves. Now he was simply quiet, watching, studying the globe of Mars dead ahead, keeping an eye on the detector displays.

She remembered her first trip with him aboard the *Cruzeiro*, in transit from the outer edge of the Solacian system to Solace itself. It had felt like pulling teeth to get him to say anything at all. She had never felt more alone than she had on the first part of the trip, with Anton Koffield for company. Things had changed since then, of course—but it was hard not to see the same self-imposed calm, the same sense of preparation for a struggle, in that face that worked so hard to give nothing away.

But maybe, somehow, he felt as if he could be alone with her, and that was why he had sent Bolt away. No, that wasn't quite right. Not alone *with* her—he felt he could be alone when she was present. Bolt would intrude, and she would not. *I'm not sure if that's a high compliment, or a dreadful insult. Assuming I'm reading his silence right.* She smiled at herself, and the convolutions she was inventing out of a man staring out a window. But there was *something* there, something more than just a quiet man.

He glanced over at her and saw her expression. "What have you got to smile about?" he asked in gentle tones.

She shook her head. "It's nothing. A whole tangled knot of things that probably aren't what they seem anyway. Just nerves and worry."

"Two concepts I know quite well," he said.

The pilot's cabin was silent for a moment, but for the purr of the ventilator and the low hum of machinery and electronics. The two of them stared at the planet up ahead, the world that had broken so many hearts, and lives, so many years before.

"Do you think he's down there?" she asked at last.

He shook his head. "I know it sounds silly after all we've been through, but I think that would be too easy. No, he's not there. There'll be another turning of the road."

"But you only took two of us along," she said. "A ground party of three, when the ship could hold four."

"The ship could hold eight, for that matter, if we didn't mind taking more risks than necessary. Three seemed enough people to endanger—but yes, we do have the room if he's down there. I accounted for that. But he's not down there. I don't have evidence that makes me say that, but it's my gut reaction."

"So what *is* down there?"

And the wall went back up, at least part of the way. His face stiffened, and his face turned harder—but then came a wan, tired smile. "It was hard enough 'fessing up about Deimos," he said. "But I made promises long ago, and I'll try to keep them, if I can. But I'll make a promise to you, too—I'll tell you what I can, when I can. Fair enough?"

"As fair as I'm going to get," said Norla.

They sat a while longer, watching the bloated corpse of a world growing larger in the viewport.

Marquez watched as the *São Paulo* moved away, down and toward the nightmare world below. What Koffield had told him about Interdict Command had him worried. There was no way they could know for sure that Deimos and Phobos were the only watchposts. And they could not be absolutely sure they could keep to a schedule that would prevent the satellites from getting a look at them. And their departure track would lead straight back to the *Cruzeiro do Sul*. Anyone who decided to take a potshot at the *São Paulo* might well decide to take out the *Cruzeiro do Sul* as well.

Marquez shook his head and sighed. Waiting and worrying were professional skills for wormhole dropship captains. He wished to hell he could learn how to get good at them.

• • •

Norla Chandray, stuffed into her inner pressure suit and outer burn-off suit, followed Jerand Bolt back up the ladder to the pilot's deck of the *São Paulo*. She had to fight against the air pressure inside the stiff suit just to lift her arms high enough to reach the next rung of the ladder. Norla had worn lots of pressure suits before, but never one this heavy-duty, or with this high an internal air pressure—or with a complete second clown-red burn-off suit worn over the main suit.

She clumped her way up the ladder. She glanced over to Koffield, seated to starboard, then at Bolt, to port. Both of them looked as absurd as she felt. Koffield's outer suit was bright blue, and Bolt's a screaming yellow. Maybe the bright colors would help them see each other, and be able to identify each other easily, once they were on the ground. Right now they looked like luridly colored inflatable toys.

She knelt awkwardly to close the floor hatch, and then waddled over to her pilot's station and dropped gratefully into her command chair. She felt as if she were sprawling up halfway out of it. It was a distinct struggle to get her seat restraints properly secured.

Suddenly, she was taken back to a moment in her childhood, during a family winter trip to Moscow. It had been bitterly cold, and her parents had dragged her from museum to museum, shrine to shrine, church to church, relentlessly determined, as always, that she see everything that there was to see. They had crowded onto trams, trains, buses, in and out of restaurants and tourist sites and hotels, and always they barely fit. For years she had been convinced that the people in Moscow were simply larger than anyone else—until, years later, it had dawned on her that it was just the winter coats, thick with insulation, brightly colored to cheer up the drabness of winter. The coats and gloves and hats and boots were so big and bulky that everyone simply took up more room.

Norla smiled at the memory, and took it as a good sign. After all, that tourist trip had been grueling as hell, but she had lived through it. Why not this trip? She looked through the forward viewport, at the looming planet, taking up virtually the entire view.

"Very well, gentlemen," she said as she turned toward her controls. "Let's go see the sights. Initiating deorbit sequence."

Mars grew ever larger in the viewports, swelling wider, taking up the entire forward viewport, and the port and starboard viewports as well. It was something of a relief when Norla pitched the ship to a stern-first, facedown attitude so the engines could be directed forward for braking. That at least swung them about so there were stars to look at again. But it wasn't long before Mars started climbing back into view in the bottom of Norla's viewport. The braking burn went smoothly, for all of being hard and fast, a four-gee kick in the stomach. It slowed them enough to kill most of their forward motion, and allowed them to drop into the atmosphere at a low enough velocity to keep the ship from melting because of air friction. The less atmospheric heating, the less chance the Interdict ArtInts on Deimos would have of spotting an anomalous heat plume.

They felt the first faint thrill of vibration as the *São Paulo* hit atmosphere, then felt something more than mere vibration as their spacecraft slammed stern first into the atmosphere proper. The air around them began to glow, and the ride became distinctly rougher. They were buffeted hard, up and down, side to side, the *São Paulo* creaking and groaning as she adjusted to the stresses. Something started banging and rattling belowdecks as the gee forces built up. *Perfectly normal,* Norla told herself again and again. *Perfectly normal.* How could it be that there wasn't a spy platform overhead right now, and how could it be that it wouldn't see something as big and obvious as a spacecraft on reentry? *Try not to think about it.*

At last the banging and buffeting eased off, as did the gee forces. The airglow died away, and their view was clear.

The planet kept climbing up the horizon. Somehow,

at some point, they crossed that blurred line, more rooted in psychology than logic, that told her subconscious that Mars was a place they were already *at*, and traveling through, and not a place they were going *to*. They weren't in space any longer, but inside atmosphere, part of the world below.

The mighty landscape below was scrolling up past the forward viewport, from below Norla's feet on up to beyond her head. They were flying tail first and eyes down, literally hanging from their restraint harnesses, nothing but the viewports between them and the lurid landscape rolling past below them.

They were coming from the west, into the sunlit side of the planet. Norla looked up from her displays to watch for a moment, and gasped in astonishment as Pavonis Mons swept past. She knew it wasn't even the largest volcano on Mars, but still, it seemed to her that she had never seen anything quite so *large*. Once, for a brief time, the caldera had been a cratered ice lake, a vast year-round equatorial winter playground for the new Martians, but the mold and the lichens had taken hold there as well, and turned the caldera a grim greenish-black. But from this high up, the squalid growth merely added a dark and dramatic contrast to the huge structure.

Norla didn't have much time to play tourist. She hadn't flown a landing like this in a long time, and, when considered as a glider, the *São Paulo* made a superb brick wall. She was managing—barely—to stay within the plotted trajectory, but the deeper they drilled into atmosphere, the harder the ship fought her. The buffeting returned, but with a different rhythm to it, a different, deeper, slower feel.

The São Paulo was dropping like a thrown rock, arcing down toward its target, tossed about by the upper atmosphere's wind currents.

They were losing forward momentum faster than projected, that much was plain. "We're going to land short," she called out.

"How bad?" Koffield shouted. Even over the suit's

headphones, it was hard to hear him over all the noise and vibration.

"About five or ten kilometers," she shouted back.

"There's no point going if we're not on target," Koffield called. "We can't walk cross-country to get where we're going. Not on this planet."

"We'll just have to do a high-hover longer and watch our propellant," she called out. As if she wouldn't have been watching anyway.

"Do your best," Koffield called out.

Not the most helpful suggestion. Norla watched her ranges, rates, altitudes, velocities, air pressures, trying to juggle all the variables by gut and guess as much as by the gauges.

They were coming up on their target now, or a bit short of it, the landscape below slowing its forward motion—but starting to get noticeably closer with every second.

"Here comes the city," Bolt shouted.

Norla swore and stole a glance out the viewport, just in time to see the jumbled ruins of Mariner City sliding past. There wasn't time to gather more than a quick impression of vast and broken structures, blanketed in the omnipresent layer of mold, lichen, and dust. Never mind, the tracking cameras would catch it all. She turned back to her displays.

"What the devil was that?" Koffield called out.

"What? What?" Norla glanced up again, but saw nothing but the eastern limit of the city sliding up past the top of her viewport.

"A crater. A big one, very fresh, right in the middle of the city. Looked more like blast than impact."

Norla didn't have time to worry about it. They were losing forward velocity far too fast—and dropping faster with every second. She could look at it on playback. If they lived that long.

"Going to pitch over," she announced. "Hang on. I don't have enough propellant to do this gently."

She hit the attitude thrusters and slammed the *São Paulo*'s nose up hard. The view out the viewport swung down and away, and they could see up, into the stars again.

The *São Paulo* was a cylinder and had been traveling base first. Now she was flying sideways, presenting a lot more surface area—and thus generating a lot more drag. The pitch-up was necessary, but it slowed the lander even more. Not good.

The pitch-up had left the *São Paulo* flying upright, but with the pilot's station facing aft. She could watch through the video screens, but it would be better all around if she flew face forward. "Doing a roll for visual," Norla announced. She blipped the thrusters hard, twice, to start the spin and then kill it almost at once. She pitched the ship forward just a trifle, angling it to bring the nose down about ten degrees, to give her a better viewing angle—and also to bring the main engines around to an attitude where they'd give her some forward velocity.

And she needed it. The *São Paulo* was now falling nearly straight down, and they were many kilometers from their target point. It would have been nice to know what the hell was *at* their target point—but that was too much to ask. All she could do was her best to get them there, and watch the terrain between here and there.

Of course, she could give herself a little help. She activated up the heads-up display, and a range-and-rate projection appeared on the viewport, with a red blinking dot indicating the target point, almost on the horizon.

"Stand by," she shouted. "Time to light the candle."

She activated the engine activation system, and watched the confirmation display show the aeroshell withdrawing, and the engine bells extending. Instantly, the buffeting grew worse as the aeroshell withdrew, exposing the jumbled plumbing underneath. When the engine bells extended, the drag on the base of the craft spiked up and the *São Paulo* nearly pitched forward before Norla caught it with a vicious blast of the attitude jets.

She powered up the rocket engines and gritted her teeth as their coughing roar filled the *São Paulo*, drowning out all the other noises. She hated the sound of rocket engines.

But noisy and inefficient or not, at least they did the job. She could feel the gee forces build as she throttled them to 25 percent power. It was enough to get them moving forward, and slow their descent to a more or less survivable rate. They were still going down, but at something less than the speed of a dropped rock.

"See anything?" Norla shouted up.

"Stand by," Koffield shouted. "Bringing up the long-range camera."

Norla allowed herself a split-second glance at the display screens, but Koffield was plainly still working to get the thing targeted. The view was jinking wildly around every corner of the landscape.

"All right," he called. "Camera slaved to the targeting system and at maximum magnification."

Norla flicked her gaze down to the camera display again. A collection of murky shapes, nothing more distinct. "Nothing! I can't make out anything. Watch that screen for me," she shouted back.

But the long-range camera was locked on the exact coordinates they had derived from the damned-fool riddles. Those coordinates could be wrong, or just not precise enough, for any of a half dozen reasons.

"Bolt! I need your eyes out the window, watching for anything that might be what we're here for."

"Doing that already," he said. "Ah, any chance of extending the landing gear?"

"Not until I have to," she answered. "This thing is draggy enough as it is."

And if you don't extend the gear, you can pull an abort that much faster. No need to waste time retracting them again. Norla wasn't sure if the voice in her head was chiding her, or trying to be helpful.

She watched her rates, and saw she was close to drifting high. She pitched forward a trifle more, translating more of the thrust into forward motion instead of lift against gravity.

The *São Paulo* slid forward and down, the landscape

an uninterrupted vista of grey-green mold blanketing the land. Off to the south, Norla could see the cold grey-blue waters of Calydon Channel, part of the long narrow finger of the Mariner Sea.

Those waters connected to the Northern Ocean, off to the north and east from here. But the channel and sea and ocean were slowly fading away, the water evaporating, falling as rain on mold and moss and lichen that held it long enough for it to leach back into the rock. More water was being frozen in at the poles, and more still was simply evaporating and disassociating to space. One day the waters would all be gone again, and even the ever-present mold blanket would die, and Calydon Channel would go back to being Calydon Fossa, part of the once-again bone-dry Valles Marineris, and the Northern Ocean would simply be lowlands again.

"Admiral! We're awfully close. Anything yet?"

"Possibly. I still can't make out what I'm seeing."

"Damned mold covers everything," Bolt muttered.

"That's not exactly a shocking discovery," Norla answered. "Bolt, you see anything?"

"Just mold on everything," he replied.

"You said that already," she muttered.

They were now not more than twelve kilometers up, the altitude air transports flew on Earth, and a bare ten kilometers from their supposed destination. The heads-up display's flashing dot on the horizon was in plain sight, dead ahead—but precious little to be seen besides the flashing dot. There was nothing for it but to press on toward a landing at that point. Norla glanced at her propellant levels. Seventy-two percent, and dropping. The later they left any course change, the more propellant it would cost them to make it—and the shorter their range of action would be. Every second that passed was another set of options burning up right along with their precious propellant.

Norla brought up a dynamic overlay display of her current landing footprint, a lopsided circle that showed the limits of her choices, given current altitude, velocity, and remaining propellant. It shrank even as she watched.

So many things could have gone wrong. They could have calculated the landing point wrong. They could have misread those damned riddles—why the hell had they bet their lives on what *riddles* had to say? Whatever DeSilvo had put here could have simply vanished after sitting on this hell-world for a hundred-plus years. Or DeSilvo could have made a mistake—or set the whole thing as a trap, some sort of revenge on—

"There!" Koffield cried out.

"Where?" Norla said. Koffield was behind her, they were both strapped down, and pointing wasn't going to do much good.

"Let me put a targeting circle on it."

A small flashing red circle added itself to the jumble of lines, symbols, numbers, and letters on Norla's heads-up, and the nav computer popped up a trajectory that could—just—get them there. She still couldn't see whatever it was that Koffield had spotted, but there wasn't time to ask questions. She brought the *São Paulo* around to her new heading and started riding down the trajectory.

She checked her propellant—61 percent. It was going to be tight. "What was it you saw?" she yelled.

"A building. A six-sided building that looked something like—"

"I see it!" There it was, dead center in the blinking red target circle. Six-sided, all right, and bearing a strong resemblance to DeSilvo's false tomb on Greenhouse.

No doubt. No doubt at all could remain.

Propellant 59 percent. Half a kilometer up. Get this thing on the ground *fast*, while they still had something in the tank, or they were going to be permanent residents. She throttled back, let them fall faster.

"Landing gear!" Bolt shouted again.

Norla felt the words like a kick to her solar plexus. She had come damned near to forgetting. She flipped open the safety door over the control and pulled the big red lever marked EXTEND LANDING GEAR. With a thrum of hydraulics and the whir of machinery, the four landing legs pushed their way out of the *São Paulo*'s cylindrical body and unfolded outward to lock into place with four solid thunks. The GEAR DOWN indicator came on.

Now Norla was glad of the extra drag, glad of anything that helped slow them down. Three hundred meters up, and they were descending too fast. Propellant 56. Don't go so easy on the thrust, you buy a crash landing.

The building was dead ahead, not fifty meters from where the targeting computer put their landing point. Hell and all! There was a boulder half the size of the *São Paulo* there. She pitched forward by a hair, and bought just enough forward motion to clear it.

But now she had to kill that forward motion, or risk the top-heavy lander toppling as soon as the gear touched. She tapped on the attitude jets, and prayed she wasn't overcorrecting.

The engines were kicking up dust and debris and hunks of roasted mold, all blowing into the sky, half-blinding her. Still coming in too fast, but it was too late to correct. Flare it out. Propellant at 54. Gun it! One last shot to kill their fall and—

The *São Paulo* hung motionless in midair, two meters above the Martian surface. Norla cut the main engines and the lander dropped down onto Mars, the gear struts smoothly soaking up the landing shocks.

"We're here," said Anton Koffield.

CHAPTER FIFTEEN

THE RUINED WORLD

Koffield and Chandray watched over his shoulder as Jerand Bolt sat at the number three command station and worked the playback on the landing video, the images showing on the big display directly in front of him.

Jerand had been all for heading out the airlock at once, but Koffield insisted they stay put for a while. They could look things over without taking needless risks, let the dust from their landing settle, and also take a closer look at what they had flown over on their way in.

"Slow it down there," Koffield said, leaning in.

Jerand made the adjustment. The images of Mariner City—or rather, its ruins—slowly eased past the field of view. A blackened circle, a crater, moved toward the center of the display.

"Freeze it," Koffield said.

"That's no impact crater," said Norla. "A blind man could see that."

"You're right, it isn't," said Koffield.

Jerand studied the image. Inside the circular zone of destruction, it looked as if the ground, and all the streets and buildings, had been lifted and dropped. Whatever it was that had done the lifting had torn through the center of the crater, leaving shards of street and building pointed straight up around the hole, as if someone had left a plate of glass on the ground and punched a hole in it from underneath, leaving a sharp circle of broken glass shards stabbing up into the sky. The building and structures had been knocked down from the center outward. "Something under the city blew up and collapsed an underground structure."

"Yes," said Koffield.

Jerand looked at Koffield. It would have been hard enough to read his expression when they were both in normal street clothes, but through the visors of their pressure suits, it was almost impossible. *One mask over another,* he thought. "Sir, you know more about this than you are saying. That's obvious. With all due respect, we're here in a place where dead cities blow up and one breath of the local air could kill us. When will our mission—and our lives—be more important than whatever hundred-year-old secret you have?"

Jerand was ready for another of Koffield's frosty explosions, or worse, one of his careful and correct replies, sharp and cutting as a bag of broken glass. But Koffield surprised him.

"It's not so much a hundred-year-old secret," he said thoughtfully. "It's my recollection of a bit of—of *folklore*—I heard closer to *two* hundred calendar years ago. And the story was centuries old even then. It might be something, it might be no more than a ghost story—though I must confess that the core of the story is starting to sound a lot more believable than that."

"But it was important enough that the first thing you wanted to look at was the playback of the city flyover, before we even looked at our landing site."

It wasn't a question, but Koffield answered it anyway. "Yes."

"Are you done?" Chandray asked Jerand.

The question was pointed, but her tone was not. He got the impression that she would have asked Koffield exactly the same questions, if given the chance. "Yes," he answered.

"Good. The point is that something happened to the

city, and the Admiral thinks it might be significant to our mission. Do you have anything to add to your analysis of the explosion crater?"

"Well—it looks old, but it doesn't look *that* old. The dust and mold and debris in the center aren't anywhere near as thick as in the undisturbed areas."

"I agree," Norla said. "Anything else?"

Jerand shook his head. "Not that jumps out at me," he said.

"Admiral?"

Koffield shook his head. "Nothing. Except—except that this makes me more certain that *he's* not here."

"All right then," Chandray said. "Run the playback forward and pause it again just before the final landing sequence."

Jerand ran the recording forward and froze it again. Norla studied the image, and then used a stylus to draw two circles on it. "Our landing site, and the structure out there."

"Structures," Jerand said. "Plural." He drew more circles around several low, rounded hummocks, scattered about the immediate area of the main structure. There were at least seven of them that he could count. "Most of those are all just about the same size and shape. My guess is there's something hidden under each one."

"That makes sense," Koffield agreed.

"The one-shot landers," Norla said. "They must still be wherever they came down. DeSilvo must have thrown domes or tents over them to hide them from Deimos and Phobos."

"But he left the—the temple, whatever you want to call that six-sided thing—in plain sight."

"He had to risk leaving at least one calling card, for those who knew where to look," said Koffield. "But letting a half dozen landers accumulate over the years would be attracting just a bit too much attention. Besides, the temple, as you call it, is one low flat building the same color as the ground around it. It'd be pretty hard to spot from orbit."

"We had to get within two kilometers to notice it," Norla agreed. "Besides, there are lots of buildings on Mars. Why not one here? But let's take a closer look at it." She reached awkwardly around Bolt and worked the controls. She brought up a wire-frame version of what Bolt at first thought was the same structure, a transparent skeleton showing sides and angles. "Those data are the basic specs from DeSilvo's phony tomb on Greenhouse, the satellite in the Solace System where they do all the terraforming research," she said. "Height, width, depth. We've got enough views of this temple from our approach so that we ought to be able to get—there." The ship's computer generated a wire-frame model of the Martian temple, then overlaid it with the Greenhouse wire model. They matched almost perfectly. She brought up a photographic image with the label DESILVO TOMB and put it next to the Martian temple. "I'd say there was a pretty close family resemblance."

"They've got exactly the same size and shape, but the Greenhouse tomb is a lot fancier," said Bolt. "Polished rock. This one is just rough stone piled up. And the one on Greenhouse has a set of steps all around it. I don't see that here."

"The steps could be under the mold," said Chandray. "You're trying to say it's just an astonishing coincidence?"

"No, no. It's a sign all right. It's like that book—something you could only notice if you knew all about DeSilvo. I'm just sort of thinking out loud." He studied the images and spoke again. "There's not much mold on that temple, compared to everything else."

"Maybe he coated the temple with something that would slow the mold down," Chandray said. "Or maybe it's just that it hasn't been here that long."

"So now what?" Jerand asked.

"Now we go take a look inside that temple," Koffield said. "And find out what surprises the good doctor has left for us this time."

Out the hatch. Swing over to the ladder of handholds set into the side of the lander. Climb down with hands and feet, one rung at a time. Get to the bottom of the lander proper. Swing over again, onto a short section of ladder set into the landing leg. Get to the bottom. Set one foot on the ground—or rather on the crusting of mold. Then the other foot. That's all there was to it.

Norla felt a certain sense of disappointment. There should have been some drama to setting foot on Mars, on the planet known everywhere as the Ruined World, but she felt nothing. Perhaps it was that the landing had left her drained, unable to feel any further excitement. Or, more likely, it was the utter, stultifying drabness of the landscape, the endless grey-green carpet of mold that draped over everything.

She knew that "mold" was something of a misnomer. The stuff that carpeted so much of this world was in truth a metasymbiote: part mold, yes, but also part fungus, part moss, part algae, with bacteria, and even viral components, thrown into the mix for good measure. The biologists still didn't fully understand how the commingling had happened in the first place, or how it worked. They still hadn't fully succeeded in replicating it in the lab.

The blend of species shifted from place to place, in response to local conditions, but one variant or another of the symbiote-molds had adapted to nearly every part of the planet. And it had certainly adapted to this part. The symbiote-mold was a thick crust, the consistency of very brittle low-grade cardboard. The rocket burn had fried a good-sized hole through the crust, and Norla could see the heat-blackened rocks and soil of the original surface below. But it was hard to spot exposed rock or dirt anywhere else. The six-sided DeSilvo Temple was really the only thing that wasn't utterly engulfed by the horrid stuff, and there were already tufts and patches growing on it. From here it was plain to see how the matted carpet of the symbiote had slowly but surely swallowed up the stairs that did in fact surround the temple. Give the stuff enough time and years, and it would no doubt engulf the temple, as it had swallowed everything else.

Koffield was coming down the landing leg ladder, and

Bolt was just coming out of the lock. He paused to activate the lock controls and seal the outer lock door. A lot
of good that would do. The lander was already contaminated. Norla peered at the landing leg and wondered if
she was imagining it, or if there was already a thin film
of spores or worse accumulating on the metal there.

Koffield dropped to the surface and paused to look
around, just as she had. But then he looked up, and to
the east. "Good news there," he said, pointing. "Cloud
cover rolling in. With a little luck, we'll have a nice solid
overcast before Deimos rises."

He had a point, but a world clad completely in grey
had little appeal for Norla.

Bolt came down the landing leg ladder and hopped
off the bottom rung, landing with both feet. He turned
and looked around. "Well," he said. "Here we are. Now
what?"

Bolt apparently derived no more inspiration from the
landscape than she did. "Admiral?" she asked. "It's your
call."

He pointed to the temple. "We're here for that," he
said. "Let's go take a look." They started walking.

They left the lander, prepared to stay away for some
time, carrying all the equipment—mainly cameras and
data scanners—they might conceivably need. They had
the gear stowed in every pocket and equipment rack that
their suits provided. They would have to remain in their
suits for the duration of their stay anyway, and there
would be no point in their wasting time running back
and forth to the ship for this or that piece of hardware.

Their footing was surprisingly unsteady. The
symbiote-mold crust had left gaps and voids underneath
its flat surface, and the crust itself was not strong enough
to support their weight. It was like walking on old
crusted-over snow. One spot you stepped on would hold
your weight, but at another, indistinguishable spot, your
foot would break through. All of them fell at least once
in the hundred-odd-meter walk between the *São Paulo*
and the temple.

Norla went facefirst down into the stuff, the front of her suit—and her faceplate—covered with the horrible dusting of spores and other reproductive forms that had doomed this world. It was a deliberate act of will to keep breathing, safe inside her suit, rather than hold her breath. She didn't even want to imagine what would happen to her if she actually inhaled a lungful of it.

Fortunately, Bolt had thought to bring a whisk broom, leading to the incongruous sight of a yellow-clad balloon-man figure valeting a balloon-woman in red, while Koffield, all in blue, looked on.

The symbiote-mold carpet was by no means smooth and uniform. It was rumpled and furrowed, and here and there had collapsed under its own weight, exposing rocks and dirt underneath. Odd growths sprouted up, seemingly at random—orange spikes, dull red fronds, brown mushroomlike extrusions, half-meter-high clumps of long, knobbly, tapering grey-blue things that resembled the fingers of an emaciated giant, clawing up from under the ground. All of it was very much alive, vibrantly, vigorously so—and yet that landscape made Norla feel utterly surrounded by death.

The carpet *was* death—death in life, life that fed on the death of a whole world. She shivered in revulsion. The sooner they were away from this place, the better.

The "temple" wasn't much of a building. Up close, it was even more obvious how crudely it was made. The stone was rough, and one block was but a poor match for the next in terms of color and texture. There were cracks in the stone, and bits and pieces of it had crumbled out to fall on the platform that supported it. Tufts of mold bloomed from it here and there. The Greenhouse tomb had been of gleaming finished stone, with elaborate carving on the exterior panels. This was just a rough stack of cut rock.

"The work on this one wasn't up to DeSilvo's usual standards, was it?" asked Norla.

"It didn't have to be," said Koffield. "All it needed to do was have the same shape as the Greenhouse structure.

Besides, let's remember that this time he had to do it all himself—though with a lot of power machinery and robotic help, I'm sure."

The three of them walked around the structure, but one side was much like another. In fact, it seemed as if there were six blank walls, with no entrance.

"Well," said Norla, "the one on Greenhouse had one open side."

"Great. But this one doesn't. How do we get *into* this thing?" Bolt asked. He thought for a moment. "Or are we *supposed* to get into it? Maybe it's solid all the way through."

"Then what's it here for?" Koffield asked.

"I dunno. Maybe there's an inscription we missed on it somewhere, under a mold patch. Maybe it's a base for a statue that never got put up."

"Or one that's already been taken away," Norla said. "Suppose we're not the first ones here, and someone else got the whatever-it-is we're here to get?"

"Then we're out of luck," Koffield said calmly. "But I don't think that's it. We've already left a lot of signs that we've been here. Footprints, the landing burn. We'll leave more if we take a look at Mr. Bolt's hummocks. Anyone who came before us would leave the same sort of marks."

"The mold could have covered their marks up."

"Not quickly. The mold-symbiote accretes very slowly, once it's buried its substrate and absorbed the easily available water and nutrient. The temple has been here over a hundred years, and *it's* not engulfed yet. The hummocks are engulfed—but if they're meant as camouflage, DeSilvo would have encouraged the mold carpet—sprayed the coverings with nutrient or something."

"It doesn't look to me as if it needs all that much encouragement," Norla muttered. She thought for a moment. "We landed just west of the temple, right?"

"Right," said Koffield.

"All right. The Greenhouse tomb was lined up so that the open face pointed due west. So if this temple is a sort-of copy of *that* one, the western face should be the entrance—except DeSilvo put a door on this one. Against the mold, I suppose. Let's go take a look."

They walked back around the temple and stumbled their way up the buried stairs to face the western face of the structure.

"You were right," Koffield said, scraping off a clump of mold. "There's a handhold carved out of the rock here—and this panel seems to be hinged somehow on the other side." Koffield wrapped both hands around the handhold and pulled hard. The panel shifted very slightly, scraping against the stone floor of the temple.

Norla grabbed at the handle, Koffield reset his grip, and Bolt managed to wedge his hands into the narrow gap that had formed.

"All right," said Koffield. "Here we go. One, two, three!" They all pulled, and the panel swung open a few more centimeters.

"Hang on," said Bolt. "I think I can do better if I brace myself in to push instead of pulling." He shifted himself. "Okay, all set."

Koffield set his feet wide. "One, two, *three*!" The panel shifted again, a bit more. "One more time. Ready? One, two, *three*!"

The panel swung open to about ninety centimeters, and stopped dead. "I think we've got it wedged against something," Bolt said. "Piece of rock or something. But we could probably rig some sort of lever to force it wider if we had to."

"Never mind," said Norla. "That's wide enough to get through. That's all we need."

The way was open, but Norla suddenly realized she was not all that keen on going inside. By the look of it, Bolt was not eager, either. Mars was not a nice place, and it seemed unlikely that he was about to work up the nerve to step through when she held herself back. She moved to go in—and then stopped herself. "Sir?" She looked to Koffield. "Admiral—ah, Anton? Would you care to go in first?"

"Thank you—Norla. Yes. Yes I would."

He flicked on his suit's helmet lights and slid sideways

through the opening. Norla and Bolt switched on their own lights and followed.

Their helmet lights, and the shaft of gloom from the open door, were more or less enough to light the interior. Inside was a plain, bare room, utterly empty, the stone walls blank, rough, unfinished, undecorated. The chamber seemed to take up half the volume of the temple, with a long interior wall running north-south straight through the center of the structure. The long wall was built of three panels. Unlike the other walls, it was smoothed down and finished off. Their helmet light cast strange, shifting, looming shadows as they looked about the chamber.

"Not quite what I expected," Bolt said. "I was half thinking we'd see the old boy himself in an open coffin."

"Well, I wasn't expecting *that*, but this isn't exactly what I envisioned, either," said Norla.

"At the risk of being irritating, it's about what I thought we'd find," said Koffield. "He'd have to put more than one level of protection between his storehouse and an outside environment as hostile as this one. But come on, let's make sure the floor is clear. I don't want the inner door jammed up on another rock."

Norla looked again. She had missed it, perhaps thanks to the shadows and the bad lighting, but sure enough, there was a handle set into the center panel of the inside wall, and smooth, recessed hinges. A door. A glance at Bolt's expression gave her the small comfort of knowing she wasn't the only one who had missed it. She looked at the inner wall more closely, and it suddenly dawned on her that the inner wall was not stone at all, but some synthetic material. Not any standard plastic— supposedly the mold-symbiotes devoured those. Norla and Bolt picked up a few small pebbles that had fallen free of the walls and ceilings, then stood back as Koffield heaved at the inner door.

It swung open easily, wide enough to close flush against the left-side panel of the inner door.

"Oh hell," she said. "Not another one."

There was an inner door—a heavy, reinforced vault

door—behind the outer sheathing. A vault door that looked as if it didn't quite belong in the temple, as if it had been borrowed from somewhere else as the nearest thing to the purpose that could be found on short notice. On it, bolted into place, was a combination lock panel, with three different rows of spin dials that could be set to different combinations. Norla was not surprised to see a mechanical lock, rather than some sort of digital device. For a location this remote, a security device that required no electricity, generated no heat, and stood in no danger of malfunctioning because of one microscopic component's failing, made perfect sense.

But it was not the vault door or the combination locks that bothered Norla. "Not another damned puzzle," she muttered.

The single word OR was stamped into the metal between the top and middle row of dials, and again, between the middle and bottom rows. The meaning was plain: There were three sets of dials, and three possible combinations, and any of them would open the door.

"That vault door must weigh thousands of kilos," said Bolt. "How the hell did he get it down here on a lander?"

"He didn't," said Koffield. "Mariner City is just a few kilometers away. He probably scavenged most of the cut stone from there as well, instead of quarrying it himself. That lock panel, though—that's a custom job. He had that made to order somewhere, and brought it in, and bolted it to the door."

"Look," said Norla. "The inside of the door panel."

There were four thick pieces of transparent material sealed to the panel, aligned vertically. Images and notices were sealed in behind them. The top one held a sign reading THE RIGHT TIME AND PLACE. The second showed an altered image of what looked to be the north interior of the Greenhouse tomb. In the tomb itself, a line of "random" characters had been the combination of the locked compartment from which DeSilvo had stolen Koffield's evidence concerning the coming Solacian collapse. Here the line of characters had been smeared out to an illegible blur. The third showed the south side of the tomb, with the "random" characters carved there likewise blurred out—they had been a lock combination stolen from Marquez. The fourth panel was another notice, printed in thick red block letters.

WARNING. LOCKS AND SECURITY SYSTEM CONTAIN EMBEDDED PIEZO-THERMAL-OPTICAL DETECTORS LINKED TO SELF-DESTRUCT SYSTEM. ANY ATTEMPT TO BREAK THROUGH LOCKS WILL INITIATE SELF-DESTRUCT.

"Boy, that makes me feel welcome," Bolt muttered. "Aside from the whole place going up if we make a wrong move, does any of this make sense?"

"Yeah, in a way, if you're as crazy as DeSilvo," said Norla. She pointed at the locks. "Three different combinations. Use combo one, *or* two, *or* three, and the door will open." She pointed to the panels. "Clues to the combinations, clues that only make sense if you've been through what we've been through."

Bolt considered them. "Probably the first one is noon on the publication date, plus the latitude and longitude of this place."

"Unless it's noon on the pub date, and the latitude and longitude for Greenwich," Koffield agreed. "Either is possible."

"Great. Guess wrong and the place blows up."

"No," said Koffield. "Not if he's playing fair. It doesn't say *guessing* wrong will set off the charges. The charges will only go off if we attempt to break in, if we try to force the lock or blow up the door."

" 'Playing fair?' " Bolt asked.

Koffield shrugged, exaggerating the movement to make it obvious despite the bulky suit masking his gestures. "By his lights, yes. He might have sent us on a lunatic chase across the sky—but it wouldn't be 'fair' to put us through all that and then blow us up because *he* left an ambiguous clue."

"Of course," said Norla, "there's the old saying—if

the sign that says 'burglar alarm' is scary enough, you don't actually need the alarm. There might not actually be a bomb."

"Not many people would be willing to take that gamble," said Koffield. "I'm not."

"The more I hear about this guy, the less I want to meet him," Bolt said. "What about the two pictures?"

"Those are interior shots of the Greenhouse tomb," said Koffield. "The blurred-out parts had strings of numbers and letters, strings that DeSilvo knew that Marquez and I would have memorized. I assume those character strings are the second and third combinations."

"Suppose neither you nor Marquez made it here?" Bolt asked.

"The top combination is the backup," said Norla. "You wouldn't need to know anything about the Greenhouse tomb to solve that."

"But you would need to have solved some of his other puzzles. You wouldn't have to be us, but you *would* have to research DeSilvo very, very carefully," said Koffield.

"Or else be a good enough safecracker to get through whatever booby trap he set up," Bolt replied. "Which makes me think of something else to worry about."

"What's that?"

Bolt gestured, waving his arm to indicate the whole temple. "Look at this place. You're saying he had to do it all alone, just using robot labor. He had to know a lot of stuff. He might have been real smart, but he wasn't an expert on security too. He couldn't count on that door being absolutely impenetrable."

"No security is perfect," Koffield agreed. "Someone with enough determination, patience, and skill can always get through. You might just set a robot to work trying every possible combination, and check back every few years to see if it had gotten anywhere. But you'd have to have a damned good reason to go to so much trouble—for starters, you'd have to come to Mars. Who but someone like us would be that determined?"

"A wealthy government with a good intelligence service, and reason to believe there was either something valuable here, or else something it wanted to keep someone else from getting."

"All right, point granted," Koffield said. "Except we've already noted that there's no evidence of anyone else having been here since DeSilvo built it."

"There's no evidence of anyone's being here in a long time. But if someone had been here anywhere within, say, twenty years of DeSilvo's building it, their footprints and landing burns and so on would have been grown over by now. But I'm more worried about someone coming in now, while we're here, now that we've pointed the way. Once we unlock the door for them."

"What are you talking about?"

"Sparten," said Bolt. "He's working for someone. Supposing he's called them in?"

"Go on," said Koffield.

"It's just dawned on me, while we've been standing here. If he has a way to feed back information, we've just led Them—whoever They are—to the big prize."

"We don't know if there's a big prize behind there," Norla said, nodding at the vault door. "It could just be a room full of DeSilvo's favorite puzzles and games."

"There's something there," Bolt said. "Maybe 'They' even know what it is."

"So 'They' wait for us to work the lock, open the door, and disarm the security system—and then they swoop in?" asked Norla.

"Or They disable the *São Paulo* and keep us from taking off. We're trapped down here, and They come and get us. Or better still, They are waiting in orbit, watching right now, hoping we'll have faith that Deimos and Phobos are the only watchposts. They wait for us to get the prize, then intercept us and take it away."

"This is rampant paranoia," said Koffield.

"Is it?" Bolt said. "That depends on who Sparten is working for, and what they know, and what they want."

"Who's your prime suspect?"

Bolt paused for a moment, then spoke quickly, plunging in before he lost his nerve. "The Chronologic Patrol."

Norla laughed. "Admiral Koffield *is* Chrono Patrol! Who do you think made him an admiral?"

"*Ex*–Chrono Patrol," Bolt replied. "And he's been working at cross-purposes to them for quite a while, hasn't he?" He looked to Koffield. "Half the reason this whole trip has been hush-hush has been the Chrono Patrol, isn't it?"

"At least half," Koffield agreed.

"Why?" Norla asked. She realized that the question had been bothering her for a while, deep in the back of her mind. The Chronologic Patrol was concerned with protecting causality, with preventing the future from affecting the past. The trials and tribulations of one badly terraformed planet weren't of any concern to the CP, and certainly shouldn't have been part of their jurisdiction. "Why *would* they be watching us?"

"They're cops," said Bolt. "Their job is to keep things the way they are, keep them from changing, keep things calm. What we're doing might change things. It would certainly upset people if the news got out. It *has* to be that there are CP agents on Solace. They're everywhere. One of them recruits Sparten. Tells him to contact the CP once he's in the Solar System. And maybe he leaves a message at Asgard Station, too. They make contact with him, and he keeps them posted. They follow us all to Mars." He pointed at Koffield. "That's why you put him on the Permanent Physical Collection job. It kept him isolated, He tried to bully me into working for him while we were there."

"I thought he might," said Norla.

"It's why he's not here, now, on this job," said Bolt.

"I've had to handle him carefully, yes," said Koffield. "But there's a long way between his working for the Chronologic Patrol—or between our suspecting him of that—and an assault squad busting in here ten seconds after we open the vault. In any event—yes, everything you have described is possible. I happen to think Sparten is working for someone on Solace, in which case he has as much interest in staying away from the Chronologic

Patrol as we do. But, assuming, for the sake of argument, that your theory is right—what is there that we can do about it?"

"I don't know, sir," said Bolt. "If I am right, I suppose it means we're already trapped. But at least, maybe, we can be on our guard. Somehow."

"It's the 'somehow' part that's the problem," said Koffield. "But very well. I promise you, we'll all try to be careful." He turned his attention back to the vault door. "But I'll be damned twice over before I'd come all this way and *not* open that door."

He thought a moment. "The second combination, I think. It's the one I know best."

He stepped to the vault door and slowly, carefully, spun the dials one by one to set up the combination. Then slowly, carefully, he checked through all the numbers, one after another. "That looks right." He stepped back, and pulled the lock-open lever. They could hear the dead bolts inside the door pull back and *thunk* into place.

Norla found that she was holding her breath. There could be anything, absolutely anything in there, from the DeSilvo-in-his-coffin tableau that Bolt had described, to some damned-fool practical joke. That would appeal to DeSilvo. It was the sort of thing he'd do.

Koffield pulled hard on the vault-door handle, and the door swung open. And inside—

Inside was an utterly empty room. There was nothing there but a set of stairs, leading down into the ground.

The three of them stood there, staring.

Norla turned to Koffield. "Don't tell me *this* is what you thought you'd find."

CHAPTER SIXTEEN
TRUTH UNDERLYING

Anton Koffield turned awkwardly in his pressure suit and looked hard at Norla. He resisted the temptation to say *"Yes, this was more or less what I was afraid we'd find."* The pieces were falling neatly into place, and it was almost impossible for him to avoid seeing the rest of the puzzle. "Let's go," he said.

"What?" Norla said.

"Let's go," he said. "Down the stairs. What else is there for us but to go forward?"

"Just like that?" she asked.

"What's he supposed to do?" asked Bolt. "Make a speech and cut a ribbon? Let's go."

Koffield, not entirely sure he was glad of the honor, led the way in.

"Hold it a moment," said Norla. She pushed the vault door open, swinging it all the way over to stop with a booming thud against the right-hand wall. Then she went to the left wall, and swung the outer door closed behind them as far as it would go, so it would block the vault door from closing and latching, if it somehow swung shut. "That'll keep the mold out, some, maybe—and keep the vault door from blocking our exit route."

The way was dark, and they had to rely on their helmet lights. They moved down the steps, slowly and carefully.

The stairs led down about five meters and ended in a small room, facing a blank wall. The right-hand wall was blank as well, but there was a doorway off to the left. With no other place to go, they went through it, and stepped out into a rough-hewn tunnel, circular in cross section and about three meters in diameter.

The tunnel dead-ended in a pile of chewed-up rubble to the right, but off to the left, it led off into the dark and the distance, the vanishing point bobbling in and out of view as their helmet lights moved about. The tunnel seemed to slope down at a very slight grade.

"Which way are we going?" Bolt asked. "I mean, north, south—which direction does the tunnel go?"

Koffield knew without thinking, but he made sure he had it straight in his head before he answered. They had come in the western side of the structure and entered moving east, then moved straight down the stairs, and turned left twice, hard right angles each time. "West," he said. "The tunnel runs due west. Let's go."

West. Another piece that fit the puzzle. He knew what was ahead, what *had* to be ahead.

He started walking, not looking back, not giving his companions time to wonder if moving forward was such a good idea—and likewise not giving himself a chance to wonder the same thing.

He could tell by the motion of the shadows they cast ahead that the two of them were still following, and gave a silent prayer of thanks for that. It would have been a wholly sensible response to stop dead, then and there, and turn back.

Anton Koffield made no brief for his own courage. He was so committed to the chase, to the hunting of DeSilvo, that there was no question of choice in the matter, so far as he was concerned. And he knew it took a different sort of courage to follow, rather than lead. And yet they came on, solid at his back. *Thanks be for that,* he thought, and felt the set of his shoulders relax. They pressed on.

After about a hundred meters, they came to a closed hatch set into the tunnel. It was a small crawl-through hatch, salvaged from somewhere and mortared into a wall built across the tunnel. Koffield came to a halt before it and waited for the others to catch up while he studied the mechanism. A lever device unlatched it, and a wheel set into the center served to seal it tight. Any near-ancient sailor would have recognized it at once.

Koffield noticed some sort of cable running along the top of the tunnel and examined it more closely. A white tube, about two centimeters in diameter. Large bright blue staples pinched into it every meter or so and held it to the rock. It seemed to disappear under the mortaring, and Koffield felt sure it ran the full length of the tunnel. He pointed to it as the others joined him. "I'd have won that bet about there being a bomb," he said. "There it is. Rope charge. It must be tied into the vault door. And I'd be willing to bet the blue clamps are piezo-sensor detonators. Cut into the rock, shake it too hard, and boom—good-bye tunnel."

"How nice," said Bolt. He tapped the wall under the hatch with his foot. "You don't look so surprised by all this," he said. "So maybe you know. Is what we're looking for behind the hatch?"

"I don't think so," he said. "I believe we've got a long walk ahead of us."

"Now I'll be the one who's not surprised," Bolt muttered. "So let's get started." He knelt down, pulled at the wheel, then pulled again, harder. It came free and he spun it out far enough to release the mechanism, then pulled the lever. The hatch opened, and Bolt climbed through it, headfirst. Norla followed, and Koffield brought up the rear.

They found themselves in a section of tunnel, a chamber about five meters long, with another hatch at the far end. There were placards attached to the sidewalls of the tunnel that read

**PLEASE SEAL HATCH BEHIND YOU
BEFORE OPENING HATCH AHEAD**

and

**PLEASE READ AND FOLLOW ALL
DECONTAMINATION PROCEDURES**

There were shelves bolted to the sides of the chamber on either side, and on them sat hermetically sealed bottles. Koffield walked over and examined them. "Bleaches, fungicides, that sort of thing," he said. "And there are sealed packets of wipe-down towels."

"Not the most elaborate setup, is it?" asked Norla. "No safety interlocks, or automated decon sprayers, or anything like that. DeSilvo usually does things with a bit more polish."

"He usually doesn't have to scrounge and improvise," said Koffield. "I'm sure he was severely limited on what he could bring in—and in what he could do by himself, even with robotic help. The rest he put together from what he could salvage from Mariner City, or wherever. You'll notice the two hatches don't match each other." He found another, smaller placard with detailed decontamination instructions—basically to wipe down carefully with this fluid, then that one. Norla was right. DeSilvo had been improvising, working close to the edge. Things were dangerous enough when DeSilvo wasn't taking chances. "Close that hatch, if you would, Mr. Bolt," he said. "We might as well get started on decon."

They left the decontamination chamber, and kept moving, Koffield still in the lead. It was difficult to estimate distances in the featureless tunnel. Koffield tried to do it by timing them and estimating their speed, but even that was almost impossible. The low gravity and the relatively low height of the tunnel made it entirely too easy to bounce up against the ceiling—and, perhaps, one of those piezo-fuse staples. They were forced to walk in an odd, long-strided gait that kept them from bouncing too high. Because the floor of the tunnel was rounded, with no effort to form a flattened path, it was impractical to walk side by side. The tunnel began to angle down more and more, making for a steeper grade and making the footing that much trickier. It was almost impossible to keep up a steady pace, let alone one wherein Koffield could guess their speed.

On they walked, and with every step they took, Koffield became surer of what they were walking into—and more determined to say nothing until there could be no doubt at all. His two companions were silent for the most part, but he knew the questions they were burning to ask. But no, hard as it was—better for everyone if they all stayed silent for now.

After a time, Koffield saw a wide space in the tunnel up ahead, and the footing changed from the bare rock of the tunnel to crushed gravel. They came up to the wide spot and paused to look.

At the lowest point in the tunnel, on the left-hand side, ninety degrees away from the main tunnel, a short, deep cross tunnel bored off down at about a twenty-degree downslope. It was half-filled with crushed gravel. "Wait here," said Koffield, then moved cautiously down the bed of loose gravel. He only had to go about twenty meters down the side tunnel to confirm what he had suspected—it dead-ended after only about a fifty-meter run. He scrambled back up the gravel bed to where Bolt and Norla were waiting.

"Drainage," he said. "To keep the tunnel from flooding."

"But there's no water," Bolt objected. "Everything's bone dry."

Norla spoke. "Things changed on Mars when they terraformed, then changed again when it all collapsed. Who's to say they won't change again? The tunnel's been here at least a hundred years—and Calydon Channel is full of water, just a few kilometers away. Water could leach through the rock—or it might start raining. DeSilvo built this right after learning all his predictions and projections for Solace were wrong. He took precautions."

Bolt nodded, but said nothing.

"We should keep moving," said Koffield, and turned back toward the main tunnel, now moving on the upgrade, toward their destination.

Norla paused for a moment, there at the low point of the tunnel, and let the others go on ahead. *Over a hundred years*, she thought. *And DeSilvo built it just for us. No— just for Anton Koffield*. Did that make sense? Did any of this make even the *remotest* degree of sense? None of it was logical, certainly—but there was, or at least had been, up to a point, an internal consistency to it. This place didn't fit. Whatever the hell it was, it was too much, too complex, even for DeSilvo.

And then she saw it. *This wasn't for us. It was for him*. DeSilvo had built this tunnel, taken the time whenever he could to do the covert engineering, the cadging of supplies, the deceptions, the disguised trips, so as to get *something* of great value *to himself*. The phony temple, the clues in the books—those were afterthoughts. *They* were meant for Koffield. And they were meant to lead Koffield here, into the tunnel ahead, to show Koffield what DeSilvo had found, and made use of— and, in some sense, to justify what he had done.

None of that made *logical* sense, either. But it had a sort of *emotional* sense that fit DeSilvo. She scrambled up the gravel, and then onto the bare rock of the tunnel, to catch up with her companions.

The tunnel climbed upward, perhaps at a steeper angle than it had on the downward leg. Before long, they came to yet another hatch built into the tunnel—and this hatch was not of the same type as either of the first two. They opened it and passed through, and, to no one's surprise, found another decontamination chamber on the other side. Again they went through the procedures as instructed on the placards, passed through yet another mismatched hatch, and on upward through the tunnel.

At last, they saw a bigger, stronger, newer-looking

hatch up ahead, a walk-through job. There was another sign on this hatch, asking PLEASE SEAL HATCH BE-HIND YOU. Something about that door said finality, the last barrier. Whatever they were after was just behind it.

The character of the tunnel walls changed as they moved toward the last hatch. There were fine hairline cracks here and there in the rock, and, somehow, it looked as if the cracks predated the tunnel, as if something had hit the rock, and hit it hard, before the tunnel was made. The cracks grew larger and larger right by the hatch. It was plain that whatever had hit, had hit just on the other side of where the hatch was now.

Norla had been hanging back a bit, wondering at the force of whatever had done this to the walls. The other two were waiting for her by the hatch, and she hurried to catch up with them. "All right," she said. "Let's do it." Bolt spun the wheel, then pulled back the four separate levers that locked down the door—left, right, top, bottom.

The door swung inward onto darkness. Koffield stepped through, then Bolt, then Norla, bringing up the rear, and dutifully sealing the hatch after she came through.

Their helmet lights faded away to shine on nothingness inside a vast underground space, the beams of light and flaring shadows almost impossible to make sense of.

Then, from somewhere near by, Norla heard the loud *clack* of a heavy-duty relay snapping shut. Some sort of detector had noticed they were there. A low hum rumbled up and through the sonic range to vanish as a high squeal as a generator spun itself up.

Then, in silence, the lights came on, from high up, bank after bank of them coming on one after another, marching across the ceiling of a vast artificial cavern.

After the dim illumination provided by their helmet lights, they all squinted, shielding their eyes, dazzled by the brightness. The cavern was too big, and too complicated, to see all at once. Norla could make no sense of it other than as a jumble of shapes, of hulking pieces of machinery dwarfed by an enormous space.

It suddenly registered that they were on top of some sort of hillside, a vast loose pile of crushed and broken rock that filled up part of the cavern. Directly in front of them was a massive steel ramp, and at its top a platform, partly buried by the loose rock on which they stood. Norla moved forward a bit and looked down. The pile of chewed-up rock tumbled out to either side, and she could see massive pieces of machinery half-buried under it.

"Well, at least now we know where the rock from out of the tunnel went," said Bolt, gesturing at the rubble.

"And what dug it," said Norla. At the bottom of the steel ramp was a massive and ugly machine, little more than a sharp-nosed drill mounted on tractor treads—a subterrene, a tunnel-cutter.

"Two minor mysteries cleared up, then," said Koffield. "I'd been assuming he dug the tunnel from the other end. I was wondering where the drilled-out rock and the drilling machine had gotten to. It must have been a real job backing it all the way through the tunnel again. Why not just leave it at the other end? Maybe he thought he might need the subterrene for something else."

"Those aren't exactly the points we're really worried about just now," said Bolt. "Where are we? What is this place?"

There was silence for a moment, and then Koffield spoke, plainly reluctant, even now, to expose a confidence. "Welcome," he said, "to the Chronologic Patrol's Technology Storage Facility. Or, the Dark Museum, to give the place its more colorful name. The Grand Library of Secrets. Making *us* come all this way is DeSilvo's way of telling us *he* found it."

"That's the secret you didn't want to tell," said Norla. "The one you didn't want to tell unless you absolutely had to."

"All right," said Bolt. "Now you absolutely have to. Explain all this."

Koffield nodded. "Let's sit," he said. "I'm tired. Tired all the way through. And we're going to have to stay in these miserable suits a lot longer than we've already been in them."

They found three rocks of a comfortable size for sitting and settled down, Koffield between the other two, looking out over the vast interior space.

"This is the lowest level, I suspect," said Koffield. "Can you see, off toward the far corner there, the big pile of rubble that's fallen through the ceiling? I'd guess that's directly underneath the blast crater we saw flying over. We were above it. Now we're below."

"We're *under* Mariner City right now?" asked Norla, surprised. It made sense once Koffield said it, but somehow she hadn't put the geometry together for herself.

"It might be more accurate to say we're *in* it," Koffield said. "This city predated the terraforming project. It used to be a domed habitat, largely underground. They used nuclear charges to blast this cavern open about twenty-five hundred years ago."

"And you knew this was here?"

"I knew the *cavern* was here. Remember, I said the information I had was closer to folklore than history—and what I had wasn't all that specific, either. It was just that the Chronologic Patrol had taken advantage of the Interdict, and put some very, very, secret facilities on Mars. Including a Technology Storage Facility."

"You mean like those are what, patent models?" asked Bolt, gesturing down at the rows of strange machinery.

"No," said Norla, suddenly seeing a bit more of it. "He means *suppressed* technology."

"Suppressed," said Koffield. "You said it yourself earlier, Mr. Bolt. The Chronologic Patrol likes to keep things the way they are. Did you ever notice anything much different about the two of us? About Officer Chandray or me?"

"Sir?"

"I was born over two centuries before you were. Officer Chandray was born about 120 years after me. The *Dom Pedro IV* is about the same vintage—though she's had some upgrades. Either of us, or the ship, ever seem particularly old-fashioned to you?"

"I'm not sure what you mean, sir."

"I wouldn't be surprised if you'd never even heard the term 'old-fashioned,' " said Koffield. "Two hundred years, and ships still work more or less the same! I've been out of circulation for two centuries, but language, technology, clothing styles—everything *is still recognizable to me*! Back before about 1300 A.D., that wouldn't have been strange—but from then on, from Late Far Ancient clear through the Near Ancient, to Recent times, right on up to the start of the Current Period—pick any two dates two hundred years apart, and human society would have changed almost beyond recognition from one to the next. But *that doesn't happen anymore*! It'd slowed down a lot by the time I was born—but I came back to an Earth that seemed a little *too* familiar."

"So, what you're saying is that the Chronologic Patrol did that by hiding a bunch of gizmos in a cave on Mars?"

"No, of course not. The whole culture is nearly in stasis. There must be a lot more reasons for that than one group, even one powerful group, suppressing technical advances. But it helped, I'm sure. Probably there were—are—a lot of nonintentional forces keeping things the way they are. But the CP is plainly a deliberate actor, working to prevent change. I'd bet all I have, and a lot more besides, that there are other deliberate actors out there, working to keep the lid on."

"But—*why*?"

"I don't know," Koffield said. "Maybe just because change is dangerous. Maybe because of nothing more than a very strong conservative streak. And no, I don't find any of those answers convincing either. I'm still thinking about it."

"Okay, never mind the general question," said Bolt. "What about *this* place? This Technology Storage Facility. What's it all about?"

"I told you," said Koffield. "Keeping things the same." He looked out at the vast cavern and thought a moment. "Let me start back at the beginning. Some I know—most I'm guessing. But just sitting here, seeing it real, in front of me—pieces are falling into place." He gestured toward the cavern's interior. "A long, long time ago—by about 2800 A.D., maybe a bit later—they got very, very good at blowing underground chambers like this. The Moon has hundreds of them, of course. The main cities are built in them. A first charge to melt the rock, a second to expand it outward—sometimes they'd do a double, or triple-stage dome. This one is a triple, I suspect. Two more levels above this one, each a bit smaller than the one below. Safe from radiation, sandstorms, whatever. Big enough that you could build whatever you wanted—and, of course, whatever surface structures you like on top of it. By about the year 3000, they were blowing underground chambers on Mars, including this one. Mariner City was mostly underground, in this chamber and the ones above."

He stared out at the chamber. "How they arranged matters here, I don't know, but usually the lowest chamber was agriculture, heavy equipment on the middle level, residence and places for people over that, and then the surface city. The city got established, and did pretty well for about three hundred years."

"Then they decide to terraform the planet," said Bolt.

"Right. They do so well fixing up Haiti—one half of a midsize island—they figure they know enough to tackle a planet. 'Round about 3300, they start the main projects. Unlocking water from the rocks, melting the ice caps, dropping in comet ice for more water, pumping oxygen into the air, breeding plants to convert the sands into something more like Earthlike soil."

"And something goes wrong."

"Not *one* thing. *Lots* of things. Not once, but many times. Time and again, they think they've isolated the core problem and fixed it. These days we talk about it as if it all happened quickly, predictably. But whole generations lived and died, centuries would pass, between the end of one disaster and the start of the next. Until the end came for good and all, about a thousand years after they started the terraforming project, and left the planet so bad off they declared the Interdict." Koffield laughed bitterly. "And, of course, we learned so much from our mistakes, we terraformed all the other worlds perfectly."

"So what finally did do them in?" Norla asked. "I've heard so many theories."

"They're all right," said Koffield. "Mutated soil-conversion species getting out of control. Oxygen-poisoning of interim species. Unexpected chemical reactions set off by flooding the lowlands to form oceans. Uncontrolled population expansion of termite colonies released for soil aeration. Unplanned microbes brought to the planet on improperly sterilized shipments." He paused again, and sat up a little straighter. "Something damned obvious just struck me. Bolt, you've heard us talk about Ulan Baskaw? She literally wrote the book on how to terraform Solace. Just thinking about the dates—she wrote *that* book, her second book, just a few decades *before* the final collapse of Mars. And she wrote her last book, warning about what could go wrong with terraforming—about nine years *after* the Great Failure. She had to have been influenced by it."

Norla cocked her head at Koffield. "If she were working in terraforming in the years just before the Failure, she probably visited Mars—and if she did that, she probably came through Mariner City."

Koffield looked back at her. "There's a thought. You're right. She very likely passed within a few kilometers of where we are right now. That's an odd little connection."

"So, anyway, Mars collapses," prompted Bolt.

"And Earth has to take in all the refugees, and there's hell to pay with all sorts of back contamination and some nasty epidemics," said Norla.

Koffield frowned, as if he had just thought of something, had just made a connection himself. "So they did. But, for our purposes, the main thing is that Mars was abandoned. And, back when I was a young officer, the story told late at night after a few too many drinks was that some bright boy thought to start socking away all the interestingly unpleasant toys they had confiscated, and doing it where no one would ever want to go look. With the Interdict in effect, and being run much, much, much more aggressively than it is now—well, there were already guards watching an empty jail—why not put whatever else that needs guarding down there too?"

"I'd heard versions of the story," said Norla. "Except it wasn't the CP hiding things. Usually it was the Earth government. There were megatons of gold that had to be kept off the market to keep the economy from collapsing, or the preserved bodies of dead aliens, or political prisoners, or a secret laboratory, or some gang of super-smugglers had their hideout here—"

"And so on, and so forth," Koffield agreed. "That's a large part of why I didn't want to say anything before I saw this was true. Too many old wives' tales that sounded too much like my theory." Koffield gestured. "But it looks like my version was true."

"I see a lot of machines down there," said Bolt, "but I don't see a big sign saying PROPERTY OF CHRONO-LOGIC PATROL. How do you know it was them?"

"I expect we'll find something to confirm it once we're down there, but I know," said Koffield. "In part, it's just that the folklore stories inside the Chronologic Patrol were more consistent, less fanciful—and the CP did provide technical support to Interdict Command. Officers and technicians transferred back and forth. Beyond that—" A faraway look came into his eye, and he spoke, as if quoting something. " *'But I have accomplished great things, and learned far more secrets than those that Ulan Baskaw taught me. There is much to be found in the most secret places of the Grand Library, and in other archives. Remarkable technologies of all sorts have been deliberately suppressed, by those who believe it is best for human society to remain nearly static, and progress with glacial slowness, if at all. Perhaps they were once right to so think, but their time is past.'* "

"DeSilvo's letter from the Greenhouse tomb," said Norla.

"DeSilvo's letter," Koffield agreed. "He wrote that letter after he had explored this place, at more or less the same time he decided to show it to me."

"What in those words makes you think it's the Chronologic Patrol?" asked Bolt. "It could be anyone who wants to keep things the way they are."

" 'Perhaps they were once right to so think, but their time is past.' The reference to 'time,' and the 'past.' It's subtle, but the psychology of using that phrasing is suggestive. And DeSilvo has always been a great one for justifying himself. When he wrote that letter, when he was preparing to show us this place, it had been about thirteen years since he'd sent his Intruder drones against a timeshaft wormhole, against the Chronologic Patrol—"

"Against you," said Norla.

"Right. Much of that letter was about justifying himself to me, explaining how good and noble it was to destroy one warship and badly damage mine, kill one whole crew, and members of my own crew. And it could only be good and justified if the organization was doing bad things—like suppressing technology. And don't forget the Intruder ships appeared to go faster than light. The CP wouldn't like that."

"That's big," Bolt agreed. "But why wouldn't the Chronologic Patrol like faster-than-light travel?"

"It would put them out of business, for one thing," said Norla. "If there were such a thing as real FTL, no one would need wormholes, and the Chronologic Patrol would dry up and blow away."

"Worse than that," said Koffield. "They'd dry up, get weaker—and still have the same responsibilities. They'd *have* to stay in business to guard wormholes that no one was using, just to protect causality. Maybe they'd be forced to destroy wormholes they could no longer afford to defend. But they'd lose their power, their monopoly control of interstellar transport. Not that they've abused that power, particularly—but power is hard to give up. And maybe DeSilvo isn't the only one who can find ways to justify self-serving decisions."

"So I think I can see the rest of the story, more or less," said Norla.

"Tell it to me," said Koffield. "Let's see if your guesswork is about the same as mine."

"There are two or three chambers, stacked one on top of another, full of technology, schematics, designs, working models, strange and powerful machines. Including, probably, a faster-than-light drive, and, probably, weapons, or things that could be used as weapons. Things the CP doesn't want used, but doesn't want lost forever, just in case. They would have gotten started something under a thousand years ago, more or less. They spent a few centuries storing away whatever they found—probably they had a lot of gear accumulated somewhere else, and needed a place to put it, and that got them started.

"But it's hard to keep something running for centuries at a time. They get sloppy, or cut their budget one time too many, or maybe something goes wrong that would have happened no matter how careful they were. One of the toys they've accumulated malfunctions. Or maybe a disgruntled worker sabotages a device. Anyway, something blows up. Something on the level above us. It destroys that level completely, and the level above that, and blasts out onto the surface, blowing a hole in the abandoned city. It partially collapses this level, over there," she said, pointing.

"It's Mars," she went on. "Just landing on the planet is dangerous enough—and supposedly it was worse then than it is now. There are multimegatons of rubble, and absolute devastation. It's plain that whatever hasn't been destroyed has been completely entombed. Probably there's bad radioactivity. Probably lots of other big nasty machines up there have disgorged very unpleasant things—poisons, solvents, biohazards, you name it. None of that makes them want to investigate too hard."

"And one other thing," said Koffield. "It's all very, very secret. No one outside knows the explosion has even happened. Secrecy makes it tougher to gather the resources to investigate too hard, and eliminates a lot of the need to investigate."

"I hadn't thought of that part," said Norla.

"One other reason they wouldn't dig too deep," said Bolt. "You called it the Grand Library of Secrets. The real Grand Library—both versions, the Permanent Physical Collection and the digital collection—they have 'em backed up. We never got to it, but there's a *second* PPC under the Lunar Farside. And there are lots of copies of the digital GL."

"You're saying there's *another* Technology Storage Facility somewhere?" said Norla. "Another one this big?"

"Maybe. It's a big Solar System, with lots of out-of-the-way places, and lots of places no one would want to visit. Why not?"

Koffield looked surprised. "I must confess that had never occurred to me, either. But it makes sense."

"Anyway," said Norla, "there's an explosion. Maybe they send in team after team of salvage workers and investigators, and lose them all, or maybe they don't even try in the first place. They abandon the place. Time goes past. Then, quite literally, enters DeSilvo." She turned to Koffield. "When, do you think?"

Koffield shook his head. "It could have been almost any time. He's had a habit of trawling through old, out-of-the-way books and data sources for a long time. The first we know of him doing that was when he found Baskaw's books. We don't know the date he did that, but he started promoting her techniques as his own, and campaigning for the Solace project, in about 4960 or so. And, of course, he could have found references to this place, and maybe done enough analysis to discover not all of it had been destroyed. But he didn't have the time or the money or the resources to do anything about it until much later."

"But once he does start the Solace terraforming project in earnest—when would that be?"

"The project officially got under way on his hundredth birthday, August 14, 4993," said Koffield. "They crashed the first comet into the planet that day. Very big show."

"Sounds like a hell of a party," said Norla. "But starting from then, and for the next two hundred years or so, he's got access to almost unlimited equipment, unlimited resources, most of it transiting in and out of the Solar System, and he's accountable to no one. He goes in and out of cold sleep and temporal confinement again and again to stretch his own lifetime—and develops something of a taste for it. He has all sorts of regeneration therapy and gets transplant replacements of practically every organ in his body, several times over."

"Some of the hardware he gets for Solace gets diverted just a bit," said Bolt, "and, for starters, maybe he borrows an uncrewed lander and a small ArtInt-controlled vertical borer, and drops the borer into Mariner City when no one is looking. He tells the ArtInt to start drilling test shafts through the rubble—while being very careful to keep all his tunnels sealed and clean against the outside."

"That way, or some other way," Koffield agrees. "He establishes there are things worth having down here and decides to come for a visit himself. Probably around the time the big push to terraform Solace is winding up, and it dawns on him he won't have unlimited access to spacecraft and hardware anymore. We'll have to guess at the details of how, but he digs himself the tunnel from here."

"But why dig the tunnel in the first place?" Norla demanded. "It sure looks like he dug it from here to the temple—unless he's just tried to make it look like that was the way he did it—and I can't think why he'd do that. If he already had a way in and out, why dig the tunnel?"

"To pile on a bit more guesswork," said Koffield, "we know the man is good at finding things out. Maybe—maybe—he discovered that Interdict Command was still keeping some sort of eye on Mariner City, watching for any changes inside the city limit that might indicate further collapse underground. Or, make it simpler—maybe he found out the automatic watch stations on Deimos and Phobos were still programmed to watch the city, to guard the storehouse even after it had been destroyed.

Repeatedly flying a vehicle large enough to carry him in and out of the city was too dangerous."

"So he finds a working subterrene on the premises and drills his way out to where no one is watching quite as hard," said Norla. "Or more likely he tells an ArtInt to do it. It would take a long time to dig that tunnel. I wouldn't want to be waiting down here the whole time for it to get dug. Maybe he never comes down here at all until the tunnel is complete. Probably he sets other ArtInts to repair the lights and so on in here. But mainly he digs a tunnel *he* can use."

"And builds himself a tunnel large enough to get some good-sized cargo *out*," Bolt suggested.

"For example, a working model of a faster-than-light star drive," said Koffield. "He builds the Intruders, the Intruders attack the Circum Central Wormhole—"

"Why?" Bolt asked.

"I don't know!" Koffield snapped. "I've spent a hell of a long time thinking about that, but I still don't know. But I can tell you it happened! I was there." Koffield was silent for a time. "I'm sorry," he said. "But that question has been eating at me since—since it happened."

"In any event," Norla said, in a gentle voice, "the Intruders attacked. And Anton Koffield nursed his crippled ship back to the Solar System in the year 5212. Then, not at all by chance, a guilt-ridden Oskar DeSilvo struck up an acquaintance. That led to your doing some research for him, and that led to discovering that he had plagiarized Ulan Baskaw's work, and that led to discovering Baskaw's work, and that led to your discovery that Solace was doomed—"

"And *that* led to DeSilvo sabotaging the *Dom Pedro IV* and stranding us in time to prevent my warning from arriving at Solace and causing a panic," said Koffield. "Dominoes, all in a row, one after the other."

"But," Norla went on, "some years *after* the *Dom Pedro IV* departs, DeSilvo concludes that he can no longer delude himself: Solace is going to die. There's enough guilt, or pride, or at least something human still in him so that he feels he has to do something about it.

But he does it in such a way that he won't endanger himself—and he can't resist making a game out of it. He builds the temple over the outside end of his tunnel. He prints that silly book, and gets it into the libraries—a message in the bottle, just for us. He seals another message into his phony tomb, shaped just like the temple, on Greenhouse."

"And that sets off the *next* row of dominoes, and ends up with the three of us sitting underground on a big pile of rocks, looking down at *that*," said Koffield. "So what the devil do we do now?"

"We go down there, obviously," said Norla, standing up. "We've got cameras and bookcatchers and other recording equipment. We use them, and get every image, every bit of text that we can."

"But DeSilvo's taken all the—"

"He can't have taken *everything*!" Norla replied. "There must be things he didn't get to. Maybe he just copied digital files and left the originals, or stole one model and there's another left."

"Wait a second," Bolt protested, standing as well. "I agree, we've got to go down and look around—but we can't get out of these damned suits until we're off-planet. We've got the remaining duration in the suits—minus some sleep time, and time enough to get back into orbit and get picked up—to look over a small city—and DeSilvo might have taken *years* browsing around. How are we supposed to match him?"

"I don't know," said Norla. "But we have to try and at least get the big stuff, the most advanced stuff. Don't you see? He set this up. He knew we'd have to come in covertly, with limited resources, limited time. We've got our nose up against the window, looking at all the goodies inside. *He already has it all*. He wants *us* to go to him, dirt-poor, hat in hand, begging him for whatever supertech stuff he's willing to dole out."

"Go to him?" protested Bolt. "*I* thought we'd find him on Mars. We don't know where he is."

"But we will," said Koffield, standing up at last, "sooner or later." Somehow the tiredness was gone from his voice, and the steel was back. "She's right. He wants us hungry, and wants us to know how much he could share if he felt like it—or if we do as he says. And I'm damned tired of dancing to his tune." He looked down at the floor of the cavern, at the gleaming, incomprehensible machines in endless profusion. "If we just charge off in all directions, we'll get nowhere," he said. "We need a plan of attack. Let's take a few minutes to think."

CHAPTER SEVENTEEN

CALLING CARD

They came down off the ramp and split up, each choosing a major east–west avenue and heading toward the far end of the cavern, each of them moving at a fast, bounding walk that took advantage of the low gravity. That ten minutes of thinking had unearthed a few things that were going help a lot. Their suit helmets had built-in longwatch cameras that could record everything the wearer saw and heard. They had kept them turned off up to now, on the theory that a record would just provide that much more evidence if they were caught. Now, of course, they wanted them on.

Not knowing what they would find, and not wishing to lose time by returning to the lander if they could avoid it, they had left the lander packing recording equipment of all sorts, along with various other sorts of hardware, like rock hammers and pry bars and climbing equipment. They dumped all the gear they weren't going to need, emptying some of the large and commodious pockets on their external suits.

"Remember," said Koffield over Norla's suit radio, "we need information, not objects. Data we can transmit—physical objects we have to abandon and destroy. So no souvenirs. Just printed text we can flatscan, or objects it would be worth doing three-dee—"

His voice cut out as Norla bounded past a particularly large and dense-looking piece of hardware. Not surprisingly, it blocked radio. It didn't matter. Koffield was reminding her of what she already knew.

"—and call out if you spot anything that might tell us what DeSilvo was interested in."

"We just went over this, Anton," Norla said, smiling at the voice in her ear, daring to use his first name.

"I know, I know. But what could it harm to say it again? There's a lot riding on this."

Norla was getting close to the collapsed area of the chamber. She slowed down and indulged herself with a half minute's look at the wreckage—heaps of stone and rubble, burned and broken bits of machinery, shattered glass. What had it all been before it was destroyed? What marvelous inventions were lost for all time, flattened beneath a pile of Martian rock? Who had spent years, decades, perfecting whatever those broken, twisted things had once been?

But there was no time. An ancient, ancient joke flitted through her mind. *A husband and wife had overscheduled their vacation, and only had an hour to get through an enormous museum. They work out a careful plan of how to get through as much of it as they can, and then take off from the entrance at a dead run. "And remember," the husband shouts. "No looking!"*

But there wasn't anything funny about the situation. She turned away and started in with the first intact display bay, concluded she could not make sense of it at all, and moved on, heading back the way she had come.

The cavern was divided into wide main avenues running east–west, and narrower passages running north–south, forming the floor into a grid of storage areas and display bays. What had seemed bright and gleaming hardware from on high was covered with dust and grit close up—especially this close to the collapsed area.

Each bay was built on a concrete pad that raised it about fifteen centimeters off the cavern floor. There was a raised curb, another five centimeters or so high, all around the edge of each pad, so that one had to step up and over the curb to stand in the bay itself. Obviously the arrangement was meant to protect the contents of the bays against minor floods and against poorly driven maintenance vehicles.

Some of the bays were totally enclosed concrete boxes, no doubt designed to protect more fully whatever delicate machines were inside. Most, however, were open to the surrounding environment, and used sealed glass cases and glass-door bookshelves to protect the contents from dust and grit. The bays were plainly designed for reference and examination—though rarely by humans, if Norla were any judge. The researchers would have used ArtInts and TeleOperators for the most part, keeping their bodies safely away from the Martian environment.

There were any number of small indicators that suggested the place had been designed more for use by machines than humans. The displays were in colors that worked well with machine vision systems, and all the things meant to be lifted or moved—dust covers, selector switches, reference systems—had the sort of oversize handles and controls intended for unskilled remote operators. A professional TeleOperator technician could deal a hand of cards or play a musical instrument using remote manipulators—but a researcher who had never used a T.O. system before would appreciate brightly colored oversize knobs on the storage lockers and handles on the book spines.

Norla noticed that most of the bays had ramps leading up into them, and the sections of curb facing the ramps were fitted with handles and were obviously meant to be removable. Clearly, all that was intended for the easy access of wheeled machines.

Norla was starting to get some understanding of the organization of the place. Each bay held one invention, or machine, or technical advance. All the paperwork, all the working models, all the dataruns concerning that one device were stored in that one bay. Some were full to bursting, some were so big they took over two, three, or four bays, and some were barely there at all, no more than one book on one shelf of a bookcase, sitting in an otherwise empty bay. But each bay had at least that one bookcase, and attached to it was a placard with some sort of catalog number, and a description of the invention. The one she had paused in front of was one of the just-one-book displays. Its placard read "CPTSF-SF-019837 AN IMPROVED METHOD OF CRYOGENIC SYSTEMS POWER CONTROL." She took that to mean it was item number 19,837 in the SF—Space Flight?—collection of the Chronologic Patrol Technology Storage Facility. But what was so exciting about power control for cryo systems? What did that have to do with protecting causality? She pulled the descriptive book off the shelf and flipped through it. It looked to be mostly plumbing diagrams.

She shrugged, set the book back on the shelf, and tried her bookcatcher wand on it. The wand beeped, and a green light came on. It had found a legible memory chip bound into the book, and had captured the full text. Good to know that at least that much worked.

She moved on. "FASTER ARTINT-CONTROLLED NAVIGATIONAL FIXES." "INCREASED PRECISION FOR HIGH-SPEED SHIPBOARD DIFFERENTIAL SPECTRAL FINGERPRINTING SYSTEMS." "ENHANCED ELECTRICAL COGENERATION AS BY-PRODUCT OF REACTIONLESS DRIVE SYSTEMS."

The next twenty bays she went past were more of the same. All useful tweaks, no doubt, and probably put together they could nearly double the profitability of a timeshaft dropship. Marquez would have loved to have any or all of the upgrades she was finding. But that was just it—there were upgrades, improvements to existing systems. *Eight-hundred-year-old improvements to existing systems, for the most part,* she reminded herself. Had things been more or less the same for *that* long?

Norla started to get more selective about the bays she would examine, let alone do a text-capture on. There was a lot still to get through, and it wouldn't do much good to waste time on minor improvements—time she ought to spend searching for real breakthroughs.

Besides, she was starting to notice some other things.

The same things, or at least variations on the same theme, were represented over and over. And some of the tweaks were already in use, perfectly standard present-day hardware.

"Admiral Koffield, Jerand," she said. "Do you hear me?"

Both of them acknowledged, and Norla reported the patterns she had noticed. "Is either one of you seeing things like that?" she asked.

"Now that you mention it," said Bolt, "yeah, you're right. I'm standing in front of the third bay describing the same damned improvement to electrostatic scrubbers in air filtration systems. The *Dom Pedro IV* has almost exactly the same system installed."

"I've noticed a similar pattern over here," said Koffield. "I think I understand. The same improvement gets invented time after time, and sat on time after time, until somehow or another it gets past their roadblocks. Once it gets out there, and put into use, there's not much point in suppressing it anymore—but they don't bother culling the collection."

"But why suppress stuff this—this trivial?" Norla asked.

"I don't know," said Koffield. "I was expecting a much smaller and more focused collection. I was expecting to find things like the Intruder drive."

"You could be two rows and three bays over from it," said Bolt. "We could all work here until our suits run out of power and still miss it."

"Agreed," said Koffield. "But we've got to *try*. Norla's observation should save us some time. If it looks familiar already, skip it. If it's just a tweak or an upgrade, skip it. Watch for bays that represent major advances."

"Gee," said Bolt under his breath, "those should be easy to spot."

The job was impossible. But what choice did they have? Norla went forward, trying to concentrate, trying to push all the puzzles and mysteries to the back of her mind. Look for the major advances. There was a faster-than-light drive down here, somewhere. DeSilvo had found it.

She moved fast down the endless avenue, barely pausing at each bay. Two or three times she stopped to run the bookcatcher when something seemed like it at least came close to being a major advance—but the Dark Museum was turning out to have a great number of exhibits that weren't worth looking at—

Norla stopped dead, almost toppling over in her tracks as she skidded to a halt. There it was: METHOD OF ACCELERATION TO SUPERLUMINAL VELOCITIES. There was something stuck over the catalog number, but she didn't study it too carefully. She stopped and looked at the bay. The absolutely dead-empty bay. Nothing there except the now-empty display tables that had plainly once held *something*, and the empty bookshelf that had been filled, top to bottom, if she could judge by the scuff marks and indentations on the shelves.

DeSilvo had not only found it. He had stolen it.

Norla swore to herself. *Damn the man.* To lead them along by the nose, to drag them to this miserable planet and this terrifyingly large cavern—just to rub their noses in it. *I have it, you don't.* But they had to keep trying. She stepped over the bay's curb, and, feeling both ridiculous and desperate, began to search every corner of its emptiness, peeking under the barren display table, on the off chance that a faster-than-light drive had fallen off and rolled under it. But what else was she to do?

Nothing. Not a damn thing at all in the place, except the placard—and the metal plaque attached to it, obscuring the catalog number, bearing some sort of mathematical formula. It was rectangular, about ten centimeters by twenty-five. It had a yellow background, with a blue line drawn around the border. In big red raised letters, it read

$$\in (oskd@(\forall X \ni X \neq Au))$$

She couldn't understand it, but she knew what it meant.

Oskar DeSilvo had left his calling card—and another damned puzzle for them to solve.

She reported what she had found to the others. Both of them wanted to see it, but she waved them off—there was nothing to see, aside from the plaque with its mathematical gibberish. She photographed the plaque, and the entire bay, and moved on.

Somehow, departing that bay was the signal for time to blur, for the task at hand to transform from meaningful work into endless rote, the same thing over and over, with no beginning and no end. She had been in this massive cavern for her whole life, cataloging mysterious machines, and she would be there until she died. Dark Museum without end, amen.

The others spotted identical placards over other bays—some stripped as clean as the Superluminal Velocities bays, others left intact. Some things DeSilvo was letting them have—others, he kept for himself.

Norla found a dozen, a hundred technologies that would have fascinated her on any other day. But with the clock running, with exhaustion closing in, nothing below the level of minor miracle was worthy of notice—and even amazing breakthroughs were only of passing interest.

There was always the hope that there was another bay, holding another, independent discovery of faster-than-light travel, somewhere in that vast space. Everything else had been invented and suppressed, over and over. It did not bear thinking about that the other instances of FTL might have been buried in the section that had collapsed. Maybe the crushed and shattered dust-covered bits she had seen on the cavern floor had been all that was left of a key to the stars.

Improved this, *Upgraded* that, *Enhanced* these and those. Endlessly onward. Another of those damned plaques over another empty bay. On and on.

Norla did not feel as if she were still truly aware of anything. Her eyes saw, her hands worked the camera or the bookcatcher, her feet moved her forward, but nothing seemed to get in at her. It was plain that Bolt and Koffield were being worn down just as hard. Just wearing a pressure suit, moving around in it, was hard work. Exhaustion was soaking into them, weighing them down. The three of them seemed to talk less and less as the weary time went on. Norla heard nothing on her suit radio but the sounds of breathing and exertion, and the occasional muffled curse from Bolt. It was therefore something of a surprise when Norla heard Koffield cry out in surprise.

"What the—" said the voice in her ear.

But there was nothing more, only silence. "Admiral?" she called. "What have you found? Anton?"

"Stand by," said Koffield. Then, half to himself—"I just can't believe this."

"Admiral?"

"Later," he said. "Later. I've got to look this over."

"Anton? Anton?" But Norla could get nothing more out of him, and she was exhausted enough not to care. She knew, deep inside some still-aware part of herself, that even an exhausted Anton Koffield would not react to anything that strongly without a good reason. But that was deep down inside, buried under all the numbed, exhausted outer layers of her mind.

She moved on.

Time seemed to come apart, dissolve into a cloud of grey effort. The suit's duration and depletion chronometer clicked off the seconds, minutes, hours, with relentless precision—and yet the precision seemed to have no relation to perceived time. Norla would glance at her suit's wrist-chron, and see that the last two hours of effort had taken all of five minutes, or that what seemed ten minutes to her had been three hours by the clock.

But finally came the moment she heard a strange, far-off beeping in her suit radio, and a red pinlight flashing on and off on her wrist display. They had reached the thirty-six-hour mark of living in their suits. None of them had slept in all that time, and they had spent the majority of that time down here, working through the display bays.

"Time's up," said Koffield, his voice husky with tiredness. "Finish whatever you're doing and meet at the base of the ramp by the subterrene." There was silence on the line for a moment. "Bolt! Jerand—are you there? Norla?"

"Wha?—yeah, okay." one of them replied. It took a moment for Norla to realize the voice was hers.

"Jerand? Jerand!" Koffield called out.

"Yeah, yeah, 'm here. See you a' th' ramp."

Norla finished her final bookcatcher scan, and stared at the wandlike device in her hand. The indicator showed it as a quarter-full. How much of that was going to be meaningless, and how much might save lives, maybe change worlds? She was too tired even to think about such things.

She stowed the catcher and her camera, and trudged wearily back toward the ramp, and the tunnel beyond that, and their ride out past that. Her suit had begun to chafe her left leg and thighs several hours before, and then gone far beyond chafing. Every step came with a burning pain. Now and then she felt something warm trickle down her leg, and she assumed it had to be blood. It didn't matter. Nothing mattered.

She spotted another of DeSilvo's brightly colored placards, stuck over a catalog number, and another, and another, as she stumbled down the broad avenue. She glared at the last of them, and swore endless revenge against the man. She hadn't even gotten halfway down one avenue. *He* had brought her here, to pick over the leavings—after he had spent leisurely weeks, months— maybe even years—studying this place, in person, and through ArtInts and TeleOperators. Wandella Ashdin's carefully constructed lifetime chronology of his movements had to have a few errors in it somewhere. He must have committed a few more frauds that she hadn't yet detected. But that didn't matter, either.

She stumbled forward, and came, at last, to the end of the broad avenue. She paused at the end, looked one way, then the other, and spotted the end of the ramp where Koffield was waiting. Far off across the caverns, she could see Bolt moving wearily toward the same spot.

"Good," said Koffield, as the two of them arrived. "Sit down. Get a good-sized drink from your water tubes, force down a food cube, and rest. Set half hour alarms, and close your eyes. If we run into problems, this could be our last chance for rest until we reach orbit."

The helmets of their suits had water dispensers, which worked reasonably well, and food dispensers that often did not. Norla sat down by the foot of the ramp, fumbled with the helmet's chin switches, and managed to get two of the gummy food cubes to go into her mouth, instead of lodging in the neck lining of the suit, the way they usually did. Bleary-eyed, she punched in the alarm timer, then leaned back against the side of the ramp. Closing her eyes seemed like a wonderful idea. If she could just sleep for—

BEEP! BEEP! BEEP!

The wake-up alarm jolted her awake, and it took her three tries before she was focused enough to shut it off. Koffield and Bolt were both still out, but both jolted awake as their alarms went off, a few seconds after hers. Norla found herself jealous of the few extra seconds of rest they had gotten.

The three of them staggered to their feet. As best Norla could see through their helmets, the two men looked to be at death's door—and she doubted she looked all that much better.

"Still alive, more or less?" Koffield asked, his voice barely more than a croak. He coughed to clear his throat, then spoke again, more clearly. "All right, then," he said. "Stimulants. Take one lozenge now. It should hold you together for a while—and don't take another without instruction, no matter how much you start to fade, or you'll do yourself—and all of us—more harm than good."

Norla hoped she wouldn't need those warnings. Spacers were trained to view stim pills with deep suspicion. They could help for a time, and this was just the sort of moment for which they were intended. But it was easy, very easy, to take a stim, let it mask your exhaustion, and then make the mistake of thinking the pill had *ended* your exhaustion. A tired spacer at least knew her judgment was impaired, and her reflexes slowed. But feed her a stim pill, and it could be all too easy to *feel* much better, without actually *being* able to think more clearly or move faster.

Norla downed one of the stim tabs from her helmet service tube and instantly gulped down the water to kill the taste. And no doubt tomorrow she'd have a splitting headache—if she lived that long. The suit designers could have put in pills that tasted good, pills that had no side effects—but they chose not to do so. As a result, few spacers took the stim pills for fun.

Norla couldn't remember the last thing she had done for fun. She sat there, too weary to move, waiting for the pill to kick in—and astonished when it did, a few moments later. She had felt so worn down she had doubted that the pill could even reach her. Obviously, it had.

She blinked, and somehow the lights seemed brighter, sharper. She stood up, and the pain in her thigh seemed to hurt less than it had. Things seemed possible again. The idea of walking back through that endless tunnel was not so disheartening. It was all illusion, of course, and she knew it would fade as soon as the stim pill wore off. But sometimes you *needed* illusions.

"All right," said Koffield, sounding a lot more awake himself. "Let's go."

They saw it as they approached the top of the ramp, on the back of the first hatch, the one leading directly out of the Dark Museum. It was painted in the same bright colors as the other plaques, but the symbols were a trifle different.

$$\rightarrow (\forall X \ni X \neq Au)$$

"How the hell did we miss that on the way in?" asked Bolt.

"It was on the wrong side of the door for us to see it," said Koffield. "The lights were off when Norla closed the hatch—and then we had other things to look at."

"Well, this one starts with a little arrow instead of a rounded-off capital 'E.' Got the first clue what it means?" Bolt asked. "Either of you?"

"For one thing, it means DeSilvo has some odd ideas about mathematical notation," said Norla.

"I doubt it is a mathematical equation," said Koffield. "Not in the usual sense. It's a puzzle, and, I suspect, a backup. Just in case we—or whoever got this far—managed to miss all the calling cards DeSilvo left down there."

"But why are the symbols different?" Bolt asked.

"He gave us three different versions of the latitude and longitude puzzle," said Norla. "Maybe the differences between the two of them is meant to give us a hint."

"Or a headache," said Bolt. He carefully photographed the plaque, then put his camera away. "Let's get this hatch open and get moving."

Norla undid the release levels and spun open the seal. The others stepped through ahead of her, and she followed. The moment she left the cavern, the lights of the Dark Museum shut off, before she could even close the hatch. *Here's your hat, what's your hurry?* thought Norla as she and the others flicked on their helmet lights. Somehow, she felt as if the Dark Museum was glad to see them go, glad to turn the lights out again and return to its interrupted slumbers.

Slumber. Even through the imaginary sense of well-being afforded by the stim pill, the very idea of sleep filled her with longing. *Sleep. Get out of this suit, get clean, and sleep.* The tunnel before them led the way toward all those goals. She started walking.

An identical plaque was mounted over the hatch on the museum side of the first decontamination chamber. It was set back in a niche over the hatch itself, so that anyone standing near the hatch would not be able to see it—but for anyone walking toward the hatch, returning from the museum, it would be plainly visible from some distance away. It appeared to be coated with some sort of hyperreflective paint. Bolt dutifully photographed the plaque and they moved on.

They spotted the first sign of trouble as soon as they stepped out of the first decon compartment. Koffield was the one who noticed it. He knelt, and looked at something on the floor.

"What is it?" Norla asked.

"I can't quite see. Shine your helmet lights here," said Koffield. He stared down at a small dot on the floor of the tunnel. "Symbiote mold," he said at last. "We must have walked it in with us."

"How could it start growing so fast?" Bolt asked.

"How could the damned stuff take over a whole planet?" Norla replied. "Not much we can do about it now. We have to keep moving. Come on."

They walked down the steep grade to the flood-control pit, and then back up all the long and weary way that they had come. They started to see more and more of the little tufts of mold, and soon they were appearing at an almost regular spacing from each other, something less than a meter apart.

Norla couldn't understand it at first. Did the mold have some genetics that made it shoot spores forward a particular distance?—then she understood, and felt foolish. No, of course not. The mold didn't need to do any such thing. Not when it could get itself stuck to the treads of a pressure suit boot, and get carried along by spacers who were obligingly unthorough when it came time to decontaminate their suits.

She couldn't help but wonder which one of them it was—but what was the point? It *could* have been any of them, and they *had* tried to check each other over. They might well have walked the stuff into the Dark Museum. Maybe symbiote molds were already growing in and around the display bays, eating into the exhibits, destroying whatever knowledge had survived the previous catastrophes.

And if they had infected the Museum, there was not a damned thing they could do about it, even if they had the time. And one look at her suit's depletion countdown clock told her they had precious little of that commodity. There was nothing they could do but keep walking.

They reached the second decon chamber, and were not in the least surprised to see yet another copy of the arrow plaque over the entrance to it.

Mold was growing inside the decontamination chamber itself. Either they had done an even poorer job of decon than Norla had thought, or DeSilvo hadn't provided the right sorts of solvents and antiseptic agents, or—most likely—the chemicals he had provided had simply been sitting on the shelf too long and had lost their potency.

They moved through the decon chamber and into the last leg of the tunnel. The mold was even more noticeable here. Norla could almost imagine that she could see the grey patches growing and spreading over the floor, walls, and ceilings as she watched.

Eager to get out of the tunnel, up from underground—and back to the ship—they hurried toward the tunnel's end, and the antechamber that would lead them upstairs.

Mold colonies were spreading out everywhere on the steps leading up to the vault entrance. They hurried up into the temple, shoved the door open—and found the temple interior almost completely blanketed in the stuff.

"What the hell made it grow so fast?" Bolt demanded.

"Maybe the waste heat from our suits," said Koffield. "Maybe when we walked through the mold crust outside we stirred up dormant spores and stimulated them. Maybe the rocket burn on landing woke them up. Maybe they found some sort of nutrient in the rocket exhaust."

"Maybe a lot of things," Norla growled. She grabbed at the vault door and started swinging it shut. "Help me with this."

"Why bother?" Bolt demanded as he grabbed on to the heavy door. "We're not coming back."

"No, but someone might, someday," said Norla, grunting with the effort of moving the door. "It'd be nice if we weren't the ones who destroyed the rest of all the knowledge down there, or made it impossible to reach. We can't decontaminate the tunnel—but maybe the stuff that's in there already will die off if we cut off air and light."

The vault door swung to with a booming crash that they could feel shaking the floor. Norla closed the lock and spun the dials, then closed the sheath door over the vault. She had to scrape four or five tufts of mold out of the way to make it close completely.

That accomplished, she followed the others out of the temple, her mind mainly on remembering to close the temple door as well. She grabbed at the door, yanked it hard, then came around to the outside and pushed it shut after her as she stepped out under the sky. She started walking down the steps—and nearly tripped over Koffield and Bolt.

They had both stopped dead on the first step, just outside the temple. They were both still as statues, completely oblivious to the fact that Norla had just run into them.

They were both looking back toward the *São Paulo*. Norla followed their gaze—and felt horror grip at her insides.

The lander was covered, landing legs to nose, in a thin, patchy covering of symbiote-mold. But that was far from the worst of it.

The ground had given way under the port-side landing leg. It must have set down in a hollow filled with mold. The whole craft was leaning drunkenly at a fifteen-degree angle. Even as she watched, she could see it settling just a trifle more. The lean angle was increasing, minute by minute.

Another few degrees and the *São Paulo* would fall over on her side.

CHAPTER EIGHTEEN

ROCKETS AND ROCKS

Anton Koffield stood there, frozen to the spot for perhaps a dozen heartbeats. His body was motionless, but his mind was moving fast—from shock and disbelief, to acceptance, to analysis, to decision—and then to command.

"Bolt! Pull all your bookcatchers, your cameras, any other recordings or objects from the Museum. Hand them over to Chandray. I'll do the same."

Bolt hadn't quite recovered his wits. "But—what—"

"Do it!"

Bolt nodded and got started pulling things from his suit. Koffield pulled all his own recording gear. "Officer Chandray, pack all this into your suit's pockets whatever way you can. Bolt, help her load up the upper torso pouches." Koffield knelt and stuffed his gear into the leg pockets of her suit, jamming them full. He stood up just as Bolt was finishing.

"Is that everything, Bolt?"

"Yes, sir!"

"Very well. Officer Chandray—Get aboard, get to the pilot's station, and get the gyros spooled up."

"But—"

"Go."

"But the gyros won't hold her up against this gravity."

"No, but they'll help steady her. Be ready on the attitude jets. If she starts to go over, use them to rock her back. *Go.* You'll be well within suit radio range. We'll keep talking as you go. And no sudden moves as you go aboard."

"No, sir. I wasn't planning on it," said Norla. She got moving.

Koffield waited until she was on her way before he spoke again. "Officer Chandray—don't stop. Keep moving, and get into that pilot's seat as fast as you safely can."

"Yes, sir."

"You are to power up all flight systems to standby status. If, in your sole judgment, the ship is about to topple, and the only way to save her is to launch at once, you are to do so. That is a direct order."

"But that'll strand—"

"We'll only be stranded until the *Rio de Janeiro* can make pickup." Of course, their suits would be completely depleted by then, and both he and Bolt would be long dead, but never mind. "If the ship does topple, and you *don't* launch to save her—we're all stranded, we likely won't have a working radio even if we wanted to break radio silence, and none of the material we've worked so hard to get will ever be seen by anyone. Keep moving. Don't slow down. Don't look back. Do you understand your orders?"

"Yes—yes, sir."

"Will you obey them?"

A pause, but then at last she spoke. "Yes, sir—most unwillingly."

"Very well," said Koffield. Taking his eyes off her for the first time since she had started walking, he looked again at the lander. One tiny blessing—the landing pad with the boarding ladder was ninety degrees away from the pad that was settling into the hollow. Going up the ladder shouldn't affect the delicate balance—much.

"Right," he said. "Bolt, you're with me."

"What are we doing?" Bolt asked, plainly eager for some sort of direction, some sort of plan.

"Those hummocks of yours. We figured those were the landers, covered over. DeSilvo had a lot of cargo to move around. Let's see if there's any handling equipment there—or anything we can use to brace the ship somehow. Something we can use to jack her up."

The two men turned and moved as quickly as they could toward the closest of the low mounds of crusted symbiote-mold, putting the *São Paulo* out of view behind them. "Officer Chandray," Koffield called. "We can't watch you as we move. Report as you go."

"Stand by," she said. "Just reaching the landing pad." They heard her over the helmet radio as she grunted with effort. "Moving slowly," she said. "The lander seems more or less steady for the moment."

"I don't need to tell you again—no sudden moves," said Koffield.

Koffield and Bolt reached the closest of the hummocks. It was a perfectly rounded dome. Plainly there was something artificial under the carpet of mold. "We have get through the mold and see what's under there. Do you see anything we could use as a scraper or a digger?" Koffield asked.

"Sir, there's ten centimeters of that mold crud over everything."

"Bare hands then," said Koffield. "Well, gloved hands." He made a fist and punched a hole in the outer crust of symbiote-mold, then stuffed his hands in and started clawing away at it. Bolt followed his lead and started his own hole. They clawed away, kicking up a cloud of broken-up mold and spores. The two of them quickly had a hole two meters across and two meters high, exposing a greenish flexible metallic covering underneath. Bolt poked at it. "I think I can punch through it," he said.

"We can't risk your cutting open your suit," Koffield protested.

"Why not?" asked Bolt. "Same logic as you handed Chandray. If that ship topples over because we can't find something to prop it up with, we're dead anyway." He made a fist and punched hard at the covering. It didn't give. He tried again. Still no good. "A rock," he said. "A sharp rock would do it."

Both men got down on their hands and knees and started scrabbling through the crust of mold. After a few moments, they exposed the surface, rocks and soil that had lain more or less undisturbed for millions, even billions, of years—until humans had shown up.

Well, it was time to disturb the rocks some more. Both men grubbed around in the dirt, kicking more mold and spores and dust up as they dug. "Here!" Koffield called out, holding out a rock with a wickedly sharp daggerlike point at one end.

Bolt took it, stood up, and slashed at the covering. It tore open easily. He dragged the rock along through the material diagonally, widening the gash in the fabric. Moving gingerly, Koffield grabbed at the flap of metal fabric. "The cut edge doesn't seem that sharp," he said. Just the same, he folded it back to get the cut edge away from his suit gloves. He pulled on it. It tore easily. Either DeSilvo hadn't bothered with superstrong material for his camouflage covering, or else a century-plus of exposure to Martian weather and symbiote-mold had done the stuff no good.

Bolt slashed another hole in the fabric and pulled the new flap toward Koffield. They joined up the two cuts quickly and pulled down nearly the whole side of the covering, showering themselves once again with mold and dust.

They could see now that the fabric had been supported by a geodesic frame, the metal struts bolted together to form a skeleton of two-meter-wide three-sided cells.

"Admiral!" Chandray called on the radio. "I have reached the pilot station and strapped in. I have the rate gyros spooling up. I have attitude jets on-line and ready to fire."

"Very good. We've just gotten into one of the hummocks—one of the storage domes, I should say."

"Do you see anything we can use to stabilize the lander?" Chandray asked.

"Stand by on that," Koffield said. "We're not in the dome yet. Officer Chandray—you did not report main engines or navigation at standby. Please report now."

"Working on that now, Admiral."

"See that you do." He turned toward his companion. "All right, Bolt. We have to move fast. Anything—the first thing—tools or equipment we might be able to use."

Koffield stepped inside the framework, switched on his helmet lights, and looked around. Bolt followed.

"Do you see anything?" Chandray asked again.

Bolt shook his head—not a very useful act during a radio conversation. "Not much," he said. "There's nothing here but an old lander covered in very dead mold."

"I was hoping for some sort of equipment hauler or winch or pallet jacks," said Koffield. "DeSilvo must have had *some* sort of load-hauling equipment we could use to jack the ship or winch it back to vertical."

Chandray called in. "If she does go over—could we boost out of here to orbit on one of the abandoned one-shot landers?"

Bolt shook his head again. "Not a hope in hell with this one. This thing is shot. I can see three kinds of leak from here. I'm guessing the other ones don't look much better."

Things were looking bad. "Officer Chandray," said Koffield. "You've had a chance to check your angles and your situation. Could you lift off from your present altitude?"

"Sir, I wouldn't want to try it on this lander. She's really a space-to-space job with legs and landing engines stuck on. A compromise. She's top-heavy. If the settled-in landing pad adhered to the surface just for a second, over she'd go. And I wouldn't want to try it unless I was well rested. I *think* I'm in good enough shape for regular flying—but if I did a liftoff like that, it would be like a half-asleep surgeon doing brain surgery."

"How about just boosting high enough to hover around to a new landing?" Bolt asked.

"No. Even worse," said Koffield. "Boosting straight

up at full power gives you some momentum and stability. Lofting up to a hover, you're trying to stay low and slow—damned hard to control, and even easier to topple. Plus we don't exactly have a lot of propellant to play with. But Officer Chandray—Norla—if you have to launch to save the ship, even if it's dangerous—*do it*. It's got to be less dangerous than letting the ship topple."

Koffield struggled to think, to come up with some solution. They had a ship that could fly, and a pilot that could fly her. It would be maddening to be done in by the collapse of a crust of mold.

But then, the whole damned terraforming project had been done in by that very same mold crust. Why should they hope to survive when so many others had been destroyed by the same enemy?

Think. There had to be a way. "We're just going to have to tear into every one of these storage domes," said Koffield. "There must be something in one of them."

"Admiral!" Norla called. "My slope indicator says it's getting worse. We're showing about another quarter degree of angle since I got here. We don't have time for searches."

"Admiral," said Bolt, "maybe we've got something here, on this lander—if we knew where to look."

"What?"

"Toolbox, sir. They use this sort of lander a lot for initial delivery to construction sites—where they're going to build a dome or something. They're expected to be dropped into unimproved fields—like this one. These days, at least, they strap on a standard tool kit, emergency hand tools in case the lander winds up in a crater, or a pallet jams. That sort of thing."

"And things stay the same. If they do it that way now—"

"They did it that way a hundred years ago."

"Let's start looking." Bolt swung to the right around the lander, while Koffield moved left, hunching down low to get between the lander and the remains of the protective dome.

Koffield had been looking at the lander as a single discrete object. Now, suddenly, it was a jumble of sub-assemblies and modules, all strapped to a spidery set of legs. What the devil would an emergency tool kit look like?

"Here!" called Bolt. "Over here!"

Koffield stumbled back the way he had come, through the tangle of landing gear and dome supports. Bolt had found it indeed. A big red cylindrical container about a meter long and twenty centimeters across, labeled EMER-GENCY TOOLS in bright yellow letters, held to the frame of the lander by two quick-release clamps. Bolt popped the clamps, and the two men hauled it out of the dome and set it down on the ground. Bolt undid two more quick-release clamps, and it swung open lengthwise.

It wasn't much. A crowbar. A length of rope. A fold-ing shovel. Some wrenches, screwdrivers, and cutting tools. A hand-cranked winch that looked strong enough to move a few hundred kilos at most. A length of accordion-pleated fuel line. A few other odds and ends. Koffield had been hoping for some sort of portable heavy-duty jack—but it wasn't there and there wasn't time. If they were going to get off the planet, they were going to do it using the tools in front of them. Koffield stared at the collection for a good twenty seconds, and then turned to look, long and hard, at the lander.

"All right," he said at last. "I think I see a way."

Bolt kept busy with the shovel and scraped away the last of the mold crust from around the fallen landing gear. It was obvious now what had happened. The crust had grown over a small, deep, crater, about two meters across and nearly two meters deep, and then more mold had grown over the first layer, and more over that, until the crater had been entirely filled in, so it looked like a smooth spot on the landscape. But the mold crusts under the top layer had partially disintegrated over time and fi-nally collapsed under the landing leg's weight. And it looked as if the pad had actually slid laterally a bit, slip-ping deeper into the crater.

"Take a break," said Koffield. "My turn."

Bolt nodded wearily, and handed the shovel back without argument. "I'll rest a minute," said Bolt, "then go get more rocks." He sat down and shut his eyes.

It was plain to see that Bolt's stim pill was starting to wear off. Koffield didn't feel so good himself. "Fine," he said to Bolt. "I'll start in on getting some gravel and soil piled up." He started digging, and called Norla as he did. "Officer Chandray? What's our tilt angle?"

"Still at 25.2," she said. "Hasn't gotten any worse in the last few minutes. Oh—I've had a chance to check the on-line manuals for the specs. Supposedly we're safe to boost at anything under eighteen degrees."

"Well, that's something," said Koffield.

"Not much. The same specs say the topple angle is twenty-four degrees."

"Not exactly comforting," Koffield said calmly. "But I'm glad of whatever it is that's holding her up." He dug as fast as he could in the bulky suit, but the heap of soil he was accumulating was pathetically small for the job at hand. Inwardly, he was far less calm about that topple angle. It could be that the only thing holding the ship up was a gentle breeze against the upper hull. Or maybe some coolant scavenger tank near the base of the ship was almost full, and a sensor was about to trigger a pump that would send the coolant, and its mass, back up into the upper deck, wrecking the delicate balance.

Or, more than likely, it was the gyros—but they couldn't be kept running at full power forever.

Bolt opened his eyes with a start. "I dozed off there for a second," he said. They had been in their suits for over forty hours. He sat for a moment longer, then stood up, and said, "I'll get rocks." He went off a few meters, dragging the empty cylinder of the tool kit behind him, towing it with a tied-off loop of the rope that had come in the kit. It came close enough to being a serviceable sledge that it probably had been designed to serve as one. There was an outcropping of rocks about twenty meters away that they hadn't gotten to yet. Bolt got to the outcropping and started loading them in.

Koffield kept digging.

"I wish I could be out there helping," said Norla. "You both look absolutely miserable."

"Remind me never to hire you as a morale officer," said Bolt with a tired laugh.

"We need you on the controls, Norla," said Koffield. What he didn't say was *And I'm afraid that if you moved out of that pilot's chair, it could be enough to overbalance the damned ship.* "Besides, once we boost, it doesn't matter if *we* get worn-out—but we want our pilot rested."

"All right, all right. Ah, ah, Admiral—the tilt indicator's moving just a hair. Closing on 25.3 degrees now."

"Very well," he said. "I wanted to have more material ready, but we're going to have to try it with what we've got." He stabbed his shovel into the ground and jogged over to help Bolt. The two of them loaded up the split-cylinder sledge with the biggest rocks they could find, then both of them grabbed at the rope and leaning into it, hauled as hard as they could in the bad footing of the mold crust.

Koffield fell down once, and it was as he was picking himself up that he noticed the thin film of something like frozen grey smoke on the arm of his suit. He stood up, looked down at his chest and his legs, and then over at Bolt's suit, leaning in to get a close look at the burn-off suit's fabric. "The mold's growing on our suits," he announced.

"What?" Bolt looked at his suit, and saw the greyish film. "I thought that was impossible."

"Tell it to the mold," Koffield muttered. "Officer Chandray—do you see any mold on your suit?"

"I can't move around much in this pilot's chair—but no. Nothing that I can see. You two have been out and around in it a lot more."

"Practically swimming in it," Bolt growled. "Wait a second. Admiral—hold still." It was Bolt's turn to lean in close. "Sir, I think there's a patch of it starting up on the far right side of your visor."

Why not? thought Koffield. *If it could grow on the*

bioresistant suit fabric, why not on the helmet? And if it could start growing—why couldn't it keep growing? Why not grow thick and full over the suit's arms, chest, visor? Why not blind me, seal me into the darkness of the suit before killing me? "Get that little broom of yours out and brush it off," he said. "Gently."

Bolt reached into one of his suit pockets, pulled out the broom—and then threw it away in horrified disgust. The thing was choked with mold, the bristles barely even visible. The two men looked at each other. "Sir, ah, I don't think I should brush your helmet off with my hand. It's probably got mold spores all over it too."

Koffield looked down at his own hands and nodded. "We've got to get out of here," he said.

The two men grabbed the rope and started to pull, leaning into the weight as if—because—their lives depended on it.

"Admiral!" Chandray called.

"What is it?"

"I'm doing checks on the interior video cameras. There're patches of mold all through the lower deck, wherever I touched things. How the hell does it grow so fast?"

"It's opportunistic, I think," Koffield said, grunting a bit with the effort of pulling the sledge. "We're presenting all sorts of new surfaces, without anything else already growing on them. And I think just being kicked around, physically disturbed, stimulates growth somehow."

"Does it matter?" Bolt asked.

"Only if we stay here much longer," Koffield said grimly. They had reached the edge of the two-meter-wide crater that had trapped the landing pad. "Okay," said Koffield. "Let's get this right over the edge of the crater, so we can dump the rocks straight in." They wrestled the sledge into position, with one end dangling over the lip of the crater. Koffield grabbed the shovel, and Bolt positioned himself at the far end of the sledge, ready to tip the contents in. "Don't let the sledge itself go in," Koffield said. "We might need it again."

"No, sir."

"All right," said Koffield. "I think we're ready. At least as ready as we're going to get."

"I really don't like this idea," said Chandray.

"We don't have time to think of a better one," Koffield replied. "Give us a countdown—and a warning if the thrusters give you trouble. Proceed."

"Yes, sir," Chandray said. "Forward lateral port-firing thruster pair to 20 percent thrust. Firing in five seconds. Four. Three. Two. One. Zero—"

The roar of the jets was astonishingly loud. Koffield looked up at the apex of the *São Paulo* to see the two side-firing thrusters belching blue flame, two jets of fire parallel to the ground. The *São Paulo* rocked slightly, shifted a bit—and then the landing pad began to lift out of the crater, slowly at first, then angling up higher and higher.

But not high enough. It wasn't clear of the ground. "Go to 30 percent," Koffield ordered, shouting to be heard over the roar of the thrusters.

The noise grew louder still—and the *São Paulo* shifted farther, the pad lifting clear. Koffield looked under the lander's stern, to the starboard-side landing gear. It was pitching downward, easing toward the ground. If it hit too hard, and bounced, then the lander was sure to tip over. "Ease back!" he called. "Twenty-five percent."

The starboard pad touched ground, and the port pad was in midair, a good meter and a half above the bottom of the crater.

Koffield did not give himself time to wonder if the next step was such a good idea. He jumped down into the crater and levered himself in under the landing pad. He tried not to think that the only thing keeping that pad from dropping down and crushing him were two noisy thrusters that could turn balky at any time. *Suppose the leg does drop on top of me and crush me. Would that get the lander close enough to vertical? Could they, would they, launch?* The horrid image of the *São Paulo* literally lifting off from his corpse flashed before his eyes. *Dig harder,* he told himself.

He scrabbled frantically with the shovel, scooping out

the last of the mold from under the pad, scraping the bottom of the pad itself clear. The pad *moved*, just a trifle, while he was under it—and he got out from under faster than he could explain. "All right!" he called. "Dump 'em!"

Bolt heaved up on the far end of the sledge, and the load of rocks went tumbling down into the crater. Koffield started grabbing rocks from the pile they had collected on previous sledge runs and heaving them into the hole. Bolt emptied out the sledge, pulled it clear of the crater, and started to help Koffield throw rocks.

"Thirty seconds into burn," Officer Chandray reported.

Has it been that long? It seemed much longer—and much shorter.

He was running out of rocks that seemed big enough to be useful. He didn't remember dropping the shovel, but now he picked it up and started frantically heaving the dirt in over the rocks. It sifted down into the cracks, filling in gaps, making the base at least a little more solid. Bolt knelt next to him and started shoving dirt and rocks into the hole, using his hands like a bulldozer.

"Forty-five seconds. Thrusters starting to show some heating."

No wonder. They weren't meant for extensive use in an atmosphere—and stars alone knew where the mold might have gotten in.

The crater was no more than half-full—but it would have to do. "All right," Koffield called. "Throttle down to zero—very slowly."

The noise slowly subsided, and the landing pad began to drift lower, slowly, very slowly. It touched the top rock in the pile and pushed it down, sending some small rocks cascading downward into the pile. Then it began to settle in, crushing down on the pile, grinding it down, rocks breaking and cracking and popping under the weight. The thrusters faded away to nothing. The pad continued settling in for a moment, the rocks still cracking and grinding.

And then it stopped. The port-side landing pad was

sitting on a platform of crushed rock. The starboard pad was still in midair, but only just. They could wedge ten or fifteen biggish rocks under it in five minutes.

"Slope angle—16.7 degrees," said Norla, breathing a sigh of relief. "Good enough for the likes of us. Come on up, gentlemen. It should be safe for you to board."

CHAPTER NINETEEN

DUST AND CLOUDS, SMOKE AND FIRE

Jerand Bolt, feeling weary to his bones, followed Koffield aboard the *São Paulo*, climbing up the ladder to the airlock entrance. At last, they could rest, rest until Deimos had safely set, then boost out of here before Phobos rose, in the thin slice of time when neither satellite could see them pass. Bolt was damned glad Koffield had allowed a few hours for—what had he called it? "Contingency management." They had used up a good chunk of that time filling in the crater and keeping the ship upright, but still, there would be time to rest.

There were tufts of moss everywhere on the ship's hull. Some of them were starting to flatten out and braid themselves together, beginning the process that would eventually produce a solid mat of the horrid stuff. Bolt saw more of it growing on the arms of his suit and brushed it off irritably.

Koffield had the outer door of the lock open, and Bolt climbed up in next to him. They pulled the door shut. Hardly any point in cycling the airlock at this point, but never mind. Bolt checked the outer door seal, and then punched the CYCLE LOCK button.

Nothing happened.

Jerand frowned, checked all his settings, and tried it

again. Still nothing. "Sir, I think the autocycle system is out. Should I go to manual?"

Koffield was staring thoughtfully at a tuft of symbiote-mold by an air intake vent. Bolt looked at it too. There seemed to be one thin tendril reaching *into* the vent. "No," he said. "Wait a moment." He turned to look at the tiny lock's extremely simple interior control panel. "Koffield to Chandray," he said. "Run an environmental systems status check. Just the basic diagnostics."

"Sir?"

"Just do it."

"Stand by—it'll take a few minutes to—" Officer Chandray's voice cut off suddenly.

"What is it?" Koffield asked.

"Sorry, sir. Just got a little thrown off there. Usually you get a blank screen that says 'diagnostic running.' This time, I got so many errors and faults they were scrolling by faster than I could read them. Still running."

There was a moment's silence.

"Ah, sir, initial diagnostic shows several minor faults that have already taken place, a dozen or so minor imminent faults, and three or four major ones threatening. Mostly short circuits and circuit failures."

"Bloody devil's hell," said Jerand. "The mold's gotten in. Can that stuff eat circuits, or insulation, or something?"

"So it would appear. Officer Chandray. Run a full ship's status check," said Koffield. "Do the basic diagnostic again."

"Already running, sir. Stand by."

A longer pause, and then Chandray's voice again, sounding slightly less worried. "One or two minor pending faults. Nothing we can't handle."

"For now, anyway," said Koffield. "But I think we have to assume that the symbiote-mold has entered the ship through the environmental system and started to take hold there. It's bound to keep spreading." He thought for a moment. "We'd better not come in," he said. "We'd be bringing in another, and probably larger, dose of the stuff and make the problem worse. We won't enter the ship's interior until just before launch. We can use the manual door controls to open the lock."

"Suppose those are jammed?" Jerand asked.

"Very unlikely—but if necessary, we could ride out the launch in here. It wouldn't be comfortable, but we'd survive it. We'd just reopen the outer door once we're in space and it's time to abandon ship. There's an escape hatch on the upper deck. Officer Chandray could get out that way."

"That sounds pretty hairy," Jerand replied.

"That stuff is eating the ship's systems *now*—how bad will it get and how fast, with a triple dose on the job?" Koffield asked.

Chandray spoke. "Sir, it's going to get worse, even with just the mold that's in here already—and the longer we wait to launch, the worse it's going to get. Plus there's the mold patches on the outside of the ship. The mold might find a way to get in through the attitude jets or something."

"Go on," said Koffield.

"The ship's deteriorating. We need to launch as soon as possible, before we get some worse system failures. We'll just have to hope that Deimos doesn't happen to be looking this way."

"Sir!" Bolt called out. "No. We can't do that!"

"Why not?" Chandray asked.

"Because they *will* be looking—what else would they be doing? It's an ArtInt system, told to watch for spacecraft launches from the surface. They'll backtrack us. They'll follow our boost trajectory and know we came from here. That wouldn't matter if DeSilvo had just put down a little box of a building with a message for us. That's what I figured we'd find. If the Interdict crowd found that, it probably wouldn't mean much to them. They're not much on security in the Solar System these days. Maybe they'd send down a probe to poke around or something, and it wouldn't tell them much. Probably they'd figure we were insane tourists or rogue archeologists, and trust to the spores to kill us before we got anywhere. They'd leave us alone.

"But if they find our launch point, they'll find the temple and the landers. If they weren't obvious from space before, they will be now—there will be the burn-off from our launch, the torn-open storage dome, and the broken-up mold crust. A few days or weeks from now, I bet all that'll be molded over enough to hide everything—but not immediately. They'll come, they'll look, they'll find our landing spot and the temple, and they'll find the vault door. *Find* that, and they'll either get past the booby traps and get in, or they'll set them off—and set off all the self-destructs. *That'll* give 'em a line of collapsed tunnel pointing straight as an arrow at the Dark Museum—"

"And if people who find that tunnel talk to the people who know what's down there—well, once they know that we've gotten in there, they'd never stop hunting us," said Koffield. "You're right. They'd hunt us down, and the *Dom Pedro IV*."

Bolt nodded. It was crowded in the tiny lock, and somehow he felt as if he were too close to Koffield for serious conversation. He tried to back off into the corner as much as he could. "But go further. Between what we collected down there, and what they'd find in the Dark Museum, and aboard the *DP-IV*, *they'd* probably be able to figure out where DeSilvo is, even if we haven't—yet. They'd scoop him up too, and whatever toys he has stashed away."

"And it would all be for nothing," said Chandray over the radio. "I think Mr. Bolt has a point."

"Agreed. We can't launch until Deimos sets."

"Sir, I won't argue with that," said Chandray. "But that's four hours from now. The way theses failure projections are running, I doubt we'll be able to launch by then."

"We still have a heavy cloud deck," said Jerand. "How about we launch, and fly east under it until we've gotten to where Deimos has already set? We don't punch out of the clouds until then. Even if the watchers are using thermal sensors, with a little luck the clouds will be enough to mask the engine burn."

"Propellant," said Chandray. "Sir, we did a fifty-three-second burn of the attitude jets, and I'm worried *that* was enough to wipe out our reserves. Right now I think we can make orbit—some kind of orbit—but I'm not sure we can make rendezvous with the *Cruzeiro do Sul*."

"Mr. Bolt mentioned propellant from the landers before we came down," said Koffield. "What are your thoughts?"

"I think hundred-year-old propellant tanks will be full of mold spores," said Chandray.

"Ma'am, sir—you're probably right. But I got a look at one of those landers. They make a model like it today. And if the old ones are like the current ones, I'd say there's a pretty good chance of at least one lander still having factory-sealed tanks of propellant—same formulation as the *São Paulo* uses. Besides, even if the tanks aren't perfectly sealed, that propellant is nasty stuff. It'll kill anything. And even if the propellant didn't kill the mold, and even if it does have spores in it, the propellant will still burn. Just not as well. Yeah, the spores might clog the fuel pumps—eventually. But this ship doesn't have much future anyway."

"Admiral?" Chandray asked. "This one's up to you. I'll fly whatever course you decide."

Koffield leaned against the wall of the airlock and shut his eyes. Jerand could see his expression clearly, even through the helmet visor, and felt it almost a violation of the man's privacy to see him so tired, so careworn, with his guard so completely down.

Jerand shifted his gaze to look at the man's suit, but that was far from comforting. The mold tufts were spreading, and there were at least three distinct patches on the edges of the helmet's visor. They dared not wipe it off. That just seemed to stimulate faster growth over a wider area. Sooner or later, the stuff was going to blind them.

Koffield opened his eyes and spoke. "Do you still have our original flight plan cued up?" he asked.

"Yes, sir," Chandray replied.

"Make sure you have reliable and redundant copies of it, as safe from system crashes as you can make it. Print out a hard copy if you can. Then start looking east for someplace it would have been plausible to land. Covert archeology or something. *Don't* pick a spot over water. Seeing a ship boost from the middle of the Northern Ocean would just be telling them we do have something to hide. Then plot a lowest-fuel-use course to that spot and a launch course starting from altitude. Get that done, and then start finding whatever you can that we can throw overboard and lighten the ship before we go. There won't be much. Marquez knew the *São Paulo* wasn't coming back, and had his people do a good job of stripping. But find what you can. Pile it by the inside of the inner airlock door, and we'll heave it all out when we come in. So. Do all that, and do it fast."

"That's a pretty long list," Chandray warned.

"I know," said Koffield. "But do it anyway. Choose speed over precision." He looked toward Jerand. "Bolt, lead the way. Let's see about those sealed propellant tanks of yours."

Norla Chandray watched on the video display as the two men headed back to the derelict landers. She felt privileged, and therefore guilty. Try as she might to tell herself that she was following orders, and that the orders made sense, and that it was all due to chance—nonetheless, she had been handed the soft side of the job. She had been resting, more or less safe inside the *São Paulo*, while the two men, already half-dead with exhaustion, had been digging ditches, stripping landers, hauling sledges, endless physical labor, under miserable conditions, with that damn mold growing thicker on them by the minute—while she took her ease inside.

It was just the sort of guilt that made Norla try harder, work faster, and it did the job this time. She had the old course stored, and a new one programmed in, before Koffield and Bolt had finished searching the first lander.

She set to work immediately looking for equipment

that could be abandoned. In a sense, in two senses, it was easy. One way or the other, the *São Paulo* and everything aboard her were going to be destroyed. There was no sense saving anything, just in case. Nothing could be saved, and there were no just-in-cases left. But there was also precious little aboard to start with. No food or drinking water, since they were going to spend the whole journey sealed in their suits. For similar reasons, most other things had been stripped out of the ship.

Norla found a stack of hard-copy repair manuals and a set of power tools that might have come in handy if they had found them sooner. There was a storage rack full of spare parts that weren't going to do any good. Marquez hadn't thought to strip out the plates and cups and eating utensils when they pulled the food. Then she stopped thinking about what was in the storage units and starting looking at the storage units themselves. It seemed that no one had thought of taking them out. The food storage locker was a modular unit that she quickly yanked out from the wall and added to the stack. The pocket galley came out just as easily. The pressure suit rack was also a quick-disconnect. Onto the stack with it. It didn't take her long to find all the other quick-disconnect fittings and get them pulled free of the hull.

Apparently, Marquez hadn't done quite as good a job as she thought—or maybe it was all stuff they would have no use for, or room for, on the other ships. What use a spare pocket galley? In any event, she had piled up at least a thousand kilos of mass, maybe more. It would help.

And they could use all the help they could get.

They found what they were looking for on the fourth lander they tried. Call it Lander Four.

Jerand Bolt was pleased, and very much relieved to be proved right. His idea of borrowing propellant tanks from one of the landers was not as far-fetched as it seemed, but it had still been a gamble. His knowledge of how the landers were built, and what they were normally used for, had made it less of a shot in the dark.

The one-use landers were built with the idea that they'd be taken apart and used for something else once they set down on the surface of whatever planet they were sent to. That meant they were designed to make it easy to pull parts off them. They were also built as cheaply as possible, with every system done in the simplest way it could be. That's why the propellant tanks were designed as they were.

When a rocket burns propellant, the mass of the propellant goes away. If the propellant is in a tank off to one side of the vehicle, this loss of mass will mean a constant shifting of the center of gravity as the rocket burns. Stacking all the tanks vertically over the center of gravity creates its own problems. It is often easier to use multiple tanks, and arrange them in a symmetrical pattern around the center of gravity. The sophisticated way to manage the balance problem was to more or less constantly pump propellant back and forth to correct for the balance shifts.

The simpler, even crude, way was to arrange the tanks in two or three pairs around the balance point. Burn the fuel in one pair of tanks opposite each other first, then burn the second pair, then the third. Anything left in the tanks can be scavenged for other uses once the lander is down. The designers had done what they could to make this convenient. The factory seal on the propellant tanks was not opened until the tanks were needed. Thus, if a given tank is not used at all, it could be pulled off the lander without any safety precautions and stored indefinitely.

And on Lander Four, Bolt found a pair of tanks with unbroken seals. The tool kit from the lander provided the wrenches needed to remove the tanks. It was far from easy to wrestle the big tanks down off the landers, but it was easy to imagine ways it could have been worse.

The two men used the tool kit cases from Landers Three and Four as sledges and lashed the tanks to them with some of the rope from the kits. The rest of the rope went for harnesses that could be looped across one arm and the torso, and they started man-hauling the tanks back. Both of them took a second stim pill before starting the job, but at best, that only made the job slightly less agonizing. *Maybe,* thought Bolt as he leaned into his pull-rope, *the stim pills can't find much of anything left to stimulate.* It was only a distance of 150 meters or so, but Jerand doubted they could have gone much farther than that.

The tool kits had fuel lines, and, for a miracle, their connectors were compatible with the *São Paulo's* fuel intake valve. Naturally, the lines were slightly too short, and they had to connect the lines from the two tool kits end to end before they would reach, but still it went more smoothly than they had a right to expect. There was a simple on-off switch for the fuel pump right next to the *São Paulo's* intake valve. For a further wonder, the mold hadn't gotten into the circuitry yet, and the pump started right up.

Moments later, Chandray was reading off the numbers on the propellant-remaining indicator as they went up. By the time the scavenged tanks were drained, the *São Paulo's* tanks were showing 63 percent full.

With a little luck, it would be enough to save their lives. It would have to be. Because Bolt knew that the effort it would take to go for another pair of tanks—even if they were there—would probably be enough to kill them both.

"Is that going to do it?" Jerand asked.

"It ought to," said Chandray. "I think I've found us a decoy launch site that's not *too* far off. New Tacoma. It's a port city, right by the water, a few hundred kilometers due east. We can boost from over the landward side of the place. If they spot us coming up out of the clouds, we'll look like souvenir hunters."

"Excellent," said Koffield as he pulled the fuel line off the *São Paulo's* intake. He slammed the access plate shut and dropped the fuel line hose down on the ground. "All right, Mr. Bolt. Unless you can think of something else that needs doing, I suggest we go aboard."

"I think we've thought of enough already, sir," Jerand replied.

"I hope so," said Koffield. "Because I'm too tired to think of anything more."

He turned toward the ladder that led up into the *São Paulo*, but then he stopped. "Mr. Bolt," he said. "I'm afraid I'm going to have to ask for your help in finding the way up. I've just discovered that the mold has grown clear over the top half of my helmet. I can't see anything at all above eye level."

Jerand didn't answer immediately. He had just looked down, to see the legs of his suit were completely covered in brownish-black mold. It looked to have eaten about halfway through the outer burn-off suit. He could still look up to see the ladder, and he did.

The hull of the ship was covered in the stuff. Some places it was so thick you couldn't see the ship at all. Other places it was just thin, hazy patches. But that wasn't going to last.

Jerand didn't say anything about what the ship looked like. What would be the point? Instead, he just responded to the Admiral's request. "Yes, sir. Let me help you up the ladder. I think we'd better get moving."

The inside of the airlock was black with mold, the interior completely covered in the horrible stuff. Jerand neither knew nor cared why the mold was growing so much darker in the airlock.

"Scrape it off," said Koffield. "We're covered in it anyway. We can't get much worse, and I want to keep that stuff out of the ship as much as we can. Officer Chandray!"

"Yes, Admiral?"

"Did you come across any sort of cloth we could wipe ourselves down with? Or something we could use as a scraper on the walls of the airlock? Or any sort of solvent? I'd be willing to try just about anything."

"Yes, sir. I think I can get you all three, if you can stand by just a moment."

"We'll start cycling the lock," said Jerand.

He had to scrape several hunks of mold off the hatch seal, and off the outer hatch itself, before the hatch

would close and seal properly. Koffield didn't even
bother trying the automatic system, but went right to the
emergency spill valves and bled ship's air into the lock.

As the pressure equalized and the hiss of the valve
faded out, they heard a series of grunts and sounds of effort over the radio, and bumps and low crashes from inside the ship. "All right," she said. "I'm right by the
inner airlock door with cloths, a few things that will do
as scrapers, and a bottle of disinfectant from the medi-
cine store."

"All right," said Koffield. "Open the hatch from that
side, hand it all in, and slam the hatch shut as fast as
you can."

Chandray did as she was told. The hatch opened, an
arm popped into the airlock holding a box, Jerand took
the box, the arm vanished, and the hatch clanged shut.
Jerand looked in the box. They had steel clipboards, a
dirty undershirt that Chandray must have found wedged
in the back of a personnel locker, and a one-liter bottle
of GENERAL PURPOSE DISINFECTANT.

Koffield looked at the bottle sadly. "One liter of this
versus Mars. Who do you think will win?"

Once again, Jerand didn't see much point in answering.

The two men scraped down the interior as best they
could with the edges of the clipboards, then doused the
shirt in disinfectant, wiping away as much of the mold
from themselves as they could, concentrating on their
helmet visors. The mold wiped away reasonably well,
but the burn-off suit's visor had turned milky-grey where
it had been.

"That's about as good as it's going to get," said
Koffield. "Bleed off the pressure and let's get this junk
out of here."

Jerand twisted the knobs on the appropriate valves
and listened as their poisoned air hissed away into the
deadly Martian skies.

"Officer Chandray," Koffield called. "I don't see any
point in maintaining a breathing-pressure atmosphere in
there, since we don't dare breathe it anyway. I'd like to

bleed off the pressure altogether. If nothing else, the air gases themselves must weigh something. Any objection?"

"No, sir, I was going to suggest it."

"Then use the manual valves and bleed off ship's pressure."

Another, deeper roar began almost at once, and kept going long after all the pressure had bled out of the lock. Even with all the purge valves wide-open, it took a while to dump that much air pressure. Jerand got the outer hatch open, and they started tossing out clumps of blackened mold and the filthy remains of their effort at cleanup. The roar of the ship's air-bleed faded away just as they were finishing.

"All right, sir," called Chandray. "Pressure equalized. Let's get the inner hatch opened."

They undid the latches manually and swung the door wide. Inside, waiting for them, was Norla Chandray— and an astonishing pile of junk that took up most of the lower deck. They could barely see Chandray standing behind it.

"You appear to have followed your orders with a great deal of enthusiasm," said Koffield. "Let's get this mess thrown overboard."

Fifteen minutes later, weary to their bones, they had thrown the last of the surplus gear overboard. Norla watched as Bolt sealed the outer airlock hatch, and followed the others as they half climbed, half dragged themselves up to the pilot's deck and into their flight seats.

"Try and strap in before you fall asleep," Norla said, trying to keep the worry out of her voice. The two men seemed barely conscious, nearly sleepwalking. Well, let them be. It was her show now. "Ah, sir," she said, "I think it's time for me to take that second stim pill."

"By all means, Officer Chandray," said Koffield as he sank back into his chair. "Please do so at once."

Norla swallowed the evil-tasting little lozenge and

started in on her preboost sequences. "Stand by," she said. "It's going to be a bumpy ride."

She ran over the checklist. Engines at ready. Event sequencer programmed to walk her through it and take over if need be. Life support—what life support? Scratch it. But it was time to do one thing that wasn't on the checklist.

Koffield had been right that dumping the *São Paulo*'s air would save some weight—but he missed where most of that air—and weight—was. Norla punched in the commands on the oxygen tank and nitrogen tank purge valves. For a wonder, none of the circuits involved had failed. The exterior purge valves opened, and the *São Paulo* proceeded to dump all her compressed breathing gas out into the Martian atmosphere. Norla hadn't wanted to do it until the last minute, for fear of giving the mold something else to grow on. She flipped another valve and dumped all the water and unrecycled waste water out as well. The viewports were half-covered in mold, but the exterior view video cameras were still working. She watched as the compressed oxy and nitrogen jetted away in dense white clouds, and the water gushed out onto the ground.

"Have some fertilizer," she muttered to the planet. "But you won't get to enjoy it."

She couldn't even tell if Bolt and Koffield were awake or not. It didn't matter. "Stand by," she called. "Engine start in ten seconds at—mark—nine, eight, seven, six, five, four, three, two, one—zero!"

She slapped down viciously at the engine start button, and gouts of blue fire stabbed down into the ground. She held the ship there for several seconds at 10 percent thrust, letting the engines steady down and purge out whatever might have started growing in the engine bells.

The mold crust around the ship, caught in the oxy-saturated air, burst into flame and flared up instantly into a monster blaze that spread out from the ship. The mold on the *São Paulo*'s exterior flared up, burned, and vanished. Norla watched as the flames ate in toward the heatproof viewports, scouring away the loathsome growth that had blocked her view and letting her see again.

Smoke and fire surged around the temple area. A line of flame hurried along the broken-up mold crust that marked their path between the temple and the ship, and between the ship and the one-way landers. The fire caught at something leaking out of the closest lander, and it burst into flame. Clear, cleansing flame, that could drive back the symbiote-mold, shrivel it, reduce it to cinders.

She throttled up to 100 percent, and the *São Paulo* leapt up out of the conflagration she had touched off and into the sky. Norla exulted in the view behind, of black smoke and orange sky, as she roared off into the heavens. She knew the burn would die in moments, as soon as the oxygen was gone, that the mold would grow back double-fast, newer and lusher, in a matter of days. But even a small victory was something. Even a moment's revenge against that horror was worth something. She had won, at least a little bit, and it felt good.

"Now if only we can get off the damned planet alive," Norla muttered, and pitched the nose of the *São Paulo* east, toward the ruined seaside town of New Tacoma.

CHAPTER TWENTY

CLEAN BURN

Norla cut the engines, retracted the landing gear, and let the *São Paulo* ride her own momentum upward and eastward. The danger would be in breaking out of the cloud deck, and thus letting Deimos see them. Unfortunately, she had no good way of knowing how high or how thick the cloud deck was. An aircraft with even the most rudimentary instrumentation would have carried the sort of radar equipment that could report such things—but the *São Paulo* was not an aircraft, just a space-to-space vehicle modified just enough to make the occasional landing. Norla wasn't sure she would have used weather radar even if she had had it. Deimos just might have a detector that could spot it.

The *São Paulo* was reaching the top of her trajectory. She'd start to fall back in a minute. Norla let it happen. The less she used the ship's engines, the happier she'd be. Between the view angle, the various upper-atmosphere effects, and the cloud cover, it would be a real job for a thermal sensor on Deimos to spot their takeoff, or any additional engine burns, and even harder to get an accurate fix on them. But the odds of getting spotted would go up every time they lit the engines.

The *São Paulo* grazed the bottom of the cloud layer and started to fall.

"Ah—Wha?" It was Koffield's voice, through the suit radio. "Did I—how the hell did I sleep through takeoff?"

Koffield was seated behind and to starboard, out of her view. Norla powered up an interior camera and pointed it at him. She laughed. "I'm just glad we all *lived* through takeoff," she said. "I didn't see any reason to wake you. You'd done your bit, and it was time to do mine."

"Ah, well," said Koffield. "Sorry I missed it."

"It was a pretty good show," Norla admitted. "I managed to touch off quite a nice little blaze."

"What about Bolt?" Koffield asked.

Norla flipped on another camera. "He's still out. He's breathing, I think. Yes, I saw him move there, a bit."

"Anything I can do?" Koffield asked.

Norla shook her head, even though Koffield could not see her. "Just relax and enjoy the ride," she said.

She noticed a thin patch of mold on the arm of her suit, and glared at it, wishing she could wipe it off. But that would just get the stuff on her hands, and from there, to the controls.

And the controls had enough trouble as it was. She checked her trouble board, and counted five ambers, two reds, and two flashing reds. The worst ones were in the environmental systems, which didn't matter anymore, but still, there were more lights coming on. The stuff was still spreading, and they had pretty much run out of things they could do about it.

Except leave, of course—and they were working on that.

The *São Paulo* was starting to develop some serious downward velocity. Norla started to bring her tail down, getting set for the next engine burn.

Twice more, the *São Paulo* lit her engines to drive her east and up, twice more she rose to the top of her trajectory and started to fall again. Norla was increasingly impressed with Jerand Bolt's ability to sleep through it all. The roar of the engines, the high gees, followed by several minutes of zero gee and near zero gee, and then the plummeting fall—none of it was enough to wake him. Norla was almost envious. She hadn't slept that well in a long time.

And speaking of time, they were getting close. The governing factor in all their calculations had been staying out from under Deimos. Phobos, thankfully, was not due to rise for about another two hours. Deimos, as seen from the vicinity of Mariner City, was westering, but still well up in the sky. But as seen from their present location, well to the east, near New Tacoma, Deimos was already safely below the western horizon.

They were still about thirty kilometers west of their intended launch point. Maybe the prevailing winds had slowed them down. Maybe she hadn't quite calculated accurately. Norla didn't know or care. Thirty kilometers was plenty close enough.

For the fourth and final time, she brought the *São Paulo* about to boost attitude, her nose pointed up and to the east. But this time the engines wouldn't just apply a gentle love tap and then shut down. "All right," she said. "Stand by for airborne braking maneuver and transition to orbit insertion. We're going to go to zero vertical speed at four thousand meters, and then immediately make the transition to the orbital insertion burn." Splitting the burn up into two pieces wasn't the most elegant way to do things, but Norla hadn't had time for elegance. Crude but effective was the watchword for the day.

She checked her laser altimeter. They were at five thousand meters, and falling fast. She throttled up to 20 percent, watching her rates and ranges, trying to come to a dead halt at four thousand—in effect, trying for a landing in midair. She was slowing down too much and trimmed her thrust down to 15 percent. The *São Paulo* fell slowly, a smooth, controlled descent. *Too* controlled. She was burning propellant too fast, playing it too safe. At this rate, she'd be pulling a pogo, making corrections too gently, and too late, so that she repeatedly overshot and undershot the zero point. Futz around too long, and she'd burn up so much propellant she wouldn't be able to make orbit.

All right then, face it. There wasn't time to calculate her maneuvers, get them plotted out all neatly on a chart. They just didn't have the time for anything but taking chances. Norla swore and throttled back again, to 5 percent, barely enough to control their descent. The *São Paulo* began to fall faster, moving faster through forty-five hundred meters than she had through five thousand. She tweaked her throttle down again, just a hair. Forty-four hundred meters. No change in velocity. Forty-three hundred.

She glanced in the video display that still showed Koffield's face. He was awake now, very much so, and wearing the expression of someone straining every nerve to keep from giving advice. She couldn't blame him. The way she was flying was getting Norla herself nervous. Forty-one hundred. What the hell had happened to forty-two? Was she that much more tired than she thought? Never mind. Forty-zero-fifty. Now! This was it. Snap roll the ship to orbital insertion attitude, and—

"MAIN ENGINES FULL THROTTLE!" she called, her voice drowned out by the sound of the engines.

The *São Paulo* roared back toward the safety of space, riding a pillar of clean blue flame.

Captain Marquez came up the ladder to the pilot's deck of the *Rio de Janeiro*. They were keeping watch from there. "Any word yet?" he asked.

Lira Wu turned and looked at him with a look of profound annoyance. What did he expect her to say? *Yes, sir, they called an hour ago. They like it so much down there that they've decided to stay and open the first Martian nudist colony. I just didn't bother to tell you.* He wouldn't blame her all that much if she had popped off like that. He had been checking in, over and over again. It was his way to relieve nervous energy—or perhaps, more accurately, to transfer it to the enlisted ranks. Wu looked pretty jumpy.

But still she kept her voice calm. "Nothing yet, sir. They're not due to lift off for several hours yet, assuming they stay on the flight plan. I'll let you know the minute we hear anything."

"I know you will, Wu. Sorry. Listen, I'm not going to be doing anything besides coming in here every five minutes anyway. Go below. Go through the airlock to the *Cruzeiro do Sul* and relax."

"Yes, sir. Thank you, sir." Wu got up from the pilot's station, seeming to be a bit hesitant about it.

"And don't worry," he said gently. "I'll let *you* know the minute *I* hear anything."

Wu blushed and smiled. "Thank you, sir. I appreciate that, too." She got up and went down the ladder.

It took Marquez a minute or two to settle himself into the pilot's station—and a minute or two longer to realize the sensors had picked something up. Something that looked a hell of a lot like the *São Paulo* lifting off from the wrong place at the wrong time—and heading straight for them.

And, most assuredly, Wu heard about it as soon as Marquez did. So did everyone else aboard the *Rio de Janeiro* and *Cruzeiro do Sul*, without recourse to the intercom system.

The *São Paulo* cut her engines and dropped into free fall. Norla had no idea if the ship's gravity system would work, and she certainly wasn't going to try any needless experiments. They had had enough excitement already. But, with the orbital insertion done, her work was over, at least for several hours. They weren't going to risk breaking radio silence, and neither were their shipmates, so there was no point trying to raise the *Cruzeiro do Sul*.

"Nicely flown, Norla," said Koffield.

She undid her seat restraints and floated up out of the pilot's chair. She had had enough of talking to people—especially Anton Koffield—without being able to see them. "Thank you, Anton," she said.

Koffield released himself from the starboard watch seat and floated up to look out the viewport at Mars.

The planet was receding—but not fast enough for Norla's tastes.

Not wishing to look at the planet, she looked at Anton Koffield. The two of them had long ago agreed to use first names together when off duty—but when was the last time that either, let alone both, had truly *been* off duty? And yet now, here they were, neither with any particular duties to perform—and effectively alone, to boot.

Bolt slept on, so profoundly asleep that Norla was starting to worry. She floated over to check his suit's bio display. He seemed all right, as best she could tell. But Norla forced herself to be honest with herself. Checking on Bolt was just a way to avoid talking to the Admiral— to Anton. And if she was being honest with herself, she had to admit she had no idea why that should be. There was no romantic attachment between them. Never had been, never would be. So what was it? She didn't know.

So she did the thing she was afraid of doing. She turned and looked at the man, straight on. He looked back at her, patient, calm, waiting, as if he knew what the problem was, and was only waiting for her.

And then *she* understood, and was ashamed. She had seen, was seeing, right now, the great Admiral Anton Koffield as he should not be seen. Anton Koffield, the man who led them, the man who drove them forward by the sheer force of his personality. There, inside the suit helmet. Tired, bone tired, looking old and worn-out, his beard scraggly, his lips dried and cracked, his skin streaked with days of sweat and grime that could not be wiped away. Anton Koffield, whose pressure suit was covered in a film of mold that was growing back again. Koffield, who had been so tired he had slept through liftoff, and might well be too weak to stand if she powered up the gravity system.

"I don't look so good, do I?" he asked gently.

And Norla burst into useless, dangerous tears. Even as she felt apart, she chided herself. It was unwise in the extreme to cry in zero gravity, especially inside a pressure suit. The tears had nowhere to go, and more often then not wound up as dried spots of salt on the inside of the helmet visor, partially blinding the person wearing the suit.

Norla wanted to collapse in a corner, but that was also hard to do in zero gravity. "Neither do I," she said. "Oh, dear God, neither do I." How dare she think, even subconsciously, of blaming Anton for weakness, when he had given up every bit of strength he had, for all their sakes. He might look terrible right now, but food, a bath, and rest would solve that. But *she* looked bad, felt bad, deep, deep, deep inside, and what soap and water could ever reach there?

"It's just nervous reaction, Norla," her friend Anton said. "It's just reaction, and exhaustion. You flew us to orbit on nothing but nerves. Rest for a time. Rest and sleep."

Norla tried to protest, to speak, to say she couldn't possibly sleep—but the words would not come. Koffield guided her gently back to her pilot's station and helped her strap back in, so she wouldn't drift off as she slept.

No, wait, you *were* supposed to drift off when you sleep. She was getting things confused. She blinked hard and tried to focus her eyes, her mind. Somehow things seemed preternaturally sharp, and yet very hard to see, all at once. There was something—something right at the edge of her understanding. Something she could almost reach out and touch. If she concentrated, really concentrated, it would give her the Answer. But, no, wait, she had forgotten the Question. She yawned uncontrollably and shut her eyes. Rest her eyes, yes. Now all she had to do was remember the Question, and the Answer would make sense—but what was the Answer? She couldn't see it. She couldn't see anything. Yes, her eyes were shut. Just rest them, rest for a moment . . .

"You rest, Norla," said Anton. "I'll take the first watch, and wake Bolt if I start to fade too much. You rest, and we'll wake you when we need a pilot again."

"Sorry," she muttered. "Sorry for crying, and everything."

"It's all right," he said. "I just want to tell you one thing, and then you can rest. I'm going to bleed off whatever atmosphere we have left. I don't see much good in keeping Martian surface air on board. Maybe vacuum will slow the mold down a bit. *Something* damned well better."

There was a low, far-off hissing that must have been the purge valves. Norla felt her suit stiffen a bit in reaction to the drop in pressure. And then she didn't feel anything at all, and so she slept.

"I still can't believe I slept through all of it," said Jerand Bolt.

"You did," said Koffield with a chuckle. "And toward the end there, we would have cut off your suit radio if we could have. I didn't even know it was possible to snore in zero gee."

"Seems to me I've heard of other cases," said Norla with a smile. It was astonishing, absolutely astonishing, what a difference a little sleep made. The Universe—even a Universe that had a place like Mars in it—seemed an altogether pleasanter and more welcoming place than it had only hours before. It helped to have the work over for the moment. They had already finished pulling all the data out of their recorders and bookcatchers, and had then beamed it to the *Cruzeiro do Sul* via secure ship-to-ship laser comm.

"I think I see Marquez there," said Bolt. "The yellow pressure suit with the blue striping."

"Those are his suit markings, all right," said Koffield.

They were only minutes away from rendezvous with the *Cruzeiro do Sul/Rio de Janeiro* complex, and all of them were counting the minutes—not until they could see their companions—but until they could get out of their suits. Nor was that strictly a matter of comfort. No doubt because of the extra physical labor they had performed, Bolt and Koffield's suits were alarmingly close to power depletion. No one wanted to say so, but it was fairly obvious that if they had waited until their originally planned launch time, they would likely have arrived dead at the *Cruzeiro do Sul*.

They watched as the *Cruzeiro* grew closer, and the end of their ordeal came closer as well.

"Can't this thing go any faster?" asked Bolt.

Marquez stood on the hull of the *Cruzeiro do Sul* and watched as the *Rio de Janeiro* undocked, headed for one last linkup with her sister ship. Lira Wu was aboard. Marquez believed in sharing the interesting assignments. Besides, this was just the sort of basic, straightforward piloting task that could give Wu some flying time and start her up the qualification ladder.

The two smaller craft linked up nose to nose about a hundred meters away from the *Cruzeiro*, after a precautionary three-second burn of the *Rio*'s attitude jets, aimed squarely at the *São Paulo*'s nose docking port. The *São Paulo* was about to dock with the *Rio*, and no one wanted to take any chances with contamination. Several hours of hard vacuum was all very well, but there was nothing like bright hot flame to make sure something was sterile. As they were about to demonstrate. Marquez watched as the *Rio* used her manipulator arm to deploy the elaborate decontamination gear.

Norla powered down the lights, the nav system, propulsion, the gyros, and every other system of the ship. She flicked on her helmet lights as the interior illumination faded. She worked carefully through the last of the power-down checklist. She wanted to do things right as she left the ship—and she wanted to be sure the *São Paulo* really was an inert hulk. Once the decontamination run was over, the *Rio* was supposed to put the *São Paulo* into a destructive reentry trajectory, then fly back to the *Cruzeiro do Sul*. It wouldn't do at all if the poor old *São Paulo* suddenly came back to life and tried to run an automatic course correction. Best to be sure everything was dead.

She set her last switches, took one last look around the pilot's deck, and then floated headfirst down the ladder to the lower deck. The others were waiting for her below, their helmet lights gleaming up at her, blinding her for a moment as she floated downward.

The lower deck, with all its fittings stripped out, would have looked strange even in normal lighting. In the ever-shifting brightness and dark of their helmet lights, it looked otherworldly. For a moment Norla was back underground, in DeSilvo's tunnel to the Dark Museum, the darkness all around, with only a small puddle of shifting, jiggling light surrounding them and keeping back the unseen terrors.

Norla shuddered. The visible terrors had been bad enough down there. She was out of that tunnel, and she wasn't going back, and that was good enough for her.

"Let's go," said Koffield, and led the way toward the airlock.

They were faced with the unusual circumstance of vacuum on both sides of the airlock chamber, but air pressure inside it: when Koffield had vented the ship's air, he hadn't thought to vent the lock itself. Bolt cranked the manual valve and spilled the lock air into the ship's interior. One lockful of thin Martian air dispersed through the volume of the ship, and then rushed out the ship's open purge valves into space.

They opened both airlock doors and saw the ends of three long poles. Norla peered up toward the *Rio de Janeiro* and saw that the far ends of the poles were clamped to hold-down points on the other ship. Each flagpole had a flexible safety harness, floating within easy reach of the *São Paulo*'s airlock. Bolt went first, clipping his suit to one of the harnesses and moving slowly and carefully up his pole. Koffield went next.

Norla was the last to leave the *São Paulo*, and, as she moved hand over hand up the transit pole, she decided it was important that she not look back, not turn her gaze toward the dark hole of the dead ship's airlock, not see the fire-blackened shreds of mold that still adhered to the hull, not look in through the viewports at the pilot's stations where she had sat. It was over. She didn't have to deal with it, or look at it, ever again. Deep in her heart, she knew perfectly well that her time on Mars would stay with her, that what she had seen and felt there were locked in her memory for all time. But just for the moment, it was a great blessing to at least know the *reality* was gone for good, and to pretend the memories would never intrude.

She looked up, and forward, at a collection of what looked like a trio of giant white uninflated beachballs, each one tethered to one of the transit poles. Bolt was just climbing into his as she watched, and Koffield was about to do likewise. Hers was waiting for her. Norla swallowed hard. She knew what was coming next, and no one—with the possible exceptions of Bolt and Koffield—knew better than she just how necessary it was. But she had the feeling she was about to create another memory that would stay with her for a while.

She had reached the end of her transit pole and arrived at her own private beachball. She started to climb in.

She was about to demonstrate why they called it a burn-off suit.

Ten minutes later, she had checked everything over four times. Her safety harness was securely fastened to her suit, and to the burn-ball's tether point. She checked the seams one last time, and made sure she had the burn-ball sealed properly. Her outer suit pockets were empty. Her suit cooling was set to maximum. She pressed the READY button on the control panel. The ball didn't have any view panels, but she could feel it shifting and bouncing as the *Rio*'s manipulator arm lifted it up and away from the ship. The bumping stopped, and the ball seemed motionless for a moment, until she felt herself drifting slowly down into the end farthest from the tether point. She knew that the *Rio*'s manipulator arm had, in effect, thrown the ball, and that the braking system on the tether had slowed her forward travel gently enough that she wasn't bouncing back toward the ship. The burn-ball was quite literally a balloon on a string—and she was inside the balloon.

The SAFE DISTANCE light came on, and Norla wondered if anyone who had ever seen that light come on had *not* asked herself or himself—*safe for whom?* One more light came on, behind a button that read PRESS TO PROCEED.

She swallowed hard and pushed the button.

A far-off hissing sound grew suddenly closer and louder as the burn-ball's interior went rapidly from hard vacuum to a high-pressure pure-oxygen atmosphere. The ball, the balloon she was in, began to expand as the pressure increased.

She heard a beeping sound, coming from outside her suit. Five beeps, very fast. Then four, each beep a bit longer, so the second sequence lasted as long as the first, then three beeps, then two, and then one long, final warning beep and then—

The suit-sparker went off.

Instantly, her suit was ablaze, a torrent of fire that engulfed her. Her outer burn-suit visor caught fire, along with the rest of the suit, and flames crackled and roared mere centimeters from her eyes. Heat punched at her face like a fist, driving out all coolness, all comfort and safety. She shut her eyes against it but still saw the glow of the flames. The light faded a bit, and she opened her eyes to see the transparent helmet itself had burned away, exposing her inner suit helmet, which she fervently hoped was as heatproof as advertised. She looked down and saw the body of her suit, the legs and the arms, burning still, filling the burn-ball with thick, oily black smoke. The smoke grew thicker by the moment, pressing up against her surviving visor, blanking out her vision of everything else. She could see a red glow from below, from her burning body, but no detail, no image at all.

She became aware of the noise of the fire, of the crackling, savage roar, even as it started to fade away, and the red-orange glow began to gutter down, the fire smothered by the toxic black smoke, starved for oxygen. She heard a new sound, a creaking, groaning sound, of fabric straining and stretching beyond its limits. The burn-ball swelled up bigger and bigger as the heat and the pressure in its interior shot upward. She heard the pop, pop, pop, of stitches pulling out, and the tearing noise of a seam giving way and then—

BLAM! It was a short, sharp shock of an explosion, the sound tremendously loud and then instantly gone, as the air pressure that carried the sound suddenly dispersed into space. The burn-ball had exploded under pressure, as it was designed to do, and Norla was floating peacefully in the dark and cool of space, safely in place at the end of her heat-proof tether.

She looked around, and saw Koffield floating at the end of his tether—and what had to be Bolt's burn-ball off beyond him. He must have been a littler slower off the mark pressing that last unnerving button. She could see the burn-ball swelling larger as she watched, the light of the fire inside glowing white-hot, then orange, then a dull, sullen red that guttered down to nothing—and then a sudden flash of light, movement too fast to see—and Bolt, there, at the end of his tether.

Hard vacuum, high-pressure oxygen, high-temperature fire, highly toxic gases under pressure, explosive decompression, and then hard vacuum again. Any microbe that could survive all that—plus the more conventional wipe-down with disinfectant-soaked towels that the inner suits would get—probably *deserved* to survive and expand out to all of inhabited space.

Norla smiled at that. It occurred to her that *she* had just survived all those things. Maybe, just maybe, that meant *humankind* had earned the right to spread out into space.

Or maybe it just meant she could get inside and finally get her pressure suit off.

The *Rio de Janeiro*'s manipulator arm handed their tethers off to the *Cruzeiro do Sul*'s arm in precisely the same manner as a child handing a bunch of balloons on a string to a parent. The three of them made their way into the *Cruzeiro*'s airlock. The outer door sealed, and ship's air was pumped into the lock. The three of them industriously scrubbed each other's inner pressure suits down with disinfectant—though Norla couldn't imagine any bug living through the burn-ball treatment. Still, she was all for being thorough. At last, at long last, it was time to open their suit helmets and breathe in something besides their own body odors. Norla popped her helmet and breathed in the airlock's air. It stank of too-strong disinfectant, and the long-unwashed bodies of her companions. But the smell of her *own* unwashed body, though it did not disappear, at least faded into the background—and that made the airlock smell wonderful.

The inner lock door swung open, and the three travelers were greeted with a round of applause. Marquez, Ashdin, Sparten, and Phelby were there, all smiles and congratulations. Norla couldn't help but notice that no one rushed close enough for a hug or a slap on the back, but she couldn't blame them for that. She wanted to get upwind of herself just as desperately as everyone else. They needed a bit more decontamination—but only for hygienic and aesthetic reasons.

Marquez had been outside on safety watch, just in case something went wrong with the transfer and decontamination. He was still in his suit, his helmet off, and smiling broadly. "Welcome back!" he said, smiling broadly. "Did you get what you were looking for?" he asked.

Norla, Bolt, and Koffield looked at each other, and nodded—and Bolt looked over to Sparten, just a little too casually. They hadn't had a chance to talk over how much they could say in front of whom.

"Oh yes," said Koffield. "We found quite a bit indeed. But we can talk about it later. I think it's time we got out of here."

Marquez nodded vigorously. "No argument from me," he said. "Just being near that place"—he hooked his arm toward the viewport, and Mars—"gets me nervous. Once the *Rio* dumps the *São Paulo* into a burn-up trajectory and gets back here, we'll be on our way." He turned toward Dixon Phelby, who was manning the pilot station. "Order *Rio* to proceed," he said, and turned back toward Norla, Koffield, and Bolt. "But you three want to get cleaned up, and eat, and sleep—"

"You two go ahead," said Norla. "I want to watch the *Rio* take *São Paulo* away." Somehow, her resolution not to look back had faded away or else no longer applied. Maybe it was the ride in the burn-ball. The contagion had been killed in fire and smoke, and somehow that had purified the *São Paulo* as well. It was safe to look now. Even as she thought of it, she knew it would sound half-mad to her after a proper meal and a good night's sleep in a real bed. But for the moment, for the time at hand, it made sense to her. She wanted to say good-bye.

She stepped up behind Phelby and watched through the viewport as the *Rio*, still docked nose to nose with the *São Paulo*, came about to a new heading and started to boost away, moving toward Mars, powered forward by the cool deep blue glow of her reactionless drive. Slowly at first, then faster and faster, the two docked sister ships started moving, back down toward the planet that had tried so hard to kill them, the planet that couldn't hurt them anymore. The *Rio/São Paulo* complex was barely more than a dot in the viewport now. Dixon brought it up on the long-range camera, and it jumped closer on the screen, close enough that she could almost touch it, Mars behind the ships in half-phase, the planet's morbid colors looking almost handsome as a backdrop to the little ship.

Suddenly the *Rio* seemed to shudder, and then to tumble violently.

"Many hits! Many hits!" It was Wu's voice, over Phelby's headphones. "I've just run smack into—"

And then the voice died.

A fireball, a second sun, popped into existence where the *Rio* had been, big enough and bright enough to blot out altogether the view of the planet beyond.

CHAPTER TWENTY-ONE

AFTERMATH

Koffield reacted first. Norla hadn't even realized that he'd been watching too.

"Captain Marquez!" he called out. "We need to get out of here. Straight line course, running directly away from a line drawn between that blast and Mars."

Marquez hadn't been watching. All he had seen was the blast, after it happened. He stood there, staring at the terrible sight. "My God," he said. "What happened?"

"Captain Marquez!" Koffield shouted again. "It was Interdict Command. *They tracked the engine burn.* They thought the *Rio* was the *São Paulo's* mother ship. They tracked the *São Paulo's* trajectory. They waited to detect reactionless propulsion in the vicinity of the *São Paulo's* course, and fired on it."

"But if we boost, they'll detect that," Marquez protested.

Koffield pointed at the still-expanding fireball. "Not through that, they won't," he said. "We have to boost now, while it's still shielding us. *Now!*"

Marquez snapped out of it. "Phelby—full power along attitude 039, 140, 002." He looked to Koffield. "Debris," he said. "We'll have to look like debris if they spot us. And debris doesn't show power emissions. Admiral—any idea on what sort of sensors they'll be using?"

"None," Koffield replied. "Obviously, reactionless drive tracking. They might have power, electromagnetic, radio, plain old visible light, infrared, gravity-wave— they might use any or all of them."

"So we'd better be very dark and very quiet. Bolt! Chandray! Power down all systems but propulsion and nav. *Everything*. Cut the grav system first. It's easiest to spot. Sparten! Stand by to kill propulsion and nav system instantly on my command."

Norla dived for the power panel and starting killing systems. Bolt had been in the refresher, stripping out of his suit, when the blast had lit up the *Cruzeiro*'s interior. Somehow, he was already at the grav control panel, dressed in nothing but the sweaty, soiled suit skivvies he hadn't had a chance to peel off yet. He cut the gravity generators, and Norla felt her stomach do a flip-flop as her weight faded away. But she didn't float across the room. Not just yet. The acceleration compensators went out with grav control out, and they were feeling the full effect of max power on the *Cruzeiro*'s reactionless drive. Norla guessed about two gees acceleration, and wondered absently how it was she was able to stand up in it. She kept flipping circuit breakers. The lights died, and the ventilators sighed to a halt.

Koffield's voice came from out of the darkness. "Off the ecliptic," he said. "They won't search as hard there. Solar south probably better than north."

"Right," said Marquez. "Mr. Phelby, you heard the man. Cut engines, come about to 039, 140, 180 and re-light, full power."

Norla did start floating as the engines died, and slammed down hard as they came on again.

"Admiral," said Marquez's voice from out of the darkness. "You're the military man. How long can we keep those engines on before we come out from behind the blast cloud?" Norla saw Koffield's silhouette float up to the viewport, and she watched him as he looked out at the blast, judging it by eyeball alone. "Thirty more seconds," he said quietly. "And I'd suggest throwing the ship into a two-axis tumble as well. That might make us look more convincing as a large piece of blast debris."

"Do it, Phelby," Marquez ordered.

"Yes, sir."

At the end of thirty seconds, the main engines died, and Phelby put the ship into a slow, wobbling, end-over-end tumble. "And now we do nothing," said Marquez. "Nothing until we get out of range—whenever that might be."

Koffield spoke again. "Captain Marquez—I'm sorry. I thought of this perhaps moments too late. Can you use the comm laser on a fixed target while the ship is tumbling like this?"

Marquez was a dimly seen form in the darkness. "Probably. If we did a short burst timed to when our tumble swept the comm laser past the target. But what did you—oh hell. Yes. Yes, we'd better warn the *Dom Pedro IV.*"

"Warn the ship about what?" asked Wandella Ashdin. Norla had almost forgotten about her in the excitement. In a sense, that was a testimonial. Ashdin had managed to keep her nerve and keep quiet in the crisis.

"Was that a potshot at us, personally, that just killed Wu, or were they just shooting at whatever random stranger it was who happened to be visiting Mars?" Marquez asked. "If it's the *first* case, and they have the sense God gave a goose, they'll be moving against the *DP-IV* right about now. Do you think, Mr. Sparten, perhaps Interdict Command might have heard a little something from a friendly organization about us? Perhaps something a well-placed inside source might have passed along?"

"How the devil would I know?" Sparten snapped.

"That is the exact question whose answer I am eager to learn," said Marquez.

Norla was shocked. *That* put the cards on the table. What had gone on in their absence?

Marquez spoke again, the anger plain in his voice.

"Mr. Phelby. Power up enough of the comm system to send to the *DP-IV*, hailing her as 'Merchanter's Dream.' Message to read: 'Case Four Bravo Subcase Charlie. Repeat Case Four Bravo Subcase Charlie.' Send it at once, and set to repeat hourly."

"What's Case Four Bravo Sub Charlie?" Wandella asked.

"It orders them to depart the Grand Library at once and rendezvous at such-and-such coordinates, toward Solar south," said Marquez. "Now I'll ask *you* a question, Dr. Wandella. Considering they *might* have been shooting at us, personally, what odds would you give on *both* ships reaching the rendezvous?"

"I haven't the faintest idea."

"Yes," said Marquez. "That is the correct answer." And then he spoke no more.

They sat, the seven survivors, in the dark, in the silence, for a long time thereafter. There was not much to say, but they all had a lot to think about.

With the nav systems powered down to standby, it was all but impossible to judge their velocity or position. The blast fireball faded away to nothing, and Mars gradually receded from view, but that gave them very little to go on. As the ship tumbled, the light of the Sun flared in one viewport, then swept past into darkness, then lit the *Cruzeiro do Sul*'s main cabin up from the other side, dazzling everyone, and then dropping them into darkness, over and over again. With the environment system down, the compartment was warming up, and the air was turning stale. Norla was starting to feel the beginnings of a stabbing post-stim-pill headache.

"Admiral?" Marquez called out. "They didn't fire on this ship at all, even after the *São Paulo* led them right to us. They only fired on the *Rio* after she fired her engines. So how good are their sensors?"

"Probably not much good at spotting us out here," Koffield admitted. "*Probably.* I expect the only reason they didn't fire on us was that they didn't see us. Assuming it was Interdict Command who fired, they targeted the *Rio* using sensors meant to watch Mars and the surrounding space. If so, we were at extreme range for them, even then. My best guess is they never tracked us at all, even as debris. They never knew we were there, and they still don't know we exist. But it's at least *possible* they are tracking us right now, waiting for us to lead them back to *our* base or mother ship."

"Lots of things are possible," Marquez growled. "But most things are pretty damned improbable—and we need to breathe. I'm gonna bet they can't detect the increased heat and power output if we get the lights and the environmental systems up and running. Phelby, get things powered up. Once you get the lights on, shutter those damned viewports!"

"What about the tumble?" Phelby asked. He looked a little green about the gills.

"Take a pill, and live with it, for now. Turning the interior lights on, I doubt they'll notice from half a million kilometers' range. But a piece of debris that stops tumbling all on its own? It'd make me curious."

"Yes, sir." A handlight came on, and Norla watched its beam jiggle and glide across the cabin as Phelby headed for the circuit breakers.

The lights came on and the shutters went over the viewports, blocking the intermittent blasts of light from the Sun. The compartment seemed suddenly larger than it had in the darkness. Norla looked around at her six companions, Phelby at the main power panel, still bringing systems on-line, the others hunkered down in this corner or that, hanging on stanchions to keep from floating off, blinking owlishly in the sudden light.

"Bolt—you were just about to get yourself cleaned up when the *Rio* blew," said Marquez. "Plumbing's back on. Go, get to work, and don't keep Admiral Koffield or Officer Chandray waiting. I don't see why you got to go first, anyway."

"I ordered him," Koffield said mildly. "I wanted to see us safely away from Mars, Officer Chandray was watching the *Rio*, and I didn't see any reason to keep him waiting."

Bolt, plainly eager to get out of his malodorous suit skivvies, got moving. He emerged from the refresher in record time, hair still damp, still tugging on his fresh coveralls. Koffield looked at Norla. "Go ahead, Officer Chandray."

She shook her head. "Rank hath its privileges, sir. Please. Go first. You've earned it."

"Very well," he said, and took his turn.

Norla smiled to herself. There was no particular reason to point out a certain obvious fact—whoever went last wouldn't have to hurry.

She didn't get to luxuriate too long in the refresher. The moment she had her suit and her inner garments peeled off, and got in under the hot water, she started falling asleep. A zero-gee cleanup was hard enough without the risk of dozing off and drowning halfway through. She settled for getting herself thoroughly clean, and attending to the badly chewed-up raw spot on her thigh, and a few other areas of abraded skin. She hosed out the interior of her suit as best she could, sealed all the joints back up, pulled the wick on a cleaner-foam bomb, threw it in, and got the helmet back on before the foam had a chance to bubble up through the neck. The suit stiffened slightly as the foam expanded out to fill every nook and cranny of its interior. The foam did a superb job of initial cleaning on a sweated-out pressure suit. She hauled her suit out of the refresher and stuffed it inside the airlock chamber, where Bolt and Koffield had stowed theirs.

The main desk of the *Cruzeiro do Sul* was one big compartment, affording little privacy, but Phelby and Ashdin were just finishing up work on an improvised bunkhouse, with blankets hung so as to block the light, and three sleeping bags strapped to the deck. Two of the three bags were already occupied, and Norla quickly made it a third. The ship's tumble was somehow more pronounced, strapped to the deck that way. It was damned disconcerting to feel the whole world tumbling, end over end like that. But it would take something a lot more distracting than that to keep Norla awake any longer. She was asleep in seconds, and dreamed, not of falling, or of Martian monsters, or exploding ships—but of nothing at all.

Aboard the Dom Pedro IV, *docked to the Grand Library Complex Orbiting Neptune*

Sindra Chon frowned, checked the lookup list again, and wished to hell there had been someone else more senior whom Marquez could have left in command of the *DP-IV.*

"Case Four Bravo Subcase Charlie" wasn't good news. In fact, of all the possible contingencies, it was one of the worst a ship still capable of sending a message might send. The listing reported it as meaning *Have Suffered Attack. Severe Casualties and Damage. Assume Enemy Listening. Proceed to Rendezvous Point Bravo With Extreme Caution.* "Subcase Charlie" meant *Report Situation If Possible Without Risk.*

She keyed a command, paging the crew members aboard the Library to return at once, and flagged it *urgent.* But she didn't send it at once. The message had taken roughly four hours to get here. They hadn't grabbed the ship yet, as they would have if it were a perfectly coordinated attack. She ought to have had a little time to think.

So, *think.* What the hell was she supposed to do?

She realized there was further meaning to be drawn from the way Marquez had sent the message. Laser messages were a hell of a lot harder to send than radio messages. In order to send via laser, the *Cruzeiro do Sul* had had to know the *DP-IV*'s precise location and aim a beam precisely, within a few tenths of a degree or better.

Radio was much easier. But laser was much safer.

Over a range of billions of kilometers, even a well-focused radio signal would have enough of a signal footprint to permit triangulating back to the source—but it was almost impossible to track back on a laser signal.

No doubt the beam had spread enough so anyone on the Grand Library could have intercepted it, but "Merchanter's Dream, Case Four Bravo, Repeat Case Four Bravo" could mean nearly anything. So, Marquez hadn't sent via laser to keep the *message* secret—rather, to keep the sender's location, *his* location, secret.

So: They had to get out of there, fast, because whoever had hit the *Cruzeiro do Sul* might try for the *DP-IV*, and, furthermore, the *Cruzeiro* was trying to hide. She would have to be careful not to do anything that might give away even the *Cruzeiro*'s general location.

Proceed to Rendezvous Point Bravo with Extreme Caution. Extreme Caution. She couldn't even really fly the ship. She could run the undock sequence, and follow the procedures for station clearance, but beyond that, all she could do was enter the flight plans Marquez had pre-programmed and watch the ship fly itself. The captain hadn't programmed in any stealth maneuvers—and the ship was a straight-ahead cargo vessel. It couldn't *do* anything stealthy to begin with. She looked at the previous instruction. *Assume Enemy Listening.*

"No," she muttered to herself. "The ship can't be stealthy. But the crew can." They had to leave in a hurry, but it would be better if she managed it without *acting* as if they were in a hurry. Don't let the "enemy"—whoever that was—know they were on to them. Of course, after what they had found in Sparten's cabin, there wasn't much doubt that there *was* an enemy. So best not to draw attention to themselves. She took the "urgent" tag off her crew recall page. Slowly. Carefully. Quietly. Sometimes, that was the best way to be urgent.

Norla awoke, having no idea how long she had slept, but coming fully awake in a heartbeat. She sat up—and noticed there was gravity again. She glanced at the other sleeping bags. Bolt was still dead to the world, but Koffield was gone.

She came out from behind the curtain of blankets to find what appeared to be a more or less normally functioning ship. Wandella Ashdin was seated at the wardroom table, by one shuttered viewport. Phelby and Marquez were in the pilot's compartment, running through some sort of checklist. Yuri Sparten appeared in front of her, offering a fresh, hot cup of coffee. She took it eagerly from him, brushing against his hand as she did. Something, somewhere inside her, made her want to draw back from the contact, but she did not let it happen.

"Thanks," she said, and looked at him steadily. Sparten was a plant—they had known that, accepted it, from day one. But his being set to watch them was a very long leap to believing he had somehow informed on them to Interdict Command and killed Wu.

"You're welcome," he said, smiling, obviously grateful for the courtesy.

Things must have gotten hard for him while we were gone, she thought. "Where's Admiral Koffield?" she asked. "In the, ah, head?"

Sparten shook his head, and hooked his thumb upward. "Once we killed the tumble and had the gravity generator back on, we rigged the temporary upper deck. That inflatable igloo job that sits on the upper exterior deck of the *Cruzeiro*. He woke up about an hour ago and went up there to read. He asked if you'd come see him when you woke up."

Norla nodded vaguely, opened the flapper top on her cup of coffee, and took that precious, life-affirming first sip. She had a lot of questions—but given the way everyone else was studiously ignoring Sparten, she had a feeling it might be easier on everyone if she tried getting the first few answers from Koffield.

She carefully closed the lid on the coffee and made her slow and one-handed way up the ladder to the temporary deck.

They hadn't exactly gone all out decorating the igloo. Koffield was sitting on one empty packing crate and using another as a reading table. There was one other box to sit on, and Norla snagged it and dragged it over to the table.

Koffield was absorbed enough in what he was reading that he wasn't aware of her coming in. It took her setting her coffee down on the table for him to realize she was there. He instantly blanked the screen he'd been reading. Norla caught only one word before the screen died. *Contraction.*

She knew him well enough not to ask, but she was willing to bet "Contraction" was something to do with the thing he had spotted in the Dark Museum that had stunned him, the thing he had refused to explain.

"So," she said, "what goes on?"

Koffield laughed. "It's hard to know where to start."

"Well, I notice we have gravity back. And I take it we're actually under boost to somewhere or other."

"The rendezvous with the *DP-IV.*"

"How do you know it's safe?"

"We got a message from the *DP-IV.* Number codes. In essence, they decrypt to 'we got away without incident. No news of you here. All well. See you at the rendezvous.' "

"We didn't hear back from *them* via *laser*, did we?"

"No, no, broadcast radio, using a prearranged one-time number code. Marquez decided that if they hadn't jumped on the *DP-IV*, they weren't shooting for us, in particular. It was just Interdict Command doing their everyday job. Therefore, they weren't likely to come after us out here. He waited a while, to make sure, then killed the tumble and relit the engines—at low power, just in case. No sense being *too* detectable." Koffield fiddled with his datapad. "Of course, we don't know—we may never know—if they have yet discovered, or will discover, what we went down there *for*. Maybe they bought into the New Tacoma ruse all the way. Maybe they believed it at first, but then they'll spot our landing site before the mold can grow back and hide everything. Or maybe Sparten will manage to signal his friends again, from here aboard the *Cruzeiro do Sul.*"

Norla's eyes widened. "Signal them *again*? He's done it already?"

"They found a transmitter in his cabin aboard the *DP-IV*. Marquez ordered Sindra Chon to search it once the *Cruzeiro* departed. That was one reason Marquez and I wanted him here. 'Keep your friends close, and your enemies closer.' "

"Wait a minute—a *transmitter*? So he was sending to someone *inside* the Solar System?"

"Exactly."

Norla let out a low whistle. She had assumed that he had been briefed to *watch* them, and report back to his superiors—whoever, precisely, they were—once they returned to Solace. If that had been true, it would have limited the damage he could do. But if he was sending to someone here, then all bets were off.

"Supposedly, Sparten doesn't know we know yet," said Koffield. "But I have the hunch he *might* just suspect. Marquez's manner might have given something away," he said sarcastically.

There was too much to think about, too many possible permutations. "But that's all off to one side," said Norla. "We can't go back. We have to assume Interdict Command *will* discover what we were doing. If they do, they'll talk to the Chronologic Patrol—and they'll never stop hunting for us. Once we make rendezvous, we have to leave the Solar System and not come back."

"Agreed, on all points," said Koffield. "But the question is—where do we go *to*?"

"Not to Solace," said Norla. "If we're on the run, that's the first place the CP would look for us. We'd have to go to some third system, probably change ships, maybe split up—maybe find a way to leave Sparten behind—and get into the Solace system coming the long way round. But for now, we can't go there, any more than we can stay here." She thought for a moment and stared at the blank rounded walls of the tempo igloo deck. "But what I'm starting to wonder is, what were we doing here in the first place?"

"What do you mean, 'here?' " Koffield asked.

"The Solar System," said Norla.

"Where else would we go? We were searching for DeSilvo. All the clues, all the leads, were here."

"Except we're still searching. We haven't found him.

And we haven't really been *searching* for him, not exactly. We've been following the trail of bread crumbs he left for us. It's not like we've been doing forensic studies. He left all the clues for us *deliberately*. 'I am hidden, but hidden where you can find me.' What sort of talk is that? When we found his false tomb, it'd been waiting for us for 113 years. Why not just leave the message—'I'm on planet Mongo, at 34 Blank Street, Mongo City. Stop by and we'll have lunch'?"

"I've thought about that," said Koffield. "And I think—I think—I have an answer. Several possible answers. The first is that DeSilvo was either completely mad or utterly sadistic. He left clues for us that led nowhere in particular, just to have his revenge on us—on me. But I don't think that's it. I think the real answer is that he wasn't leaving a trail of bread crumbs. *He was leading us on a guided tour.* There were things he wanted us to see—things we *needed* to see—before we confronted him." He glanced at the datapad he had been reading.

"So what was it we needed to see?" she asked. "Did we see it all? Is there something we're supposed to understand now?"

"Yes. No. I don't know. And I'm the one who's supposed to know, the leader with the vision, the one who can see the way forward—and I can't even follow a trail of bread crumbs." He was silent for a moment. "It might be something as simple as seeing how lovely Earth is, and then rubbing our noses in Mars, the Great Failure, the cautionary tale about what Solace and all the other terraformed worlds are going to become."

"Maybe that's part of it—I'm *sure* it's part of it," said Norla. "But not all. And—what about the next bread crumb? Where do we go from here?"

"I think we've seen it already."

"Oh. Right. So you think it was the plaques?"

"Probably. I haven't had two minutes together to think about them, let alone look at them." Koffield picked up a datapad—not the one he had been reading—and handed it to her.

She switched it on and stared at the screen. Obviously,

Koffield had been thinking about them, at least for long enough to pull up their images from the stored data. The screen showed both plaques, one image of each type.

$$\in (oskd@(\forall X \ni X \neq Au))$$
$$\rightarrow (\forall X \ni X \neq Au)$$

"They're certainly not much as math," said Norla. "Neither one parses as an equation."

"Agreed," said Koffield. "But that's about as far as I got. I'm not much good at puzzles."

"But you're the one who always solves them," Norla protested.

"Only because I'm stubborn," he said. "I'm not much good—but I don't give up. And I take whatever help I can get. Do you see anything else?"

She looked at the images a while longer.

"Well," she said, "everything inside the inner parentheses is the same in both versions. I don't remember what you call that rounded-off capital e thing, but it means 'belongs to the set of.' An arrow can mean about a million things, depending on context. 'This is important,' 'look at this,' 'go this way'—and given that this is a puzzle, the answer could rely on any of them—or be a pun or play on any of those."

"But whatever it was, it was important enough for DeSilvo to go to a lot of effort to make sure the arrow version was seen by anyone *leaving* the Dark Museum through *his* tunnel."

"And in any bay *he* had taken something from," said Norla. "You don't get to see it until you've gotten that far. Until you've passed whatever sort of test that represents—"

"Or until you've seen whatever it was you were meant to see," said Koffield. He stared at the images again. "Are we assuming it's a location?"

"I suppose I was assuming that—mainly because I'm damned if I know how else we'll figure out where to go next. What else could it be?"

"A number, if you figure out the trick or the joke that lets you correct the equation so it's solvable. The title of a book, maybe. But—'oskd.' That could be a person. A certain person."

" 'Osk. D.' *Osk*ar *D*eSilvo. Yes, you're right. But wouldn't the normal form of his initials be 'O.D.' or maybe 'O.d.S.'?"

"I suppose," said Koffield. "But if my initials were short for 'overdose' and the variant could be pronounced as a worse insult—maybe I'd use a different version. Or maybe I'd just do something nonstandard to throw off the people trying to solve my puzzle. But if it is a form of his name, that gives us 'belonging to the set of Oskar DeSilvo at-sign' for the first part of the first puzzle."

"Puzzles!" Norla cried out, and dropped the datapad back down on the packing crate. "We've got a crew member dead, two ships destroyed, a lunatic who is hiding somewhere with a faster-than-light drive he *might* give us if we can find him—and what do we do—we work on puzzles! Puzzles and games. Why are we doing this?"

She propped her elbows on her knees and cradled her forehead in her hands. "I'm sorry," she said. "I'm just not sure how much more I can take."

"It'll take more than one night's sleep to get over Mars," Koffield said gently. "And to answer your question, we're doing it because there is nothing else we can do. If you can see any other line of inquiry open to us, I'd be glad to hear about it."

"I don't know. We got digital copies of all those thousands of books on terraforming. Maybe there's something in there."

"That's a lot of reading," said Koffield. "And it doesn't really fit the pattern that DeSilvo's developed. Nothing's been hidden, exactly. It's been in places where you couldn't help but spot it if you knew the right information ahead of time. Besides, if the plaques aren't the next puzzle for us to solve, what are they? What are they for?"

Everything he said made sense, in an infuriating sort

of way, but Norla wasn't in the mood to be entirely reasonable. "Maybe it's just that we haven't—"

But she was interrupted by Jerand Bolt's head popping up through the deck hatch opening. "Breakfast to be served in five minutes," he said. "That is, if you're hungry."

Norla's stomach suddenly reminded her that she hadn't eaten anything but what came out of a pressure suit's helmet dispenser for a long, long time. She looked toward Koffield. "Think this will keep until after breakfast?"

He smiled. "I think so," he said. "I've spent half the morning trying to remember what food tastes like."

Norla turned to Bolt. "We're right behind you," she said.

The *Cruzeiro do Sul*'s regular wardroom table wasn't big enough for seven, but it could be folded out to double size, and that just about allowed everyone to get wedged in around it.

The food was the blandest of shipboard concentrates, cooked up by Wandella Ashdin, who was thus proved to be a most indifferent cook. Norla didn't care; in fact she barely noticed. Freeze-dried this and reconstituted that— she didn't care. *Everything* tasted good.

The mood at the table, however, was tense in the extreme. Marquez was at one end of the long table, the viewport at his back, and Sparten was at the other, with everyone else forming a sort of human neutral zone between them. Phelby and Ashdin were chattering away about the food in Germany, where Phelby had recently visited. As Wandella had never been there, and was not likely to do so soon, it was hard to see why she was interested. Norla got the distinct impression, from their polite chitchat on a topic of very slight interest, that Phelby and Ashdin were continuing a previous policy of relentlessly pretending nothing was wrong. Things must have gotten rather grim during the days her group had been away—and a lot worse since the *Rio* blew up in front of them. And it seemed to her that it could get damned tricky to keep the topic safe. Phelby, for example, would be well advised to avoid mentioning the food in Rio de Janeiro. . . .

However, fortunately for Phelby and Ashdin, the two stay-behind neutrals now had a whole new source of conversation.

"So, tell us, please, Officer Chandray," said Ashdin. "We've been *very* patient while the three of you rested up. But we are all most eager to know what you *found* down there. What happened?"

Norla, seated between Phelby and Bolt, looked carefully at Koffield, who was sitting next to Ashdin, but his face was as much a study in neutrality as the breakfast-table conversation had been. No leads from there. Was it even *safe* to talk in front of Sparten? Maybe it didn't matter, now that his cover was more thoroughly blown. "I really don't know where to begin," she said. "We found—more than we expected."

"And a lot of things I'd just as soon not talk about while eating," Bolt growled. "Especially during my first meal back. Could you pass the bacon patties?"

"He's got a point," Norla agreed. "Mars itself wasn't exactly pleasant."

"Was there any sign of DeSilvo?" Ashdin asked. "Was he there? Had he been there?"

"Oh, there were all sorts of signs of him," said Norla. "He had very definitely been there—but he was long gone."

"Gone where?" Marquez asked, speaking for the first time. "Admiral Koffield, when you left, you said you didn't expect to find him, but you did expect to find some sign of where he was. Did you?"

"Officer Chandray and I were just discussing that," he said. "We found what looks like a clue—but we're honestly not sure."

Marquez raised one eyebrow and snorted. "Why am I not surprised? Even now, Oskar DeSilvo is not through playing games with us."

"True," said Norla. "But the Admiral believes that perhaps the games have a purpose—that we have been meant to see things, to find things."

"To prepare us before our meeting with the Great Man himself?" Marquez demanded, almost sneering.

Norla nodded, very slightly. "Something like that."

Marquez turned toward Ashdin. "Well, what about it, Doctor? Did *you* find anything we need to know? Anything important, hidden from the public view, that we couldn't have learned by checking the local news feeds?"

"Oh, yes," she said. "Very much so. I should have thought that would be obvious."

"Maybe not to all of us," said Phelby. "What is it you found?"

"That terraforming is a dying art—"

"Not exactly news, that," said Marquez.

"—and that killing it is a deliberate policy," Ashdin finished up, without missing a beat. "We couldn't have seen the proof of that without sending a team to do a physical inspection of the books in the PPC, and to establish that no one at all had used the Geology and Terraforming Reading Room within a normal human lifetime."

Koffield considered for a moment, then nodded. "I hadn't viewed it in quite that way—but you're right. You're absolutely right. You know, one thing that didn't occur to me until much later—the decision to zero out the work priorities for the terraforming section at the Permanent Physical Collection could have taken place years before I visited, 128 years ago. It might easily take decades for the results of abandonment to be noticeable."

"Or, it could have happened, say, thirteen years after your visit," said Norla. "I don't think it was anyone's deliberate policy but DeSilvo's."

"No," said Koffield, "I disagree. One, his primary motive is always to protect himself. He was about to fake his own death and vanish. He had no need of protection—and I can't see what other motive he might have had. There has always been some sort of motive, some sort of logic to his actions. If he did it, it was mere caprice—and that's out of character. Two, we saw lots of *other* signs that pointed toward making terraforming a lost art, things DeSilvo *couldn't* have done. For starters, there were no completely new books or datasets or other information published on the subject. I ran some statistical studies. Everything, and I mean *everything* my ArtInts examined was at least in part a rehash or re-working of older source material. My ArtInts didn't have a chance to examine all the material—but, statistically speaking, they established a very high confidence level. *Less than 1 percent* of the material in the terraforming books and data published since my last visit to the PPC was new. And 1 percent is the *maximum* level. Probably there was far less."

"But why?" asked Jerand Bolt. "Why would the study of terraforming die?"

"You saw why on Mars," said Norla. "Because it doesn't work."

"Yeah, maybe, but do *they* know that?" Bolt asked. "I thought the main reason you—we—had to keep this mission quiet was to keep people from finding out that this Baskaw character proved that terraforming always fails. We didn't want to set off a panic."

"*People* don't know about Baskaw's work," said Koffield. "We'd have heard about it, otherwise. We'd have seen references to it—or people would have told us about the riots that had been touched off by the news. On the other hand, it has always seemed unlikely to me that DeSilvo was the first and only one to find Baskaw's work and understand. And someone else could have made the same discoveries. For that matter, DeSilvo *didn't* understand it, not completely. That's what got Solace into trouble. But governments, organizations, policy groups—maybe it wasn't all that secret from them."

"So a few organizations decide to back off from terraforming. They turn off a few money spigots, kill some research grants. That's all it would take. After a while, terraforming isn't current technology—it's historical, something we don't do any more because we don't need to, like hydroponic farming."

"All right, all right," said Marquez. "I get the point. So we did find something out."

"Several somethings," said Koffield. "Mostly things about as subtle as the death of terraforming."

"But what do they mean?" Phelby asked. "What do they *tell* us?"

Koffield shook his head. "I don't know. I want to say 'I don't know yet'—but I'm not even *that* confident. Suppose we didn't find every puzzle piece? Do we have enough of them to put the picture together?"

"What about—" Yuri Sparten spoke for the first time, but then cut himself off. "Um, never mind."

Norla looked at him. At a guess, he had gotten interested in the conversation, forgotten his own troubles, and then promptly remembered them as soon as he spoke. "What about what?" she asked gently.

"What about—whatever it was you saw on Mars? Did you find any puzzle pieces there? Anything that adds to the big picture?"

"Possibly," said Norla. "We really haven't had a chance to study what we found. There's a lot of it."

"So how long will it take?" Sparten asked.

"I'm sorry, I don't follow. How long will what take?"

"How long until you—we—figure out where we go next? We're still trying to find him, right?"

There was silence around the table.

Jerand Bolt looked around at the carefully neutral faces all around him. "What's the problem?" he asked. "It's a fair question. What *do* we do next? Where *do* we go?"

Norla toyed with her fork, pushing the last scraps of food around on her plate. She'd lost her appetite. "Yes, the question's fair—and so far as I know, the answer is— we don't know yet. We rendezvous with the *Dom Pedro IV*—after that, I have no idea. The problem is with the questioner. The problem is that *we* know that *you* don't know that *he* doesn't know that we know."

"What?" Bolt stared at her.

"The same old game of who knows what," said Norla, throwing down her fork. "And I've just decided I don't want to play anymore. It's too damned hard to keep it straight what you're supposed to pretend and with whom, and I'm just too damned tired to care. Mr. Sparten—Yuri. They searched your cabin aboard the *Dom Pedro IV*. They found the radio transmitter."

Sparten turned deathly pale.

Marquez jumped up out of his seat and glared at Norla. "You had no right to tell him that!" he shouted. "We were going to keep it quiet until—"

"Quiet?" asked Koffield, cutting in. "You've been shouting it from the rooftops since we got here. If Mr. Sparten didn't know the particulars, he knew *something* was wrong."

Marquez seemed to be working up toward another explosion—and then the air went out of him. "All right. All right. You've got a point. At least now we can talk about it." He looked toward Sparten. "We all knew you were some kind of plant. You got shoved down our throats a little too hard for it to be anything else. But we—well, I, at least, figured you'd be reporting back to whoever it was *after* we got back—if we got back—and maybe that the someone in question might have a legitimate right to know. After all, the Solacian government paid to refit the *DP-IV* and send her out. Maybe they were just making sure they had an independent source of information. I got an extra officer out of the deal, and his pay didn't even come out of my budget. Fine. But a radio transmitter. That means you're sending to someone in the Solar System. *That means you can betray us.*"

"But it doesn't mean I *did*," said Yuri. He stared down at the table, looking very scared, and very alone. He was silent for perhaps twenty seconds, then looked up, seeming more resolute. "All right, game over, cards on the table." He looked over at Bolt with a weak smile. "You won the first game we played too." He looked to Marquez, and then Koffield. "SCO Station Intelligence," he said. "My old boss, Karlin Raenau. Or actually, *his* security chief, Olar Sotales. And you had it figured right. I was supposed to watch you, report back, be a back channel. Solace Security had—has—I guess, some sort of agent-in-place, or part-time officer, or something in the Solar System. I don't know who or where. I don't even know much about how the transmitter worked. I didn't *want* to know. I was just supposed to enter coded reports into it when I could, and it would handle transmitting automatically. It had a transmission schedule programmed into it."

"So you'd write up a report, and the transmitter would take care of getting it sent?" asked Koffield.

"That's right. The reports would be forwarded on to Solace via the next ship to make the run."

"How many ships have gone from the Solar System to Solace since we've been here?" asked Norla.

Sparten shifted in his seat. "One. Just after our arrival. And there's another boosting out next week."

"So it hasn't been very useful, so far," said Marquez.

"Probably both those ships will get back home before we do," said Sparten, a defensive tone in his voice.

"And all that tells us is that the setup hasn't been all that useful for the purpose you were told about," said Koffield.

Sparten looked puzzled. "Sir?"

"All *you* know is that the transmitter was supposed to send reports off automatically," said Koffield. "You don't actually know who was listening. And even if it was only Solace Security listening—you don't know who they shared with."

Sparten's eyes grew wide, and there was suddenly a thin sheen of sweat on his forehead. "I—I never thought of that," he said.

"Solace is a small-time operation, son," Koffield said gently. "Solace Security is even smaller. They're not going to have agents in every port. They'd have intelligence *sharing* arrangements with the locals. Pick up our report transmissions for us, see if there's anything you think is interesting, then pass the report on to us."

"So your letters home have all been read by someone at this end," said Marquez. "Now do you see the problem?"

Norla watched Yuri Sparten as he struggled to find something to say. She thought he had never looked quite so young or vulnerable. "I—I—didn't—"

"You didn't know, and they used you, and they lied to you," said Koffield. "For what it's worth, Captain Marquez, I suspect Sparten hasn't really made things all that much worse for us. What we found on Mars is important enough—and still hot enough—that we have to *assume* they'd be after us anyway. And if SCO Station Intelligence was willing to trade us to their friends in the Solar System while we're here, I think there's a pretty good shot they'd turn us in once we got back anyway." Koffield looked at Sparten thoughtfully. "He may even have done us a favor. I, for one, was expecting that we'd be welcomed back to Solace with open arms. Now we know to be careful—and we have at least some idea where the enemy fire might be coming from."

"I'm not your enemy!" Sparten shouted.

There was something of the petulant schoolboy in his tone, getting angry at the teacher who caught him stealing the test answers. He seemed near tears. *That shouldn't surprise me,* thought Norla. *All of us have been rubbed raw. Everyone's emotions are out in the open.*

"If you're not our enemy, what are you?" Marquez asked. "A spy working for our friends? With friends like you—"

"No! I'm not a spy, either. That's not why I'm here. Not anymore, anyway." He took a deep breath and calmed himself down. "I didn't trust *him,*" he said, nodding toward Koffield. "My family is from Glister. I grew up hearing them blaming Anthon Kolfeldt—that's what they called you in the stories, spelling shift or something—Anthon Kolfeldt made their planet die. There were nursery rhymes about Terrible Anthon, who wrecked the Circum Central wormhole and stopped the relief supplies from getting through—and, and all that. So when your ship showed up at Solace warning about all sorts of things that might go wrong, they were suspicious, trying to figure out how it might be a trick. They wanted a watcher and they sent me. Figured I wouldn't trust you anyway."

"So you watched," said Marquez. "What did you see? What did you report?"

"That's—that's just it," said Sparten. "I didn't get to see much. The inside of the Permanent Physical Collection, a lot of dust, some books—and then the inside of the *Cruzeiro do Sul*. I haven't made any reports since I came aboard here, obviously. You kept me bottled up pretty well. I knew the quarters would be tight in here. That's why I didn't want to risk bringing the transmitter. Obviously I didn't think about the other side of the risks."

"So we searched your quarters and got lucky. *We* didn't trust you, either," said Koffield.

"The point is, I couldn't report much because I didn't learn much." He turned to Bolt. "That's one reason I pushed you so hard, ordered you to get information. *I* wasn't getting anywhere—and I figured you'd be trusted more, get to see more."

"And you were right," said Bolt. "But your orders are not the ones I have to follow. Never were, in my book."

"So what did they learn from you?" Koffield asked.

"That you followed all the rules getting rid of Renblant. That you signed up three new crew on Asgard. That you were looking for material on terraforming, and DeSilvo. That your people needed to search to find proof that you, Admiral Koffield, had been at the PPC. Proof to make *them* happy, I guess. That the terraforming section was messed up and abandoned. And ah, that three crew went over the side—two when we got here, and one on Earth." He looked to Marquez. "I never got a chance to report on the clues in the terraforming book, or anything about Mars."

"Did you give them names on the new crew that came aboard, and on the ones who left?" Koffield asked.

"Yes, sir. Full names and ID information."

"That could be the biggest problem," said Koffield to

Marquez. "It might take them a while—a long while—but if the Chronologic Patrol *wanted* to track down our deserters, they could—and deserters who get caught usually are very well motivated to cooperate."

"The others bailed out before the fun really started," said Marquez. "The only one who might be able to tell them a lot would be Clemsen Wahl."

"Wahl isn't going to want to be found," said Phelby. "And if they do find him—well, I don't think he was paying enough attention to his work to tell them all that much. And he left before you found the book."

"But I made queries about that book to a number of institutions," said Koffield. "Those would be enough to tell them I was interested in it."

"It sounds like more of the same," said Norla. "A nice, murky grey. We have to assume They're after us—but we don't know for sure who 'They' are, or how badly They want us, or how much of a trail we've given them."

Marquez looked at Sparten. "You said before you didn't trust the Admiral. Still feel that way?"

Sparten looked at Koffield, but seemed to have trouble meeting his gaze. "I think I've learned enough about terraforming to know that Admiral Koffield didn't kill my parents' world by destroying the Circum Central wormhole," he said. "That's folklore. A few shiploads of supplies didn't get through, and so it took longer and was harder to get back and forth to Glister. But the planet wouldn't have lasted much longer, no matter how many relief expeditions had gone in. Beyond that, I don't know what I feel," he said. "I know I'm part of the reason there is so much distrust—but there have been so many tricks and lies and secrets and double and triple agendas that I'm not sure of anything anymore. I'm not even sure why we're here now."

"I'm starting to think like Officer Chandray here," said Marquez, pacing back and forth along one long side of the table. "I'm tired of all the secrets. So I'll *tell* you some secrets—I'll tell the whole story, flash-bang. We're here because we're running like hell after one of my people got killed, and two of my auxiliary ships were destroyed. And all *that* happened because we're after Oskar DeSilvo, *because he's got a faster-than-light drive.* A *real* one. No wormholes, no timeshafts, no danger of time paradoxes. Just from here to there, moving faster than a laser beam. And we know he has *that* because *he* was the one controlling the Intruders at Circum Central. And what we found in that phony tomb of his was a confession—in it he said that it was the Intruders, *the robot ships he controlled*, that destroyed the wormhole. He let all of Settled Space, and Admiral Koffield himself, go on believing that Koffield had done it—but that wormhole would have been destroyed if Koffield's ship was never there at all!"

Sparten went white. He swallowed, opened his mouth, and struggled to speak. "But—I don't—if that's true, then—"

"Then what your whole worldview is based on goes away!" said Marquez. "Terrible Anthon the Worldkiller! Except he *couldn't* have killed your world, and it turns out he *didn't* wreck the wormhole. Nothing is what you thought, and everything you thought isn't there at all!"

Norla looked sharply at Marquez. What did he say? *Everything isn't there.* Another phrase popped into her head. *Nothing is, but what is not.* "Hold it!" she cried, jumping out of her chair. "Wait a second!"

"What is it—"

"Quiet a second! Just a second! Let me think. I can't let it get away." She stood there, stock-still, not daring to move a muscle, as if the idea she had were an easily spooked animal that would run off at the slightest provocation. It was like her fitful worrying of the night before, when the Question kept escaping every time she had the Answer cornered. If she could just hold the thoughts in her mind a second longer, string the beads on the thread—

"Wait here! Just a second!" She turned and shot up the ladder to the temporary igloo upper deck, where she and Koffield had been talking just before breakfast.

Voices percolated up from the main deck. "What the hell got into her?" "What was that all about?" "I don't know."

Norla ignore the voices, grabbed at the datapad, and stared at it. Yes! Yes! That was it. She rushed back down the ladder, nearly turning her ankle as she landed. She turned the datapad so everyone could see it. "We saw these plaques on Mars," she said. "Time enough for the whole story later. Admiral Koffield and I had gotten as far as thinking the first part of the first one might mean something like 'Belongs to Oskar DeSilvo.' "

"What of it?" Marquez asked.

"Something you said made me think of a quote from one of the pre–near ancients. Dr. Wandella—DeSilvo admired a writer named—what was it—Sharkspar?"

"Shakespeare," said Wandella.

"That's it! There were some of his words floating around in my head, and something Captain Marquez said brought them to the surface—and the words the captain said made sense of this plaque—*and* if I remember right, I think this is Shakespeare too. I remember reading something on Solace about it being endlessly misquoted. They always get one word wrong."

"Sounds like your subconscious is working overtime," said Koffield.

"Or else it's just blown a gasket altogether," she said. "But look at the part inside the parentheses. It's the same for both plaques."

$$\in (oskd@(\forall X \ni X \neq Au))$$
$$\rightarrow (\forall X \ni X \neq Au)$$

"That upside down 'A' means 'for all,' " said Phelby. "So it reads 'For all values of x wherein x is not equal to a times u.' So what?"

"No. That 'Au' isn't mathematical," said Norla.

"*A.U.* means "astronomical unit," said Bolt. "One A.U. is the average distance between Earth and the Sun.

So that would be, ah, all of the somethings that are greater than or less than one A.U. Doesn't really make sense."

"No. Not astronomical, either. Think chemical. Elemental, you might say."

"Gold!" said Bolt. "That's the chemical symbol for gold."

"Right," said Norla. So we have 'for all values of x that does not equal gold.' "

"Solve for x . . ." said Koffield. "All x that are not gold—" Suddenly his eyes lit up. "Yes. Yes! Then stick on 'belongs to Oskar DeSilvo at' for the first one, and I guess that arrow on the second just means 'go to' or 'this way to.' Norla, you said you weren't any good at puzzles."

"I still don't get it," Phelby protested.

"Brush up your Shakespeare, Phelby," said Koffield. " 'All that X is not gold.' "

"It just jumped out at me," said Norla. "Well, it jumped after I thought about it long enough, and something put me in mind of it." She turned to look at Sparten. "Yuri—what do you say we all go take a look at where your parents came from?"

INTERLUDE

OLAR SOTALES

The second report traveled by every bit as roundabout a route as the first, and Sotales paid more attention to it when it finally arrived. Unlike the first, it contained hard information—but that information would not be particularly welcome to those who had sent Sparten out on his joyride. They had wanted proof that Koffield was a fraud—and Sparten's second report made it more than clear that the expedition was going to bring back solid proof of Koffield's veracity. Once that proof arrived back at Solace, all reasonable people would have to accept the truth of Koffield's information. *So they'll have all the reasonable people on board,* Sotales thought. *But it won't be enough. They'll still need a majority.*

He leaned back in his chair and stared at the wall opposite. *So,* he asked himself. *Whose side are you on?* But that wasn't right. Not anymore. *There can't be sides anymore,* he told himself. This wasn't any routine political battle. This wasn't right versus left, city versus country, rich versus poor, upper versus lowdown. This was life versus death—and death was winning.

Throughout his career, Olar Sotales' job had been to keep the lid on, to suppress what needed suppressing, to maintain order. Put another way, his job had always been to preserve the status quo. At the end of the day, it

was those who benefited from the status quo who paid
him, protected him, supported him.

Now that game was over. The status quo wasn't there
anymore.

Which merely meant it was time for a new game to
start. Sotales powered up his wallscreen and summoned
up a view from an external camera. There was Solace—
tired, dying, Solace, still lovely, but plainly not a healthy
world. It was too late to save that world. Sotales was finally coming to accept that. Now the challenge, the
game, the new game to be played in deadly earnest—was
to save the people of that world—somehow.

It would be massively complex. Technology, politics,
engineering, economics, ecological engineering, public
health, news and propaganda management, intelligence
gathering—there would be endless problems to deal with
in all those areas, and many others. It would have to be
a game played deep, and played, not for the quick score,
but for the long haul.

And there would be parts of the game that would
have to be played dirty, where an excessive concern for
the niceties could get people—a lot of people—dead.

Playing dirty, thought Sotales. *That's where I come in.*

Then and there, he started his planning, started thinking as many moves ahead, as many years ahead, as he
could.

He didn't intend to play any games he couldn't win.

CHAPTER TWENTY-TWO
ALL THAT IS NOT GOLD

They rendezvoused with the *Dom Pedro IV* in the outer regions of the Solar System a week and half later and departed at once. They took the long way around.

Forty years in temporal confinement brought them to the Sirius Power Wormhole Farm. They held their breath a bit harder and longer than normal as they passed the Chronologic Patrol ship on uptime station. It was highly unlikely, but just barely possible, that the Chrono Patrol had received orders to stop them. But the CP ship did nothing.

Down an eighty-year wormhole at Sirius, and the last of the *DP-IV*'s original enlisted crew went ashore at Sirius Power Station Gamma—Aziz, Sherdan, and Tugler. No one was happy to see them go, but no one could blame them for departing after the *Rio*—and before whatever it was that was going to happen next. They were certainly within their rights. They were, after all, merchant crewmen, not a combat team. The *DP-IV*, distinctly undercrewed, went on her way.

Another forty years of temporal confinement, another endless day locked up in the TC chamber, brought them back to their departure date, and arrival at the Five Goddess Network Hole Farm for a fifty-year drop into the past, followed by fifty more long and weary years of temporal confinement, and once again, return to the date of their departure—and arrival at Glister. The journey took two and half months total subjective time—but the ship had aged 130 years.

Back and forth, up and down, around and again, they sailed the Ocean of Years, always coming back to when they had been.

Just another routine heroic saga, thought Norla, one evening toward the end of it. *Just another incredibly long, complex, dangerous journey, crossing time and distances vast beyond human comprehension, trusting in a madly complicated and terrifyingly powerful system of artificial wormholes that grabbed space and time and tied them in knots for our convenience.*

She stared out a viewport at Glister's star, a fat point of light that would swell into a blazing sun in the days to come. *How the hell did such a way of travel become accepted, become normal? Flying up and back through a human lifetime, or more, and then diving down a wormhole—a wormhole!—to negate it all. Wipe the years and the sweat and the pain away, make them as if they had never happened—and then travel right back through them again.* Depending on how you looked at it, counted it, there were certain decades of time she had passed through four times on this trip. Were there, somehow, four of her, passing in the night out there?

And it's all breaking down, she thought. That was what her gut told her. All breaking down, as surely as the planet they were approaching was dead, dead and buried under the failed ambitions of humans who had dared try to make a dead ball of rock into the twin of living, breathing Earth.

Somehow, she knew, that was the key to it. That was the theme that pulled it all together. But like the Question and Answer that still came close and then ran away in her fitful dreams, it was a key that would come no closer, that would not let itself be taken in her hand or fitted or turned in a lock. Not yet, anyway.

She sighed, smiled, and laughed at herself. She did tend to get a bit overpoetic when she stared out at the

stars. But even so—they were close now. No one ques-
tioned that DeSilvo was down there, somewhere, on
Glister. And whatever the Answer was, whatever the
Question turned out to be, they were close to it—and
that was reason enough to reflect on all that had happened, on all they had been through.

And all that might happen next.

Glister's sun grew in the viewport, and soon it was possible to pick out the planet Glister from the background of
stars. Not long after that, Glister was a world growing
closer, brighter, bigger in the overhead dome. Captain
Marquez found himself spending a lot of time on the
ship's main command deck, contemplating the cold and
wasted planet as it grew larger.

Koffield found him there one evening, sitting in the pilot's chair. He went over to sit beside him, join him in
staring up at the frost-grey world. " 'All that glisters is
not gold,' " he said. "Therefore, all that is not gold—is
Glister."

"That doesn't quite make sense," said Marquez.

"You don't think we got the answer wrong, do you?"

"No. Glister is it. But I won't pretend to understand
the way DeSilvo's mind works. I've never met the man,
but my whole life has revolved about him ever since—"

"Ever since I bought a ticket on your ship, asked if
you could take me to Solace—and he sabotaged your
ship to stop me. None of this would have happened to
you if not for me."

Marquez waved away the apology. "Don't worry
about it. It's been interesting. More interesting than
hauling freight. Whatever ship you chose would have
gotten the treatment. I'm almost glad it was the *Dom
Pedro IV*." He paused for a minute, and frowned. "Except for the crew that died. The two when we came out
of cryo at Solace, and Wu, killed on the *Rio*. That's
blood spilt, and it can't be made good. Not ever. That's
on DeSilvo's hands."

"And a splash or two of it on mine," said Koffield. "If
not for me—"

"No," said Marquez. "If not for you, DeSilvo would have gotten away with a terrible crime. That's all. Thanks to you, sooner or later, the universe will know that—and, just incidentally, you did manage to get a warning to Solace. DeSilvo made sure it got there late— but at least it got there before the place looked like *that*." He pointed up at the eternal winter of Glister. There was only a narrow band at the equator that was clear of snow and ice. The rest was dirty-grey clouds over gleaming white snowfields, cold dark hard lines of mountain ranges stabbing up through the whiteness, the chaotic jumble of the sea ice—smashed and broken ice boulders, ice sheets, ice peaks, remaining just where they were when the sea had at last frozen solid from the surface on down, until there was no water left below the ice, and the ice above simply collapsed under its own weight.

Neither man spoke for a time.

"I wonder if we're the first ones here," Koffield said at last.

"*What?*"

"We still don't know if the Chrono Patrol or Interdict Command knows about us. Judging from the way we weren't pursued, the *Rio* looks more and more like a normal shoot-down of an unauthorized visitor, not an attack on us in particular. But if they started looking, and looked hard enough, they'd be able to find our landing site. If they did *that*—sooner or later, they'd find those plaques of DeSilvo's. And if *we* can solve the puzzle, so can the Chronologic Patrol."

"I hadn't thought that far ahead," said Marquez. "Is there anything we can do?"

"We're an unarmed, undercrewed merchant vessel with fairly good sensors, and exactly one auxiliary craft left aboard. If the Chronologic Patrol is waiting for us, they'll have us outgunned by more than just a little. And if they have gotten here first, somehow, that means they'll already know everything we know, and probably more. No sense sacrificing ourselves to protect knowledge that's already compromised. If they're here, I would suggest we surrender, we answer their questions—and then we'll probably get 'resettled' in a very isolated habitat somewhere. But I can't see why they'd wait until now to take us. They'd have grabbed us the moment we came in-system. So I think we're all right."

"I suppose that ought to be comforting," said Marquez. "But your point about our not being armed makes up my mind about one thing. It'll be just as dangerous on planet as aboard ship. I'm going to declare the landing party 'all hands welcome.' Volunteers only, but all volunteers accepted."

"I suspect they'll all come, if you give them the chance," said Koffield. "Are you willing to leave the ship uncrewed?"

"She'll be in standby mode in a high orbit. Either nothing will happen, in which case it won't matter if no one is there, or else someone will fire a weapon or board her, in which case it won't matter if anyone is there, and I'd be just as glad not to get anyone else killed."

"They could get just as killed on the surface," said Koffield.

"And they know it. But if they want to go, they're going."

Koffield nodded. "Fair enough." He looked up again at the cold, dead planet overhead. "Now all we have to do is find him."

Oskar DeSilvo had spent a great deal of time designing and building his detection system, providing it with the most powerful equipment he could find, and programming it to deal with all the likelier contingencies. Needless to say, first among these was the arrival of the *Dom Pedro IV* in-system. He had provided the detection ArtInt with full data on all of the *DP-IV*, along with full data on how the ship's detectable characteristics might change if she were modified in this way or that. He had told the system all about the earliest date she might arrive, the possible approach vectors she might use if she came via this routing or that, everything he could think of. He wanted to be sure that the system would be able to distinguish the *DP-IV* from other ships.

He needn't have bothered with so much detail. Glister was a lonely place, and there were precious few other ships that visited in all those long years—and when the *Dom Pedro IV* slid into orbit around Glister, his system spotted her drive signature all but instantaneously.

Oskar DeSilvo had calculated very carefully as to the first possible moment that the *DP-IV* might arrive, if everything happened in the absolute minimum of time. Even though he knew it was absurd, he had been sitting there, waiting, ready, for an hour of confinement time before that first possible moment came, waiting for it, just to be sure—while eight months passed outside. He had been sitting there for a further two and a half hours since then, sweating it out as two full years passed on the outside. The comm center's message detector pinged repeatedly, but DeSilvo did not bother with the incoming reports. It could take half an hour for a full page of text to come through. Why bother hovering over the incoming traffic display watching one letter at a time appear, when, at any moment, time itself might change, accelerate, make everything—

A temporal confinement field shuts down rather abruptly, as seen from the inside. In the flicker of time between one moment and the next, it is simply gone. DeSilvo let out an involuntary gasp and stood up suddenly.

Like a soap bubble pricked by the sharpest of pins, the invisible wall of nothingness and energy that had shut Oskar DeSilvo off from the outside universe was suddenly gone. He peered through the viewport of the inner chamber, the viewport that had shown nothing but blackness in all this time. The outer chamber that housed the confinement was suddenly there to be seen. He looked to the incoming message display, and saw it suddenly sprout a dozen MESSAGE RECEIVED flags as the system caught up with the traffic that had been cued up, waiting to be fed in, one letter at a time. *I've arrived,* DeSilvo thought. *The time is finally now.*

DeSilvo unsealed the hatch and stepped outside the confinement chamber for the first time in over a century.

He hurried over to the main detection display, powered up the system, and excitedly checked over the detection report. Yes. Yes. Modified here and there, slight changes in some ways, but there could be no doubt. The *Dom Pedro IV* had arrived in-system. He had to get ready—and there was a lot to do.

He was going to have to hurry.

Oskar DeSilvo set to work at once, delighted by the irony of having so much to do—and suddenly having so little time to do it.

Yuri Sparten stared at the screens, watching the world of his parents roll past. The *Cruzeiro do Sul* had settled into a polar orbit, with the orbital period keyed to the planet's rotation. Every orbit brought up a new swath of real estate, each pass overlapping slightly with the one before. It would take them about forty-five hours to get a daylight look at the whole surface. In all probability, the *Dom Pedro IV*'s ArtInt could have been trusted to spot any anomalies of interest, but there was always the chance that a human eye would notice something a machine would not.

Yuri had volunteered to take the first watch, not quite knowing why, beyond the fact that it would get him left alone, undisturbed and able to think by himself—and for himself. The transit from the Solar System had been far from easy on him.

He stared at the ice fields sliding by, trying to find some sort of calm. *I wish I could blame them for being so angry with me,* he thought, for something more like the thousandth time than the first. It was hard enough to fight down his own, irrational anger at them. It made no sense for him to blame them for what had happened—but the fact remained that he would not be in this mess, if all of them—especially Koffield—had just stayed home and not stuck their noses into things that did not concern them. *And if they had done that, Solace would never have known the truth—and Solace would kill as many as Glister had*. But for all of that, still he was angry at all of them.

And angry at himself. He had spent a lifetime believing Koffield had killed Glister and that DeSilvo was the savior of the Glister survivors. After all, DeSilvo had terraformed Solace, and Solace had made a home for the Glistern refugees. And now that was turned on its head. Now he knew who the villain was, and who was, perhaps, the hero—and who had been fooled. It mattered not a whit to him that millions of others had been fooled just as badly. Someone had done a bad thing, and the bad thing had happened to *him*. What had happened to everyone else didn't enter into it. He felt entitled to take it personally.

But even in the midst of that anger, old beliefs died hard. It was difficult to throw away the old familiar lies and mistakes. It was almost easier, more comforting, to wonder if it could all, somehow, be a trick, that the evil Anthon Kolfeldt was scheming even now to destroy the memory of the saintly Oskar DeSilvo.

The dead surface of Glister rolled past. The ruins of a small city went by. The wrecks of a few tall towers, knifing up through the snow, were the only surviving sign of a place where thousands, perhaps even millions, had once lived. But *what* city had it been? Perhaps his parents had been born there, in the place he was looking at now. Perhaps they had lived their whole lives there, until the Evacuation. Perhaps they had never set foot in the place. Where *had* they lived, anyway? Yuri was coming to realize just how ignorant he was concerning Glister's geography and history, and about his own family's history. Embarrassing, given his heartfelt passion over the crimes committed against Glister.

And, then, underneath it all—the secret he still held, the truth that still survived, still hidden under his last remaining cover story. Had Koffield guessed? Had Marquez? Were they plotting, now, this moment, how best to neutralize him? Or had they failed to detect him? Was he free to fulfill his duty, if need be? Was he capable of performing that duty? And if so, how would he judge the moment, the situation? How could someone so full of confusion and doubt be sure?

The *Dom Pedro IV* left the dead and buried city behind, and tracked over a cold and massive storm, with huge wheeling arms of cyclonic winds and clouds over a cold, hard eye. Yuri felt some of that upheaval in himself, and he watched as the storm slid past, and the ship crossed into darkness.

Around and around went his thoughts, around and around went the spacecraft, girdling the planet again and again. He stared, fascinated, unable to look away from the endless, frozen devastation below.

—Until he spotted something different on their fourth night-side pass. It popped up on infrared. A hot spot, a big one, just to the east of their current orbital path. Yuri blinked, came back to himself, and checked the instruments. A *very* big hot spot. Marquez and Koffield had expressed some quite reasonable concern that DeSilvo might be hard to find—one man tucked away somewhere on an Earth-sized planet. But as Yuri stored the images into the analyzers, he realized that they need not have worried and would have little need of the daylight imagery, for that matter. It *had* to be DeSilvo's HQ. It was the size of a small city, blazing away in infrared and shining just as bright in visible light.

Yuri paged Koffield on the intercom. "Sir, I think we've got it," he said. Koffield was there in minutes. The city—or whatever it was—had fallen below their horizon by then, but Koffield took a look at the playback and nodded. Marquez came in while Koffield was looking.

"He's sure as hell left the light on for us, hasn't he?" asked Marquez. "For a guy who's supposed to be hiding out, he's being a little bit obvious."

"Maybe not exactly," said Koffield. "I've got a feeling that he turned the lights *on* to attract our attention. I'd bet a fair amount that that site was a lot darker and harder to see before we entered the system. He's telling us that he's spotted *us*." The playback ended, and he reset it to the beginning and ran it again. "Unless, of course, we've got the whole thing entirely wrong. Let's do the full-planet scan, just for the sake of thoroughness—but I'd be very surprised if that wasn't the spot."

Two days later, the scan was done, and they had found no other candidate sites. The whole ship's company gathered round the video displays for the daylight pass over what had already come to be known as DeSilvo City. The pass gave them more geographic information, but nothing particularly useful. DeSilvo City had been built inside a large impact crater, in the form of a five-kilometer-wide bull's-eye, with a round central dome and a large auxiliary structure, surrounded by six raised rings. The rings appeared to be bulldozed dirt berms that seemed to have no function other than to be visible. The central structure looked very much like a standard domed-in landing field, the sort that opened up to let ships in and out, and otherwise stayed shut against the outside environment.

"That's a lot bigger than I was thinking it'd be," said Phelby.

"How many people has he got *down* there?" Norla asked.

"My guess would be one, counting himself," said Koffield. "He's here alone. I'm sure of it. He wouldn't trust people if he could help it."

"But that place is huge!"

"And it has to be huge for one reason—so we can see it from orbit."

"One man couldn't build all that," Marquez objected.

"One man could," said Wandella Ashdin, "if he were in charge of a whole-planet terraforming job like Solace, and stole and diverted one-hundredth of 1 percent of the automatic earthmoving and construction equipment they used. And he probably sent some of the ArtInts and robots out to scavenge whatever he could out of Glister's cities. DeSilvo thinks on a grand scale—but he acts alone."

"You surprise me, Dr. Ashdin," said Koffield. "You're usually the one defending DeSilvo."

"Well, there are limits," she sniffed. "And I've had a lot of time to think and look over what we've learned. A good scholar must be prepared to accept new evidence and discard discredited theories."

Norla raised her eyebrows and caught Koffield's eye. He just shook his head, plainly as taken aback as Norla herself. To hear Wandella Ashdin say such things was almost as shocking as the size of DeSilvo City.

Marquez moved the *DP-IV* out from her close-in orbit to a stationary orbit over the planet's equator, directly over the longitude of DeSilvo City, thus affording them a constant watch over the place. They remained there for a full day/night cycle, watching, listening in on all the standard comm channels, trying to gather as much data as they could before the final move. There was no visible activity during the day, but as soon as local sunset came, the lights came on again—but this time, they did more than shine. There were lights strung along the top of each of the circular berms, and they started flashing: the outermost circle first, then each circle toward the center, and then the lights of the central dome would come on. The pattern repeated over and over—and then the central dome split open into six sections that folded back out of the way, then closed up again, then opened, then shut, as the lights blinked on and off.

"It's just possible he knows we're here," said Marquez, watching the light show.

"And it looks like we're invited," said Koffield. *DeSilvo was down there.* The endless pursuit was drawing to an end. Somehow, it seemed to him, there should have been some way to mark the occasion, some event or ceremony—though certainly not a celebration.

But there was nothing he could think to do or say that seemed appropriate, and that was probably just as well.

Never mind. Let the event itself serve to mark the occasion. He nodded to Marquez.

Marquez turned to his crew. "Mr. Sparten. Bolt. Chon. Start final checkout on the *Cruzeiro do Sul,* and prep her for departure. It's time to go down there."

Anton Koffield stared at the locker for a full two minutes before he opened it. No one else would have been able to tell, but he had no doubt whatsoever that it had been tampered with. That he knew in the first few seconds of his examination. The rest was merely rechecking to be sure, to confirm that he had seen what he had seen, and not what he hoped for—or feared.

He worked the lock and opened the locker, and carefully counted the contents, twice. Everything there. But he was also quite certain that the contents had been disturbed, examined, and replaced, and plainly with less skill than the perpetrator had hoped for.

He sighed, a tired man whose fears had been confirmed. He thought back to his time as a very green lieutenant, and the wisdom that a grizzled old chief petty officer had given him, when it had fallen to Koffield to manage a bad situation belowdecks. *Hide the stuff as hard as you want. You can't stop a drunk from finding booze,* the petty officer had said. *Sometimes it's better to let them find it, and just check every day to see how fast the bottles are emptying. That way, at least you're monitoring things. The level drops too fast, you know to move in. Hide the stuff where the drunk can't find it— and he'll find a supply you don't know about, and you'll have lost whatever little control you had.*

Well, this wasn't booze. This was worse. Much worse. But the point still held. If he cleaned out the locker, he'd be sending a formal announcement to the perpetrator that he'd been caught—and he'd be forcing the perp to look elsewhere, probably somewhere Koffield didn't know about, for what he needed.

So leave the contents where they stood. And—yes. *Adjust* the contents. Take it all down a notch, and make sure it stayed there.

Decision made, Koffield acted quickly, then replaced the adjusted units—doing so with greater skill than the *last* person to handle them.

Games within games, thought Koffield. And each one deadlier than the one before.

The *Cruzeiro do Sul*'s main engines shut down, and the lighter began the long, spiraling fall to the planet's surface. Marquez was flying the *Cruzeiro*, and taking them in via the most propellant-saving course he could devise. He had no way of knowing when or whether he'd get a chance to top off the tanks, and was operating on the assumption of no replenishment.

"Very well," he announced after checking his displays. "We are on course. You are free to unstrap and move about the cabin for the next several hours."

"So—you're the expert," said Jerand Bolt as he unstrapped himself. "What do *you* expect to happen down there?"

Wandella Ashdin undid her straps herself with nearly as much skill as Bolt himself. Even she was aware that she had started out as a fumble-fingered ninny when it came to life aboard ship. Not anymore. She had had plenty of practice. It seemed as if she had been in and out of this ship and that all her life. In a sense, she had, for she was living a completely different life than she had before being summoned by the Planetary Executive herself to assist Admiral Koffield. *That* Wandella Ashdin had scarcely ever flown in an aircraft. The new Wandella Ashdin thought not a thing about flitting from one star system to another. It had changed her, in a lot of ways.

Mind you, of course, some experiences were still novel—such as strapping herself into a flight chair in preparation for landing on a strange, dead world to face a man who was supposed to have died long years before she herself was born.

"Expect?" Wandella Ashdin echoed. She shook her head. "I think I've given up altogether on expecting anything." She smiled to herself, and laughed.

"What's funny?" Bolt asked.

"Oh, meetings and expectations and all that," she said. "It put me in mind of a moment—oh, two or three lifetimes ago, it seems. I was a very young and eager student. I suppose I was eighteen or so. I was at one school, and the one true love of my life—up to then—was transferred to another campus. It was very hard to go see him—no money, no time, no way to coordinate my free days with his—the usual student problems. I would lie awake imagining the moment we'd see each other again for the first time. I never got past that first moment, that first embrace—but I imagined it happening every possible way. We'd meet in the town square, or at his dormitory, or mine, or we'd both travel to a village midway between. It would be glorious daylight, or a very romantic foggy evening—on and on and on. Then we finally *did* arrange that I would take the speed train to go see him on such and such a day."

"So what happened?"

She smiled again. "It was a long time ago. I remember we had a lovely, splendid, romantic few days together— and that we parted swearing eternal love, and then drifted apart for no reason either of us quite understood. All normal, adolescent romance. The very odd thing is that I *can't* quite remember the moment of reunion itself. I can remember two *distinct* moments, so different from each other they can't both be right. They're mutually exclusive. One, where he swept me into his arms on the train platform, and just *held* me, while imaginary violins played in my heart. The other, at a cafe near my college, where we had arranged to meet, and we held each other's hand and ate the cheapest thing on the menu. And I know two things for *certain*: One of them is a fantasized meeting, one that I had imagined over and over and over again, in every detail. The other is how it *really* happened, and I am *quite* sure in my mind that I *never* once imagined anything like the way it really happened. But now, so many years later, I can't recall which is which. Which of the two scenes etched in my mind is the memory, and which is the fantasy? I honestly don't know anymore."

She did not speak again for a moment. "I spent my professional career believing that DeSilvo was an historical figure—dead, gone—from an academic perspective, he was *complete*. He was done doing things, and so, it was, in a sense, possible to learn all he had done without one's work being overtaken by events." She thought a moment. "I was an architect, studying a building that I thought was complete, *done*, a full statement of the designer's intents as tempered by effort and event. And then, one day, I walked around the back and discovered a huge construction tarp over the rear of the building and work-robots swarming in and out of the tarp's entrance flaps. They've started up work again. The building was under construction once more, and I was not allowed to see the work in progress."

"I get it," Bolt said.

"There came the day when I discovered that DeSilvo was probably still alive. And then came the day when I was assigned to this mission, a mission sent to track him down. From that moment to this, there was at least the theoretical possibility of *meeting* Oskar DeSilvo, the man I spent my whole life studying. It was as if Julius Caesar or Leonardo da Vinci were in cold sleep somewhere, just waiting for me to come and start the revival sequence." She frowned again. "And, along the way, I've found that my alive-again hero is a madman or a criminal, or both. I've learned things about him no scholar ever knew. I've asked myself, again and again, *what's the first thing you'll ask him?* The question keeps changing—and I find myself imagining his answers as well. Mostly I imagine answers that are apologies, explanations.

"And I imagine the first moment when I see him, when we meet. I've set it in a thousand different places, played it out a hundred different ways. But all I know for certain is that the real event will be nothing like what I imagined."

Bolt nodded toward Koffield, observing their flight from the copilot's seat, his face calm, his movements careful and deliberate. "You've got all *that* running through *your* mind," he said, speaking quietly. "With all *he's* been through, just think what's going through *his* mind right now."

Wandella Ashdin shook her head. "That," she said, "I honestly can't begin to guess."

The *Cruzeiro do Sul* spiraled down toward the planet, making a full circuit around Glister, performing a braking burn at the periapsis, or low point, of the orbit, then looping upward again over the planet, and firing a second braking burn at the high point, apoapsis, thus forcing the periapsis low enough to dip into the atmosphere. Running their planetary approach this way cost them time, which, as Marquez pointed out, they had plenty of, while conserving propellant, which was in potentially short supply.

The *Dom Pedro IV* remained in her synchronous orbit, and their orbital track twice took them behind the planet as seen from the *DP-IV*, and thus out of line of sight with the ship. On their second and final emergence from behind the planet, as they reestablished radio contact with the main ship, they realized something was wrong.

"What the hell is that?" Marquez demanded as he stared at the data display. None of the *DP-IV*'s telemetry system data were making any sense at all.

Koffield look at the data displays and instantly brought up the *Cruzeiro*'s long-range cameras and trained them on the *DP-IV*.

The *Dom Pedro* showed as a long silver cylinder, small and toylike, the image clear and sharp. But the *DP-IV* was not alone. There was a perfect swarm of smaller vessels all around her, and several seemed to be attached to her hull. As they watched, two more craft docked with her.

Marquez stared in astonishment for the space of a few heartbeats and feverishly began working to compute a flight plan back to his ship.

Koffield looked down from the video display, watched Marquez for a moment, then reached out and put a hand on his shoulder. "No," he said. "Don't. It won't do any good."

"But I've got to get back to my ship—"

"And do what?" Koffield demanded. He punched up a display of their orbital position relative to the *Dom Pedro*. "Look at the orbital tracks! If we abort our landing now and reboost to the ship, it would take us fifteen hours on a minimum-fuel burn, and something like seven hours for a minimum-time mission that would burn so far into our reserves we wouldn't be able to risk a landing afterward! In seven hours, they'll be done with whatever they're doing."

"*Who* are they?" Norla asked from just outside the pilot's station. Not too surprisingly, given Marquez's reaction, everyone else on board was crowding in behind her.

"And what the hell are they doing?" Phelby asked.

"DeSilvo's ArtInts," said Koffield. "As for what he's doing—I haven't the faintest idea. But he's had *years* to browse through four centuries of suppressed technology. Who knows what he found? And he's had decades to plan out what to do if and when we arrived, figuring through every possible contingency. One fairly obvious possibility—even probability—was that we'd arrive in the *Dom Pedro IV*. So now he's acting on those plans. And you'll recall he broke through the ship's security before. He's got full data on the ship."

"But my ship—"

"It's not your ship anymore," said Koffield. "I'm sorry. He's stolen it. And we're unarmed."

"But—" Yuri Sparten started to protest, then stopped himself.

"But what?" Marquez asked sharply.

"Well, ah, what are we supposed to *do*?" he asked. "Just land in the middle of his compound and ask nicely if we can have our ship back?"

Koffield nodded. "Believe me, if I could come up with a better plan, I'd suggest it. Even if we were armed, I don't know that I'd want to take on whatever firepower he's been able to put together. But we knew coming in we were walking into the lion's den. All we *can* do is walk up to him and ask him nicely—about a lot of things," he finished, making no effort to hide the bitterness in his voice.

They spoke no more. But Anton Koffield could not shake the distinct impression that Yuri Sparten had been about to say something very different when he stopped himself.

The *Cruzeiro do Sul* dropped toward the frozen carcass of Glister, sliding out of orbit and slamming into the upper atmosphere, a hard, fast entry trajectory that slowed them down quickly and was more than a little rough on the passengers—but it saved on propellant.

They were all strapped in for entry and landing, and all struggling to hold their emotions in as tightly as their flight chairs held their bodies. The gee stresses built up rapidly, and stayed high. The noise was terrific as the *Cruzeiro* bulled her way through the atmosphere, her hull roaring with vibration. Her viewports were shuttered, but the glow of frictional heating on the hull was plainly noticeable on the feeds from all the exterior cameras. Finally, the gee forces eased off, and the *Cruzeiro* was falling through the cold upper air of Glister, dropping exactly like a well-aimed stone, directly toward a bull's-eye on the ground.

Down below, it was early morning, the flashing lights of the night before were gone, and the six segments of the retractable dome roof were opened in earnest, no longer cycling open and shut.

Even Anton Koffield had the sense they were uncomfortably low and moving unnervingly fast, before Marquez killed all of their forward motion and most of the speed of descent with a vicious blast of his main thrusters. He killed the engines and they commenced falling again, straight down this time, directly for the center of the opened dome. He let the *Cruzeiro* drop hard for what seemed like far too long a time, then popped open his landing gear and fired his main rockets one last time, starting at full throttle, and easing smoothly back down to zero, killing the engines just as the landing gear was setting down, so smoothly and perfectly there was no jolt to tell the passengers they were down. It took them a few moments to realize they had landed, precisely in the center of the dome.

Koffield was rarely impressed by piloting, but Marquez had just managed some rare flying indeed. "All rates nulled out precisely at touchdown," he said, reading the displays. "Zero forward motion, zero laterals, zero vertical motion, all at exactly zero altitude," said Koffield. "That's as near a perfect landing as I've ever seen."

"I focus on my job when I'm angry," said Marquez. "Now let's go. I gotta talk to a guy who's going to give me my ship back."

"Make that 'ships,' " said Norla, who had already unstrapped and gotten up. She was pointing out the viewport. The segments of the dome were swinging shut again, this time with the *Cruzeiro do Sul* inside.

"Well, you had to figure that was going to happen," said Marquez, sounding oddly philosophical. "A place with weather this bad, they'd have to keep the doors shut."

"Let's hope that's all it is," said Koffield. "Whatever else might happen, at least the service is good." A roll-up servicer ArtInt, a standard unit seen at every planet-side spaceport on every world, was moving up to the side of the *Cruzeiro do Sul*. A hose extended itself from the front of the servicer, and Koffield watched on the external cameras as it plugged itself into the *Cruzeiro*'s propellant line.

"I guess we don't have to worry so much about propellant now," said Norla.

"Assuming they're not tanking us up with surplus from their waste disposal system," growled Marquez, already busy powering down the *Cruzeiro*'s flight systems, getting the lighter into standby mode.

Another familiar vehicle was headed toward them. It

was a self-elevating passenger ground transport, a sort of cross between an elevator and a glorified bus. The vehicle came to a halt directly under the *Cruzeiro*'s main airlock and the transport's passenger compartment began to raise itself on its lifter jacks until it was even with the lock. A flexible skirt pushed itself out from the end of the compartment and cozied itself up to the hull of the ship, forming a seal against the cold and unbreathable outside air.

They could hear the muffled thuds and bumps of the skirt forming itself to the ship, and then the far-off hum of air compressors as the skirt matched pressure with the passenger compartment. Other automated servicing vehicles rolled themselves up to the *Cruzeiro*, attaching themselves to various umbilical ports, and opening inspection hatches—and effectively preventing the *Cruzeiro* from taking off again, even if the dome did reopen.

Marquez made no protest, made no move to stop the servicers. He just went on with the power-down sequence, putting the lighter safely to sleep. At last he unstrapped from the pilot's chair, stood up, and nodded to Sindra Chon, who was waiting for his cue. She started the *Cruzeiro*'s airlock cycling. The inner locked door opened.

"Last chance to leave someone aboard, just in case," Koffield said to him.

Marquez shook his head. "Just in case of what? We're locked down here. You said it—we just walked into the lion's den. Or jackal's den, maybe. Either way, we walked in knowing we'd be at his mercy. Besides, everyone here has earned the right to be in at the finish—or whatever the hell this is going to be."

"I certainly don't know," said Koffield. "I've been spinning theories for the last two months, and I haven't the faintest idea."

"All right, everybody," said Marquez. "Let's go." They all crowded into the lock, and the inner door closed itself and made a tight seal. The pressure differential between the ship and the transport's passenger cabin wasn't much, and the outer doors opened almost at once.

The transport had extruded a steel bridge for them to cross over to the forward doors of the passenger cabin, and the party from the *Cruzeiro* stepped across into it.

Sindra Chon waited until everyone else was aboard the transport, then worked the *Cruzeiro do Sul*'s outer lock controls, sealing the outer door. Koffield watched as she carefully set the security locks as well. A lot of good that would do them. DeSilvo had gotten past much more impressive security in the past.

The compartment had a row of forward-facing seats along each side, with a narrow aisle in between. The whole interior of the vehicle looked worn and shabby. A few of the seats had gotten torn, and then had been inexpertly sewn up again. The carpeting on the floor was threadbare, and here and there in the aisle it had worn completely through. Koffield looked around the woebegone vehicle. "Scavenged from Glister Spaceport after the Evacuation, I expect," he said.

"Yeah, just like the vault doors and hatches on Mars," said Bolt. "This guy's pretty good at playing vulture."

Though its internal appointments weren't all they could be, the mechanical parts of the transport seemed in good working order. It closed and sealed its access doors, withdrew the flexible pressure skirt from the *Cruzeiro*'s hull, and lowered the passenger compartment smoothly down onto its undercarriage. The moment the compartment was down all the way, the transport backed away from the lighter, turned itself around, and headed straight for an airlock door in the perimeter of the dome, and whatever—and whoever—waited beyond.

They were almost there.

INTERLUDE

KALANI TEMBLAR

The pieces of the puzzle were starting to come together, but Kalani Temblar couldn't make any sense at all of the picture that was starting to emerge.

Start with the ship, the *Merchanter's Dream*. There were damn few spacecraft of that make and model still in service. Most of them had been scrapped generations ago, in favor of newer, more efficient models. Working from the shipyard records that gave the number of ships actually built, the various planetary ships' registries, the reports from scrap yards and breaker's yard, and all the other sources, Kalani had quickly pared things down to a list of exactly twenty-three similar ships that were at present unaccounted for.

Of that twenty-three, twelve she could eliminate at once with the use of a little common sense. They showed all the signs of one or another of the classic dodges. Some shady companies carried whole fleets of scrapped and destroyed ships on their books, claiming them as being in active service for this or that complicated tax reason. Other ships on the list she could match with almost perfect confidence against ships of unspecified make and model that had popped up on the registries out of nowhere a year or a month or a day after the last reported sighting of one of the "missing" ships. Some of those were just sloppy reporting, some were fraud or theft or tax evasion. But none of them was likely to be the *Merchanter's Dream.*

By the time she had filtered out all the probable and possible underreported registrations and frauds of one sort or another, she was down to four ships that might have been renamed as the *Merchanter's Dream.*

And one of them was the *Dom Pedro IV*, last reported lost, 129 years before, en route to Solace—where the *Merchanter's Dream* had launched from.

Kalani had never heard of the *Dom Pedro IV*, but Intelligence Command's Archive ArtInt certainly had. Kalani found a dozen references to conflicting and plainly inaccurate versions of how the ship had vanished mysteriously.

One datum all the versions agreed on was that Anton Koffield had been aboard her when she vanished—and Kalani Temblar had very definitely heard of Anton Koffield. It would be impossible to serve at ChronPat IntCom HQ and not know all about IntCom's most famous former officer.

Which brought her to the most intriguing snippet of data she had: The Earth authorities had been even more slow and lackadaisical than usual, but there had been a report out of Berlin. One Alber Caltrip, who appeared to have traveled to Earth aboard the *Merchanter's Dream*'s lighter, had claimed to be Koffield's remote ancestor— and had tried to visit Koffield's old house! Kalani was working to track down whatever she could on Caltrip— if there even was such a person. She had theories on that point, but she wasn't ready to commit them to writing just yet. She wasn't in the mood to get herself sent down for a psych check.

And one other tenuous little set of facts, a sequence of events that meant nothing each alone, but that became highly suggestive when strung together on a time line. The aux vessel that had carried Caltrip to Earth departed, apparently bound for the outer system, within a day of the time both of the *Dream*'s smaller aux ships undocked from the main ship and departed from the

Grand Library, bound for the inner system. None of the auxiliaries had been heard from since—and then the *Merchanter's Dream* had undocked from the Grand Library and headed off into deep space, *without* her aux vehicles.

An aux ship from Earth heads out. Two aux ships from Neptune move in. Mars is in the middle. There was some sort of large explosion near Mars—and, twelve hours after the explosion, the *Merchanter's Dream* files a departure flight plan. It was altogether too vague, too easy to explain away as it stood. Probably it would turn out to be nothing—but it was worth checking out. Kalani had queries into Interdict Command, to see if they knew anything—and if they were in a mood to cooperate.

All of it, of course, could turn out to be nothing. Except for the infuriating and stunning news she had just received this morning, in response to a routine request-for-info-on memo she had circulated to various departments two weeks before. The Passive Sources Division reported that they had received and relayed encrypted pass-and-share messages, intended for delivery to Solace, from a transmitter *aboard* the *Merchanter's Dream*!

She would have to get copies of those messages from the archives, and then go through half a dozen layers of approval before she would be allowed to get them decrypted, but that almost didn't matter. The mere fact of the messages was enough. It told her there was, in fact, a spy of some sort already aboard the *Merchanter's Dream*. Someone was plainly up to something, and it seemed increasingly unlikely that it was all just innocent research.

Kalani started to prepare a full report for her boss, Burl Chalmers. With all the information she put together, he would *have* to approve a field investigation—one that might take months, even years.

There were plenty of areas that might well prove productive if investigated. There was the report out of Rio—one of Caltrip's assistants had run away there. And two others had bailed out as soon as the *Merchanter's Dream* had arrived in-system—and, according to the routine reports filed by the *Merchanter's Dream* herself, they had put down an officer—an officer!—at Asgard Five Station, in the Thor's Realm Wormhole Farm. Yes, indeed, she had a lot of ideas about where to start on the job.

But she hadn't the first idea where it might end.

CHAPTER TWENTY-THREE

A PACK OF SILENT DOGS

Wandella Ashdin's heart was pounding as the transport came to a halt. *This is it,* she thought. *Here and now is where it happens.* She thought again of her long-ago college romance, and how she had imagined every possible variation—except what really happened. Already, this was nothing like what she had thought it would be. . . .

DeSilvo, flying his own spacecraft—perhaps named the *Novo Cidade de Ouro*—up to dock with the *Dom Pedro IV*, gallantly welcoming his visitors, humbly submitting himself to their judgment. DeSilvo, striding arrogantly aboard the *Cruzeiro*, claiming them all as his prisoners. DeSilvo, resplendent in his pale yellow scholar's robe, standing on a high platform, gazing down from behind a grand lectern as his visitors—his supplicants—entered from the far end of the great hall that she had imagined, and approached when he summoned them, crossing the fearfully wide chamber in order to plead for his indulgence. Absurd stuff, overblown nonsense, straight from the potboiler romances she had devoured as a schoolgirl.

Nothing like this. Nothing like a worn-out, workaday passenger transport rolling up to a perfectly ordinary airlock.

Somehow, her companions in her imagined encounters had been but shadowy, faceless creatures, there to fill out the scene between herself and DeSilvo, spear-carriers in the background. She had not imagined being here with this band of brave, ordinary people, thrown together by chance and choice, ready to face their fate, their destiny. She looked at them. They were lining up in the aisle of the transport, waiting for the doors to open, precisely like any crowd of slightly anxious, slightly bored commuters about to disembark the shuttle train that took them to the office every day.

Not like this, she thought. There were so few of them left, this far into the journey. Death, fear, anger, tempta-tion, chance—all had thinned their ranks. Now those few who remained stepped out into the lair of their quarry, their objective, their tormentor.

Up until the moment it opened, she had no idea at all what to expect on the other side.

The transport's door slid open, then the door to the interior, and they had arrived.

One after the other they went. Koffield, Marquez, Chandray, Sparten, Phelby, Bolt, Chon, and, bringing up the rear—was she just that little bit more afraid than all the others?—Wandella Ashdin herself. They filed out of the transport, into a waiting area that could have been in any spaceport or airport or surface transport center, on any world.

And there, at last, was Oskar DeSilvo, standing there calmly, arms at his side, smiling at them.

The moment slowed, froze, and Wandella Ashdin seemed to have an infinity of time to contemplate the tableaux in every detail.

She looked first to DeSilvo and took in the sight of the man in the flesh that she had come to know so well through the printed word and recorded images.

He looked *young,* far too young for who he was, but she knew that all his vital organs had been replaced or revitalized at least once, and several of them many times. She could have recited the dates, times, and details of most of his surgical procedures. It would be impossible to judge DeSilvo's age based on his appearance. But there was something that did not quite ring true in that glow of youthfulness. His skin, his eyes, his teeth, were too perfect, and the very slightly yellowish cast to his complexion told Wandella his last skin regen was wearing out—and the next one might not do much good.

Somehow, she was not surprised that he seemed smaller than she expected. He was such a hugely important figure that she had subconsciously thought of him as a physically large man, though she knew perfectly well he had always been of medium height, with a wiry physique. He looked fit. The thick, luxuriant, shoulder-length black hair she had seen in all the pictures of him was gone, cut back to a most utilitarian crew cut. Though he was clean-shaven in all the photos she had ever seen, now he wore a small, neat goatee, black with a streak or two of grey. It suited his square-jawed, high-cheekboned face, his piercing blue eyes and thick black eyebrows.

He was dressed in a very plain, very utilitarian ship's coverall, very similar to the ones worn by the *Dom Pedro IV*'s crew. Odd in a man who had always taken such pains over his appearance. Perhaps he felt the scruffy surrounding called for a workaday appearance. Or was it all part of the show, the theater—short hair, a beard, working clothes? What part was he trying to play?

She looked then, more briefly, to the faces of all her companions, drawn up more or less instinctively in a semicircle, facing DeSilvo. Emotions, strong emotions, were playing over all their faces—but it was plain to see Marquez, Koffield, and Sparten were most affected. Anger, betrayal, confusion, doubt, and fear were all there to be read. *And what are you feeling?* she asked herself. *All the same, and more.*

And all of it, all of that pain and hurt and rage and fear, focused squarely on DeSilvo. If he noticed it at all, he did not reveal it. He had either lost all contact with human behavior, or he was a magnificent actor. Both, perhaps.

The frozen moment drew to its close, and time started up again as DeSilvo spoke.

"Welcome," he said to them all, spreading his arms

slightly, palms out. Absurdly enough, he actually seemed to mean it.

Somehow, to Wandella, the moment almost made sense. If no combination of words, no number of words, could *possibly* mean enough at such a moment—why not use just *one* word, and one that meant as near nothing as possible?

"Thank you," said Anton Koffield, his voice as hard as steel. "We've had quite a journey. And lost several companions along the way."

"Dead because of you," said Marquez. "Two dead before we got to Solace, and one more at Mars."

"My sympathies," said DeSilvo, and the smile dropped away. "I'm sorry about that. Truly. The fault is mine. But their deaths were not—intentional."

"What about my ship?" Marquez demanded. "What are your robots doing to her?"

"They are doing no harm. They are installing upgrades. Improvements. Doing replenishment of your supplies. And, just incidentally, installing a faster-than-light drive."

"*What?*" Marquez was stunned. "But, I—"

"We will talk more about it later," said DeSilvo dismissively, as if it were a very minor matter. "There are other issues we must deal with first."

Wandella frowned to herself. There was something odd about his manner of speech, as if he were out of practice addressing human beings. He'd been isolated a very long time. He seemed to decide to try and start again. This wasn't working out quite the way *he* had imagined, either. "I suppose it is unnecessary to introduce myself," he said, "but I believe it is always helpful to observe the formalities. I am indeed Dr. Oskar DeSilvo—the man you came looking for." He looked around the rest of the group. "Admiral Koffield and I are old acquaintances, and I believe I can at least guess some of the others, but perhaps, Admiral, you could present your comrades to me?"

Koffield did so, indicating each of them, giving their names, but no other information.

"Dr. DeSilvo, I presume," Bolt muttered under his breath as Koffield was speaking, not loud enough for anyone but Wandella to hear. "What the hell goes on with this guy?"

"Shh," Wandella whispered back. "I don't know, but behave yourself. This is going to be tricky enough even if we just play it straight."

"I bid welcome to you all," DeSilvo said. "But this is a poor place for talking. Come, please." The smile, false as a dawn in the west, snapped back into place. "There is a more comfortable room nearby, waiting for us. Come."

Unaware of the rage boiling all around him, he turned his back on the group to lead them on, clearly not understanding just how dangerous that might be for him.

And Wandella Ashdin realized, in her first meeting with the man who defined her life, that she had not asked him anything or spoken a word to him at all. And *that* was indeed something she had never imagined.

Norla Chandray followed toward the end of the group, and could not help but feel there was something oddly anticlimactic about meeting DeSilvo. It went beyond the disconcerting discovery that the icon, the Great Man, the great hero and villain was just a man after all. She had half expected that going in. Oskar DeSilvo was supposed to be the grand architect of gleaming spaces and intricate, self-referential geometry. Here, all was shabby and worn. Maybe DeSilvo had felt no need for show here. Perhaps the titanic effort of building this place had been all he could manage. Or perhaps he no longer cared for such things. Perhaps something deep inside the man had changed.

He brought them to a very plain conference room, nothing more than scruffy walls and a collection of mismatched chairs around a large round table. Norla noted there were far more chairs than needed. Apparently, he had not been sure how many would be coming.

DeSilvo sat down at one side of the table and waited for the others to pick out their seats and settle themselves in. There was an odd little moment, a pause, and Norla half expected DeSilvo to start with that old, old, old, line—*"You're probably wondering why I've asked you here today . . ."* Norla suppressed a hysterical giggle and forced herself to calm down.

"There are so many things I would like to ask you all," he began in a cheerful voice. "I would very much like to know if you—"

"No," said Anton Koffield. "We did not come here to be interrogated."

DeSilvo's pasted-on smile faded away. There was a pause of several seconds before he recovered, forced that itchingly insincere smile again, and spoke. "Ah, but you did, Admiral. One hundred and fourteen calendar years have passed since last we saw each other. I'd estimate that you have actually lived about three years of personal time, biochron time, since then. I have lived something more. About ten years, all told. And all that time I have been preparing to ask you certain questions. I brought you here because I want—I need—your opinions."

"That's as may be," said Koffield. "But you'll get no answers from me. Not until I get some from you."

"I see," said DeSilvo, speaking carefully. "Very well. Ask away. I will answer frankly—and then expect the same of you when my turn comes."

"Why did you send the Intruders to destroy Circum Central?"

Norla raised her eyebrows in surprise. The question was one that Koffield, no doubt, had been burning to ask—but it was Yuri Sparten who had spoken. Koffield seemed as startled as Norla, but he leaned back in his chair and let Sparten take the lead.

"To seal it shut, and make it that much more difficult to reach Glister," DeSilvo said calmly. "I believe you used temporal confinement to travel here, which is far less stressful. But in those days, as you know, it was nearly all cryogenic storage—and without Circum Central, Glister was a very long way from anywhere that was remotely central, if you'll pardon the expression.

Without Circum Central, transit to Glister took long enough to be near the safety limit for cryo duration."

"And why do that?" Sparten demanded. "Why cut off a living world?"

"Your people are from Glister?" DeSilvo asked.

Sparten nodded. "My parents."

"I thought as much. You are too young to have been one of the evacuees. But your question is a central one. Much turned on it. The short form is that I thought Glister would already be dead by the time I closed the uptime end of the timeshaft, and I had chosen Glister— the future Glister, as seen from that time—as a safe place to hide certain valuable objects. My plan was to conceal those things in the *future*, on a world that would be dead by the time my automated ships arrived."

"Why did you want a dead world that *had* been inhabited? Why not just choose a planet that had never been inhabited or terraformed?" Norla asked.

"Look around," said Marquez. "Everything here has been salvaged from the stuff abandoned on-planet after the collapse. Our host developed a taste for scavenging on Mars. You can't find conference tables or airlocks or lighting systems free for the taking on a world that never had people."

DeSilvo glared at Marquez, but calmed himself down and proceeded. "Crudely put," he said, "but essentially accurate. I needed a place that had manufactured resources already available. I had found Baskaw's work, but, I now confess, I was nowhere near as good at applying her ideas as I thought I was. I failed to account for the effects on Glister of closing the timeshaft. After the event, I *did* perform such calculations—and found that they jibed quite well with the course of real-life events. Closing the timeshaft actually *prolonged* the survival period for Glister's terraformed climate. There were still settlements on Glister when my cargoes arrived—but none of them were in any shape to waste time investigating freighters landing in an uninhabited crater."

"Cutting off the relief supplies *prolonged* the planet's survival? But how could that be?" Sparten demanded.

Koffield answered. "No relief means more people die sooner," he said. "That leaves fewer survivors, and fewer descendants. Later on, that means fewer mouths to feed, lower population density for disease vectors, reduced demand on dwindling resources. That sort of thing." He frowned for a moment, and then a look of stunned surprise lit up his face.

DeSilvo smiled craftily. "I believe that the Admiral has just had the insight it took me years to have. But we'll come to that later."

"What were these 'valuable objects' you had to conceal?" Norla asked. "The data from the Mars vaults?"

"Yes, for the most part," DeSilvo said, "and various working models and engineering test objects."

"And the ships that came to be called the Intruders," said Koffield. "They had a double mission, correct? To deliver the data and models to Glister, and then to go back and smash the uptime end of the timeshaft?—to slam the door shut?"

"Quite correct. They were a fleet of small freighters—about the size of your *São Paulo* or *Rio de Janeiro*, Captain Marquez. They were used for transporting material during the Solace project. They had been declared surplus, and I obtained them, and stored them away on a small satellite of one of the Solacian system's outer planets. I had access to essentially unlimited resources, and that made it quite easy for me to set up various covert, wholly automated bases. I did it several times. For the freighter base, I used various remote systems to manufacture faster-than-light drives and install them on each ship. Some were meant as decoys. The rest carried cargo. Each cargo ship carried a complete set of the data I had collected from the Dark Museum—and a few other places. Each also carried robotic construction machines. The essential thing was the data, and each ship carried that. A mere handful of the freighters actually made it to Glister, but if only one had, that would have been enough. The main idea was to preserve and conceal the data. Getting a start on building this place was secondary."

"But all this was before Solace went sour, before

Admiral Koffield found out that you had Baskaw's material. You were planning to disappear even then?" Bolt asked.

"I was planning to—retire. To have a place with sufficient privacy and security that I could bring in specialists of one sort or another to perfect this device or that, based on Dark Museum data."

Bolt nodded. "And then you'd find a way to introduce your 'invention' in such a way that the Chronologic Patrol wouldn't be able to suppress it, and wouldn't be able to connect you with the Dark Museum. Being a century or two away from the thefts would make it safer and easier to take credit for the inventions."

DeSilvo looked annoyed. "You are putting the worst possible interpretation on the plan, but yes, that was the general idea."

"It might have worked. We saw a lot of things that got invented more than once down there," said Norla. "Some of them devices now in general use. The CP can't always stop the stuff they don't like—but they do slow it down."

Bolt cocked his head to one side. "What was it they didn't like?" he asked. "I thought the idea was to suppress technology that could cause time paradoxes or upset causality. There were a lot of gadgets down there that didn't meet those criteria."

"Let us not get confused on side issues. Consider that another point we will come back to later," said DeSilvo.

"All right," said Bolt. "I'll stick to the point. I'll even sum up. You spent years sneaking around in the wreckage of the Dark Museum and scooping up goodies. You made a bunch of copies of the data, stuck them in freighters equipped with Dark-Museum-based faster-than-light drives, and sent them *uptime* through a wormhole, sent them from the past to the future. They delivered their cargo to Glister, to right here, where we're sitting—then went back to wreck the uptime end of the wormhole. Is that about it?"

"All correct," he said. "Then I—"

"Wait a second," said Norla. "Why send the FTL

freighters through the wormholes to reach the future? Why not just leave them in storage for a century, or whatever length of time it was?"

"I considered that," said DeSilvo. "But not all hardware is as robust as a timeshaft-wormhole ship," said DeSilvo. "Your *Dom Pedro IV* is designed to last for centuries, even millennia, of elapsed shiptime. These were ordinary freighters with jury-rigged, prototype FTL drives. I was concerned they would deteriorate if I left them in storage—especially their power systems. Furthermore, I needed them to make calibration runs through the wormhole. It was the only way for the ships to collect certain data they needed to disable the wormhole."

"You've confirmed some of the theories that got spun back then," said Koffield. "You make your little freighters sound quite innocuous. But they killed everyone on board the downtime CP vessel, and aboard the freighters who were caught in the middle—and crew aboard my ship. You marooned the survivors in the future, cutting them off from their families, their lives, forever. And there was the damage you did to Glister. You might have inadvertently extended the survival time for the climate—but at the cost of tremendous and prolonged suffering for those who *did* survive. Quite a price to pay so that you could have a secret lab for bootlegging suppressed technology."

"My motives were not selfish," DeSilvo snapped. "You have seen the technology in question. It has been suppressed for too long. It would have—it will—benefit a great number of people. But yes—I made a number of miscalculations. The harm I did was unintentional."

"You sabotaged my ship," said Marquez. "Left us stranded 127 years in our own future, and killed two of my crew who died on cryogenic revival. Was that unintentional?"

"Solace is falling apart *right now*," Sparten half shouted. "You built the planet. *You* stopped Koffield from getting a warning to us, let the planet lurch forward until it's on the point of collapse—while *you* hid out here, waiting in temporal confinement. That was *all* deliberate. You knew what you were doing. You can't call that harm 'unintentional'!"

DeSilvo's face flushed, and his expression turned angry. He stood up and leaned his fists on the table. "I did not bring you here to serve as judge and jury over me!" he shouted, and pounded his fist into the table. "Mistakes! Delusions! Miscalculations! Yes! Self-deception? Yes, absolutely! I plead guilty, to all of it! There—you have your confession!" He paused for a moment, got back some control of himself. "And I will confess further. Look at all that I did, in all the cases you've just thrown up at me. What are the common themes? What did I do, again and again? Answer: I saw what I wanted to see and blinded myself to the unforeseen, the unintended. I acted too soon. And that *is* why you're here, why I have hidden myself away for so long."

"What in the hell are you talking about?" Sparten demanded.

"I will explain," he said, "but I must touch on one or two more points first." He turned and faced Marquez. "When I sabotaged your ship, Captain, I did so wishing to prevent Anton Koffield from spreading needless panic. I could easily have programmed my invasive programs to kill everyone on board, and then told myself that your deaths would prevent the deaths of thousands who would die in panic riots and other disturbances. Instead, I chose a solution that was meant to be more humane. It got you to your destination—127 years late. I intended for all your ship's party to get there alive."

"Intentions won't bring them back," said Marquez. "And putting new equipment on my ship, no matter how fancy it is, won't give my crew back to the loved ones who lost them forever."

"I agree," said DeSilvo. "*Now*, I agree. Back then, I would have brushed such points aside as irrelevant, told you the fates of a handful of men and women are meaningless compared to the safety of a planetary population."

"So what changed?" Marquez asked.

"What changed," he said, "was that, years after I sabotaged the *Dom Pedro IV*, I discovered Admiral Koffield had been right. The Solacian terraforming project had been doomed from the start—and *all* terraformed worlds were doomed. Untended, they would collapse in roughly the same amount of time it took to establish them. That is a gross oversimplification, and many other effects mask that relationship, but that is the basic underlying rule that Baskaw discovered, that I refused to believe, that Koffield warned against—and that turned out to be true. The accelerated terraforming techniques used on Solace merely meant the world would survive a shorter span of years. Solace was to be my great achievement—and it would be a catastrophe, a humanitarian catastrophe with my name on it."

Norla took note of DeSilvo's last phrase. Even in the midst of his self-described confession, the man's raw egotism was there for all to see. Plainly, a good deal of what upset him was not the collapse of a world—but the damage the collapse would do to his reputation.

"We already knew that much," said Marquez.

"What you do *not* know is that I spent the thirteen years between Admiral Koffield's departure for Solace and my own supposed death confronting those facts, studying them, thinking best how to make some form of restitution. It was too late to save Solace. I decided I would have to do something else, something more."

DeSilvo paused, collected his thoughts, and went on. "In my studies, I started to see other patterns, other even more disturbing truths, and—perhaps—a solution. A way out of the trap in which humanity finds itself. That possible solution, I will not speak of today. But it is there. It is a desperate option—but these, I believe, are desperate times."

"But if you saw both a problem and a solution," said Wandella Ashdin, speaking to DeSilvo for the first time, "why didn't you act?"

"Because I have acted before—and as you have pointed out—I have done great, and unintended, harm. I had to give it time—years, decades—to see if, in *this* case, my calculations and projections and predictions were right. I decided to use temporal confinement, to let the years pass by without me, and then see how accurate my modeling was. For what it is worth, I can tell you that all the checks I have made so far show that it has been distressingly accurate.

"Since I needed to wait so many years, I decided to wait long enough for Anton Koffield to arrive—while making certain backup arrangements. I wanted the insight, the opinion, of the man who had been right before, of the man I had wronged. So I designed my false tomb for Greenhouse. I designed and built its rough twin on Mars, and set the plaques with the clues pointing to here in the tunnel, and over all the technology bays of interest that I had found in the Dark Museum. Just to be on the safe side—and to provide greater incentive for you to come, and, frankly, to improve my bargaining situation now, here, today, I removed the information on certain technologies, so you'd have to come to me to get it.

"I used my own FTL-equipped ship to come here, without recourse to the timeshaft wormholes, bringing various pieces of construction equipment with me. The robotic construction machines brought by the freighters had made a good start. With the aid of the equipment I brought with me, I completed construction of this place. Its main purpose has been to serve as a place for me to hide—but it also shelters a large amount of technological data and working equipment.

"I worked here, alone, for about two years, completing my studies, refining my predictive models. Then it was time. I programmed my ArtInts to monitor certain communications links and ordered them to bring me out of confinement if a ship approached the planet, or if certain other events took place. And then I entered temporal confinement. I was brought out a few days ago, when my detectors spotted your ship."

"Why the scavenger hunt?" asked Koffield. "Why not just leave a note in the urn that supposedly held your ashes, telling us to come straight here to Glister?"

"Because," said DeSilvo, "you needed to see certain

things, see them for yourselves, and not be told about them. Especially not told about them by *me*, a man you have no reason whatsoever to trust. *I* needed someone I knew could find and judge data to go where the information led him. I needed—I still very much need—to see if the trends I had spotted were really there at all, and to see if they have moved in the ways that I expected." DeSilvo paused and looked around the room. "This time," he said, "I had to be sure I was seeing things right."

He turned to face Koffield directly, brought himself to attention, then bowed stiffly from the waist. "Admiral—what it boils down to is this: I have brought you here so I could ask one question, and hear your answer: *Did you see what I saw?*"

The question hung in the air, unanswered, for what could only have been a few seconds, but seemed much longer. At last, Koffield spoke. "I ran across a book in the Dark Museum," he said. "Every other bay had an invention, a design, a working model, or a book describing how to build *something*—a description of a machine. But in one bay was nothing but a book, a book about nothing more than ideas."

"You were quite fortunate to have found it," said DeSilvo. "My ArtInts spent years cataloging the contents of the surviving portion of the Dark Museum, and there is only one book treated as an exhibit of suppressed technology in the entire collection."

Koffield went on as if DeSilvo had not spoken. "It was called, simply, *Contraction*, written by one Ulan Baskaw. A long-lost fourth title from our mysterious long-dead researcher. I read that book three times, on our journey from Mars to here."

"Contraction of what?" asked Sindra Chon.

"Interstellar civilization," Koffield said quietly. "Baskaw treated the matter on a wholly theoretical and mathematical level, but one need make only the smallest of steps to go from her theories and numbers to a projection of the retreat of humankind from the stars, back toward the Solar System. I've spent most of our passage here pulling data out of the Grand Library datacube the *Dom Pedro IV* was supposed to deliver to Solace, doing every cross-check I could think of, confirming the retreat."

"Yes," said DeSilvo. "Yes."

A change had come into the room. Norla looked to Koffield, and Marquez, and she could see it. The anticlimax of the first meeting with DeSilvo, the unexpressed anger, had retreated—though not all the way, and not for all time. But they had found something bigger, better, than the revenge they had been dreaming of, all the endless nights they had sailed the Ocean of Years, coming toward this moment. They had found *answers*. Answers that had eluded them for so long suddenly were there for the taking.

"Retreat?" Bolt protested. "What retreat?"

"It's been true for a while now. Migration inward is higher than migration outward," said Koffield. "The authorities don't like to talk about it much. I always thought—no, I didn't think, I *assumed*—that their silence was just the bureaucratic instinct for hushing up bad news. But I am starting to think it was, and is, deliberate policy."

"What, not talking about contraction?" asked Wandella.

"No," said Koffield, speaking slowly, choosing his words carefully, "As I sit here now, this moment, I am starting to think that contraction *itself* is official policy."

The room was silent for a moment. Norla was too amazed to speak, and so was everyone else. Except DeSilvo. He was not surprised. He was eager, excited, watching something he had waited a very long time to see.

Koffield was thinking, nodding to himself, putting the pieces together. "Yes. Yes. I believe that what Dr. DeSilvo wanted me to see—and what I am starting to see, now, in this moment—is that it is the long-term policy of the Chronologic Patrol, and the governments of the Solar System, to shut down interstellar civilization. To manage the orderly withdrawal of humankind from the stars."

The room erupted in shouts, in protests, everyone up out of their seats, trying to speak at once. Only Koffield, DeSilvo, and Norla were silent. Koffield remained in his chair. DeSilvo, still standing, still leaning forward with his fists on the table, was staring at Koffield with that fierce eagerness, his eyes locked with Koffield's. Neither seemed to hear, or even be aware of, the tumult around them.

"Quiet!" Marquez shouted at last. "Everyone, pipe down. Sit down and be quiet. We need to hear this. Admiral, what the hell are you talking about? Why would the CP and the Solar System governments want to shut down the other planets?"

Koffield looked toward Marquez. "They don't *want* to. But if the evidence and the theory can tell *us* that Solace is failing, that all terraformed planets will eventually fail—then Earth and the Solar System can see the evidence as well. Perhaps their policy makers read Baskaw. Perhaps their people made the same discoveries she did. Or perhaps they have no mathematical models at all, and they just saw what was coming in the lines on the graph."

"But why would they care?" Sparten asked. "They're the one place that *won't* be affected by it."

"The hell they won't," said Norla. "When Glister collapsed, the refugees wound up on Solace. When there was a premature rumor that Solace was going under, the orbiting stations were hit by a wave of refugees—and they'll be hit even harder when the *real* collapse starts. When the orbital stations can't take the population stresses anymore, and *they* start to fail—where are the refugees going to go? Maybe Blue Haven, maybe Beacon—if those planets will have them. But when Blue Haven starts to have problems, where will *her* people go?"

"And in the meantime, the un-refugees, the well-off people who can afford interstellar travel, will be on the move as well," said Marquez. "The ones who can afford passage will decide they've had enough of bad weather and peasants rioting and ugly politics. They'll go back first, at least a lot of them, and take a lot of money and resources with them."

"Yes," said Koffield. "That's it. If Baskaw's models hold up—and they do—the other terraformed worlds will start deteriorating, more or less in reverse order of their establishment—because the later worlds were terraformed faster. We knew that much already. But we *didn't* think much about where the people would go."

"And you're saying this whole collapse is Earth's *policy*?" Marquez asked.

"No, no, not at all," said Koffield. "The collapse is inevitable. Earth's policy is to contain it, to manage it, to prepare for it."

"How?" asked Dixon Phelby. "I was there, on Earth. I didn't see anyone preparing for anything. No one there was talking about getting ready for refugees. They didn't even much care about Clemsen Wahl running away."

"No, they didn't," said Koffield—and then a light seemed to come on inside him. "Logically, they should have. That should have told me something." He looked toward DeSilvo again. Their host had slid quietly back down into his seat, still watching the proceedings eagerly, listening with an almost manic intensity.

Norla watched him too. Koffield nodded at DeSilvo, as if DeSilvo had spoken. But Koffield did not appear to see DeSilvo, or anything else in the room. His eyes were focused inward, at the answers that were emerging, at the truth. "I can think of a lot of absences that should have told me things," he said. "There's a series of mystery stories, old and famous stories from the middle Near-Ancient period. They've been translated and reworked over and over again, to place the action in this place or that place, this or that time. In one of them, the hero remarks on the remarkable incident of the dog in the night—the incident being that the dog *didn't* bark at a stranger, when it should have. The clue was in what *didn't* happen, but should have. Mr. Phelby, you and I walked through an entire pack of silent dogs on Earth. We not only didn't hear them—we didn't see them."

"What were they?" DeSilvo asked.

"Some were there on the ground, in plain sight if you knew where to look," Koffield said, still looking at that inward spot. "The more I sit here thinking about it, the more connections I see."

"For example?"

"The lack of security, of all sorts," said Koffield. "The astonishingly relaxed attitude toward immigration. Clemsen Wahl was over the horizon, and no one seemed to care. No search, no investigation. No authorities came after us, or tried to delay us in hopes of catching Wahl and packing him back aboard our ship—all the perfectly standard things that would happen to a crewman who jumped ship anywhere else in Settled Space."

"After he ran, I kept getting told they didn't chase jumpers much because the population is in decline," said Phelby.

"And doesn't *that* strike you as odd?" asked Koffield. "I checked the figures. Earth's population today is about half a billion. It *used* to be close on ten billion, thousands of years ago—if you can even imagine that. It peaked out toward the end of the Near-Ancient period. In fact, some historians date the end of the Near-Ancient as the first year of declining population. It kept falling until it stabilized at about a billion, and stayed at about that level for well over a thousand years—but then it started dropping again, about three hundred years ago. It's still declining.

"Half a billion is still larger than the combined population of all the terraformed worlds, but Earth has *half* the people she once had—and the population is still in decline. Every source I checked observed that current levels were well below various theoretical 'optimum' or 'sustainable' levels—but look at taxation, look at what gets funded, at what gets encouraged and discouraged, and it's plain to see the continued decline has the tacit approval of what passes for government. The population has been in decline for three centuries, and children are still discouraged and rare—unfashionable. In lots of places on Earth, it's *still* a crime to have sexual relations without taking contraceptive precautions."

Koffield went on. "And even as the population declines, they're maintaining all sorts of surplus infrastructure. The transportation systems, the street grids in the cities, the reserve production capacity in practically every category. Whenever I asked why about anything, I kept getting explanations that seemed more plausible than they really were. I was told it was cheaper and simpler to keep the machines busy and functioning, so you'd know they were working when you actually needed them. Maintaining a city that was twice the size needed for the inhabitants was easier than turning off a few automated systems! Or else it was explained away as 'long-standing cultural bias' or, less pompously, 'tradition.' I once read somewhere that 'tradition' is the traditional explanation for anything the anthropologist can't explain."

"So there's some Earthwide conspiracy to keep people from having babies?" Chon asked, plainly dubious. "And another conspiracy that makes people welcome offworlders? And the Earth governments are playing along—and it's stayed secret all this time? Come on. People don't keep secrets that well."

"No, they don't," Koffield agreed. "And there's no conspiracy, not the way you mean. Just people who are set in their ways, generation after generation, and a whole social structure set up to keep it that way. Keep it going along long enough and it's tradition, and people don't need a reason to keep doing it. They'll keep doing it until you give them a good enough reason to change.

"But machines do keep secrets well, if you tell them to. As for the government—Earth has *incredibly* small and weak governments at all levels—there's *another* dog that's not barking. I kept getting told that government is not very much needed when everyone is rich and healthy and free. That sounds nice—but how true is it? No matter how rich everyone is, there are still jobs only a government can do properly. And it's ArtInts doing a lot of those jobs. They manage a lot of government operations—and there is a great deal more government than people realize. It's just that it's automated."

"So what?" Chon asked.

"As I've said before, ArtInts are like honest cops—they 'stay bought.' Once programmed a certain way, they won't change their views with time. They will stick with a given policy far more completely and permanently than a human would. For centuries at a time. And Earth doesn't like to turn off machines if it can help it. You don't really need a conspiracy, once the machines have been told what to do."

"So what does all this add up to?" asked Bolt.

"Don't you get it? *They're emptying out the planet*," said Norla. "Getting ready for the flood of refugees. Population down by half, birthrate in the tank, no immigration or security controls, molding public opinion and tradition to welcome newcomers and not to feel threatened by them. No one will even notice when it starts—or maybe it has started, already. Earth could take in the whole population of all the terraformed worlds, if comes to that—"

"And it *will*, sooner or later," said Koffield. "And Officer Chandray is right—it *has* started. The influx probably isn't even enough yet to make the population rise—but it will. And one day, people will wake up and notice how many offworlders there are in the neighborhood. But they'll have a tradition going back for centuries of welcoming strangers, of letting them in—and they'll have enough room, enough resources, ready for them."

"All right," said Chon. "So they're preparing. But you also said 'containing.' How?"

"By discouraging things that make the problem bigger," said Koffield.

"Like what?" she asked.

"Like terraforming," said Norla and Bolt, almost simultaneously. She looked him and smiled faintly. "You go," she said.

Jerand Bolt looked around the table. "Terraforming's becoming a theoretical science," he said. "No new studies or research on how to do it. Some work—not much—on maintaining existing climates. But most of the titles we saw in the Permanent Physical Collection were from a hundred years ago, or earlier. And what new titles there are aren't being placed in the Grand Library digital collection, or in the copies of it shipped out to the various planetary libraries. Admiral Koffield said it, a while back—terraforming is turning into something you read about in history books."

"And there's more," said Norla. "A lot more. The Dark Museum. The suppressed technology. It was supposed to be for technology that might threaten *causality*. But it turned into where they kept technology that might threaten technological *change*. Technological *improvement*."

"Exactly," said Koffield. "It's the mirror image to how Circum Central's destruction let Glister last longer, because more people died sooner. If more people live longer, then the crisis and collapse will arrive sooner." He looked to Chon. "Think it through. Eventual collapse is inevitable. But the better a given transportation technology is, the more people will move into space, and the more planets they'll settle. But more people, more planets, would only make the collapse come sooner, hit harder, and last longer. Temporal confinement that's cheap enough for the whole crew made interstellar travel easier and safer than cryogenics—so they suppressed it as long they could. But they couldn't buy out or sit on all the inventors and engineers on all the planets, and twenty microscopic improvements can be as significant as a single major breakthrough, so they suppress incremental improvements just as hard."

"But some breakthroughs—like FTL travel—are more than major," said Norla. "If a usable, economic, true FTL drive ever reached the market, I can't even begin to imagine what would happen."

"I can," said Koffield. "The timeshaft wormholes would be abandoned. All the timeshaft ships would be made obsolete in a heartbeat. The economic upheaval would ripple out from there. There would be a massive increase in trade and travel between all the star systems. More star systems would open up. It would suddenly become far cheaper to terraform candidate planets. Starships could be cheaper and lighter, because they wouldn't have to be built to last thousands of years. And then—"

He paused. "And then the Chronologic Patrol would go bankrupt, because it would still have to guard the wormholes to protect causality, but would have no sources of income to pay for it. Even destroying the timeshaft wormholes might be enough to bankrupt them.

"Even in my day, the Chronologic Patrol was getting set in its ways, more akin to a priesthood protecting the sacred truths than a conventional military force. But it was and still is very important. It's the only force, the only authority, that reaches *every* populated star system in Settled Space. If the CP falls apart—or even is severely weakened—it wouldn't be able to maintain any semblance of order when the crunch came. And when the collapse does come, and the contraction starts, it will hit sooner, harder, and longer."

"So that's why they don't want FTL," said Bolt. "I guess I can see their point. If we're all going to die, and you can't stop it—at least try to make the end less painful."

"Yes," said Koffield. "It's not much, but it might be all that's left to us. Limiting the damage."

"No," said a quiet voice, a voice Norla did not even recognize at once. She looked to DeSilvo. "It's not all that's left," he said. "And it's not enough."

"Why not?" asked Koffield.

"Because," said Oskar DeSilvo, "things are worse than you think."

He stood again, and walked toward the door. "Come with me," he said. "There's something I want to show you."

The others stood to follow him, curious, eager, interested, willing to put off their quarrels with DeSilvo until another day.

DeSilvo. Norla stared at him. Not at all the man she had expected—and, she was coming to believe—not at all the man he had been.

Norla watched him as he crossed the room—but

something else caught her eye, as he passed by Yuri Sparten. She saw the look on Sparten's face. *Hatred.* Venomous, searing hatred—aimed directly at DeSilvo's retreating back.

It looked as if Yuri Sparten had finally managed to find someone he could blame for all his troubles.

CHAPTER TWENTY-FOUR

LAST MAN STANDING

DeSilvo led them briskly down a shabby-looking hall-
way, past doorways that led to rooms full of strange-
looking machines, none of which DeSilvo offered to
explain. At last he came to a firmly shut solid door. "I
need to keep the light out," he explained, as if someone
had asked why a man who lived alone needed doors.

He pulled it open and led then into a room about
twenty meters by twenty. An elaborate projection system
stood at the center of the floor. There was a control
lectern for a standing operator between the projector
and the doorway. The walls were rounded in the corners,
smoothing out the hard angles, and were made of the
sort of gleaming perfect white sheathing material used in
high-end simulation projection systems—which the
room obviously was.

DeSilvo waited until they were all in the room.
Sparten brought up the rear, and didn't seem happy to be
with them at all. DeSilvo nodded to him. "Close the
door, if you would," he said. Sparten did so, and managed to do it sullenly. Norla noted that the inside of the
door was made of the same material as the walls.
"Thank you," said DeSilvo.

He turned to Koffield. "Admiral, what I am about to
show you is in fact based on the math and the theories of

that fourth book of Baskaw's, the one you found in the Dark Museum. Obviously, I did most of this work a century and more ago—but since your ship was detected and the ArtInts switched off the temporal confinement field, I have spent much of my time here, in this chamber, feeding in new data that had accumulated while I was under slowtime conditions. Later, I will ask you to check out everything—my methodology, my data, the simulation programming, all of it. But for now—let me show you what I have found, what I have learned."

He turned to the control panel and activated the controls. The room faded down to black—and then worlds started to appear in the firmament. Sharp, clear, and bright, the perfect three-dimensional globes materialized in the darkness before them, one after another, here and there in the air, faster and faster until Norla could no longer keep track of their appearances. Some were blue and white and green, the colors of life. Others looked far less healthy.

"Fifty-three worlds," said DeSilvo. "Earth, Mars, Solace, Glister, Beacon, Blue Haven, New Kenya, Starland, all the others." Labels showing their names appeared under each world. "One world, Earth, made by nature. All the others remade by humans. They are arranged roughly by degree of proximity to each other."

A data-display panel popped into view under each name label, displaying various parameters—*Oxygen Level*, *Atmospheric Density*, *Gross Biomass*, *Mean Temperature*, *Population*, *Climatic Health Index*, and so on through a number of measurements Norla had never even heard of. "Please note," DeSilvo said, "that the population figure for each planet is actually the figure for the entire star system in which it resides, counting space stations, domed settlements, and so on."

DeSilvo turned toward his audience again. "The planets as shown in the simulation right now reflect their approximate appearance, and their state of health, as of about the time the *Dom Pedro IV* started out for Solace—roughly 130 years ago. As you can see, Glister is already on its last legs. Several other formerly terra-formed planets are effectively dead. Solace appears reasonably healthy, as do most of the other worlds. Using the Baskaw formulae, I am now going to project them forward to the present day, at the rate of one year a second. But first, let me reduce the number of variables being displayed."

He made an adjustment, and all the values but *Climatic Health Index* and *Population* vanished. "Just to help you interpret what you'll see, the Climatic Health Index—the CHI—is a weighted average of ten core measures of climatic health," said DeSilvo. "Earth in perfect health scores about 100 percent, and can sometimes score higher than that for brief periods, if everything comes together just right. A totally uninhabitable planet would have a CHI of zero percent. The best CHI ever measured for a terraformed world was 32 percent. At its peak, Solace scored 25 percent. I'll now run the data forward to the present day. Watch the numbers and the general appearance of the planets' images."

DeSilvo started the run, but there was very little of drama about it. Glister died almost at once, starting out with a CHI of 8 percent that had nowhere to go but down. The population started out at eighty thousand, but thirty seconds into the run it was down to three digits—then two, then one—and then zero. Norla glanced to the display for Solace in time to see the corresponding upticks in population as the Glister refugees arrived there. She turned back to watch Glister's CHI drop to zero only a little later than the population had done so, just as the last warm color left the planet's image, leaving it a study in cold greys and whites and dirty browns.

The CHI numbers under Earth twitched and jittered a bit, mainly flickering up and down between 98 and 99 percent, as the population ticked slowly downward. The CHI value blipped over 100 percent once or twice, and flirted with 101 for a few moments before settling back down.

Solace slowly deteriorated, her CHI starting at 23

percent, dropping almost at once, and never reaching that high again. The planet slowly lost its livelier appearance as the years ticked by, leaving the world a study in muted green-brown landscapes, and dull, blue-grey oceans.

"We have arrived at the present," said DeSilvo, and paused the display. "I have been showing you the results of my data projections. However, I can tell you the real-life data have generated all but identical results. While you watched, three planets died." Norla blinked and looked around the room. She was stunned and, irrationally enough, a bit ashamed, to realize that two other worlds had zeroed out while she was concentrating on Solace and Glister.

"Wait a second," said Sparten. "You said Glister lasted longer because there weren't so many people, right? The Glister refugees coming to Solace wouldn't have any effect, right? There were so few of us—of them."

"I'm afraid they had a very definite effect. Solace was on a knife edge. The refugees tilted the balance years sooner than would have happened otherwise." He turned back to his console and did not see the play of emotions on Sparten's face. "Now we move into the future," said DeSilvo. "I am tripling the speed. Now, three years per second."

Even with the speed increase, the rate of change was not noticeable—at first. The population and CHI numbers for Solace drifted downward—and then crashed down to nearly nothing. At the same time, the worlds closest to Solace experienced a slight upward spike in population, as first voluntary back-immigrants, and then refugees, arrived. But it was plain that Solace had lost far more people in total than her neighbors had gained. The rest, of course, died. The image of Solace turned wholly grey and brown as she reached a Climate Health Index of zero. Her population stabilized at a few thousand and held there for a time, before drifting slowly downward.

"The diehard factor," DeSilvo said quietly. "The people who simply will not leave. Some hunker down in domes on the surface, some keep habitats going. There are still a few here in the Glister system, even if the Glister display shows zero. There are so few they are in effect a rounding error at the level of accuracy for this projection. But they can't hold out forever. It is merely hard to make them die, not impossible. Sooner or later, the universe finds a way." The population number for Solace dropped to zero.

They were now about fifty years into the future. Two other worlds began sudden declines, and the same pattern as with Glister, and then with Solace, began. Neighboring worlds absorbed some, but not all, of the population as the dying worlds continued to fail. The worlds entered final collapse almost simultaneously—and then one of the nearby worlds, the one that had absorbed the most refugees, failed suddenly and drastically, collapsing altogether in less than ten years. They were a hundred, a hundred fifty, two hundred years into the future. More worlds failed, and more, and more.

"One by one, the lights go out," DeSilvo said quietly. "Obviously, this becomes more and more speculative as we reach farther into the future. Any number of things—politics, an unexpected plague, a natural disaster, a war, a medical or technical advance—will alter the details. But the overall pattern will be as you see it here. One by one, sometimes two by two, the lights go out."

Five hundred years, and two-thirds of the planets were gone. DeSilvo paused the display again. "Baskaw suggests that various psychological effects will take hold at about this point," he said. "Most people will have come to realize their worlds are dying. Some will fight harder to save their worlds—and probably merely make the end come sooner. Some will realize that an influx of refugees makes the end come faster. Overfill the lifeboat, and it capsizes. They will try to save themselves by holding back outsiders. Probably there will be wars fought on that basis, fighting over possession of a house that's on fire, if you'll forgive another analogy.

"Some will decide to emigrate sooner, rather than

later. They will be the well-to-do, obviously, and that will drain wealth from the systems they leave. Politics in the Solar System will play a very large role as the incoming flood of final-stage refugees reaches its peak. Will they still be welcoming? Will they try somehow to seal the borders? Impossible to say. This variant of the projections ignores such things. When I have factored them in, they end the same. It merely comes sooner or later.

"I will say this: Sometime between today and five hundred years from now, it is likely that FTL travel will be invented again, perhaps several times. If the Chronologic Patrol does not suppress it whenever it pops up— well, I think we can assume that we have reached the point where FTL will mainly serve to increase the speed and volume of travel Earthward. When I run the simulation with *that* variant, the end comes far more quickly, and far more violently."

Six hundred years, seven, eight. There were only a handful of terraformed worlds left, all of them as feeble as candles in the wind, guttering down to darkness.

Norla looked to Earth, and was astonished to see that the population had skyrocketed, to nearly two billion— more than the current combined population of Earth and all the terraformed worlds. Earth's Climate Health Index had dropped, dipping down toward 92 percent, 91. "What's happened to Earth?" she asked. "All those people, and the index dropping."

"Earth has absorbed population from all the outer worlds—and all the outer worlds have cultures with traditions of much higher birthrates. I have also assumed a survival rate to adulthood in between the higher levels of Earth and the somewhat lower levels of the terraformed worlds. More babies are born, and they live longer. Keep that up long enough, and a degraded Climate Health Index will take care of itself."

Nine hundred years, a thousand. Blue Haven was the last to go, her bright color fading away into drab brown and oily green-grey.

Only Earth survived. DeSilvo paused the simulation

again. "Obviously, this projection simplifies some things," he said. "There will still be a few remnant populations out there somewhere. They ought to be able to survive quite a long time. Centuries. Maybe longer. But we know, beyond doubt, that an artificial environment requires some sort of periodic replenishment from a natural one—and there is only one natural environment. Earth. If the remnants fall out of touch with Earth, they'll die."

"But we knew all this!" Sparten protested. "You've shown us a lot of pretty pictures, but we knew all this coming in!"

"The simulation isn't over yet," DeSilvo said quietly. "Watch Earth. Refugees from every failed world have come in. They've had rushed decontaminations, or no decon, or maybe not even a health check. Earth's population will have no natural immunities to the imported diseases. The refugees have been overwhelming the public health system for generations. Probably every other planet and habitat in-system has caught a plague or two as well. And then, of course, there are whatever other molds, spores, viruses, bacteria, insects, and what-have-you that have adapted to harsh environments off-planet for a millennium or two, and then suddenly come back to the easy life on Earth. Organisms that don't attack people—but do attack plants, mammals, birds, fish, indigenous microorganisms. And then there's interbreeding with the root Earth stock. The result will be hardy and aggressive hybrids.

"And, of course, the likelihood that, sooner or later, the Interdict will fail. Someone will get to Mars, avoid death on-planet, dodge the guns of Deimos and Phobos, and land on Earth, bringing along a few hitchhikers. It's happened several times in the past, of course, and they've always managed to stamp it out. But with the planet in turmoil, with the Chronologic Patrol effectively out of business because there is little or no interstellar traffic, with a restless population that has much cause to be angry and no ingrained loyalty to Earth—the odds of attempted violation go up, and the odds of successful intercept, or successful containment if the organisms do reach Earth, go down. Roll the dice often enough, and you lose."

He started the simulation forward again. Eleven hundred years in the future. Earth's health index numbers started to fall again, declining rapidly even as the population continued to increase. And then, something *happened*.

"It varies from run to run a bit. Sometimes it comes later. Sometimes it starts even before Blue Haven is dead. But it always comes." DeSilvo hesitated, then said something rather odd. "I never did care for my father much. A cruel man. But he did say one thing that has stuck with me. 'If it just means you're the last to fall, it doesn't mean much to be the last man standing.' "

Earth's bright blue oceans turned dark, and the lands took on a terribly familiar greenish-grey cast. The cloud cover vanished. And the population numbers crashed, dropped below a billion, below half a billion, below a hundred million, down under a million, and then—*Population Zero*.

Earth hung in the darkness, next to her sister world. "We opened the age of terraforming by trying to make Mars look like Earth. Under the policies currently being pursued, or anything remotely like them, that age will end—and so will the age of humanity—when we have made Earth look like Mars."

The silence and the darkness lasted a long time, until at last DeSilvo brought the light up a bit, but left the images of the ruined worlds hanging in midair.

Wandella Ashdin was the first to speak. "Don't they know? The Solar System governments and the Chronologic Patrol—if you can project it out, so can they."

"I don't know the answer to that," he said, making minute adjustments to the console, fiddling with machines, rather than looking at people. "Maybe they know all about it, and they don't believe it. Maybe they haven't bothered to run a fifteen-hundred-year projection. Maybe they've concluded that there is nothing they can do to stop it, other than to limit the suffering in the years to come. Maybe they have a secret plan. Maybe I have gotten the projection wrong."

"But you've run it many times," said Koffield.

"Yes," said DeSilvo, and turned to look at him. "I've checked and rechecked and reworked everything, over and over. Run endless variations. Different things happen, and happen sooner or later. But the contraction always ends with the death of Earth. I want you—all of you who have any expertise at all—to check my work. *I want you to find out I'm wrong.* But, unfortunately, I think you'll find out I'm right."

Koffield nodded hurriedly, as if it were a given, and there was no need at all to ask. "Of course. But—I have two questions."

"Ask them," said DeSilvo.

"You said you had a solution. Do you?"

"Yes. One I will not speak of—yet. But I did not lead you to this place—or fit out Captain Marquez's ship with an FTL drive—merely to depress you with tales of doom a thousand years in the future. I want you to study the problem first, understand it, check all my work, see what you find that I missed. *Then* we'll discuss my solution. Understand the problem, and perhaps my solution will not seem quite so lunatic."

"Fair enough, I suppose," said Koffield.

A device clipped to one of DeSilvo's pockets beeped. He glanced at the screen. "Come," said DeSilvo. "My service ArtInt informs me that luncheon is served, back in the conference room."

They all moved out of his way as DeSilvo moved toward the door, opened it, and headed out into the corridor, not stopping to see if his guests were following. They hurried to catch up as he walked briskly along.

DeSilvo noticed after a moment that he was leaving people behind, and stopped to let them catch up. "Forgive me," he said as they all rejoined him. "I've been living a rather hermetic existence for quite a while. I'm not quite used to having other people around. Please do bear with me. I'm bound to make all sorts of blunders until I get back in practice." They started walking again, at a better pace for a group moving together. "I believe you said you had two questions, Admiral. What was the second?"

"I'm sure I'll have several thousand as we go along," said Koffield. "But the other I wished to ask right now is this: Several times in our conversation today, you have said things that implied you had fairly recent knowledge of current events, of our travels, of the state of things in the outside universe. But you've been on this very isolated planet, and in temporal confinement, for over a century. How do you know what you know?"

DeSilvo slowed, stopped walking, turned to Koffield, and smiled. Something of the trickster showed through that smile, through the half-forgotten urbane manners and the overlay of a hermit's abrupt behavior. Norla saw that smile, and knew, beyond doubt, that DeSilvo had changed—but not completely. They could work with him, perhaps, in the days to come, and perhaps even trust him, to a certain degree. But caprice and low cunning still lurked in the dark corners of his character. They always would. "I'm sorry," he said. "I thought I had mentioned that. I've imagined my, my—reunion with you so often that I'm neglecting to tell you things in real life that I've told you over and over in my own imagination."

He laughed, and pointed to Yuri, who was standing as far from DeSilvo as possible while still being part of the group. "Why, Mr. Sparten has kept me informed with his reports. Quite detailed, too. I read them over the moment I came out of slowtime. I've had other sources for other material, of course—but thanks to Mr. Sparten, I know all about *you*."

Sparten was stunned. "But—but—I—" He looked to the others. "I never—I wasn't working for *him*! I did my report for Sotales! The security officer on SCO Station! Not him!"

Marquez looked toward DeSilvo, all the fury he had

forgotten, or put to one side, or let go of, suddenly back in full force. "What the hell was Sotales doing sending information to *you*?" he demanded.

"Sotales didn't know he was," Koffield said, his voice suddenly grim. "But DeSilvo *built* SCO Station. When we were there, I was told that the ArtInt running the station was so dug in, so intertwined with the hardware that runs the station, that they've never dared try to replace it or upgrade it. Brain surgery would be simpler. And ArtInts, as we've discussed, are honest cops. They stay bought. The station ArtInt listens. When the station receives intelligence reports, they go through a system the ArtInt can access. It collects whatever DeSilvo told it to collect, and it sends it on."

"But—but Solace is light-years from here!" Bolt protested. "No signal could have reached us from there!"

"No radio signal," said Koffield. "But if there was an FTL ship drive in the Dark Museum, why not an FTL communications system?"

DeSilvo smiled and bowed slightly to Koffield. "You are quick, Admiral. And you are right. I long ago started placing FTL message relays into whatever comm systems were installed in my designs, and wherever else they might do me some good. The Sotales tap gave the frequencies and so on to tune my general Solar System tap to pick up and relay Mr. Sparten's reports directly. There's another tap in the DeSilvo Room in the Grand Library that tells me who uses it, and what they do. Dr. Wandella, your scholarship has been most dogged and impressive."

"I'm not exactly sure I should say thank you," Ashdin replied coldly.

"*Where else?*" Marquez demanded. "My ship. When you sabotaged my ship, way back when, did you plant a bug?" He stepped toward DeSilvo, hooked his thumb upward, pointing toward the sky. "Are your robots installing one *right now*?"

DeSilvo was at last getting the idea that he had reminded everyone of their anger. He held his hands up, palms forward, toward Marquez. "No. No! There *is* no tap on your ship, and I *will* not put one there. I swear it. All I know about you I got from my taps on Mr. Sparten, and—"

"No!" Yuri shouted, and lunged for DeSilvo. Somehow DeSilvo dodged out of the way, and Yuri Sparten went flying past him and tumbled onto the floor.

But Yuri was back up in a moment—and there was a gun in his hand, pointed straight at DeSilvo's heart. "I didn't work for you. You killed this planet! You killed my parents' planet, you bastard! You came damn near to killing *them*. I've got relatives out there somewhere, aunts and uncles and cousins, who died from the cold, froze solid, and are still lying where they fell, thanks to you. You and your ego built Solace as a monument to Oskar DeSilvo, and you told us all to love you very much—and when you finally admitted to yourself that you got it wrong, you hid out here and let the farms and the farmers die, let Solace City half wash away, because you figured it was too late to do anything about it, so why bother trying?

"So I'm going to kill you." He raised the pistol, lifted it to aim for DeSilvo's head and—

Sparten crashed to the floor, tackled blindside by Jerand Bolt. The gun came out of Sparten's hand, hit the floor, and went off with a sound like a loud cough, punching a small hole in the side wall of the corridor. Bolt landed on top of Sparten, then scrambled over him to lunge for the gun. He got to it, then rolled sideways to give himself a clear shot at Sparten.

But Sparten was moving fast too. He jumped to his feet, grabbed for DeSilvo, slammed him against the wall, his head right next to the still-smoking hole—and suddenly he was holding a knife to DeSilvo's throat.

"Put the gun down, Bolt!" Sparten shouted. "Throw down the gun or I kill him right now."

"You're going to kill him anyway," said Bolt. "No, sir, I keep the gun. I'm not subject to your orders, Mr. Sparten."

"Please! Please! Don't hurt me!" DeSilvo cried out.

"You need me! You need me *alive*. You need what I know! There's—there's a deadman sender stuck to my back. If—if it stops reading my heartbeat, the whole place goes up!"

"Fine," said Sparten. "I've got one too."

"What do you mean?" Koffield asked.

"Deadman sender, sir. I've got a sender too, keyed to bombs hidden in the *Cruzeiro do Sul* and the *DP-IV*. Little ones, just big enough to wreck the propulsion systems for good. Sotales told me to activate the system if I thought the *Dom Pedro IV* might be captured and turned against Solace—and we saw *his* robots do the capturing. I should have blown the ship this morning. I should have. But I wanted to see *him* for myself, see Glister. So I rigged the deadman system. I die, the ships die, and we all die, here."

"Don't do it," said Koffield. "Put the knife down."

"This place is a trick, Admiral Koffield," Sparten said, tears of anger and frustration welling up in his eyes. "I don't have it all worked out yet, but this is all another DeSilvo trick. *He* wants to rehabilitate himself, be the hero again! All hail DeSilvo! That's all *he* wants."

"You might be right, Sparten," said Koffield, standing carefully back from the action. "But that's a small price for saving humanity from extinction, don't you think?"

"That simulation was all wrong!" Sparten cried out, nearly sobbing. "How could *he* know all that? *He* made it up! It's some kind of crazy trick!"

"Maybe it is," said Koffield. "We'll find out. Now put the knife down."

"No, sir. I'm going to kill him. *Someone* has to kill him."

But he didn't use the knife. Fear, uncertainty, the simple unwillingness to kill, to draw blood with a knife, held him back.

The moment was balanced on the tip of Sparten's knife. If his blade moved forward by only a few centimeters, DeSilvo would at last be dead indeed—at the exact moment when he could finally do some good by living. He'd take everyone else, and all the treasure he had gathered in this place, with him. All that, and, perhaps, humanity's future survival.

"Think it through," said Koffield. "If he dies, his deadman sensor will touch off the self-destruct for this whole place. We'll all die. You'll die. And when you die, the *Cruzeiro do Sul* and the *Dom Pedro IV* will be wrecked. Anyone who did manage to survive the self-destruct would be stranded here forever. Put down the knife. Put down the knife."

Sparten's arm relaxed, by the merest fraction of a centimeter. "It's a trick," he said. "It's all a trick. I can see it in his face. *He* doesn't have any deadman sensor. There *isn't* any self-destruct. All *he* wants to do is live, and be loved by everybody. *He* wouldn't ever hurt himself. No. I'm going to do it." But still he did not act. "Make him put his gun down or I'll do it right now."

"Mr. Bolt!" Admiral Anton Koffield did not take his eyes off Sparten and DeSilvo as he spoke.

"Sir!" Bolt was fiercely alert and focused, staring at Sparten, his gun still trained on him.

"You refused to obey Mr. Sparten. Do you regard yourself as bound by *my* orders?"

"Sir? Yes I do!"

"Bolt—I know you pride yourself on proper obedience to your superiors."

And on finding loopholes and technicalities that can save you, thought Norla. But it wasn't the time to point that out.

"Sir, I do!"

"Very well, Mr. Bolt. I am going to give you an order. You are going to carry it out. Do you understand?"

"What?"

"Bolt—answer me! And *that's* an order."

"Yes, sir! You will give me an order, and I will obey it! Understood."

"Very well," said Koffield. He was silent for a moment. "Mr. Bolt—shoot Mr. Sparten."

The world froze for a split second, and then exploded into motion.

"No!" cried DeSilvo.

Sparten jerked his hand away in surprise, and nicked DeSilvo under the chin. "What? No!" he shouted.

"Sir?" Bolt yelled the question. "Are you—"

"Obey your order, Bolt!" Koffield shouted.

Jerand Bolt fired. The gun barked, another loud, angry cough. DeSilvo started to raise his arm to defend himself. The shot caught Sparten in the side of his ribs, and threw him hard, headfirst, against the wall. The knife fell from his hand, and nicked Oskar DeSilvo again, in the right forearm, just below the elbow.

DeSilvo cradled his arm in his left hand, then felt the blood seeping through the coveralls. He dropped his right arm in horror, touched himself under the chin, and found the blood there as well. He held his blood-smeared hand out in front of his face, and stared at it, wide-eyed. He opened his mouth to speak, but no words came out. He took a step forward—and then Dr. Oskar DeSilvo, the last man standing, collapsed in a heap on the floor.

The others swarmed in to check them both over. Norla got to DeSilvo first, with Marquez right behind her.

"Come on, DeSilvo!" Marquez shouted. "Make it just a clean faint. No fatal heart attack! I didn't come this far to get blown up by a deadman sensor."

"Good strong beat," said Norla, her hand on his chest. "That's half our worries. What about Sparten?" she asked, still bracing for the far-off *whump* that would signal the *Cruzeiro do Sul*'s destruction. And it could still come. A deadman sensor usually had at least a few seconds' delay built in, forcing the system to reconfirm before it sent the destruct signal.

Koffield was kneeling over Sparten, checking him, but not appearing too concerned. "Out cold," he said. "But a cracked rib and getting your head slammed into a wall can do that." He turned to Jerand. "Next time, Mr. Bolt, don't put *quite* so much effort into confirming my orders."

"But, sir I—if he had died, then we'd all—"

Koffield held up the gun and smiled. "Never bet on youth over experience," he said. "He stole this from the

Dom Pedro's armory locker, *after* I had locked all the guns in it down to low-stun mode. I'll admit to missing the deadman sensor—but I found the bombs on both ships and disarmed them during the flight from Mars to here."

CHAPTER TWENTY-FIVE

THE SHORES OF TOMORROW

Norla was not very surprised to find Anton Koffield in the simulator room, and Wandella Ashdin with him. "*Neither* of them had a deadman sensor," she said. "Bluff and double-bluff."

"They both could have," said Koffield, not looking up as he examined the controls. "And DeSilvo could still be bluffing."

"About his secret solution?" Norla asked.

"Or about Earth being doomed in the first place," said Wandella, gesturing at the planet images. "It takes some nerve to project a thousand years ahead. Bluff and double-bluff. Anyway. Where are Punch and Judy?"

"Patched up, sedated, and sleeping it off, locked up in rooms as far as possible from each other," she said. "Marquez and Bolt are both pretty good jackleg med techs." Somehow, the compound felt safer, calmer, more reasonable with DeSilvo out of the picture, at least for a little while. They could think things through without being chivvied along. Norla nodded at the images of dead planets, still hanging in the air. "*Was* he telling the truth—about the disease, or the cure?"

Koffield shook his head. "I don't know. But he could have been. We have to check it out, very carefully. And there are lots of other interesting toys tucked away in this place. Ah. There it is." He had figured out how to make the adjustment he wanted.

He blanked out the images of all the other worlds and made the image of Earth swell up until she was nearly three meters across, almost as tall as the room itself. He pulled her back in time, back from the deadly, hypothetical—and quite possibly inaccurate—future that DeSilvo had ordained for her. She regained her color, her cloud cover, her oceans, her beauty. "There we are," he said. "That's the way it should be." He spoke again, still keeping his eyes on Earth of the present day, having banished the shadow of an Earth that might be, at least for the moment. "We'll have to see about DeSilvo's claims," he said. "We'll take advantage of this bit of time, with him out of the picture. The man has a way of sweeping you along, making it seem as if what he's doing is the only possible choice."

Wandella Ashdin made a most unprofessorial snorting noise. "I can't think of anyone else like that. Can you, Officer Chandray?"

Norla laughed, and after a time, so did Admiral Anton Koffield. "Point taken," he said. "But still, we do have to think it all through. Some of what he claims is real. Marquez is going to have to learn how to fly an FTL ship. Think of that."

"Think of that," said Norla. And FTL communications. And any other number of wonders that had been hidden away too long. Yes. A lot to think about.

"And no more timeshaft wormholes," said Wandella. "Not for the *Dom Pedro IV*, at any rate. Though I see the arguments about not letting it out into the great wide universe."

"And those arguments could be a bluff as well," said Koffield, still studying the control system. "Every major invention has upended things—especially in transportation. But none of them has wrecked civilization. And there *are* a few disadvantages to the timeshaft wormhole system—especially when it goes wrong. Norla and I could both tell you all about it. I for one won't miss going backward when I'm trying to go forward. If I can manage never to go through the same year twice again, I think I'll be a happier man." He looked up at the lovely Earth, and for a moment Norla thought there might have been tears in his eyes. "We'll take care of you," he said, in something close to a whisper. "We'll start on it, first thing tomorrow."

They all stared at the mother world for a moment, and then the moment was gone, never to return. The way time was *supposed* to work.

"We missed lunch," said Norla. "Let's go see about dinner in this place."

They left Earth still shining in the darkness, and went out into the corridor, moving forward.

Forward. Perhaps there would be reasons, good reasons, to make use of the timeshafts again, sometime in the future, but Norla knew she would be most reluctant to do so.

The *future*. She willed herself, willed all of them, *forward*, toward the shores of tomorrow, just over the horizon, sailing out and away, leaving the old routes and the old ways behind them. *Forward*, to find the answers, to fly in present time, to travel straight toward their destination, no more to sail against time, no more to beat back against the currents that flowed endlessly onward, across the Ocean of Years.

THE END

GLOSSARY

ArtInt—Artificial Intelligence. Any machine or device with sophisticated decision-making ability, and the capacity to interpret and execute complex orders. Generally speaking, ArtInts are deliberately built and programmed so as to be regarded as appliances and tools. Thus, while it is possible for them to speak and understand speech, they are usually designed to discourage any tendency to treat them as human.

Bookcatcher—A data-reading device designed to capture the entire text of a book off a digital copy of the text stored in a memory chip, built, for this purpose, into a physical copy of the book.

Burn-off suit—An isolation suit, for use in extremely hostile environments, worn completely over an inner pressure suit. At the end of a period of exposure, the wearer enters a burn-ball filled with pure oxygen. The burn-off suit is made to burn, incinerating any unwanted life-forms and—usually—leaving the inner suit and its wearer intact.

Buzzbrain—Derogatory slang term for an ArtInt or especially ShipInt. The term refers to an Int that is hyperparanoid or excessively suspicious, "buzzing" with false data and other static.

Chronologic Patrol—The military organization assigned to protect the timeshaft wormholes, and to defend against any deliberate or accidental attempt to abuse time travel so as to damage causality.

Cidade de Ouro—A private ship, belonging to Oskar DeSilvo. Capable of long-range interplanetary flight, but not interstellar transit.

Circum Central Wormhole Farm—The timeshaft wormhole linking Glister to other worlds, usable for transit to Solace as well. The name is an optimistic misnomer. Circum Central is not central to anything, and there is only one timeshaft there, though the term *wormhole farm* usually refers to three or more wormholes clustered near each other at a main transfer point. Circum Central was supposed to be much more important than it turned out to be.

Comfort—A large gas giant planet in the outer reaches of the same planetary system that holds Solace. The satellite Greenhouse orbits Comfort.

Cruzeiro do Sul—Large auxiliary ship, or lighter, carried aboard the *Dom Pedro IV*.

Dark Museum—Informal name for the Chronologic Patrol's Technology Storage Facility, a vast underground complex on Mars where suppressed technology is stored for future reference. Badly damaged in an explosion centuries ago, it was assumed to be completely destroyed. The lowest level, however, is partly intact.

Deadman sensor—A variant on a deadman switch. In a classic deadman switch, the operator pulls or pushes some sort of control that will set off a bomb if the switch is released. So long as the operator is alive and maintaining his hold, the bomb won't go off. The most common form of deadman sensor is a heart monitor, attached to the chest or back. If it fails to sense a heartbeat for some prescribed time, or is removed without a safety code being entered, it sends a signal to a detonator.

Dom Pedro IV—The timeshaft-wormhole dropship—i.e., the starship—commanded by Felipe Henrique Marquez. Flies under the assumed name "Merchanter's Dream."

Downtime—Referring to events in or travel toward the past as regards a timeshaft wormhole. For a hundred-year timeshaft connecting 5100 A.D. and 5000 A.D., 5000 A.D. would be the downtime end.

Glister—A terraformed planet near Solace that has suffered a climatic collapse.

Grand Library—The ultimate storehouse of human knowledge, housed in a massive habitat orbiting Neptune. Two Permanent Physical Collections, or PPCs, serve as backups in the event of the Grand Library's destruction. One PPC is in a different orbit of Neptune, while the other is buried in an undisclosed location on the far side of Earth's Moon.

Greenhouse—A rocky satellite of the gas giant Comfort, used as the research station and breeding support center for Solace.

Interdict—The policy, enforced by Interdict Command, of completely forbidding all visits to the planet Mars. Though still enforced, the Interdict is more than half-forgotten, and Interdict Command is not the force it once was.

Intruders—Name given, more or less by default, to the thirty-two ships that attacked and went through the Circum Central Timeshaft Wormhole, transiting from downtime to uptime, past to future.

Malf, Malfunction—The private term used among themselves by the group marooned on Asgard Five by legitimate ship malfunctions, rather than by supposedly "voluntary" departure. See *Vol.*

"Merchanter's Dream"—False name for the disguised Timeshaft Dropship *Dom Pedro IV*.

Near-Ancient, near-ancients—Referring to a period of remote human history, or the people of that period. The Near-Ancient period is considered to start roughly with the Enlightenment, and end roughly with the establishment of wormhole transit. Thus, from about 1740 A.D. to 3000 A.D.

Objective time—The time or duration as measured by an outside observer. Typically used in regard to timeshaft-wormhole travel. A timeshaft ship might travel for one hundred years of self-chronologic time, and experience significant relativistic time dilation, but arrive only a week or so after departure in objective time, thanks to passage through a timeshaft wormhole. See *self-chronologic time* and *subjective time*.

Rio de Janeiro—One of two smaller auxiliary ships carried aboard the *Dom Pedro IV*. [see *São Paulo*.] The *DP-IV* also carries one larger auxiliary, the lighter *Cruzeiro do Sul*.

SCO Station—Solace Central Orbital Station—the largest and most important of the spaceside facilities in orbit of Solace. It houses thousands of people and has a great deal of technical expertise in ship handling, ship repair, cargo services, and so on. A natural trading center, it is in effect the capital of the Solace system space habitats.

Self-chronologic time—The accumulated duration or age of an object, a person's life, or an event, as it would be measured by a chronometer physically attached to an object or person, and ignoring the actual calendric time and date and relativistic time-dilation effects. Put another way, self-chron is a measure of how much an object or person has actually aged, regardless of time travel or cold sleep. A person who traveled, over the course of several trips, for five centuries in cryosleep, but traveled down five one-century wormholes, would have gone through five centuries of self-chron time, but experienced virtually no subjective time, and might well end up in the same objective year from which he or she started. See *objective time* and *subjective time*.

ShipInt—Alternate term for Ship's Artificial Intelligence. The term has arisen since the *DP-IV* was marooned in the future.

Slowtime—Slang for temporal confinement. Time moves very slowly for anyone inside a temporal confinement field.

Solace—A newly terraformed planet.

Solace City—Capital of Solace.

Subjective time—The apparent time or duration as experienced. A passenger aboard a starship might be in cryosleep for a century, but only be awake to experience a few weeks of subjective time. See *objective time* and *self-chronologic time*.

Symbiote-mold—The generally accepted term for the complex of commingled life-forms that have, somehow, formed into a symbiotic whole that has engulfed virtually all the habitable land surface of Mars. Molds, fungi, bacteria, and other forms of various species have merged into a meta-life-form that adapts to differing landscapes and climates by expressing whatever combination of member life-forms is best suited to the local environment. It is unclear exactly how the symbiote-mold came to be.

Technology Storage Facility—See *Dark Museum*.

Thor's Realm—A large Timeshaft Wormhole Farm, near the Tau Ceti star system.

Timeshaft wormhole—A wormhole linking past and future. A hundred-year timeshaft would allow one to travel back and forth exactly one hundred years—no more, no less. In the year 5000 A.D., the downtime end of a hundred-year timeshaft would link with the year 5100 A.D. on the uptime side. A timeshaft experiences normal duration, such that both ends are moving normally through time, from past to future at the normal rate. In 5001 A.D., the same timeshaft would link with 5101 A.D., and so on. A hypothetical twenty-four-hour timeshaft would link 4:15 P.M. Tuesday with 4:15 P.M. Wednesday. Two days later, 12:05 A.M. Thursday would be linked with 12:05 A.M. Friday. Move from the downtime to the uptime end of a timeshaft, spend five minutes on the uptime side, and then return to the downtime side, and it will be five minutes later there as well.

C.P.S. *Upholder*—The Uptime Chronologic Patrol Ship, commanded by Koffield, that survived the attack of the Intruders at Circum Central.

Uptime—Referring to events in or travel toward the future as regards a timeshaft wormhole. For a hundred-year timeshaft connecting 5100 A.D. and 5000 A.D., 5100 A.D. would be the uptime end.

Vol, Volunteer—The derogatory termed used by the Malfs to refer to members of the group marooned on Asgard Five who supposedly elected to leave their ship by their own choice. The term is sarcastic; the Malfs assume that most or all of the Vols were thrown off their ships for incompetence or insubordination. See *Malf*.

CHRONOLOGY
OF KEY EVENTS

3300 A.D.—Start of central effort to terraform Mars.

3800—Approximate start of timeshaft wormhole system.

4000—Founding of Chronologic Patrol.

4306—Ulan Baskaw's first known work, *Statistical Analysis of Species Populations in Artificial Environments,* is published.

4316—Ulan Baskaw's second book, *A Proposed New Method of Terraforming,* is published.

4350—The Grand Failure: collapse of Mars Terraforming Project.

4359—Ulan Baskaw's third book, *Ecologic and Climatic Stability of Artificial Environments Formed by Certain Means,* is published.

4823—Explosion at Technology Storage Facility, Mars.

August 14, 4893—Oskar DeSilvo born in Rio de Janeiro, Earth.

4932—DeSilvo discovers Baskaw's books and uses ideas in them to put forward idea of terraforming Solace.

He jumps in and out of cryo and temporal confinement to stretch his own life span.

August 14, 4993—DeSilvo commences terraforming of Solace on his own hundredth birthday.

5101—DeSilvo commences covert project to investigate Technology Storage Facility on Mars.

5129—DeSilvo concludes that Glister is going to die.

5132—DeSilvo sends thirty-two robot ships from 5132 to 5211 bearing stolen data. Ships cache the material and then return to wormhole and destroy it.

5211—The Circum Central Wormhole is destroyed, stranding Koffield and his crew in their own future. Koffield flies his ship, the C.P.S. *Upholder*, back to the Solar System.

5212—DeSilvo befriends Koffield. Koffield finds Baskaw's books, realizes their significance, and heads off to Solace to warn of the dangers the planet will face. DeSilvo believes he can prevent Solace from dying. DeSilvo steals Koffield's report and sabotages the *DP-IV*'s computer.

5225—DeSilvo realizes that Solace is doomed, but concludes it is too late to call a halt. He plans his own false death, and leaves clues to his real plans on Greenhouse and at the Grand Library, Earth, and Mars.

August 3, 5225—Purported publication date of *The Science and Art of Terraforming* by Anon Nemo.

August 3, 5226—Death of Oskar DeSilvo reported at Grand Library. He enters temporal confinement and starts waiting.

December 24, 5254—Oskar DeSilvo checks on status of his projections from inside temporal confinement.

5339—Koffield and company arrive at Solace System aboard the *Dom Pedro IV*, 127 years late.

5340—Koffield meets with Neshobe Kalzant after return from Greenhouse with letter from DeSilvo.

5341—*Dom Pedro IV* transits Thor's Realm Wormhole en route to Earth.

Here are the two puzzle-formulae mentioned in the text, with their solutions.

"All that Glisters is not Gold."

$$\in (oskd@(\forall X \ni X \neq Au))$$

Belongs to (Oskar DeSilvo at (for all values of X
such that X does not equal gold))

$$\rightarrow (\forall X \ni X \neq Au)$$

Go to (for all values of X such that X
does not equal gold)

ABOUT THE AUTHOR

ROGER MACBRIDE ALLEN was born September 26, 1957, in Bridgeport, Connecticut. He is the author of eighteen science fiction novels, a modest number of short stories, and one nonfiction book.

His wife, Eleanore Fox, is a member of the United States Foreign Service. After a long-distance courtship, they married in 1994, when Eleanore returned from London, England. They were posted to Brasilia, Brazil, from 1995 to 1997, and at present reside in Takoma Park, Maryland, just outside Washington, D.C. Their son, Matthew Thomas Allen, was born November 12, 1998. As of this writing, plans call for them to move to Leipzig, Germany, in the fall of 2002 for a three-year posting.

Visit the author's website at www.rmallen.net.

DON'T MISS
THE DRAMATIC CONCLUSION
TO THIS SERIES!

LOOK FOR

THE SHORES
OF TOMORROW:
Book Three of the Chronicles of Solace

IN STORES IN 2003.

"Help us," said Commander Raenau. "Help us, and we'll help you."

"With what?" Elber asked.

"Not so much with 'what' as with 'who,'" Sotales answered.

He handed Elber a datapad. It was looping a security camera recording, showing the very start of the Long Boulevard riot, when Zak Destan brought a wine bottle down on top of an enforcer's head and touched off all the trouble.

Zak. Zak Destan. Now, at least, Elber was beginning to understand. An enhancement grid locked onto one scared-looking, blurry face at the edge of the action and brought it into sharp focus. It was his own face—dirty, half-starved, terrified. Elber at the absolute worst moment of his entire life.

"We had the faces," Sotales said. "But no names, no records. We got lucky when we checked station records. We want to talk with you about Zak Destan."

Whatever tiny shreds of hope Elber had begun to feel were swept away. Suddenly, once again, the future was nothing but blackness. Elber had done nothing wrong that night, but Zak had done plenty—and in the world of the lowdowns, association was all that it took to draw a guilty verdict—and a long, unpleasant punishment.

For Elber, that punishment had just begun.